STAR-SPAWNED

LOVECRAFTIAN HORRORS & STRANGE STORIES

Mark Howard Jones

"He feared that his presence would be discovered. That the doors would burst open, and he would be dragged away to participate in some unimaginable scarlet ceremony. Or that he would be condemned to join the frozen figures, petrified in place forever while his soul screamed in agony, immortal and trapped within.

Night was here now, black as raven feathers embedded in tar. Small dark waves lapped against the stonework at his feet as if against a shore of utter desolation, an island of pariah souls.

Something was being borne along gently by the rise and fall of the bizarre inland sea. A flash of whiteness would rise above the surface for a few seconds before being obscured again. He bobbed his head from side to side, trying to identify the object. As it drifted closer to where he stood, an awful realisation dawned.

It was the body of a woman, her eyes white against the overwhelming blackness of the fluid. He couldn't be sure because he hadn't been close enough to see her face, but he suspected this was the corpse of the young woman he'd seen running through the poppies earlier. Her face rose towards him on the soft swell of the waters, and he could see that something had used her as food. "

First Edition

For those that we have lost -
Eddy C. Bertin, Willum H. Pugmire, Sam Gafford, John Pelan,
William F. Nolan, and Bryn Fortey.

Publication History

Beneath Black Spires (I) was first published in *Cyaegha No.11*, edited by Graeme Phillips—Summer, 2014.

Beneath Black Spires (II) was first published under the title *You Shadows That in Darkness Dwell ...* in *Black Wings VI'*, edited by S. T. Joshi—PS Publishing, 2017.

Put on the Mask was first published in *Dreamglass Days*, edited by Rachel Kendall—ISMs Press, 2016.

The Turn of the Tide was first published in *Black Wings III*, edited by S. T. Joshi—PS Publishing, 2015.

The Cobwebbed Bird House was first published in *Weird Fiction Review No. 8*, edited by S. T. Joshi—Centipede Press, 2017.

The Last Ones was first published in *Madness of Cthulhu 2*, edited by S. T. Joshi—Titan Books, 2015.

Sunday (Early Evening Ecstasy) was first published in *Weird Fiction Review No. 7*, edited by S. T. Joshi—Centipede Press, 2016.

Taking the Cure was first published in *Lovecraft eZine No.12*, edited by Mike Davis—March, 2012.

The Rolling of Old Thunder was first published in *Gothic Lovecraft*, edited by S. T. Joshi and Lynne Jamneck—Cycatrix Press, 2016.

Red Walls was first published in *Black Wings V*, edited by S. T. Joshi—PS Publishing, 2016.

Out of Stock was first published in *Weird Fiction Review No. 2*, edited by S. T. Joshi—Centipede Press, 2011.

Finest Garments Repaired was first published in *The Last Review; The King In Yellow @ 125*, edited by D. J. Tyrer—Atlantean Publishing, 2020.

In the Deeps of Dreams was first published in *Lovecraft eZine No. 37*, edited by Mike Davis—March, 2016.

By a Scarlet Thread was first published in *Phantasmagoria No.19*, edited by Trevor Kennedy,—Summer, 2021.

Side 1, Track 3 was first published in *Fungi No. 22*, edited by Pierre V Comtois—Summer, 2015.

Treading the Lost Path (Descending Aklo Songs) is previously unpublished.

A Meeting Beneath the Moon was first published in *His Own Most Fantastic Creation*, edited by S. T. Joshi—PS Publishing, 2020.

For the Love of Insects was first published in *Creeping Crawlers*, edited by Allen Ashley—Shadow Publishing, 2015.

Late Night, Caradoc Street was first published in *Cthulhu Cymraeg 2*, edited by Mark Howard Jones—Fugitive Fiction, 2017.

The Sixth Guardian was first published in *Cosmic Horror Monthly*, November, 2021.

Doorgrave to the Bittersea was first published in *Oculus Sinister*, edited by C. M. Muller—Chthonic Matter, 2020).

Preface

Firstly, I would like to thank S.T. Joshi for his always unstinting support and for kindly agreeing to write the Foreword to this collection.

Many of the stories included here are influenced by the work of H.P. Lovecraft and Arthur Machen. There is even a story where the two meet—an event that never actually took place, unfortunately.

The influence of other authors will also be evident to some readers but, whoever I have been inspired by, I like to think that I have placed my own stamp upon these stories.

Finally, I would like to point out that the three stories that are now collected under the title "Beneath Black Spires" were written at different times and saw print in very different publications. The reason I have chosen to bring them together here is that they all feature, in one form or another, a very particular example of arcane architecture.

- Mark Howard Jones
Cardiff, Wales
November 2021

CONTENTS

Foreword

The work of Mark Howard Jones is a distinctive contribution to the weird fiction of our time. Quirky, infused with powerfully bizarre imaginative touches, and written with a quiet elegance that allows for intense emotive effects, his tales span the spectrum from pure supernaturalism to dreamlike fantasy to grim psychological terror. H. P. Lovecraft is a strong influence, and I have been proud to include several of Mark's tales in my *Black Wings* series; his fellow Welshman Arthur Machen is also an influence, both in the use of landscape to evoke horror and in drawing upon the heritage of history to summon up weirdness from the depths of time. But Mark is no mere imitator or pastichist; he is able to subsume his influences, using them as the springboard for the articulation of his own moods, conceptions, and imagery. In this sense, Mark draws upon the storied legacy of weird fiction while at the same time generating work that addresses contemporary concerns regarding identity, intimate relationships, and the eternal theme of humanity's place in an indifferent cosmos.

There is a seeming effortlessness in the development of Mark's tales, but this is the art that conceals art: it is exceptionally difficult to fashion a narrative that appears to progress from beginning to end as if it were an actual event. His dialogue is sharp and evocative, contributing its mite to the overall horrific scenario; indeed, Mark follows in the footsteps of Poe, Lovecraft, and every other notable writer of short fiction in rigidly excluding everything—sentences, paragraphs, entire incidents—that do not have a strict bearing on the denouement. There is never a wasted word in his tales.

While it may seem a trivial matter, the brilliance of the *titles* of Mark's stories has to be noted. The fashioning of an effective title for a story is a much-undervalued skill; a pungent title sets the stage for what is to follow, initiating the sense of unease in the reader that the text must enhance. In the corpus of Mark's writings, we have such titles as "The Cobwebbed Bird House," "The Rolling of Old Thunder," "Beneath Black Spires," "Treading the Lost Path," "For the Love of Insects," and the highly poetical "Doorgrave to the Bittersea." With titles like these, Mark has already gone a long way in creating the atmosphere of weirdness that envelops a reader of his tales.

Mark Howard Jones has been writing for more than two decades, but in the realm of authorship he still qualifies as a relatively young author. The several books he has published and the dozens of stories that have appeared in magazines and anthologies have already established him as a presence in contemporary weird fiction. This volume only cements his reputation as a writer whose every tale is worth seeking out by those who find delight in literary terror and strangeness.

—S. T. Joshi
Seattle, Washington
November 2021

Beneath Black Spires

I

While the nightbird listened to whispers in the midnight station, he slipped out to slink down to the tiny nightclub. The place lay in the basement of a cheap, run-down hotel where only hopeless cases resided. Not the best place in town—any town—but he couldn't get what he now needed anywhere else.

Predictably the club was called "The Black Cat" and its customers largely consisted of things that any self-respecting feline would have refused to drag in.

Smith stood for a moment at the bottom of the steps. Above his head was a wooden sign with the club's name and a very badly painted image of a black cat. The cat's head was simply the wrong size and shape for any feline he'd ever met. He put the misrepresentation down to the artist's lack of ability.

Once inside, he was hit by the sound of smoky jazz that filled the air. His lungs were filled with an equally smoky atmosphere and there was a strong undercurrent of mustiness. Only a handful of bedraggled customers clung to the edges of the small club, nursing their drinks and bad memories. Despite their shabby clothes, some of them looked as if they might be part of the decor: stuffed and sitting strategically to make the place look fuller on quiet nights. Like tonight.

The barman was large and bald and snorted heavily with each outward breath. Smith didn't know if it was painful to wear a face like that, but it was certainly painful to look at.

"Gimme a whisky," he muttered and passed over his very

last note. "And keep the change." The barman pawed at it, slid a drink across to Smith and murmured "Thanks" in a ruined baritone.

On a small stage in one luridly-lit corner of the club was the woman he'd come to see. A drummer and a bass player worked diligently to provide an adequate backing for the woman in the tight blue dress and long dark hair. She called herself Sage Sagitarria and her voice was working its way through the dying chords of an old song.

It was a tune Smith certainly recognised, but he couldn't put his grubby finger on it just now. He knew it was a tattered Torch song, something Judy Garland used to croak out in her downtrodden, desperate last days, like Dorothy's death dirge.

After muttering something about returning after a short break, Sage walked across to the bar. Her eyes actually seemed to grow larger in her head when she caught sight of him. She regained her composure and asked the barman for a Screwdriver.

Taking a single sip, she turned to him. "So what brings you to this broken neck of the woods?"

"Shall we sit down, Sage?" he asked, indicating a vacant table near the door.

She smiled to try and hide her discomfort. The crow's feet cracked at the edges of her eyes, dislodging flakes of caked make-up. She seemed shocked at his dishevelled appearance, constantly running her eyes over his filth-spattered clothes.

"So what can I do for you, Mr. ...?" she asked once they were seated, knowing he wouldn't dare use his real name. She was obviously being cautious but something about her nervous hands betrayed the fact that she'd given up all hope of ever seeing him again.

"Smith," he said. But he seemed troubled by the name, as if it was an overcoat that was uncomfortably large for him.

"Smith?! Really? How unoriginal ..." she laughed. Then she paused, leaning forward and staring into his eyes for clues. "You really don't remember who you are, do you?"

He looked down, shaking his head. But he remembered her face, had found her name on a card in his pocket, a name straight out of a comic book. She was the only one who could help him, he was sure. "No, but you do. I need your help … now."

"Of course. But not here." She drained her glass. "And I've got a show to finish first."

He looked her straight in the eyes. "Why do you sing in this dive?"

"Because people here don't ask awkward questions."

He twitched his mouth in return, his last cigarette dangling from his fingers. The paper table cloth began to scorch.

She scowled at him. "Hey, cut that out—I don't want to get in trouble with the owner. And I certainly don't want to die in a fire started by an idiot."

He snorted. "Die! Die? You!? That's a good one …" He wasn't sure why he'd said it but somehow he was convinced the comment contained an unarguable truth.

She seemed agitated and was obviously anxious to be rid of him. "Meet me at the Temple in an hour."

He looked blank. "The Temple …?"

"The old Cornerstone Church on Spider Street," she said in a frustrated tone. "In an hour. You know it?"

He snorted derisively. "Oh yeah, like the back of my head."

"Which, incidentally, could have a big hole in it soon enough." She sounded angry but also concerned. He took that as a good sign.

His life had been a long series of betrayals and retreats, though he found it almost impossible to recall any details. That had something to do with *her*, he knew. With what *she* had done.

But he also remembered that, before the accident, he'd been a devout man. Though it escaped him which religion or denomination he'd belonged to.

He'd asked an old man on the pavement outside the nightclub for directions to the place Sage had mentioned. They'd sounded complicated, so he was surprised when he found the place so easily. Maybe he'd been here before.

Spider Street was little more than a miserable back lane, dark and cramped with several boarded-up doorways. At the end of the street was a large and imposing Victorian church.

Although the spire was in proportion to the church, it made Smith shudder when his eyes fell on it. He turned his back to it and stamped his feet in the cold.

The false bravado he'd shown at the club had melted away in the dark and the cold. Keeping his eyes down, he walked towards the church and sheltered in its large porch. It did little to keep the cold at bay.

Above the doorway he noticed a badly carved relief. It featured three stars arranged in an odd conjunction. Below them stood a four-legged animal that he was appalled to see bore a passing resemblance to the poorly-painted cat on the nightclub sign. What on earth was it meant to be? Surely not a cat on a place of worship ....

He pushed his hands deep into his pockets and tried to remember what had happened to him. He knew it had something to do with a car crash—he'd found the keys in his pocket, tucked inside a hospital envelope. There'd be a lot of pain—a hell of a lot. Then there were the bandages. He'd sneaked out of the hospital as soon as the nurses' backs were turned. He'd always hated those places.

But before that there'd been her face. Sage had been there. By the car. As he was lying on the road. But ... what? There was nothing else; no recollection before that, only fragments here and there. She must know who he was ... had been.

As best he could tell, that was almost a month ago. Now, each time he closed his eyes, his mind was invaded with images of a gargantuan building, night black, gaunt and insanely tall. His mind's eye was always drawn up to the impossibly twisted spires, towering for miles, high above him. It seemed as if, at any moment, they must crumble under their own weight and come tumbling down, crushing everything below. He felt as if his neck would snap if he ever succeeded in seeing the peaks of this overwhelming, nightmare architecture.

Yet he daren't let his gaze fall, for fear of seeing the plague of misshapen human vermin that covered the ground before the structure, all drawn inevitably towards its giant, dark mass.

And when he dared to sleep, his dreams were even darker. The night that his screams woke his fellow derelicts, he was certain he'd glimpsed the dreadful thing that clung to the top of the loftiest of those dark spires ....

Every night drew him further into that terrible place, revealing new dreads, new agonies. He hadn't slept for three nights now, for fear he might never be able to wake again, that he'd be imprisoned in his poisoned dreams.

Suddenly—too suddenly—Sage was there at his side. Then he noticed that the door to the church was open a crack, explaining away her magic act. The blue dress had disappeared, replaced by a dark skirt and blue sweater with a curiously-designed logo embroidered on it.

"Why meet here ... why a church?" He shivered. The darkness behind Sage seemed to shift and swirl at the question. Smith instinctively took a step back.

"It is no longer a church—it has been de-consecrated. And consecrated anew by our Order." Sage appeared calm enough but was oddly tense below the surface.

"Well, can we go inside? It's freezing out here." His regret at having no overcoat grew as the temperature fell.

She shook her head. "Not yet, no."

He seemed put out but didn't let her manner put him off his stride. "All right. I was in an accident about a month back. You were there—I know it. Nobody can tell me who I am. Your card was in my pocket. I've got no one else's name. It's as simple as that. Who am I?"

After the crash she'd used the knowledge granted to her by her worship of the Great Old Ones. She'd thought she wouldn't have to explain that ... not to him, of all people. He'd drunk too much after their last successful ritual, during which there had been certain manifestations. She wished now that she'd insisted on driving.

Puzzled by her silence, Smith spoke again. "Tell me! You were there. The accident. That day I ..." It was the first time he'd ever actually put it into words instead of just rolling it around inside his head. And those words had acted as a beacon, lighting up the farthest corners of his understanding. "The day I *died.*"

Smith's shoulders sagged with the weight of realisation. "Dead. I was dead. And you brought me back. *Why?*"

He looked up at her but there was no answer in her expression. She simply shook her head, unable to tell him the truth.

Shards of memory rose to the surface of his mind, but none explained who he or Sage were. Or why she'd done what she had. Feeling broken, Smith finally realised there was only one route of escape left open to him.

"You gave me this life—take it back. Now! I don't want it ... I've seen the black spires ... I've frozen in their icy shadow... I-I know what they do to the children .... please, just take it away ..."

She seemed shocked by his words. "You are privileged to have been granted a vision of the place of true worship. All followers aspire to go there," she said. Doubts rose in her mind— if he did not even recognise the hallowed ground, then maybe her abilities were not all she'd thought them to be. She'd failed.

Smith was appalled to hear the word "worship" come from her lips. He shivered at the thought of what could possibly be worshipped in such a foul place. "No! No. I want it to end. End ..."

Sage stepped forward and spoke quietly. "Are you sure this is what you want? Absolutely sure?" She hadn't felt this nervous since she'd discovered he'd walked out of the hospital and vanished.

Smith nodded. Tears began to run down his face, and Sage raised her hands. "It begins," she pronounced and began to chant softly. "Ahn ahn et'rhu Yog-Sothoth ..."

At the sound of the words, Smith's weak frame shook like a toy. He gasped and fell forward, drooling open-mouthed into the gutter, on all fours like a ruined old drunk. "O—oh Guh-god ... oh fu—"

"Which god are you praying to, Mr. Smith?" She didn't wait for the obvious answer, but instead opened her palms. "Please accept our God, with my compliments ..."

She reached forward and gripped his shoulders, her low voice gaining volume with each word. "...vi'dch ahn Nyogtha im'ykh ..."

Though they came from her mouth, the words were spoken

in an ancient voice, cold and commanding. They tore through him like the vibrations of an enormous bell, pealing slowly and persistently. She struggled to hold him as he began to pant heavily and pull away. "... c'aes nyhoo Cyaegha, sath'lei cor'pa ..."

A sheen of sweat covered his forehead and face as the ceremony reached its climax. "... et'rhu Yog-Sothoth ... Y'-Sothoth! Y'-Sothoth! Y'-Sothoth!"

As the last syllable left her lips, his struggles finally ended and the chaotic whiteness at the heart of everything flowed into him, emptying him of whatever he had been.

He knelt before her, as still as a stone. He did not struggle now as she raised him gently to his feet and turned him to face the right direction.

"Enter the temple," she said in a firm tone. His eyes were glazed with incomprehension as he walked towards the large double doors. Just beyond, the inviting darkness waited.

As he moved away, she murmured softly to herself: "Forgive me, I *couldn't* let you go. Better to serve the Old Ones like this than to be cast into outer darkness forever."

She followed him through the doors, closing and locking them behind her. At least he would be near until the time came for them to worship beneath the black spires together.

"Welcome home, father."

II

He'd wanted to get lost, certainly, but not *this* lost. The map he'd procured when he hired the boat was now useless.

After the strain of the last year, five days away, all alone, seemed like a good idea. A chance to clear his head. And God knows nobody would miss him. Certainly not his insolent daughter or her disinterested younger sister. Only his distant wife had raised any concerns, and those were mainly financial; she was in the midst of divorcing him, after all.

A hiking holiday would get him away from all that. It was intended to help him focus on what was important in his life. The trip down river had been almost spur-of-the-moment.

He'd come upon the small boatyard by accident after getting lost. Despite some initial language problems, the old man who ran it had been very helpful and told him where he'd taken the wrong path. But before he could begin re-tracing his steps, he'd been drawn to a small boat with a motor.

A keen canoeist in his youth, he was sure he could handle the small boat. And it wasn't the boat that was the problem. He had now sailed off the edge of the map—literally and metaphorically.

Simply turning the boat around was not an option; he'd hit some white water earlier in the day. He'd never be able to make his way upstream past that … and the banks were too steep simply to haul even his small boat onto dry land and go around.

At the first likely-looking spot, he'd heaved to and dragged the boat up onto the shallow bank. Making sure he'd tied it to a sturdy-looking tree stump, he'd set off to find someone who could tell him where he was … and where he should be going.

He panted as he laboured up the rise. There was no sun, but the air was filled with a clinging heat that seemed intent on persecuting him.

All around him grew black-petalled flowers. Although he'd never seen anything quite like them before, he felt sure they were a member of the poppy family.

He stopped for a moment, hands leaning on his knees. Once he got to the top of this rise he'd be able to see what lay ahead. A town, he hoped. His thirst was growing with every step, and he was so tired.

He looked down at the flowers. They weren't even nodding their heads. As there was not even a faint breath of wind, the only thing to disturb them was him. They were all around him, stretching to the horizon on all sides. Maybe this was their only home, this hollow in which he found himself.

Their petals were a lustrous black that he didn't think was possible in plants. He imagined that somehow he was the first to discover them. And maybe he'd be given the honour of naming them. *Papaver noctis* sounded right. The night poppy.

He pushed himself back up straight and forced his legs to

take him onwards. As he was approaching the top of the rise, he saw several spires of a huge building rising before him. The building was unlike any architectural style he'd ever seen, the spires so unnaturally tall that they disappeared into the light grey clouds above.

As he got to the top of the rise he came across a huge, dark plain as far as the eye could see. Covered in black poppies.

In the centre stood an enormous cathedral or abbey. Even though the cloudbase was low, the spires must still be many miles high. *Impossibly* high.

Whatever its architectural peculiarities, it was the only building in sight. And the only place where he might find help.

He'd been walking for just a few minutes when he saw someone else crossing the plain. They must have been over half-a-mile away and coming from the opposite direction, but it heartened him to see another person.

There was a kind of heat haze over the flowers, and he had to stand very still and concentrate to see what the figure was. Squinting and straining his eyes, he could make out the shape of a young woman. She evidently had more energy than him as she was hurrying towards the huge structure. Then she stumbled and disappeared into the mass of black blooms.

He stood still, watching for nearly a minute but she didn't get up. Maybe she'd collapsed from exhaustion and was unable to get to her feet again. Even if he'd wanted to help, even if he had the strength, he'd lose his bearings in this black wilderness as soon as he began to move. He'd never find her.

He decided the best thing to do was reach the building and report the woman's accident to whoever was in charge. Meanwhile, he continued to scan the plain of poppies, in the hope that she'd reappear.

The giant building still seemed miles away, even though he'd been walking for over 30 minutes. He stopped for a second and looked around him. The ocean of black petals barely moved around him, as if they were all part of some enormous piece of sculpture instead of living plants. To reassure himself, he bent and plucked a single poppy, grinding its petals between his fingers. Thin, black juice was smeared on his fingertips.

Wiping his fingers on his trousers, he resumed his trek. As he went on, he felt sure the poppies were growing darker. A colour darker than black? He knew it was impossible but ….

He peered down and realised it was the space between the stalks that was darkening, not the flowers themselves. Its colour was completely opaque, impenetrable. At first he though the darkness was rising from the earth. It was only when he looked at his hand that he realised it was falling like rain from the grey sky. Two or three black marks appeared on the back of his left hand, to roll slowly and sluggishly off.

He rubbed the back of his hand with his fingers. The "rain" had a peculiar silky feel to it. And it was certainly not a liquid. Nor was it a dust. Or a gas. He searched his fuddled mind for a description but came up blank. He stooped and dipped his fingers into the layer that had settled on the ground. It clung to his fingers for a fraction of a second before sliding off.

The heads of the poppies were only barely above the level of the black stuff now. Suddenly he realised that, if it kept raining, he'd be unable to see where he was walking within an hour. He daren't risk that. If he stumbled over or into something … Or simply into the "fog" ….

He hadn't been scared of the dark since he was a child, but he didn't relish being swallowed by it, blinded in the blackness. He began to pump his legs in panic. He had to get to that building. No matter what appalling things he might find there. It was his only possible haven.

Maybe the black stuff was fallout from some nearby industry, he thought. Pollution might also explain why the clouds hung so low in the sky. He didn't want to take the chance that it was toxic and tried to push himself harder to reach the huge dark building, pulling his jacket over his head as he went.

As the building gradually drew closer, its strangeness impressed itself upon him. Though its design suggested a religious use, besides the enormous spires there were very few attributes of the sort he was used to in a place of worship. There were no windows visible, which was almost unheard of in such a huge building. And there was an uncanny smoothness about it—an old building was usually covered in statuary or decoration of some sort, often depicting religious figures ... but not this one.

Finally, he felt like he was within a reasonable distance of the building. Panting heavily, he crossed the final few hundred feet to reach its vast bulk. He stretched out his one arm, symbolically splaying his fingers against the icy stonework. This soon turned into genuine support as he leaned against the wall to regain his breath. One beneficial aspect of the strange architecture meant that he could shelter under an overhang, safe from the dark rain for a while.

The architecture had seemed unusual, even odd, from a distance. But close up it had a disturbing aspect to it. Arches seemed to overflow each other, while buttresses tried to loop inside each other, as if someone had plucked the designs from the nightmares of some half-insane architect and rendered them solid.

In fact, from a certain angle, the whole building seemed to be lurching forward, as if getting ready to break loose of its foundations and hurl itself headlong across the flower-filled plain.

He'd seen lots of old buildings over the past decades—usually at his wife's insistence—and their surfaces wore their age openly. They were weathered, pitted, scarred. Yet the curious black stone of this structure looked like it had been quarried only yesterday. But surely nobody built on such a grand scale any longer?

He had no idea the architecture in this part of the world was so distinctive. He didn't remember any of the guide books mentioning it. He fished in his jacket for the pocket guide which had been so helpful in the past weeks. It was gone.

Slipping off his jacket, he checked all the pockets twice. Then he looked about him, as if it would be possible to spot the book if it had fallen out on his walk here, as if the black flowers would relinquish *any* prize. He realised that he must look like some over-enthusiastic mime artist to any spectator. Self-consciously he glanced about him; there was no one.

Standing in this strange place, he suddenly felt cut off from his own world. The guide had been his link to home, in a way.

Without it and surrounded by these odd blooms, he felt truly like a stranger. Lost and friendless.

He decided the only thing to do was to find a door into the huge building. There might be a tour guide or a caretaker who could tell him exactly where he was … if he could make himself understood to them, of course. He imagined English was a rarity in this district.

His missing guidebook had also contained a selection of useful phrases, but he didn't trust his memory to recall them correctly. He might even accidentally conjure up an insult by mispronouncing something. Glumly, he realised he'd probably have to fall back on his previously unrehearsed skill for mime once more.

Pulling his jacket over his head again, he began to make his way round to the front of the building. When he'd started his journey towards the building he'd hoped to head straight for the entrance, but the bizarre design had defeated him. However, after several minutes of following the curves and angles of the wall, he found himself at his destination.

The front of the building had an enormous doorway set within an oddly angled porch. The overhang was more than enough to provide him with shelter. He walked up the four broad steps leading to it.

In the archway he noticed a detail that filled him with admiration for the craftsmen who created it. The top half of a human cranium had been carved into the curious black stone, to act as a macabre doorstop. A memento mori also, he guessed. Indeed, the top of the skull had delicate cracks lining it, as if the heavy door had begun to fracture it, like a spoon when it first hits a fragile eggshell at breakfast time. He half-chuckled to himself at the playfulness of its creator.

The thought of breakfast made him realise he was hungry. Once more his hand plunged into his pocket, retrieving the remnants of a chocolate bar. He pushed the last few pieces into his mouth, turning his head to gaze out across the dark field that surrounded him.

The field had disappeared. In place of the black blooms that had stretched from horizon to horizon now stood a broad dark lake. It had drowned everything except the architectural monstrosity on which he was standing. He had become trapped on an island.

Exhaling a huge sigh, he sat down on the broad step. His only hope was to wait for the water to subside. The rain had now stopped so, hopefully, the lake of black fluid should drain away. If it behaved as water did, of course.

He might as well make the best of things and play the tourist while he waited for the lake to subside, he supposed.

To one side was an arched entrance way cut into one of the bizarrely-angled buttresses. It led to a wide platform set into the wall of the enormous structure. Cautiously, he peered around the corner of the archway. There was no sign of anyone and nothing that looked dangerous, so he stepped through the opening.

Just a few steps past the archway stood a pair of unusual objects. Set into the floor were two enormous, curved shapes, rising to a height of about seven feet. As he walked around them it became clear they were two enormous horns, facing each other. He doubted whether they could ever make any sound as they were made of the same cold, black material as the building itself. They were obviously a piece of sculpture, though what they were meant to represent eluded him.

Between the two fake instruments was a narrow, raised platform. It sat in the ten-foot-wide space between the bowls of the horns. Worryingly there were two large metal rings set into the platform. There appeared to be some dried liquid on it. He walked past the rings, not wanting to think of their possible use.

Clustered just beyond the horns was a set of figures, dark and still and slightly forbidding. Some were of nearly full-length figures. Others had been formed as if they were cut off at the knees. Still others were simply a head and part of a flailing arm.

At first he thought they were sunken statues, impossibly mired in the black stone. He couldn't think how stone could be softened enough to allow such large sculptures to sink down into it like rocks in mud. Yet, instinctively, he knew they had not been carved. He backed away from them in fear when he finally realised that they were the remains of those who had come here before him and stayed too long.

He moved away from them, his arms tucked into his sides, as if they were contagious or unclean. While backing up he bumped into another archway. Looking around he saw it led to yet another platform.

This area contained something that couldn't possibly be human. The giant dark hand was three times the height of even the tallest man.

Only when he stood to one side and looked at a particular angle could he see that, carved into the tip of each great finger, was a face. The expression on each of them was twisted in anger or agony, maybe both.

It was as the wind suddenly picked up that he discovered its true purpose. As the breeze changed direction, each malformed mouth began to moan. He clapped his hands over his ears to block out the painful sound. The vibration was inhuman. It shuddered through his body, causing pains to rise in his stomach and chest as his ribs vibrated in sympathy.

Other sounds seem to join in, as if the foul voices had been joined in accompaniment by some monstrous instrument that scratched at his brain like tin and old pain. It was the coldest music ever created; each impossible note held one crisp-edged corner of the night, ready to fold it over him, smotheringly, trapping his breath in his lungs, never to move again.

He twisted from side to side, adding his own voice to the unearthly cantata of despair. His feet started to work seemingly on their own, desperate to get him away from the overwhelming din.

He stumbled past the two enormous horns that he had seen earlier. To his horror, they had both burst into life, emitting gargantuan notes that shook the stone beneath his feet. The impossible instruments had been given horrific voice. Anything caught between them would be pulverised with sound, dead within minutes.

He fell to his knees, pushing the material of his sleeves into his ears to afford some relief. The vibration still shivered painfully through his body.

And now he saw that the sound was indeed a summons. From across the lake, he saw a procession of figures approaching. At first he thought they must be a mirage brought about by the mind-jarring noise because they seemed to walk on the surface of black fluid itself, in a parody of the divine. But when the figures refused to fade away, he realised this mock miracle was actually happening in front of his eyes.

As they came closer, he realised they were walking along a raised path that led across the plain. This was his chance. As soon as it was safe he intended to take that same path away from here.

The procession drew closer with each second. They were not moving at a respectful, stately pace but seemed to be rushing to worship, as if answering an urgent summons.

Their unnaturally long legs moved swiftly like branches tormented by a high wind. Their garments drank in light, as if made of the black rain, cowled around faces of fog and shadow.

Behind them, dragged along as if on invisible chains of air, were a small herd of human vermin. Their clothes tattered and filthy, their faces shoddy masks that could not hide their despoiled souls. They were the very lowest apostles of depravity. He was sure he recognised some of the faces.

Fearing discovery, he slid back behind the archway cut into the smooth, cold stone.

From where he now stood, the swelling threnody of bleakness threatened to overwhelm him. He pressed his head against the cold stone, seeking relief. If he were to smash his head open against the unyielding wall, maybe the torment would stop. That was the answer—if he could just dash it hard enough to split it open, maybe the obscene music would spill out of him, every last drop, leaving him in blessed silence at last.

When the figures were within a few feet of the enormous doors, the deafening cacophony stopped suddenly. He dared to breathe a sigh of relief, though he did not hear it. His ears rang abominably, as if someone standing next to him was singing in a preternaturally high voice.

From his hiding place he dared to crane his neck, catching a glimpse of a red-lit interior. He had the unmistakable impression that the procession was descending and moving to the left. He was puzzled why a building that stretched up so high would also need to descend into the ground.

The last of the figures passed out of sight. Once the procession was inside, the gigantic doors closed with an overwhelming crash, that he felt more than heard.

He unblocked his ears and massaged his temples. Then he yawned to try and return his ears to something close to normality. Within less than half a minute his ears were more-or-less back to normal. But then he almost wished that he'd lost his hearing.

From inside the building came an awful sound. It reminded him of enormous hooks scraping against stone. From time to time, it sounded as if they caught, digging into the hard surface and dislodging material, which tumbled down noisily.

The unsettling sound continued for a short while, punctuated by the sound of words chanted in an unnatural rhythm. Then both gradually and mercifully faded.

He was certain he heard the sound of hands pounding against the enormous door. There followed a sudden babel of voices. Only one cut through the rest; it trailed off in despair after shouting "… there *is* no outside!"

This was followed a few seconds later by the sound of the voices receding quickly into the depths of the enormous building. In the sudden silence, he heard the wind pick up, whispering its message of despair to him.

There were only a few seconds of this respite before a single voice could be heard from within the cathedral.

It was lost somewhere between a chant of praise and a cry of terrible agony. It phased alarmingly, becoming something not quite human just before the chilling noise stopped altogether. His mind reeled at what might have happened to the owner of that voice.

Then a chorus of others joined in, adding their pain and their devotion to the lone acolyte's song. Whether in support of condemnation, he preferred not to know.

Within the catechism of despair, he'd recognised peculiar names. The last time he heard them was in the mouth of one of his daughter's boyfriends. He'd assumed in his arrogance that they were fictional bogeymen, conjured up to scare and delight impressionable children.

But in the mouths of these devotees, among words tinged with both devotion and terror, the names had a cold, awful power—one devoid of any human idea of mercy.

The names themselves became unnaturally amplified, rising on volume until they became a huge column of sound. Once more he clapped his hands over his ears and ran to the edge of the lowest step. It was as far as he could go to get away from the sound.

Eventually the liturgy died down, and he lowered his hands in relief. He felt as if his mind had turned to fog by the onslaught. One thought fought its way to the front, and then he remembered the earthen causeway used by the sinister procession.

He ran to the edge of the broad steps and peered down, seeking his path to freedom.

Moments before, it had begun to rain once more. The blackness started to rise almost at once. He stared at the raised pathway as the blackness began to spill over it. He tried to muster his courage, standing with his feel half hanging over the edge of the lowest step. All it would take would be to extend one leg and step onto the path. It was only a foot or so below him.

He had no evidence that the black fluid was dangerous. But his sense of revulsion at touching it sounded like a bell in his head, drowning out any rational thoughts.

Breathing heavily, he tried to force himself to place his foot where he knew the path must be. Then it dawned on him how long the journey across the plain would take. And he had no clear destination. The black flood would have taken him long before anything like salvation appeared to him. He clung desperately to his fears, afraid to let the fluid—if that's what it was—touch his skin.

He suddenly became aware that it was twilight. The light was going, and he struggled to fight back a wave of anxiety. The thought of spending the night in this place horrified him. But what choice did he have?

He feared that his presence would be discovered. That the doors would burst open, and he would be dragged away to participate in some unimaginable scarlet ceremony. Or that he would be condemned to join the frozen figures, petrified in place forever while his soul screamed in agony, immortal and trapped within.

Night was here now, black as raven feathers embedded in tar. Small dark waves lapped against the stonework at his feet as if against a shore of utter desolation, an island of pariah souls.

Something was being borne along gently by the rise and fall of the bizarre inland sea. A flash of whiteness would rise above the surface for a few seconds before being obscured again. He bobbed his head from side to side, trying to identify the object. As it drifted closer to where he stood, an awful realisation dawned.

It was the body of a woman, her eyes white against the overwhelming blackness of the fluid. He couldn't be sure because he hadn't been close enough to see her face, but he suspected this was the corpse of the young woman he'd seen running through the poppies earlier. Her face rose towards him on the soft swell of the waters, and he could see that something had used her as food.

He looked away, clamping his eyelids tight shut. When he opened them again after an uncertain period of time, the waves had carried their grisly cargo off into the blackness, offering her up to the night's mercy.

That was the fate that awaited him if he tried to brave the unnatural lake. He felt grateful that he hadn't sought an escape across the causeway into the uncertain night. His thoughts were interrupted by a sound, and he turned his head to follow it.

From far above him he heard sounds of movement. He raised his head to peer upwards, but even the light from the faint stars failed to help him penetrate the darkness. The sounds continued but he could see nothing. His imagination painted pictures of enormous night birds with penetrating vision, many times better than his own. They might do him harm or even kill him.

Clutched suddenly by a shiver of fear, he retreated along the side of the cathedral, pressed close to the wall. Taking care not to touch the half-buried petrified figures, he slid down the wall behind them and pulled his knees up to his chest.

After many minutes he was seized by a kind of sleep. Inside his unquiet slumber, he dreamt that something came to him, easing its huge body almost gracefully between the immovable figures. It touched him, leaving an invisible stain on his flesh.

He jerked awake, fearful and cold. Instinctively, his hand went up to his face at the place where the dream creature had touched it. He could feel nothing, though the spot tingled and stung. Pulling his jacket even tighter about him, he forced himself to believe his imagination had got the better of him.

If such a creature did exist, if it had come to him in the darkness, surely he wouldn't still be alive, he reasoned. Unless it was saving the pleasure of his death for later, of course.

He had to get away from here before he became a part of the building or a victim of something unknown. Before he was unable to leave.

He already felt that this non-place, leaking through a rent seam in reality, had sucked him almost dry. It was nearly too late to escape.

For all of one second, he contemplated plunging into the blackness and "swimming" for it (if that was the right word). Even the awful fate that awaited him there was better than the uncertainty that was torturing him.

The hairs on the back of his neck rose suddenly as the scent of blood reached him on the night wind. He could never mistake that smell. It reminded him of hunting trips with his father. The scent had overwhelmed him as the animals died, surrendering their lives too quickly. The smell had made his stomach turn over, and it threatened to do the same now. He covered his nose and mouth with his arm and moved back from the edge of the steps.

He wondered who or what had been killed. Had they been killed by the creature he was sure he'd heard earlier? The fear that he might be next froze him in place. He stood, pressed against the vast doors, for an unguessable span of time.

The coldness of his own death touched him, making him

feel small and old. He didn't want to die here, alone in this ugly place, far from those who loved him … even if only a little.

He was seized by a sudden wave of anger. He felt mistreated, abused by this place.

This shadow cathedral, this gathering place of obscenity, must not be allowed to remain standing. Though he could not imagine how much force it would take to demolish this leviathan citadel of night, he knew he had to try and persuade someone—somewhere—that it must be utterly destroyed.

Its very existence seemed to blacken the world, in his mind. Those who had been taken inside were now surely lost. Though he had no sympathy for their type, he knew that others must be spared the same fate … whatever it was.

And whatever dwelt within or around it must be destroyed, too.

Sullenly he sat on the step, the cold seeping into him from the stone, staring out into the nothingness around him.

Gradually he saw a shape appear out of the darkness. He was preparing to retreat through the doorway that led to the place of the petrified figures when he saw it was a boat. Crouching down, peering anxiously, he saw that it was *his* boat, the one that had brought him to this accursed place. A small part of him wanted to sink the damned thing in misplaced vengeance. But it was his only way out of here.

The tiny craft was eddying and turning, frustratingly out of reach. Taunting him with a dream of escape.

For minutes he watched, as it slowly came closer but still remained out of reach. Carefully he emptied his jacket pockets of his few possessions, then wound the jacket around his right hand. As the boat looked as though it might drift right past him, tantalisingly out of reach, he lashed out with the jacket. The one sleeve caught on part of the outboard motor. He tugged at it, giving the boat enough momentum to drift his way. When the side of the boat hit the step with a clunk, he thought it was one of the most beautiful sounds there could ever have been.

Making sure to always keep one hand on the boat, he slipped his jacket back on, scooping up his few bits and pieces and dropping them back in his pocket.

Afraid that the blackness might not hold up the weight of the boat with him in it, that he'd sink into the ebony lake, he gently placed one foot down. Ready to leap back onto the steps at the first sign the boat was sinking, he leant more of his weight on the tiny vessel. It sank only a few inches.

He eased himself into a seating position in the boat. Then, mustering all the strength he could, he pushed against the cold stone of the step.

Looking around in the boat, he realised that his rucksack was gone. All his food and water had been stored inside it. He sighed heavily, consciously fighting off the despair that threatened to cover him. One or two items had obviously fallen out and lay in the bottom of the boat, including his watch.

He'd slipped it into an outside pocket of the rucksack when the strap had broken yesterday. He picked it up. The illuminated dial showed him it was just gone 9:30. It should have been light hours ago. He shook his head, puzzled.

Sitting up straight to look behind him, he allowed himself to feel some relief as the enormous spires, blacker even than the lightless night that surrounded them, began to recede into the distance as the boat drifted farther away.

This was the first time he'd ever thought that any architecture could be predatory. But the idea fitted this carnivorous dark structure perfectly.

He reached out to start the small outboard motor, then quickly withdrew his hand. Part of the side of the motor was missing. It looked as if it had been torn off as if it was simply paper. He imagined that it had been done by whoever, or whatever, had taken his rucksack. The perpetrator obviously possessed enormous strength.

There was nothing left to do but sit and wait to be taken wherever the boat would take him. He looked back in the direction of where upriver might have been. Nothing waited for him back there. He wondered what waited for him up ahead as he drifted into the overwhelming darkness.

He pressed the button on his watch to light it up once more. He was incredulous that the dawn hadn't broken. Only darkness was allowed to reign here, obviously.

By the weak light, he noticed that the map he'd used to get here had fallen out of his pocket. As he picked it up he noticed there was another fold to it. He carefully unfolded the part that had been tucked inside—maybe on purpose—and peered at it closely, struggling to see. The prospect of undiscovered territory ahead at least offered hope.

There were the rapids he'd had to struggle through this morning. The fields were marked with tiny blobs representing black flowers. Yet there was no sign of any large building. That the nightmare spires could have escaped the eye of any cartographer, however amateurish, was beyond belief. Unless that person had intended it to stay "hidden," to come as a surprise to anyone unlucky enough to find themselves there.

Then his heart froze as he saw that the river was swallowed up before it reached the edge of the paper. All drawing and writing ceased, swallowed by an enormous stain of black ink. Whether this was on the original map or was just a product of poor photocopying was impossible to tell in the gloom. But neither possibility could explain how the stain now began to spread ominously across the map, devouring all the badly drawn details in its path.

But I am already sailing through that darkness, he thought. The map was only now "catching up" to reality, whatever that was. He was unsure whether this place was "real," His cold numbed body and his fevered mind were both unsure of what was any longer defined by that word.

Obviously the laws that governed the world he was used to didn't apply here. What laws did apply would be a dreadful new discovery, he felt sure.

The ancient names he'd heard chanted earlier echoed repeatedly around his head, making it feel like an empty eggshell, waiting to be crushed. In his gut he knew that any answers he might seek were hidden within the dreadful syllables of those names. If he had the courage to seek them ….

Looking at himself with new eyes, the thought of ever returning to his old life sickened him. Yet his cowardly, sick self baulked at what lay ahead.

He crouched in the bottom of the boat, covered his head and sobbed.

Drifting. Days buried under bruised nights. The dark tide too merciful to drown him, too jealous to release him.

Years later, or maybe only hours, a dim shoreline lashed by black rains rises at the farthest reaches of the ebony tide.

Up ahead, a black dawn is breaking. Up ahead, the shadows gather in procession.

III

A world created out of ash-black and charcoal remnants. A sky of distressed twilight.

Moments before he had been sitting in the solitary chair of his dark, unheated room. Now the heat was stifling as it poured into his lungs and scorched the bottom of his feet.

He knew the difference between a dream and something merely masquerading as one. The furnace-hot air that made his skin prickle with sweat and the dark stink of ash were too real, and too harsh, to be part of any dream.

Despite the oppressive heat, he found himself shivering. Dreams didn't crawl across your skin like that, either. Only nightmares did that.

Though there seemed no point in moving in this near-featureless landscape, he put his left foot forward.

Pain provided further proof of the reality of his plight when his foot sank into the ash, twisting his ankle to one side. He slumped down, raising a cloud of ash, massaging his foot. He winced at the bitter taste as he spat out a few flakes of ash that had landed on his lips.

Pulling his bare hand back from the burning ground, he looked about him.

Shapes half-buried in the ash could be what was left of either machines or animals. He had no desire to find out the answer, to intrude upon their death.

Black, grey, and charred brown were the only colours in this world. The only fitting hues to represent the archaeology of an apocalypse. Anything brighter might seem like a blasphemy in this barren place.

And hanging over it all was a black sphere of incredible size. It cast a bizarre, penumbral light as if it had, impossibly, eclipsed itself.

If pressed to describe the colour of the canopy in which the swollen sun hung, he'd be forced to admit the truth by muttering the word "Unknown."

He shielded his eyes and looked through shaking fingers at the sun. The black circumference roiled and shifted, becoming something even darker than black, something even more absent.

He'd never heard of a scientific phenomenon like this. It didn't fit into any easy category. By rights, any sun that had burned itself out should be any colour except black. And this one was still burning, as the stifling heat proved.

Over the course of several minutes, the globe had swollen. Now it filled far more of the sky, nearly touching the horizon. He had no way of knowing if it had drawn dramatically closer or was expanding in size. Whichever it was, it had happened with astonishing rapidity—far more quickly than any normal astronomical event. He pushed to the back of his mind the awful thought that maybe it was responding to his presence here.

He dared to raise his eyes to look directly at the great black circle once more. Its surface looked as if a million snakes were writhing over each other with a never-ending malignant energy. He didn't know if he should really call the radiation it gave off "light," but whatever it was, the dark illumination had increased painfully.

"Never stare at the sun," his mother had told him when he was a child. She couldn't have imagined anything like the nocturnal light of this dark sphere, but maybe the advice was still good. He lowered his eyes, clamping his eyelids shut to get some small relief from the aching illumination. Behind his eyelids, bright white snakes writhed away from an enormous white globe, like sperm desperately trying to escape a hungry ovum.

His eyes ached and throbbed within their bone cage, as if they, too, longed to escape.

Within the light there was something else. He could sense its endless, tumbling, mindless ruminations on nothing. There was a kind of vacant hunger, too.

For better or worse, this orb was alive. He became aware, buried within the chaos of its consciousness, that it craved worship … that it considered itself a god.

Sinking into a state of mild shock, he prayed that it was just his imagination, because the implications were terrifying if what he sensed really was the truth. If this is God, then who will help us?

He knew that his own ambition must have played a part in his fate. The revelation of a god that was also a star demanded something beyond science. Beyond the sane and the possible … it was something that he'd found only once before, within the pages of an insane tract.

He had read a very old book once by a man called Dee— itself the shadow of a much older text—and he'd thought he could do better. He'd laboured at it for years. This place was an answer, of sorts, to his arrogance.

His own work had brought him here. Through some unknown, unwitting conjunction of thoughts and practices and a bumbling combination of blasphemies he had condemned himself.

He cursed himself as he walked up a dune of dirty ash. Such stupidity deserves no other fate, he thought. Now he was trapped here and would die a charred, lingering death.

As he reached the top of the rise, he saw a wide flat expanse of nothingness. Yet there were strange shapes rising out of the desert of grey and black.

Eight thin pyramids rising from the plain of emptiness. They could easily be the tips of eight spires, their full height buried like icebergs beneath the sea of ash.

They reminded him of eight enormous fingers, pushing up through the ground, reaching for the bloated black sun. He began to walk towards them, shading his eyes in the peculiar light, hoping to pick out some detail.

Once within the shade of one of the spires, he could rest his eyes for a few moments. They ached and strange shapes danced across his vision. After a minute or so of respite, he raised his head to stare up at the strange shapes.

Toward the tip of each spire, ten or twelve feet off the ground, there were a series of letters written in three distinct alphabets. One was English. He walked laboriously from spire to spire, his lungs complaining at each step, and read what was there.

Many of the letters had crumbled, leaving the cracked alphabet of desolation now unreadable.

Only six of the eight elongated pyramids still held letters that were uncorroded and legible. He spelt out the word Z-A-T-H-O-T to himself. Puzzling over it for a few moments, he was on the verge of dismissing it as nonsense when a faded memory pushed its way forward, bringing the two missing letters with it.

A name, remembered from a clandestine book—a name masked by a thousand others—slotted exactly into the empty space in his mind. A perfect fit. Azathoth.

The name was weighted down with centuries of fear; from that name all darkness would rise. A name definitely not to conjure with, and never to speak out loud. This then was his crumbling throne, his rusted crown, the pain hidden behind the secret words. This place, at the end of time, was the death of every hope. A garden of ashes.

A shiver of fear ran through his body. He remembered sketchy details of the words he'd read, but none of them was good. He needed to escape from this place … but he didn't have any idea of even how to start. Without his books he was useless. And he daren't try any half-remembered formulae.

At the far side of the final spire, he was met with a sight that sent a cold chill through him, even in this scorched landscape. The remains of twelve figures knelt on the blackened surface, hands clasped before them as if bound, or perhaps joining together in some obscene prayer.

All of their heads were raised to the sky, staring straight at the black orb that burned darkly overhead. But their sightless eyes had been burned black and blinded a thousand years ago.

He forced himself to step forward, trying to drive from his mind that the blackened things before him had once been people. Their skin was a collection of fragile flakes, barely clinging together to form a shell. He imagined that their skeletons, buried within the ashen crust, must be similarly desiccated and charred.

He stood next to one figure. Like the others it was kneeling, blackened hands clasped together at its chest. It was impossible to tell what sex it had been.

Forgetting himself, he reached forward and placed his hand on the head of the figure. A few scorched remnants of cloth crumbled as his fingers brushed them. He withdrew his fingers, realising that the body itself might also be as fragile, and that he had no appetite for disturbing the dead in that way.

He had pulled his fingers away too late. Even that slight disturbance of the air was sufficient to provoke the destruction of the calcined cranium. The bone beneath the desiccated covering crumbled, leaving the darkened skin horrifyingly intact for a moment, the face sagging and deforming before it, too, flaked away to nothing.

What remained of the head became a small cloud on the wind. He quickly closed his mouth and held his breath as he turned away, not wanting to inhale the corpse dust.

He felt ashamed at having disturbed the corpse. He realised that ideas like respect and dignity had been scorched from this place long ago, but he couldn't help feeling a pang of pity.

Sorrow filled him as he stared at the figures. He had no way of knowing if they were priests or prisoners … or some final sacrifice to the dark deity that they saw as their ruler. If the latter was true, their offering had been in vain.

As he turned his back on the awful scene, he saw a thirteenth figure. This one had clearly been bound, though any bindings that held him had corroded ages before. It was clear from the way the limbs were twisted, spreadeagled, that they had been secured to the tall black pyramid. Blackened remnants of teeth were visible in the gaping mouth, no doubt opened in one final desperate scream of defiance. Like the other figures, the eyes were hollowed dark shells. He dreaded to know what the figure's final sight had been, before his sight had been cruelly burned away by this hellish place.

Something from an ancient book pressed its way to the front of his mind. He gasped in a lungful of burning heat as it dawned on him at last where he was. The pieces had come together—this was his world. And it was the last of a million charred worlds, sacrificed to the idiot greed of a god.

Yet hunger was all he felt pouring like befouled light from the dark star above.

Surely to have devoured a billion minds, blinded two billion eyes—to have a silenced a billion times a billion voices—surely this was enough for any god?

The truth was inescapable. God wasn't dead: he was simply mad, deranged. Hope was now just a four-letter word.

He noticed that grey blotches had begun to appear on the backs of his hands. Pulling up his sleeves, he saw that they were on his arms, too. Like ink spilled on antique paper. The alien radiation—whatever it was—had begun to claim him.

Suddenly, an astonishing sound reached him on the seared air. Voices, or something very like them. Vaguely human voices at that. He turned back to the cremated figures, astonished to find it was they who were making the sound.

Their mouths all hung open in what he had assumed was their final death agony. Even the figure bound to the spire was emitting the horrific sound. Not agony then, but praise. That seemed far worse to him.

More of a drone than a chant, the dead, dry throats croaked a ragged requiem to their uncaring god. Even death was not the end of their devotion. They were still called on to recite this empty litany in an alien tongue—allowed no rest, no final peace. For him, that was the ultimate cruelty.

Old gods die hard, damning us for starving them of devotion, failing to sate their greed for obeisance. This deity demanded an eternity of obedience and service, like an eternal slave-master driving those under him with a brutal disregard.

The obscene choir was accompanied by an odd, wavering piping sound coming from the distance. He looked around, but nothing and no one could be seen in the featureless burnt landscape.

His eyes moved from one ruined face to the next, convinced

that the souls that had once lived behind them must have long since rotted away, leaving them mere blackened automata. His stomach turned over at the inhuman sadism of their tormentor and the bleakness of their plight.

A soft, hot wind stirred up a feeble tornado of ashes just in front of him. Even though he covered his face with his greying, grimy hands, the stink of despair on the wind still reached him.

The blackness above continued to roil and grow, shapes within it writhing over each other in an eternal dance of madness. A never-ending turbulence of empty thought emanated from it, unthinkingly sucking in all life around it.

This greedy god had made him want to end his life. To escape somehow. But he had nothing with him that he could use to even harm himself slightly, let alone end his life.

Madness then, is the only route out of the maze that his racing thoughts could find. But how long would that take?

He felt like a man sliding down an endless wall of black glass, with nowhere to grip on to and no way to signal anyone on the other side who might aid him.

He would force this obscene dark god to release him. Burning his mind out was the only thing left to him!

He turned, eyes wide open, and stared straight at the gargantuan black disc. Holding his head there, shaking with pain, he looked straight into the black nothingness that was the face of this blasphemous deity.

His mind raged with the emptiness and chaos emanating from the swelling blackness. The pain in his eyes began to cut through him, like steel slicing into the centre of his skull.

A searing whiteness spread through his mind, leaving a trail of utter darkness behind it as his sight was burned away. Whimpering in agony, he slumped forward into the burning ashes, which now felt cool in comparison to the white-hot agony inside him.

In a reflex of pain, his muscles pulled him up into a kneeling position. Spasms of agony held him in place, unable to move. His neck arched back with cramp, forcing his face to point skyward.

Gazing at the sun he could no longer see, he heard his voice join the choir of worshippers as he cried out in his final, eternal agony.

Having glimpsed the ashen future, he awoke to blackness and a chill that would never again leave him. The crumpled page beneath his fingers seemed to burn with an ancient and cold fire.

Lifting his fingers to his eyes, he sobbed in relief that his sight was still intact. But what now was worth seeing? Anything beautiful was simply a hollow mask hiding the withering chaos behind it.

His vision of the empty centre of everything had left him with the conviction that his eventual death would be no release at all.

No, God isn't dead.

And neither will he allow us to ever taste the mercy that death brings.

Put on the Mask

Tickets for the performance can be found scattered all over town, though no one dares pick them up for fear of becoming the supporting act. Not that there ever is one. Not in the way you or I would understand it, at least.

Lift the mask to your face, peering through the waiting eye holes. Put it on. Secure it in place. Wear it, uncertainly, uncomfortably, each day for the rest of your life. For fear that people see the truth in your face.

Motionless, he lies in the dream of days, unmoving and uncertain. But there is no rhythm of night and day for him, just endless grey. Since his accident, colour has been a thing only seen in memory and occasional dreams. Sounds increasingly hold less and less meaning.

He is aware of being the victim of something, if only of circumstance. Gathering his feeble energies, he concentrates on regaining the power of speech. But even that seems to be futile.

The doctor and two nurses who attend him, all masked, remain silent the whole time. One even refuses to answer questions, dismissing him with a slow shake of her head.

There is a clock on the wall opposite his bed. He makes careful note of the large black number in the date display. Whenever he is awake, he watches its slow progress as it crawls towards the top of its small window on the clock face. Only boredom and illness can provide the clarity needed to notice its tiny incremental movement.

Unaccountably, he awakes on the third day with his body healed. He feels healthy. There is no bruising, and nothing is broken. His muscles don't ache in the least. His vision is clear, and his hearing seems as sharp as it ever was. He knows he's been in some sort of accident, but the details are missing.

At first he waits for the doctor or the nurses to appear. After an hour and a half, he decides to rise from the bed. He dresses slowly in the clothes draped over the room's single chair, which he assumes are his, despite their unfamiliarity.

Poking his head out into the corridor, he sees no one, so he walks down the corridor to the reception desk. Still there is no one to be seen. After standing at the desk for five minutes watching another clock, expecting a nurse or receptionist to appear, he decides to discharge himself. To his surprise the front door of the hospital is a mere few steps away.

Once outside he looks back at the door, hoping for a clue as to his whereabouts. There is no sign on, above or to either side of the entrance and he finds himself standing on an ordinary street. It is as if the hospital is trying to deny that it is one, he decides. For a moment he thinks it must be a private medical facility—then concerns about the hospital bill float into his mind. He shakes them off. Whatever the cost, it feels worth it. He doesn't know exactly what medical care he's received, but he's never felt better.

The street is surprisingly empty for near midday, so he decides to try and find a sign that will tell him where the railway station is. He's sure he recognises one or two buildings and, gradually, more and more things become familiar. This isn't his home town, but he suddenly remembers his brother's house is just across town. Even if his brother isn't there, he can wait for him.

His mind made up, he heads in the right direction, deciding to stop for some food on the way. He digs in his pocket but comes up empty—no money and no wallet. His brother is his only hope, in that case, he decides. He'll just have to go hungry until then.

He stops at a junction, waiting for the lights to change. The cars and other vehicles that crawl past the lights are a mixture of old and obsolete vehicles. Their drivers all seem in a state of torpor. Not bothering to wonder why, he looks down at his shoes, waiting for the lights to change.

There, at his feet, two brightly coloured pieces of paper seem too enticing to ignore. He bends and, at the instant he plucks one from the floor, he stops. His name. The piece of paper has his name on it. His old name. And a time. And a place. And the promise of some sort of performance. But that's impossible.

"For One Night Only." He exhales suddenly, a half-snort of disbelief. This is impossible. He is no longer a performer and, even if he still had been, how could this have been arranged without his knowledge? He knows the address printed on the ticket but is certain there is no theatre there. At least, there hadn't been the last time he …

This is a mistake. Or a joke. Some sort of hoax, maybe. He can't imagine who would want to do this—he is loved, respected—but he intends to find out.

The only people he sees on his way there all seem to be ill or old, their faces grey and lined, most of them stooping or turning their gaze away. Every shop is dark; either closed, and looking like it will never open again, or boarded up. It seems like the town and its inhabitants are slowly dying.

He tries to shake off the feeling, doing his best to convince himself that it is simply a type of "hangover" from the treatment he's received. That maybe the residue of some drug still in his system is causing him to suffer from some sort of mild depression. But he can't ignore the evidence of his eyes. Or his nose.

The fallen leaves that clog up all the gutters are the colour of rotting meat. The suggestion is so strong that he sometimes imagines he can smell the awful throat-clutching stench.

Further down the street, he notices a brightly lit building. Convinced it was in darkness only minutes earlier, he makes his way towards it. The neon is bright but not gaudy, and he recognises the name from the tickets he picked up—Théâtre Du Monde De L'Ombre.

There in the display case beside the door is a poster with his name on it. The stage name he hasn't used in years. "For One Night Only" is emblazoned across the poster. "They'll be lucky," he thinks. He'll confront the manager, demand an answer.

From the name and the design of the facade he thinks that perhaps it's a Burlesque theatre. Behind the polished wood and chrome door he imagines a delicious den of modern demimondaines, tattooed and tempting. While he has no intention of treading the boards himself, he smiles at the thought of seeing a pleasing performance or two. He'll demand free tickets as some small compensation for the impertinence of the poster, of course.

The doors swing shut behind him with a satisfying thud. The lobby has wine-coloured carpets and cream walls, and, like the hospital reception area, it is deserted. Another clock stares down at him from above the ticket office window. He watches its hands for a few moments before tapping the window and shouting "Hello?" Nobody comes.

He paces back and forth, wondering what to do next. Out of the corner of his eye, he catches a glimpse of someone looking at him from around a corner. He turns in time to see a head bob back out of view.

A memory rises like a startled bird. He is sure he recognises the girl. That platinum hair. Surely it's her.

He runs to the corner where she's been. Double doors stare back at him. Above them is written the word "Stalls." Fearing a sudden shock, he reaches out and pushes the door open gently. Gloom stares back at him from a quiet corridor. Its floor has a gentle upward gradient.

He puts one foot through the door, despite his nervousness. An unexpected reserve of courage pulls the rest of his body through after it. "Hello?" he calls, softly. The door swings shut behind him, shutting out most of the light from the lobby.

The end of the corridor holds a velvet darkness that drinks in his gaze and gives him nothing in return. He puts out his hand to touch the comforting solidity of the wall, then makes his way slowly into the gloom.

He stops for a second. Was that someone moving in the darkness? He couldn't be sure if it was just his eyes playing tricks as they adjusted to the dark. Or was there really someone there? He feels something brush against him and he gasps, surprised. A hand grabs his lower arm.

"Is that you? Hehe …" It must be the girl with the platinum hair. Then more hands grasp him, pulling at his arms, tugging his clothes. He tries to pull away.

"What …? Who are you?" He begins to feel panic. It is answered by a volley of whispers, a dozen voices emerging out of the darkness, luring him on. "This way. This way. This way. This way."

Something about the way the air moves past him convinces him that the corridor has disappeared. He is somewhere else now.

As a tiny hand touches the top of his head, he jerks it sharply to one side. Trying harder to pull away now, he cannot move; the darkness already has him in its grip.

He'd met her first in a cafe. She was with friends; he was not. At first his broken-backed, limping words seemed to have no effect on her. Then she looked again and seemed to recognise something in him that she desired.

Her friends, all nearly identical with their dyed platinum hair and heavily painted eyes, seemed to melt away at some point during the evening until they were alone. Together.

Whenever she ordered food it was like eavesdropping on someone's prayers, murmured in pain. She toyed nervously with the thick gold bangles around her wrists. They talked about nothing, really. Inconsequential. Idiotic.

Then. "Come back with me," she'd said in her child's voice. She seemed so young. But so ready for his love. She seemed to be just what he wanted. What he needed.

Frightened of his pleasures, he is too drunk with them to stop himself. "No names," she insisted, pulling him towards her.

The rain entered her room, soaking them through as they lay together and kissed. "Wear the mask for me," she said. "F-for you?" Placing it over his face, she replies "Yes. It's your body I want—I don't want to have to look at your filthy feelings." It was clear to him now that he was merely a toy of flesh to her. A reverse of fortunes indeed. "Put on the mask now, Phantom.

Step onto the stage and prepare for a song you will never sing; lie on my bed and prepare for the ecstasy that will never arrive." A threnody of broken gasps and cries reaches his ear, a hit single of co-mingled despair and shock. There is nothing but darkness around him. Sounds reach him through the thick velvet nothingness.

The voices are all small. Some are angry; others simply broken, damned. Locked in. No escape from his hands.

Some of the voices are his own. "You're so much prettier than your mother."

"Don't be afraid."

"It's a secret, OK? Just you and me. No one else."

A shuddering chorus of angry denials, screams, shouts shakes him like a train rumbling by, right over the grave of his still-living corpse.

He remembers crows cawing on the heath as he walked to school when he was a child. No matter how fast he walked, he could never outdistance them. He felt that same way now. They will always be there.

The voices crowd in on him now. They threaten to suffocate him, drown him out forever. They crush his mind, and he screams.

The eye holes have grown bigger. There is a tear at one corner of the mouth. The mask is not what it was. And what if one day it should come to pieces in your hands, as you struggle to put it on? People would see your true face.

He awakes in the theatre. In an aisle seat. The dust and dryness of the old place fill his mouth and nose. There is someone at his side. Startled, he gasps, and turns his head. She is standing, leaning forward. "You fell asleep," she says, reaching out her hand to him. "Come on, you're due on stage."

"O-on stage? Me ...?" He allows himself to be helped to his feet and towards the waiting spotlight. As they move forward, the empty auditorium around them seems to fill up. The same shadowy faces, the same whispering as in his dream. The same barely suppressed anger and pain.

She tugs at his hand. Nods. Smiles. "Yes. Come on. They're all expecting you."

He allows himself to be dragged forward. "But where did you ...?" he begins to ask. His words don't seem to matter as they head towards the steps leading up to the stage. He has to prepare for his impromptu performance, trying to remember all the little tricks that made him so popular back then.

He almost trips as she pulls him up the short flight of steps. "Slow down, please."

Once on stage everything seems very different. The flats are punctured and razored in long tears, rattling in the merest breeze. Antique, desiccated vermin crunch beneath the soles of anyone unwise enough to venture onto this ghost-crowded stage. Secret pacts made in the dark are briefly revived, reverberating around and beneath the seats, echoing down the bricked-up corridors of misplaced lust.

He feels uneasy. Outside the theatre looked brand new, nothing like this near-derelict husk. "I-I just want to see the manager. You see, nobody's booked me. I've just come out of hospital this morning. Nobody's said ..."

She holds up a hand, smiles reassuringly. "Don't worry. The owner will be along very soon. Then it will all become clear."

He stands awkwardly, like a schoolboy who has been waiting outside the headmaster's office for most of his life. He becomes so used to the silence that when she speaks it is like a gunshot.

"Did you hear them? Did you dream of them? Even your own daughter. You bastard!"

He turns to look at her, startled. "What? What did you say?"

With a few strides she is at his side. "You heard me, you filthy old bastard." There is a darkness in her eyes that scares him. How could she possibly know anything about his ... tastes? They'd spent just one night together.

When in doubt plead for mercy, that's what his mother taught him. Not that it had done her any good once his father had emptied the bottle. But he can't think of any other way out right now.

"Look. I don't know what you're talking about. Please— I'm just not up to this right now. I've only just got out of the hospital." His words seem to elicit no pity from her, so he adds, slowly: "I had an accident. I was lucky to survive." At that, a slow cruel smile creeps along her lips. The smile seems to plant an image in his mind.

The accident. Is it an accident when someone pushes you, trying to silence your tongue, your words smashing apart on a hard concrete floor at the end of a long fall down a stairwell? An accident. That was what he'd called it, but now …

She stands before him, shaking her head. "No accident. I was sent to fetch you." A flicker of understanding passes through his mind, but before he can grasp its meaning, she grasps his chin and forces him to look at her.

Then the girl with platinum hair removes her mask and he sees the truth at last. Hope falls, reeling headlong into a deep pit. He hasn't seen her since they took her away. He hasn't been allowed to.

"You! B—but we …," he begins.

"Not for the first time!" she hisses, anger nearly strangling her words at birth.

He draws in his breath sharply. "But how are you here? You're still alive."

She slides the wide gold bangles from her wrists and holds them out to him. They bear the ugly deep scars of fatal wounds. They hadn't told him—he hadn't even been allowed that.

"D-dead," he breathes, in a voice as hollow as his every promise.

"I don't want to see your disgusting fucking face! Put on the mask, he's coming; the ultimate audience, the final critic."
He looks up and the small theatre is suddenly full. There must be hundreds of them. None of their faces are clear. There is a light in his eyes, but he can still make out that they are all children. Every seat is filled by a small figure, just like the children's matinees he used to perform at. Some are smaller than others, but they are all silent. All gazing at him.

He looks behind him. She is standing there like some wardress, ready to punish any infraction of the unguessed-at rules. He realises that he is dressed in his old stage clothes, now spotted with mould and hanging in tatters.

A bang at the back of the theatre makes him peer into the darkness. A door has just slammed. The figure who has entered strides forward purposefully. As he passes each row of seats, the figures of the phantom children evaporate into nothing, leaving not even a wisp behind.

Now the man has reached the front row. His appearance causes the ragged figure on stage to gasp and back away in fright, only to be intercepted by the girl and forced back to his former place.

To some the man would seem smartly dressed, to others it would appear overdone. Gloved and hatted. His movements are slightly too precise, as if considered by an actor, calculated for maximum effect. But the face itself is hardly finished. The gloved hands appear imprecise and clumsy.

The shabby figure on the stage does not dare turn around again but does not want to look at his "audience" either. He stares into the painful glare of the spotlight, praying for blindness. He can feel her hate-filled gaze upon him. "The stage is yours, old man. This is your time. Give us one of your standards. Sing "Light As a Feather"," she instructs.

She looks at the solitary seated figure. "For your pleasure, sir," she says, indicating the pathetic figure in rags stood before her. The man nods enthusiastically. With a wave from him, the tiny orchestra pit suddenly becomes peopled by musicians.

Every member of the small orchestra looks emaciated and terrified. Their sharp elbows poke through the faded cloth of their striped clothing. The leader, hollow-eyed, looks up at the figure on stage for a moment before turning to his companions. Bows begin to scrape dryly, the horns emit a few spare, wheezy notes.

It is a tune he is familiar with, he thinks, though it is hard to make it out at first, given this near funereal rendition.

The sudden impact of her shoe in his back reminds him he is expected to perform. Afraid to begin, yet more afraid of what might happen if he doesn't, he begins to croak out the first line of his most famous song. His voice catches, and he stands shamefaced while his body shakes with a coughing spasm.

The solitary punter looks up. In a voice rough and rusty

he asks, "What's this? Has the actor forgotten his lines ... the singer, his song? No!"

More afraid than ever of the consequences of failure, the tattered performer begins again. The orchestra begins scraping away once more. His dry old vocal cords begin to grind out the words.

"When we're—togethe-e-er, I (cough) feel as light as—a—feathe-e-er, My heart is—" The words stop as his chest fills with pain, his throat with the dust of desolation and disappointment. Falling to his knees, he struggles to keep his spine straight for a few seconds, then falls flat on his face, choking.

She steps forward, looking down at him with glee as he jerks with pain, his eyes rolling back. When he is finally still, she clasps her hands together in front of her. She kicks the limp body just once. The impact dislodges the mask he has worn all his life, revealing the ugliness and corruption it has covered for too long.

From the front row, the call of "Encore! Encore!" is spat through brown, sharpened teeth. The solitary audience member's gunshot-loud clapping sends clouds of dust up into the air, drifting slowly towards the stage to rain down upon the collapsed figure lying there.

The punter stands, picking up the expensive-looking coat laid across the seat beside him, and turns to leave. He glances once over his shoulder at the heap upon the stage, the man's daughter standing over him, trembling, hands clasped in prayer to some imaginary god of revenge and redemption. Both victims. He grins in malicious satisfaction, enjoying the symmetry. As he walks towards the exit, he yells over his shoulder: "Your finest moment!"

The heavy door swings shut with a final thud as he leaves the theatre. He spares a single glance at the poster beside the door. Across it a cheaply printed two-colour red-and-white banner reads "Tonight—and every night!"

The street down which he walks has changed beyond all recognition, as if a theatre flat had fallen to reveal the truth hidden behind it. Along its length a million other theatre fronts show a million identical banners.

The Turn of the Tide

At first, none of us could work out why the tide was so strange that evening. It rushed at our feet, devouring them in a fuss of foam, when the tide tables said it should have been nearly a half-mile away across the beach.

We wandered up and down the shoreline, scanning the sky and sea as if an answer would suddenly present itself, and we could all laugh and sigh in relief before going home.

But by the time darkness began to close in, and Rosemary had to leave to begin her drive back home, we were still none the wiser.

The following morning, when Kate returned from her customary walk, she was nearly in tears. Ed and I stood and listened, leaning forward now and then to hug her, as she told us of the disturbing flotsam she had come across on the beach.

There was a fish, she said, that was all fins. Just fins and a mouth; no eyes that she could see. It was lying dead by the big rock.

Then further on she'd found two birds, each with just one wing. One was flapping helplessly, cawing loudly in distress, the other was dead. "It was like they'd been one bird, and someone had pulled them apart somehow ... and just abandoned them. But all the life was left in just one of them. It was horrible!"

After a sit down and a strong cup of coffee, the three of us bundled up and went down to the beach. We looked for a long time but there was nothing.

Kate turned to us: "They *were* here!" Ed suggested that maybe another freak tide had come and gone, taking the strange things with it. I nodded in agreement, not believing a word of it.

I had hoped that Kate's suggestion of three weeks in a cottage overlooking a picturesque old fishing harbour might be good for all of us.

It would also serve to give my ex-wife Rosemary a break. She'd been acting as Kate's guardian ever since the accident that killed her parents. That was two years ago, and I could see more strain in Rose's eyes every time we met up.

There was a small gleam of hope in the back of my mind that I might get some worthwhile work done myself. Spending time with two unpaid models (though I *was* paying the rent) might lead to some interesting drawings, I'd hoped.

But now this incident with Kate had me worried. Perhaps it was a glimpse of what Rosemary had been struggling to cope with.

My pencils and sketch pad remained in the back of the car for the time being.

On the local news last night, they showed pictures from a farm about 20 miles away. A lamb had been born, more-or-less inside out. Yet it was still alive, running around in the field.

Ed looked squeamish, while Kate hid her eyes and made little noises of protest.

The item made the national news, too. They should have issued a warning beforehand. The pictures were revolting, truly disturbing. Something inside me wanted to scream out at how wrong they were. To me, they seemed to be the worst sort of pornography; nature inverted, mocked, life turned so obviously into a sick joke.

We didn't need our faces rubbed in it, did we?

Kate had arrived with nothing more than a small bag and a pile of wormy old books, which I presumed were for her thesis (I could never remember what she was studying, but it was something to do with archaeology).

In contrast Ed had almost filled my car with half the contents of his flat. It was a good thing Kate had driven down with Rose, or she'd have had to sit on the roof for the whole of the journey.

The town was tiny, more of a village really. It sat on a promontory with the old harbour visible from the living room of the cottage. There was a long, pale gold beach back down behind the cottage, reached by a maze of narrow, steep streets.

It was never really busy, but at this time of year the place had already waved goodbye to most of its tourists.

Ed and I have both been enslaved by Kate's deep green eyes and sweet lopsided smile. We both do whatever she wants with little protest, knowing that whatever sacrifices we have to make will be more than compensated for by the time we spend with her. Whichever of us she chooses, whichever night.

Perhaps we are both fools. Or just keenly aware of how lucky we are.

I think of them lying together, their bodies smooth and unblemished, maybe sleeping with their limbs entangled. But I don't feel I have the right to feel jealous; she should be with him.

God knows why she's even interested in me, this sad old sack of raddled flesh. Perhaps because, to her, I'm so old that I represent some sort of continuity, the lie of permanence, and the hope that there is something left when the flash and dazzle of youth have gone.

Well, she got what she wanted—me and my nephew together here at the bitter end of summer. I wonder what she'll do with it?

Towards the end of our first week there, Kate spent two nights with me.

On the second night I'd grown accustomed enough to things to notice that when she reached climax, she muttered some phrases in an unfamiliar language.

When we were lying together afterwards, I asked her about it. She was evasive and denied that it was some obscure old European language like Basque or Welsh. Soon afterwards we both drifted off to sleep.

The next day I gathered my courage and asked Ed if she did the same when she was with him. He seemed embarrassed and uncomfortable, which was unlike him. He denied that she did.

"She just says my name," he insisted. Though I can always tell when he's lying. Just as I can with his father.

A few days later, Kate and I were talking in the lounge of the cottage. She'd been fascinated by reports in the newspapers of the events at the nearby farm earlier in the week.

She said she thought someone or something was changing things, experimenting with them. "You know. Making them better."

I was puzzled how she could think that way, be so calm, after how upset she'd been. I flopped down into a chair. "What? You mean nature?" I asked, knowing full well that evolution was a game played over thousands and thousands of years, not a matter of mere days.

She stood looking at me with her green eyes, clutching one of the old books she'd brought along, her mind working around the idea. "No. Not nature. But something like that."

I puffed in frustration. "There's nothing *like* nature, Kate. There's just nature."

"We don't know that, do we?" she said rhetorically before turning on her heel and walking into the kitchen, my sarcastic "Oh, I thought we *did*" left unsaid. She added "I'm going to find Ed" as she left.

She knew he would give credence to her irrational idiocies, if only because he was so besotted by her.

I'm normally an early riser. Ed and Kate are not. I had discreetly made sure that Ed and I slept as far away from each other as the cottage allowed but I had to pass his door to get downstairs.

As I crept down to breakfast one morning I could hear Kate sobbing in his bedroom. I suddenly felt angry that he'd upset her. What had the little idiot done to her?

For a second I wanted to burst into his room and confront him, but then common sense prevailed. I settled instead for some guilty eavesdropping. The voices were muffled, of course, but I managed to catch a few of Kate's sentences.

"… miss them so much, Ed. You don't understand, do you? I was wrong. I just want them *baaaaack*."

Content that it wasn't Ed who'd upset her, I gathered up my guilt and sneaked downstairs as quietly as I could manage.

Late that afternoon I found Ed at the back door, a pair of binoculars held up to his eyes.

"You'd be better off waiting for dark if you want to catch any unwary blondes stripping off." He ventured a half-laugh but kept the eyepieces pressed to his face.

I endured a further minute of silence then asked: "What are you looking at?"

He lowered the binoculars and handed them to me, pointing at the hill that rose just beyond the houses. "Up there. Something seemed unusual about that hill. Look at the trees."

I adjusted the lenses for my older eyes and peered up at where he had indicated. "The trees all seem to have joined together in one mass," he said.

I could see the branches wound together seamlessly, one tree becoming another, all moving as one when the wind passed through the leaves. What I could see of the trunks below them seemed to have lost their roundness, flattening out as if reaching for their companions on either side. I couldn't think what could have caused those changes but something inside me didn't like it.

"One mess, you mean," I said, handing the binoculars back to Ed in disgust.

"Shall we go up there and take a look?" he asked, as I walked back inside.

"No!" I yelled over my shoulder. That was the very last thing I wanted to do.

During a solitary walk along the beach behind our cottage, I began to feel a sense of deep unease.

I'm not given to being spooked, easily or otherwise. For a painter, I suppose I've got a very poor imagination, at least in that regard. But the wind that afternoon seemed to carry on it a scent of something awful, a slight tang of uncertainty, the taint of uncleanliness.

I dug my hands into my pockets and tried to ignore it,

walking back towards the cramped streets of the town. I noticed that a small group of men had gathered outside one of the pubs on the front, gesticulating in an odd fashion.

Turning to look out to sea, I saw a line of grey clouds settling themselves along the line of the horizon. I was sure they should mean something to me, like a set of signals that are perfectly clear to anyone with any sense.

I disliked the feelings that were tugging at me, so I drowned them in a glass or two of whisky at the pub a few doors down from the cottage.

Meal times at the cottage were a rudimentary affair. I'd have liked us to eat out every meal, but it was simply too expensive, so I usually shopped at the market every morning.

On the menu this time were lamb chops with potatoes and runner beans. Neither Ed nor Kate seemed very keen on this simple fare.

Eventually I felt compelled to ask if there was anything wrong with it. They both shook their heads but there was evidently something wrong with something, even if it wasn't my cooking.

"Ed keeps going on about the "weird things" happening. He keeps trying to explain them away and I just think he should just shut up," blurted Kate after a short pause. He looked across at her, peeved.

"Weird things?" Even though I'd asked, I knew perfectly well what they meant. But it might give them a chance to clear the air.

Ed detailed the catalogue of unusual things we'd witnessed, discreetly leaving out Kate's odd orgasmic utterances.

"Hmmmm. I see what you mean," I said.

"Well, I just don't think they add up to a pattern like you do, that's all. That, taken in isolation, they wouldn't seem so "weird" after all. They're just coincidences," he said.

Kate laughed, obviously unimpressed by his argument. "Maybe it's … a warning. Maybe the world has finally had enough of us. Maybe this is the way things are supposed to be." There was a look very like triumph on her face.

Ed turned to look at me and there was genuine fear in his eyes. Maybe it was the implications of what Kate had said, that the world he was so sure of would now become unrecognisable. Or perhaps it was the fear that she might simply be losing her mind; that he might be losing her.

I could offer him no answers and turned my attention to the undercooked runner beans on my plate.

Despite there being only a few years between Ed and Kate, it seemed like a gulf at times. They were both bright, of course, but she sometimes seemed as if she was made of different stuff to him.

He was already working in my brother's law firm and was beginning to make a name for himself. But he found Kate's moods unfathomable. It made me chuckle sometimes to see him struggling with her, particularly as his befuddlement meant she'd soon be seeking solace in me.

I suppose I must have a streak of sadism in me somewhere.

They had been arguing on and off all morning. Kate was adamant that there was "something" abroad causing all the strange phenomena that seemed to have haunted the summer so far.

Ever rational, Ed demanded that she agree that it might all just be a huge coincidence.

I dragged them into a small corner shop and bought ice cream for us all in an attempt to cool things down, literally. It didn't seem to work.

Ed decided to throw down a fresh challenge. "All right, all right ... if there is some "evil genius" at work, why haven't they shown themselves? Why are they so shy?"

Kate was gazing out at the sea. "What if we're looking at them right now?"

Ed looked puzzled.

"I mean, what if they're there? Just above the surface of the water, but we just can't see them?"

Ed shook his head. "But where would these giant invisible "things" have come from, Katie?" He only called her Katie when he was very annoyed with her.

"Well, maybe they've always been here, but they've only now woken up from a long sleep and here we are ... everywhere ... and everything's changed. And maybe they don't like that. You'll see."

She fished a few stray strands of auburn hair out of her mouth with her long fingers. "And don't call me "Katie" like that!"

I tried to remain as nonchalant as I could, licking my ice lolly, doing my best to look as if I was ignoring a little lover's spat. Though nothing is ever that simple with us.

We continued rambling along the side streets of the town. When Kate disappeared into a junk shop, I drew Ed aside, pretending to draw his attention to a box of books out front.

But when I suggested Kate might simply be letting her imagination get the better of her, he seemed outraged at my interference (that's what he called it— "interference"!) and stalked off into the gloom of the shop, following her.

Ed seemed aloof with me for the rest of the day, and he and Kate went off for a drink on their own that evening. I had dared to criticise his goddess.

I was evidently asleep when they returned. The next day I kept myself to myself. At least until the afternoon.

A sudden commotion from the kitchen interrupted me halfway through the sixth chapter of Vian's "Autumn In Peking." I put the book down and went to see what all the fuss was about.

Ed was kneeling in front of Kate as she sat on a kitchen chair, tears running down her cheeks. He dabbed delicately at the soles of her feet. She was dressed as usual, in a skimpy top and some shorts.

"What's wrong?" I asked, gazing down as he bathed her feet like a character in a Bible story. It would have made a very bad Victorian painting.

"Kate's feet are all cut up," said Ed, matter-of-factly.

Kate sobbed. "The beach was all hard. It had turned to glass. I felt the sand cutting me and tried to get back to the road. It was huh-huh-huh …" Her words became lost in more sobbing.

I patted her shoulder in comfort and bent to look at her feet. The soles were covered in tiny cuts, weeping blood.

"You must have trodden on some glass," I said, trying to brush off the impossibility of her words.

Kate continued sobbing. "Nuh-no. It was *all* glass!"

Ed held out the blood-stained towel for me to see. Sure enough, there were a few tiny fragments of glass glistening among the drying blood, but that didn't confirm Kate's story.

I felt it was my job to nod in a reassuring manner.

After we had both sat comforting Kate for a while, I left Ed to take care of her. I put my jacket on and headed down to the beach. Even after the recent strange events, I hoped to find a rational explanation for the state of Kate's feet. There would be a broken bottle that had been ground against a rock, the sharp detritus then scattered unnoticed across the sand, I was convinced.

But as I walked down the few steps from the road onto the beach, I noticed the sand made an unusual crunching sound under my shoes.

The place was deserted except for me. I knelt and gingerly rolled a few grains between my fingers. Instantly, blood appeared.

Wiping my hand very gingerly with my handkerchief, I carefully flicked off the last few grains clinging to my skin or stuck in the pooling blood. One or two grains remained on the white cotton handkerchief, and I examined them closely. They glistened like tiny diamonds in the morning light. They were glass.

The whole beach beneath my feet seemed to have been turned to glass. It was a hideous impossibility, but the stinging in my fingers told me it was true.

Walking on a few steps, I could see that there were tiny creatures stuck in the shining sands. Half kneeling, I could see they were some kind of mollusc, but one I'd never seen before, with a longish shell from which emerged tiny tentacles; all made of glass.

My head began to spin. I stood up and it seemed as if the

very skin of the world crawled with horror beneath my feet.

I steadied myself against a rock while I examined the sole of my shoe, pulling my hand away quickly at the strange sensation beneath my fingers. I peered at it, but the rock looked the same as it had yesterday, when I'd passed it while out walking.

My exploring fingers soon found that it was soft, yielding easily beneath even a very slight pressure. It had become like a giant sponge, discarded on the beach by a careless bather. Stepping back, I wiped my hand on my trousers. There was nothing on my fingers, not even water, but I wiped them again, just to be sure.

I walked further down the beach, wondering what the hell was happening to the world around me. Or happening to small pockets of it, at least. I briefly imagined it might be some sort of previously unknown pollution; God alone knew what monstrosities industry or the Government cooked up in their labs, or what by-products they dumped in the water. I nearly sniggered at my own paranoia.

After several minutes, I turned to look back at the town. Then I noticed there was a track across the beach. It was wide and slightly discoloured, cutting across the sand and part of the rock I had leant on earlier. As if something had passed this way, just as someone walking through tall grass leaves a trail of bent stalks behind them.

Squatting, I examined the sand at my feet. Just sand.

Later, when I was back on the beach road, I examined the soles of my shoes. Just like Kate's feet, they were tattered and torn.

Looking down on the beach, I could see the discoloured path clearly, stretching from the tideline to the sea wall. Yet the road was completely unaffected.

Whatever it was, wherever it had touched nature, it had changed it. Man's world, his structures and roadways, had remained untouched. But they, too, were made of natural materials, simply rearranged—how could they be anything else?

Perhaps that process of man-made change had granted them some immunity; maybe there was an unknown law that said only one metamorphosis of certain materials was allowed to take place before they became fixed forever.

Kate hobbled around gingerly on bandaged feet for a day-and-a-half. Her wounds healed astonishingly quickly. I supposed that the cuts had only been very shallow.

Ed was very solicitous, as I'd expected he would be, hovering around her, organising things, and never leaving her alone for a second.

I felt left out of it all and spent most of my time alone, reading.

Thinking back over the last few days, of how different things felt, I couldn't help thinking that for so long the tide had been going out. But now it was coming in and we were right in its way.

I tried to get out of bed without waking Kate, hoping I could move my arm slowly enough not to wake her. It was all I could do to stop myself from tracing the line of pale freckles on her left cheek with my finger, wanting to join the dots before kissing her on the nose as usual.

When I finally managed to extricate myself, I pulled the sheet back over her so she wouldn't get cold. It was then that I noticed the skin on her throat had become coarse and red. Strange that I hadn't noticed it before.

Over breakfast later I asked her about it, and she insisted it was a flare up of her eczema. Shortly afterwards she disappeared into her room and came back wearing a silk scarf. I hadn't meant to embarrass her and tried to reassure her. But she insisted on wearing it all day long.

I phoned Rose today. Even though I hadn't intended to before I spoke to her, I asked if she could manage to come down earlier than planned.

She thought I was talking about a few hours, but when I said I thought it'd be better if we left four days sooner, she was unsure whether she could make it.

"But why do you want to come back four days early? What's wrong?"

I made up some nonsense about us not having a good time and told a half-truth about Ed and Kate arguing all the time. But there was no real reason, of course—at least nothing I could put into words—so we left things as they were.

When I'd heard Rose's voice on the other end of the phone, it had been a straw that I knew I had to clutch at. I'd had an unusual feeling of unease at being in this place. I felt only she could rescue me; all of us. From what, I didn't know.

I knew it was a dream, but it felt like one of those lucid ones, where you think about waking up and then you do. Except that it didn't work this time.

Ed and Kate were at my side as I walked down the narrow main street of the town that led to the sea. But things weren't quite right, I felt.

Then, as one woman walked towards us, she began to blossom with strange fleshy growths, her skin stretching hideously. It was as if the meat she was made of was imitating things that had no business being on a human being, transforming her into a walking tree of flesh.

Around me everyone seemed to be going through a similar transformation. A man with enormously long arms tried to wave before being weighed down by the bulk of his obscenely unnatural limbs, laughing as he tumbled forward.

Another man seemed to be dragging his family along behind him, a woman and two children becoming lost as they grew into him, his face changing to become them as well as himself.

Two women who had been talking began to meld with the building they were standing in front of, just as a decorative bush nearby grew through them and took parts of them with it as it left.

I couldn't decide whether these people were becoming more or less than human. Even the seagulls overhead seemed to have been affected, their cries becoming chilling and unearthly.

Everything was becoming mixed up. There was a fine mist

of blood in the air, and I panicked at the thought I might breathe it in; so far I had avoided the changes being wrought around me, but this mist might be the catalyst.

I felt like I wanted to run but something prevented it. I was forced to carry on walking at my normal pace as if all this was inevitable, as if something didn't want me to be spared the fate of these others.

In a doorway, a limbless shape huddled in a corner, trembling and threatening to become something even more repellent.

We were nearly at the seafront now. I had deliberately not looked at my two young companions, fearing the changes that might have occurred. But now Kate turned to me and smiled with what her mouth had become. I couldn't scream.

"Wonderful, isn't it?" she asked. Then she pointed to the sea and said "Look!"

I looked but I couldn't see anything. There was something there, though, I could feel it: something gargantuan. The water parted as something unseen rose from it, enormous and overpowering, threatening to crush our minds as well as our bodies. Although I knew I would be prevented from doing so, I tried again and again to turn from it ….

I woke sweating and kicking, moaning incoherently. The things I'd seen still seemed to be there in the dark, holding back, staying just outside my vision. I sat up in bed and strained to see into the darkness, trying to penetrate it and make the shapes appear.

The dark had never held any fears for me, even as a child. But now I felt like a child, sitting there afraid to get up and put on the light in case whatever was in the blackness seized its chance.

As the sweat cooled, I began to shiver. I gathered my courage and leapt out of bed suddenly to flick on the light. Those two short steps to the light switch seemed to take longer than anything I'd ever known.

There was nothing hiding in the dark. I went through to the kitchen to make some coffee.

I sat alone in the dark for a few hours, sipping coffee and

wondering what on earth I was thinking in agreeing to come here. The old saying about there being no fool like an old fool had been proved agonisingly correct. I was just in the way.

Then there was the feeling that Kate *knew* something or was somehow drawn here. I had no idea what her game was, beyond the obvious one of having two men attending to her whims, but I determined to challenge her about it in the morning.

On returning to bed, I eventually managed to drift off for a few fitful hours. They were mercifully free of dreams.

I was awoken rudely by Ed bursting into my room just after seven without knocking.

"She's gone!" he yelled. It took me a few seconds to drain the last dregs of sleep and find my way to the waking world. The uneasy feelings left by my earlier dream still clung to me.

"Wha …? P'raps she's just gone out for a walk," I offered.

Ed seemed convinced otherwise and kept shaking his head. "She was strange last night," he said. Despite myself, I snorted in derision.

He continued: "She kept talking about the sea. And how she now knew what she had to do. I was so tired that I didn't take any notice of it."

As soon as I'd pulled some clothes on, we ran down the steep street at the back of the cottage. A kind of shared instinct told us where she'd gone. Above us, the perfect cloudless sky threatened to tilt forward, spilling out whatever lay behind it, to bury us forever.

When we reached the beach we stood panting, our gazes sweeping the sands for any sign of Kate. There was nothing, and I was unsure whether to feel panic or relief.

The sea was unusually calm, as if a storm had recently passed over. But if there had been a storm, it was unseen and unfelt by the inhabitants of the town.

I walked along the beach for a short distance, then stopped as I noticed something lying by a large rock. I called Ed over.

We looked down at the pathetic pile of fabric scraps for what seemed like several minutes, not wanting to acknowledge the awful implications. She was gone.

Then we saw the line of footprints that led across the beach. They struck me as strange, as if Kate had been moving in a manner other than her usual elegant gait. They stopped several yards short of the high tide mark. It was as if she had suddenly jumped into mid-air, leaving no trace behind her. Or ascended heavenward like some ancient mystic.

Ed and I stood side by side on the shore, staring out at the secretive sea as it held its tongue. She was out there; we both knew it. She had to be.

I just hoped that she had changed, become "better" as she would have put it, because God help her if she hadn't.

The Cobwebbed Bird House

Whenever she looks out of the window she has a view of a street emptied of houses. The holes where the shells fell are beginning to harbour a small forest of weeds and young trees. Occasionally a bird or small animal will venture through them, hoping for a scrap of food or some other advantage offered up freely by nature; they are seldom lucky. The woman sometimes cries while standing at the window, but there is no one now left to care or to wipe her tears. When the sun shines it merely irritates her and she prays hard for winter.

The photograph in her hand shows a dark-haired boy and a man in his mid-30s. The man has light stubble, and the boy has a brightness in his eyes that she remembers so well. The photograph is crumpled and creased badly along one edge where she struggled to free it from the grip of an angry woman. Yesterday, she saw the boy standing in the small scrap of garden that remains at the back of the house. His eyes were as bright as ever; quite different to when she saw him last. She quickly closed the curtains and turned away.

When it is cloudy and the sunshine is weak, she stands in the tiny garden. Then she tries to remember it as it was, the ghost ground stretching away under her feet. She has never seen the boy while she's been in the garden; only from the window and only once, so far. The remnants of the flowers strain to appear beautiful, reaching for the sun. She hasn't seen a bee in the garden for well over three years. The abandoned woman stands in the abandoned garden waiting for the sunset. Then she will go inside and face the dreams.

The walls talk to her, but it is hard for her to decide whether she is inside or outside of her dream. When she sleeps there are always images of the two of them, man and boy, walking towards her through cold morning mist. A crow accompanies them: it could be warning them or merely waiting for them to fall. Their slow footsteps are never numerous enough to reach her. The ground cannot support their weight. They fall and her heart falls with them. Then there is blackness, in the dark of the dream and in the hot small room.

The alarm clock on the night table tells her another long day is here. Often she wishes she had no eyes so that she didn't have to look at its accusing face. The sweat of her dream still clings to her. When she stands in the shower and turns on the tap she counts it a small victory that there is water today. She washes quickly as the supply might end at any moment. Sometimes the water turns brown or red as if it contained excrement or blood. Then she presses herself against the cold tiles to avoid its touch.

It is only when her vision blurs and her cheeks grow warm that she realises that the face in the mirror is her own, crying. The face displeases her; she remembers as a child wishing that all the world's pretty things would disappear, so that she would be the prettiest thing left. The tear tracks cut through the filth on her cheeks. Despite endless washing, the layer of grime always remains. The air is thick with it, settling upon her skin constantly. She wonders if the water in the lake, just a short walk through the trees, will cleanse her.

The trees stand frozen in mid-dance, limbs twisted fancifully, straining towards gracefulness. Many are dead and have now been engulfed by the hungry moss, egged on by the dampness from the nearby lake. She clambers over those trunks that have fallen, recalling her lonely childhood forays into another wood, far from here. When she suddenly finds the water is at her feet, she stops and steps back, wanting to turn away. But she forces herself to approach it, staring down now into its black mirror. For the first time since she was a very young girl, the water frightens her.

The dark water reflects a night canvas back at her, swallowing the blue mid-morning sky and refusing to show it to her. Ripples bend the mirror, remoulding it from moment to moment, and playing hideous games with her face. Despite her unease at being next to the water, she finds the courage to reach out her hand and slap the surface, creating her own explosion, fragments of the day flying away. Eventually the water settles into a placid smoothness. In the depths of the mirror, she sees a speck of white that may be the grudging reflection of a cloud.

Forgetting her intention in coming here, she kneels and peers down into the water. The white shape dances slowly as if caught in the secret nocturnal tides of the lake. It is no reflection of the sky but something that is wholly of this place that keeps things to itself. The object is moving towards her, falling upwards now, shaken loose from its submarine nest. A moment before it breaks the placid mirror, she realises it is a tiny bird's skull. It bobs before her, a reminder of her own death and her cherished dreams of flight from this land.

Lifting it carefully, it drips into her palm, like tears from the dead. She turns it over slowly, examining the empty orbits and the perfect curve of the beak. She remembers the boy holding out another bird's dry bones to her after his return from the park that once stood near the house. She had taken it from him and wiped the cobwebs from it. He'd told her of the birdhouse, hidden under the darkest tree at the edge of the park, and of the small avian skeleton secreted within. Dead too soon, she'd thought, like so many things here.

The empty eye sockets stare at her, sucking in her own gaze, negating her thoughts. She peers into the space behind them and feels how lovely it would feel to be so empty, so free of any painful duties of memory or feeling. The tiny cranium nestles in her palm, slowly leaking water onto her skin. The pool reflects the bone white accuser, reprimanding her silently for disturbing its rest and its lonely dreams of nothing. The sharpness of the small beak has been blunted by time and disuse. She thinks of how like this freshly liberated relic she is.

A chorus of birds seems to protest at the disturbance of their dead ancestor's remains, angry at her casual desecration of this avian relic. Then the woman notices that a man has emerged from the trees and realises it was a warning passed between beaks. Looking at him as he walks slowly towards her, she remembers the words of a childhood story: "Suddenly a wolf came from out of the dark forest." The man is shabbily dressed, and something covers part of his face. She catches her breath as she sees, just for a moment, the boy walking beside him.

The man clambers over fallen trees and splashes through the swampy shallows towards her. As he comes closer, she can see that what she thought was some sort of mask or an item of clothing over his face is really a scar. The sun catches the still livid areas of the old wound, giving him a frightening appearance. There is no boy with him, of course, and she thinks how stupid she was to have thought so. Soon the man is within a few feet of her. He stands, panting from his exertions, and breathes a woman's name; "Teresa."

She doesn't know what this man expects of her and turns away from him quickly. He repeats the woman's name, and she wonders if he thinks she is that woman. She looks at the bird's cranium in her hands and, turning, holds it out to the man. Maybe she is making an offering to him, but maybe she hopes he can tell her something significant about it. He peers at it for a moment, uncertain of whether to take it from her, and then his damaged face creases in painful recognition. This time it is a boy's name he breathes.

There is something hidden behind the names which the man has spoken that plucks at her memory, like an insistent child at its parent's sleeve. She looks around at the shining flat lake, the surrounding trees, the white objects collected on the far shore, and wonders if she should even be here. But her memories stay stubbornly submerged beneath the surface; she wishes she could shake them free like she had done with the bird's skull. She feels the man's hand in hers, softer than she might have imagined it would be, and he says the woman's name once again.

The touch of his hand makes her feel wanted for the first time in a hundred years. All she can think of is the photograph of the man and the dark-haired boy, together. She looks up at the sky, reflecting blue, and tries to clear her mind. The sudden confusion of faces makes her want to weep. After a few moments, she forces herself to look at the man. The scar is horrific but, behind it, she sees at last the man in the photograph. His face is older now, much older than it should be, but it is him.

Although he is talking to her, she cannot follow the train of words. "Wife" and "home" mean nothing to her. She fights with her memories, struggling to get them to make sense, to stand in line as she's certain they should. She remembers him pulling at her arm, insisting that his way was the best; that it was best for all of them and that things would calm down again within a few months. It wasn't the fighting, or the soldiers, it was him. He had taken the boy away from her; this man had robbed her of her son.

He moves forward and takes her by the arm, expecting compliance. But now she hates the memory of her hands on him and refuses to go back to that place. She pulls away sharply and he shouts, forcing her footsteps to take her into the shallows of the lake, water welcoming her with its soft grip. He begins to follow her, huge boots breaking the water noisily. There is fear in her face, and she remembers what she is holding in her hand. Bringing it up, she drives it into his one smooth cheek, the tiny beak splintering in flesh.

The man yells in pain and advances further. She clambers onto a fallen tree at the water's edge in an effort to escape his anger. The tiny fragments of bone that she still holds drop from her hand and are forgotten. The blue sky frowns down. Memories of the boy's screams mingle with those of her own as the man stretches his hand out towards her. Her footing is unsure, and she slips backwards off her perch, avoiding his fingers by a whisper. He begins to clamber over the obstacle, losing his footing on the wet wood and falling hard.

She clambers out of the water, on all fours, and is ready to run. But all she can hear is the birds singing, no sounds of human anger, or pain, or renewed resentment. She dares to creep back to the tree and peers at where the man has fallen. His face is buried in wood, his head at an unnatural angle. Blood mingles with the dark water, darkening it further. She dares to reach out and touch him; the movement of his torso as his lungs fill and empty is missing. She climbs onto the tree. He is simply still.

"Water cannot stain'" is her only thought as she watches

his blood swirl slowly out. His absence has allowed her escape but only down a lonely path, no son and now, no husband. She thinks of the house: it is the only thing waiting for her. After several minutes, her feet begin to carry her away from the lake. Gradually she makes her way back to the house. She stands in her room, praying that the rain will hold off and gazing out of the window at the scrap of ruined garden, hoping to see the boy appear once more.

The Last Ones

The sea-scented air blowing through the open side window almost served to clear away the cobwebs of the three-and-a-half-hour drive. The small office in the Midlands university where he'd started his journey seemed ridiculously far away as the vista of deep blue sea and sky opened before him.

He'd have been tempted to stop and drink it in, if it wasn't for the belligerent-looking farmer on a tractor following close behind him. The weather was very clear for this time of year, he mused. Particularly for the west coast of Wales, where things could get a little wild.

Just before he began the descent down the steep hill into Narmouth, he glanced across at the headland. There were two figures standing there, waiting to dive into the wildly crashing waves. They looked like a woman and a young girl, their figures obscured periodically as the foam flew up around them. Surely they would be dashed to pieces if they dived there, he thought; the rocks looked like razors. But then the figures were gone, and, within seconds, they could be seen swimming strongly away from the jagged shoreline. They were obviously practised hands.

Despite the small size of the town, Patrick had trouble finding the guest house. It was tucked away up a grey side street. The proprietor had tried to liven the place up by painting it light blue. But that was obviously years ago, and the paint was now peeling badly, as if the house had very bad skin.

There seemed to be no other cars around, so he parked on the slight gradient outside the guest house. The houses opposite looked grim and uninviting. Several broken windows told him they must be abandoned.

He walked up the steps of the house and noted the name painted above the door in black: "Glan Mor," which he knew meant "Seaside," It was the only hotel or guest house he could find listed in Narmouth, despite extensive enquiries and online searches. Even if it turned out to be a pit, he was only going to be here for three days.

He rang the bell and waited. After a short while, the door opened a fraction and a face with very smooth skin and a perfect little mouth appeared before him.

"Hello." He extended his hand which she declined to take. "Professor Patrick Neede. I rang last week to book a room."

Her eyes were the lightest grey he'd ever seen. He thought the colour almost ethereal, as if she were a deity, used to merely gazing down on the ants below her rather than moving among them. He found her intensely beautiful.

At length she nodded and swung the door open. "Please come in, Professor."

He tried not to stare at her as he heaved his heavy bag up the last step. "Thank you. And, please, call me Patrick."

"Elin Williams. I spoke to you on the phone." She indicated a door to the left, and Patrick struggled and fussed his case through to a small but comfortable lounge. He collapsed on a sofa, regretting bringing so much with him.

Elin stood looking down at him. She was striking and wore a simple white dress that ended below her knees. "I'm the owner, Prof … umm, Patrick. I hope you'll like it here. You wanted the room for two nights, didn't you?"

Once again Patrick found it difficult not to stare openly at her, being unused to such beauty. He nodded eagerly before Elin said, "Some tea" and disappeared into the rear of the house.

As they sat and sipped, Elin asked him why he had chosen such a lonely place and out of season at that.

"Nobody really comes here anymore," she said. "It was popular in Victorian times." She indicated a photograph on the wall that showed a pier, now long gone, crammed with promenading peacocks and peahens. A small steamer was moored at the far end, eager to take trippers on a jaunt around the bay.

"But the new road means most people just drive straight past now," she added. What she called the "new" road had been built back in the late 1950s, he remembered.

"I'm here to research your local celebrity," he beamed. Elin looked puzzled, her eyes searching the air for answers before Patrick stepped in with "Saint Deigion."

The woman seemed to stiffen in her chair. "Oh. Dyn y mor. Our 'man of the sea.'" She seemed slightly downcast at the news. "I suppose you'll be wanting to see the stones."

Patrick hesitated for a moment. "Err... the crosses, yes. You've seen them then?" This was the first concrete evidence of their existence beyond mentions in a dusty volume or two. There were no photographs and only one very bad drawing done by a local fisherman in the early 1900s.

"Yes, I have. You'd be better off leaving them be. It's very dangerous out there. People get drowned all the time around here. The beach falls away sharply, so it's very deep. And the tides coming round the headland are so strong ..."

Patrick nodded, glad of some local knowledge. "I'll be going at the neap tide tomorrow morning. I should be safe, because the water will be very low then."

There was an awkward silence. Patrick broke it with: "This is a sort of homecoming for me, in a way ... even though I've never been here before."

Elin looked at him as if he had just disclosed some awful secret. Her voice was very small and quiet when she spoke again. "Oh? How so?"

"Well, my mother was born here. In Bridge Street. She left a long while before I was born, of course. Do you know where it is?"

Elin nodded, seemingly with a sense of relief. "Yes. It's only two streets over. You should be able to find it easily."

"I don't know—it's quite a maze. I had trouble finding you. Perhaps you'd be kind enough to show me tomorrow?"

Elin clattered her cup into her saucer and stood up suddenly. "Rhiannon," she cried, quite loudly. Within seconds a girl of about 9 or 10 appeared in the doorway. It was clear from the family resemblance that the girl was Elin's daughter. But in contrast to her mother, the child was peculiar-looking, with huge, liquid eyes so large they stopped just this side of being monstrous. He felt uncomfortable looking at her. She reminded him of a doll that had the wrong eyes pushed into its head.

"Rhiannon. Show Pa ... the Professor to his room, will you?" The girl nodded and stepped to one side to allow Patrick to steer the large case past her. He followed her up the narrow stairs to a door on the first floor.

"Here we are," she said in a slow manner as she opened the door for him. After a nodded thanks, the girl departed.

His room was small but comfortable. Patrick's heart lifted when he saw that he had a view over the dismal row of houses opposite to the sea beyond.

He began to unpack the oversized suitcase, placing the object that had drawn him to this odd little town on the bedside table.

The book had a rubbed cloth cover with letters in faded gold— "The Lives of the Early Welsh Saints." It had been written in 1875 by the Reverend Eli Morgan and contained a 15-page chapter that was of special interest to him: the story of Saint Deigion.

The clergyman's over-elaborate Victorian English revealed that Deigion was "inspired by God" to erect a line of crosses on the beach at Narmouth. It was in the very same spot several years later that he walked into the sea during the throes of a religious ecstasy, never to be seen again.

It was claimed that the present town had grown up at this remote spot precisely because of the "miracle of Deigion."

But Patrick was most fascinated by the hints of several other scholars that Deigion had kept alive elements of the old Celtic religion, alongside the Christianity he professed to spread. Yet nobody had ever produced any evidence for this. Puzzled at his colleagues' lack of intellectual curiosity on this point, Patrick had become intrigued when Reverend Morgan's book revealed that the inscriptions on the crosses were written in ancient Celtic. If not carved by Deigion's own hand, they would certainly have been made under his direction; Patrick had decided he had to see for himself.

After consulting a meteorologist colleague, he'd discovered that the only time the tide would be low enough to see the crosses fully was at the neap tide of the Spring or Autumn equinoxes. He'd planned this expedition for four years but had always missed the dates due to other commitments.

Today was September 21st and tomorrow would be both the equinox and a full moon. The waters would be at their very lowest. And at this time of year any seaside resort was bound to be empty of tourists, which was an important bonus as far as he was concerned.

He took his shoes off and lay down on the bed to rest after his long drive. The tea had revived him somewhat, but a quick nap wouldn't hurt, he thought.

The town was tiny and seemed half-dead, with meagrely stocked shops that opened for just a few hours each day. The streets were mostly deserted. He supposed this was due to its isolated position, though he was surprised the picture postcard views didn't draw the tourists in.

Then again the view seemed cold and empty without the basic human comforts. And they were something this town seemed to ignore. Even the pubs—usually the mainstay of such communities—had doors that were resolutely barred to visitors.

At last, he found a tiny corner newsagent's shop that was open. He pushed the door, and an old-fashioned bell rang to announce his entrance. It was very gloomy inside the cramped space, and it was several moments before the proprietor emerged from the dimness.

The man had a large wisp of white hair on top of his head and a pair of gooseberry eyes set in a pale face. His colourless cardigan had obviously been a comfortable home to several generations of moths.

Patrick nodded to the man and muttered a subdued "G'morning," even though it was now mid-afternoon. The place had a smell like old sardines, and he felt reluctant to touch anything. He looked over the magazines on display, recognising the cover of one as being at least six months old.

There didn't seem to be newspapers on offer, so he asked

for his usual title by name. "Not today," croaked the seedy little man.

Patrick felt slightly crestfallen. "Will you be having a delivery later?" The man merely stared at him, as if unused to dealing with customers, before shrugging his shoulders.

"Thank you," muttered Patrick, turning to the door. As he reached for the handle, he heard a whispering begin. He knew he should simply ignore it, but he felt uncomfortable at being talked about and turned to glance back at the man, expecting to see a companion or co-conspirator at his side. The man stood alone, staring. The shop was silent once more.

Patrick pulled open the door and was glad to be back out in the daylight, able to breathe in a lungful of clean air.

After a few minutes' walk, he finally came to Bridge Street. Number 3, the house where his mother said she'd lived, was brown and shabby; it looked abandoned. No wonder Mum left this place as soon as she could, thought Patrick. The phrase "narrow horizons" seemed to have been invented for it, despite the view out over the bay.

He continued his exploration of the maze-like streets, eventually coming upon a small square where several streets met before continuing their near-precipitous descent to the quayside.

Patrick could see the back of a figure and welcomed the opportunity to strike up a conversation, hoping for a nugget or two of "local colour." As he approached, he realised his hopes would be dashed.

The man stood at the corner, face pointing straight up as he opened and closed his mouth in rhythm, gulping great mouthfuls of sky into himself. He looked as if he was drowning in air.

Dressed in shabby old clothes, the man was either deranged or in distress. Patrick was uncomfortable with the afflictions of others, so he backed slowly down one of the streets, unnoticed by the stranger. Feeling guilty at being such a bad Samaritan, he continued his exploration of the peculiar town, clustered around its tiny bay, guarding it jealously.

Some of the buildings looked very old, but nowhere did

Patrick find a single church, chapel, or other place of worship. As an academic theologian he always looked for such places—they told him a lot about the people who built it. It wasn't that he was a particularly devout man, but for a town that had been founded in honour of a Christian saint, the omission seemed puzzling to him. It was possible that the old clergyman had been mistaken on that point, of course. Maybe the entire town was in fact trying to hide from God.

After wandering around the corpse of a place in the cutting wind for nearly half an hour, he returned to his room and read for the rest of the afternoon.

As he ate the tasty but spare evening meal provided for him in the small dining room, it became clear that he was the only guest currently in residence. Elin appeared to tend to his needs periodically.

When he asked her why there were no places of worship to be found, she gave a vague answer about the townspeople "not having got round to building any." Patrick began to wonder if the town's founding fathers, the followers of Saint Deigion, had been closer to Pantheists than Christians, preferring to worship in the presence of nature than in any house of God.

Patrick smiled to himself as he ate, convinced more than ever that the town was a goldmine of pre-Christian worship. There was at least a brace of articles if not a book in it: a few more jewels for his crown.

As he walked back up to his room, he anticipated eagerly the secrets that the crosses might yield to him tomorrow.

Before retiring for the night, Patrick set his travelling clock for the ungodly hour of 6 am. He turned the light off and stood looking out over the water, lit eerily by the full moon.

There seemed to be no activity in the tiny town. No streetlights, no cars. But then he noticed that there were people moving about, more than during the daytime in fact.

The strong moonlight was throwing deep shadows, so he couldn't be sure. But it did seem as if there was movement, almost as if some broken procession was making its way along the street as it headed towards the shore.

Patrick wondered what their mission was. Possibly some nocturnal fishing. Then he noticed the small boat drifting on the silvery-grey sea. It was being drawn inevitably towards the shore, it seemed to him. He had no binoculars with him so he couldn't take a close look, but he was certain he saw something, or someone, lying in the bottom of the boat. He strained his eyes uselessly in the pale light, unsure of whether he'd seen a movement in the prow.

Under the tiny vessel the sea twisted and shrugged, a huge animal struggling to slough its troublesome skin. He watched it drift and turn in the moonlight until the sky clouded over and the boat became obscured by heavy rain. As rain bullets pinged dully against the window he smiled to himself; it always rained in Wales.

That night he was awakened by the strengthening rain and his clock told him it was 2:25 am. He plumped up his pillow and attempted to return to the dark depths of his unconscious.

But just as he was drifting off, he heard voices whispering. This went on for several minutes without ceasing. Frustrated, he sat up in bed and strained to catch what was being said. It wasn't English, that was for sure. And even though he couldn't speak Welsh, he knew the sound of the language from childhood hiking holidays. It definitely wasn't Welsh either.

He got out of bed and walked across to the door of his room, thinking the voices were coming from the corridor. But as he approached the door, he fancied the voices were coming from the room next door, through the wall. Cautiously, he edged the door open a crack. The corridor was filled with only darkness and silence.

He closed the door softly and stood listening once more. Gradually the whispers grew quieter before fading altogether. He stood there for several more minutes in the dark, to ensure they didn't return, before climbing back into bed, puzzled.

It reminded Patrick of what had happened in the shop that afternoon. He listened to the sound of the rain on the window panes filling the night before sleep welcomed him back.

The rest of the night passed in shallow sleep and half-dreams of perfect white crosses, etched deeply with Celtic writing, rising unbidden from the sea.

He rose very early and dressed warmly. He struggled into the waders he'd bought the previous morning and waddled down the stairs, feeling like a monster from some old horror movie.

As he reached the bottom of the stairs, he was surprised to see Rhiannon in the hallway. It wasn't yet seven, and he'd expected her to be in bed at this time of the morning instead of standing before him, staring at him with her solemn, large eyes.

"Oh, uhh ... hello," said Patrick. "Is your mother not around?" He felt suddenly that if he could gaze into Elin's wonderful grey eyes, it would be an omen of good luck.

The girl shook her head slowly. "She had to leave," she said, equally slowly. It seemed to be her only speed, he thought.

As he edged past her, Patrick said "Well, can you tell her I'll be back before lunch, please?" He tried not to notice the girl's strange glare but was sure he caught her nodding out of the corner of his eye.

Once outside, Patrick felt much easier. He quickly made his way to the end of the street and then down the steep lane leading to the beach. The rain had stopped during the night, leaving a sky that was light grey and gave an even, milky light.

The narrow band of shingle at the top of the beach soon gave way to a greyish sand. A dozen yards further on, he could see the sand become even greyer in hue. Elin had been right: the beach did fall off sharply not that far from shore, and he found it necessary to take the descent quite slowly.

He scanned the beach, his hopes falling with every second, before he finally spotted the crosses. They were just a line of darker grey stumps against the sand, but his pulse quickened in excitement at being so close to his goal at last.

Then his boot sank into the ground, and he discovered that the darker grey stuff wasn't sand at all, but a foul-smelling mud.

He rushed forward as best he could while the mud sucked at his feet, gripping him for seconds at a time before releasing him again. By the time he got near to the stone crosses, he was panting with exertion, his shirt damp with sweat.

They stood in a line, like five figures heading out to sea. There was a space between the third and fourth stones where another might once have stood.

Gazing out to sea, he thought that he spied what might be the sixth cross, just sticking up out of the water. But it might have been a trick of the light or a piece of driftwood, he thought. In any case, it would be impossible to reach.

Patrick fiddled around in his canvas bag and pulled out a notebook in which he began scribbling.

Reverend Morgan's book described them as crosses, yet they clearly weren't. Even taking account of natural erosion, or the fact that they might have started as the distinctive circular design of Celtic crosses, these were quite different. Pillars would be a better description, he thought. He took a step closer and off to one side. Somehow, even under the layers of encrustation left by the sea, the "crosses" seemed to have a peculiar twist in their design.

These couldn't be what the old clergyman was describing in his book, could they? They differed markedly from his description. For a moment he thought he'd come to the wrong place. But then he dismissed that as nonsense—after all, how many lines of stone crosses could there be that were visible only once or twice a year? His best chance was to clear away the detritus that had grown on the stones, he decided. The inscriptions would tell him what he needed to know.

He brought out a small hammer and chisel from his bag and, standing awkwardly to maintain his balance, began carefully chipping away at the limpet shells and detritus that covered the first cross.

For a second or so, he imagined that the stones didn't lead down into the sea at all but instead pointed the way towards the town. Something about their orientation struck some vague chord within him. But what use would they be to anyone? They wouldn't be visible to fishermen, except at a time when they couldn't use their boats. And swimmers would be unable to see them in the murk of these tidal waters.

As he worked away, certain figures could be seen emerging

from under the accretions of time. Slowly a full line of figures was nearly legible. He took off his gloves and brushed at the dark stone with his fingers. As the last bits of filth dropped away, Patrick saw a line of figures making up a strange conjunction of angles and loops. He was puzzled by what he saw. It might be Old Aberdareian or even a form of Runic, but it couldn't possibly be Celtic. He shook his head.

Could it be that Reverend Morgan had never seen ancient Celtic and simply imagined that this was what it looked like? Or was he simply trying to hide something he didn't understand?

He spent a further 20 minutes taking photographs for later study and then, vaguely annoyed at having found more questions than answers, and puzzled at his predecessor's slapdash research, he turned to head back to the town.

Patrick spent the rest of the morning in his room, staring out sullenly as the tide came in, inch by inch. The place where the crosses stood was hidden from his view by houses, but he knew they would now be submerged.

There would be another low tide this evening and he wondered if he should go back then. Maybe he'd given up too soon, he thought, but couldn't help feeling defeated.

He still felt downcast when lunchtime came. Elin greeted him and asked how his morning had gone. When he shook his head and said, "Not well," she seemed unconcerned and asked about his choices for lunch.

Every time she appeared in the dining room, Patrick asked Elin another question. He was fairly sure she wasn't holding out on him, but he was sure he was missing something.

Frustrated at his lack of progress, he asked "Is there a local library?" Elin shook her head. "Not anymore," she said. "Not since I was small."

"And there are no pictures around of Saint Deigion, that you know of?" Again, Elin shook her head. Patrick would normally ask about stained glass windows dedicated to him in a local church, but he knew that was useless.

When she came in to clear his dishes away, she sat down at the table opposite him. Her grey eyes hypnotised him once more. "Maybe you should go and see old Miss Jenkins. She's got a lot of books and her family have lived here since I don't know when," she offered.

Patrick almost choked on his coffee. "Yes. Yes. Please. Anyone who can help ..."

Elin nodded. "Rhiannon can take you in a little while then."

After lunch Elin told her daughter to take him up to old Miss Jenkins's place. Patrick didn't relish spending time with Rhiannon, but it would have seemed too rude to make any excuses now.

Fortunately, the girl remained silent, and Patrick did nothing to stimulate conversation, not wanting her to turn and look at him. He walked a step behind her as she led him to a street behind the guest house, stopping at the bottom of a long, twisting road leading up the hill. Patrick looked with dismay at the climb ahead.

They began the slow ascent of the dismal street, cramped grey and brown fisherman's cottages with small doors hemming them in on both sides. Just a narrow strip of sky was visible between the rooftops, so narrow was the street. Occasionally a curtain would twitch as they passed, but mostly the dwellings seemed soulless, uninhabited places. A heaviness sank down over Patrick's soul.

After nearly ten minutes of fairly steep climbing, the houses suddenly stopped, giving way to a path between the tangle of bushes and wind-stunted trees. Patrick looked around, almost dazzled by the daylight after the dark street, and glad to be away from it. They were above the town with a glorious view out over the bay and the sea beyond it.

Rhiannon led him around the corner of the path where a large two-storey house came into view. It had large gateposts with a rusty pair of gates propped permanently open. These gave onto a short driveway and a small garden. There was an antique Ford parked to one side with weeds growing up into the rear wheel arch. The car had obviously not been used for some time.

Patrick was drawn to two large stones, sitting among the

grass and flowers. They bore similar strange markings to the stone crosses, and he determined to ask Miss Jenkins about them.

Rhiannon rang the bell of the large door and stood dutifully waiting for it to be opened. By the time it was pulled open, sticking slightly as it came, Patrick was standing beside her. A woman with sober clothing and white hair gazed at them from the opening.

"Mum said to bring you the Pruffesur," Rhiannon said in her slow way.

Miss Jenkins bent to the girl and placed something in her hand. "Thank you, Rhiannon. Now you go straight back home, won't you?" The girl nodded and began to walk away.

The white-haired woman looked at Patrick with eyes that were a shade darker of grey than Elin's. "Please come in … Professor, is it?" Patrick stepped forward, smiling and shaking his head. "Oh no, no … please call me Patrick."

The woman closed the door decisively behind him. "You'll forgive me if I call you Professor, won't you? I find informality both too modern and too familiar for someone of my age."

Patrick found it difficult to judge her age as he followed her into a comfortable sitting room; in some lights she looked to be in her late 40s, while at other times she could be twice that.

She motioned him to a chair in front of a large bookcase, choosing herself to sit at a writing desk placed in the bay window, turning her chair to face him.

"I'm not looking at you askance, Professor," the woman chuckled. "It's just that I am blind in one eye, so find it more agreeable to hold my head this way."

Patrick found it vaguely discomforting that she could laugh at her affliction in such a way, so he merely smiled politely. He speculated that maybe the old lady's eyesight had been taken by a stroke, as she also wore her left hand gloved in black lace.

"Ummm … Elin … Miss … er, Mrs. Williams, that is … she said …" he began. Miss Jenkins nodded. "I know. I know. Elin rang me to say you were on your way."

Patrick found her gaze slightly cold and alarming. He wasn't sure how welcome he was meant to feel, but on a scale of 1 to 10 he felt a chilly 2.

In an effort to ingratiate himself, he said "My mother was from here originally. Bridge Street. Nia Evan-Hopkins."

This elicited a small smile from the woman. "Yes, I remember her. Mair's daughter. Such a shame she had to leave. She had freckles and red hair, didn't she?"

Patrick nodded and smiled, memories of his mother swimming to the fore. "That's her, yes."

"How is she? Will she be joining you here?" the old woman asked.

Patrick coughed twice with shock. He hadn't been expecting to be asked that. "N-no. She died last year. Of cancer."

Miss Jenkins looked slightly surprised at the news and shook her head. "That shouldn't have happened. I'm so sorry. So she's passed the baton on to you, eh?"

Patrick wasn't sure what Miss Jenkins meant by her remark, so he let it go.

After a pause of a few seconds, he decided he'd best get down to business. "It wasn't family business that brought me here, actually. I'm following the trail of a local divine ... Saint Deigion. I've got the Reverend Eli Morgan's volume on ..."

Miss Jenkins immediately cut him off with a wave of her hand. "It's a mistake. He should never have been included in that book. The old priest was clearly a fool." She almost spat the words out. The subject was clearly one that rankled in her family.

"He came here to talk to my great-grandfather, Gwynfor Jenkins. He was the local minister and magistrate at the time. He told old Morgan to leave well enough alone, but he insisted on scribbling a lot of nonsense about Deigion being inspired to create the crosses and so on. He trod on a lot of toes."

Patrick hadn't expected such a response and was speechless.

The woman fixed him with her gaze once more. "Elin said you were keen to see a picture of our so-called saint. Well, reach up to the third shelf behind you and take down the sixth volume along. That was my great-grandfather's Bible. It's too heavy for me now ..."

He stood up and selected the volume, struggling to shift it down onto a small table nearby.

"There's an image of him inserted into the front endpapers," added the woman. Patrick eagerly turned the pages.

The engraving was elaborate, but from the date it was obviously based on an earlier source. It showed a figure with a sort of halo around his head, dressed in the garb traditionally associated with Christian saints. But the man had enormous eyes, which seemed more in keeping with stylised Byzantine art. In his hand, he carried a large book which Patrick assumed was the Bible. But there was something not quite right about the hands. Given the skilful execution of the rest of the engraving, he doubted this could be put down to the fact that the artist found hands difficult to capture accurately.

Above the image were the words "Saint Daegon." Patrick gasped with mild surprise. He'd never seen it spelt that way before. "Daegon," he said out loud. Miss Jenkins tilted her head to look at him, seemingly puzzled by his own confusion.

"But why is it spelt that way? Everywhere else I've seen it spelt D-E-I-G-I-O-N." Patrick was really only thinking out loud but was shaken out of his reverie when his host began speaking.

"My great-grandfather objected to the locals 'Welshifying' the name, apparently. He insisted on sticking to the original spelling. That's what I was told when I asked the same question as a little girl, anyway. I was a little clever-clogs and was always trying to catch people out," she chuckled, then turned away to gaze out of the window.

"The original spelling. This is fascinating," muttered Patrick. Below the engraving was a verse from the New Testament. "'Come follow me,' Jesus said, 'and I will make you fishers of men'—Matthew 4:19." Below it, in faded black ink, was a line of symbols very like those he'd seen on the cross earlier.

"Miss Jenkins, this writing … do you know what language it is? I noticed that it's on the stone in your front garden, and I saw something very like it on the beach this morning?"

She turned to him once more. "On the beach? You've seen the crosses then?" Patrick nodded, hoping he hadn't committed an indiscretion that meant his access to further information would be curtailed. "I don't really know very much, Professor. You should have spoken to my great-grandfather. He was a real scholar and spoke several languages. He'd have been able to answer all your questions. But he's long gone ... of course."

He felt a change of tack was needed once more. "The population was a lot larger in his day, I expect?"

She nodded. "Yes, of course. There aren't many people here now. Not anymore. Those that are left are the guardians, I suppose."

Patrick didn't understand what she meant. He didn't want to push her too far, but his curiosity overcame his caution. "Guardians? Of what, Miss Jenkins?"

The old woman chuckled. "Of the past, Professor. The betrayed past."

Patrick sensed he had touched a nerve as the woman was still staring out of the window, refusing to look at him.

He decided to change the direction of the conversation slightly, hoping to steer it onto safer ground. "So where did all the people go?" he asked, expecting, maybe even hoping for, a conventional answer about the decline of the fishing industry.

Instead, the old woman merely raised her arm and pointed out at the bay. "Out there."

Patrick didn't know if he was being told of mass emigration to Ireland or asked to believe in a religiously inspired suicide pact. He couldn't think what to say. Elin had led him to believe that Miss Jenkins could provide him with answers, but he felt as far from the truth as ever, maybe farther.

"I don't wish to seem inhospitable, Professor, but I have many errands to complete, so if you've seen enough ..."

Patrick mumbled some apologies and placed the heavy Bible back on the shelf.

Miss Jenkins showed him to the door, said goodbye and closed it firmly behind him. He stood looking out over the bay for a few moments, feeling deflated and bewildered, wondering what he should do next. He realised he had to go back to the source. Another examination of the crosses might bear some fruit.

It was only when he was halfway down the lonely hill that he realised that he had heard whispering in the house.

Patrick set out from "Glan Mor" as soon as he could. The conjunction of tide and twilight was awkward, with the waters not subsiding sufficiently until the light was already beginning to fade. He would only have about 10 minutes on the beach at most before it became too dark to see properly. And he was nervous about getting back up the beach safely in the darkness, despite having a torch.

Even though he now knew what to expect, it was still a struggle to get out to the crosses, with the mud fighting him at every step. After several minutes of struggle, he stood before the ancient stones with his hammer and chisel ready. The third cross along seemed to be a few inches higher than the rest, he now noticed, as if it was the most important one. Patrick decided to concentrate on that one.

Bracing himself in the mud, he began to chip away gently at the ocean's leavings. As chips of old rubbish fell into the water at his feet, Patrick let out a small gasp of satisfaction. He was beginning to uncover what looked like the carving of a standing figure. It was in low relief and stood about 12 inches high, near the top of the stone pillar. He retrieved a brush from his bag and began working at it. Within a minute, he'd revealed enough of it to recognise it as the supposed saint. But it looked unspeakably pagan.

The image was even more unsettling than the version he'd seen in Miss Jenkins's Bible. This Daegon had huge eyes and strange, stunted limbs. To Patrick, he looked more animal than man. The thing was repellent. The early Christian pilgrim of the Dark Ages was obviously a fiction, just the wishful thinking of a Victorian clergyman. The reality was something very different indeed.

Suddenly he felt like he was being invited to attend a picnic in hell. A sense of deep unease gripped him. Now he knew he shouldn't be there. He wasn't meant to be gazing on these ancient stones at all. A chill deep inside told him they weren't meant for him and his kind. He wanted to leave.

He turned and struggled to make progress towards the shore, the mud gripping him once more, hindering his progress.

Within moments a strange mist began to rise from the mud. He'd never seen anything like it before. It rose very slowly and, if it had been alive, he'd have used the word sluggish to describe it.

Then the mud began to bubble slowly. He imagined small creatures just under the surface, mouths opening to gulp in air or bite off chunks of the new day.

He took a step forward and yelled in shock as the ground gave way beneath him. He sank up to his waist, as he stepped into an open pit filled with the foul mud. Patrick twisted and struggled, lifting his arms above him to prevent them being trapped in the enveloping slime.

He tried not to panic, keeping perfectly still. He was sure he'd heard that struggling would only suck you under in quicksand. He presumed it was the same with mud. Gathering his wits, Patrick threw his canvas bag towards the shore, grasping the strap firmly and hoping it landed on more solid ground. His heart sank with the bag as it was swallowed immediately by the grey filth.

He felt himself sinking slowly. Now his arms lay across the surface of the mud. His only hope was that someone in the town would spot him and come to his aid. But looking at the town he could see it now for what it really was—a graveyard, empty, abandoned.

He began to moan to himself, unready to die yet unable to do anything else. And drowning in this foulness would be the worst possible death, he thought. Then the mud ahead of him seemed to part, as if something was swimming through it. Impossible, thought Patrick. A head broke the surface and a female figure stood before him, dripping with water and covered in grey muck. He gasped as he recognised her. It was Elin.

The grey mud trickled from her naked body, revealing the skin beneath. It had changed somehow. The porcelain perfection he'd noticed yesterday had gone, replaced by a rougher texture. She now looked much more like a part of nature, something born of the oceans, than a woman. Yet her grey eyes were still as entrancing as ever.

He stretched his arms out to her in a pleading gesture as he sank even further down. "Please. Help me!"

She moved towards him as the mud sucked him even further under. Now just one arm was still free. He strained his fingers towards her as she seemed to sink slowly towards him.

She was within a few yards of him now, and it was plain to Patrick that she was not human. Or not wholly human. But she was his only chance now. Again, he pleaded with her. "Please, Elin."

She moved still closer to him. "Now do you understand?" she asked. Then she reached out and touched his face with hands that were not hands at all.

The stones began to whisper, and he turned to them as Elin guided him. Moving closer, his lips pressed against the ancient stone and his mind turned black, burning inside.

He collapsed on his back in the water, plunging below the surface. In his head the stones continued to whisper, and he could hear Elin's voice joining them. "Now do you understand?" And he did. Now he knew that not just his mother's blood flowed through his veins but that of something far, far older. It was only a trace, but it was enough. And it was becoming a tide, surging through him, changing him.

As he sank, his lungs stretched to bursting, he could feel his limbs cramping, transforming. Itching chunks of frail flesh fell away in a bloody soup, revealing a new and different body beneath.

He had been Patrick but now he was a new creature, perfect and strong, that could breathe in a huge gulp of water and not drown. Now he was ready.

He had answered the call of the ancient stones. And he sensed they were far older than they seemed. Merely brought here by one of his messengers, waiting half-submerged for century after century, calling quietly but insistently in the dark and in dreams, to those who would hear, to men and the things that were more than men. A whispered clarion from the fathomless ocean of time, calling them home.

He and the others left in Narmouth, were among the last ones. They were all gathering now from across the water-girt globe, at a place he could see in his mind; at the deepest part of the ocean, far deeper than man's nets or his poisons could reach, a dark blue flame burned, summoning them.

The time was nearly here, said the voice of the stones. He would soon rise, and they would be needed. Vast dark legions of them.

He turned in the direction of the pit of blue fire and, with the creature that had been Elin at his side, began the long swim homeward.

Sunday (Early Evening Ecstasy)

The window was streaked with rain as he sat watching the late afternoon light fade. The single framed photograph on the windowsill was now just a silhouette. He watched another day leave him behind.

The bottle was almost drained dry. A small golden pool lay at the bottom of the glass grail he clutched in his left hand.

A slight pain suddenly shot down his left arm, making his hand jerk. The glass slipped from his fingers and tumbled to the floor. Groaning in frustration, he remembered how much he'd spilled over the last few weeks—he probably had the drunkest carpet in town.

He sighed deeply at the realisation that there was no more. It had been the final glassful of his last bottle. He felt a peculiar kind of pain rise within him.

The truth was, he'd given up the bottle for the woman. It was no surprise that when the woman died he'd turned again to his first love for solace. The gold in the bottom of the glass was the only song he could bear to listen to now, a music in his blood that blunted the sharp edges life had used to slice him open with. Except there was that voice … again.

There were no words exactly. But he recognised the tone, the timbre.

At first the voice seemed a long way off, but within the last few days it had come closer. Now it seemed as if it might be just the other side of the wall. Though the words were uncertain, he was sure they held a secret that he needed to hear.

Sometimes he pressed his ear against the wall. But when he did, the voice was silent.

It was an outside wall. He thought at first the voice might be coming up from the street. But he was four floors up. And it surely wasn't possible for one voice to separate itself from the cacophony of the street. Even on a quiet, rainy Sunday the street below never ceased its chaotic chorus.

The truth was, he feared he was mad. Walls don't start talking by themselves.

He put his ear to the wall. The brick beneath the wallpaper was cold. He could still hear the voice, but it was loudest in the ear that he didn't have against the wall. Moving his head downwards, kneeling now, he pressed his ear against the wooden panelling that covered the lowest part of the wall.

Yes. Now the voice was clearer. His breath caught in his throat, refusing to move. It was her. HER!

But she was dead. Long ago. No, just three weeks now ... but on days like these it seemed like a million years.

She was trapped in the wall. He didn't know how, and he didn't care. His fingernails scrabbled uselessly at the wooden panelling. He stopped, drew back and punched the thin wood hard. It split vertically. He nursed the knuckles that he'd bloodied on the wall just behind the panel.

He looked around for something to use as a tool. In the kitchen he spotted a large knife lying on the work top. Grabbing it, he started to stab at the wood as if trying to murder it, twisting the blade to prise away a wider splinter. Finally, a section about half an inch across came away. He wormed his fingers into the gap, grazing his knuckles once more.

He pulled. The wood splintered, cracked loudly, and came away in his reddened hands. He threw the broken thing to one side, stopping to pick a large splinter from his forearm. Droplets of blood splashed onto the carpet and disappeared into the overly ornate pattern.

Frantically he tore at the wood, cracking and splitting it away before throwing the pieces behind him. After several minutes he stood panting, the panel in pieces on the floor around him.

The wall was solid. Brick and age-blackened mortar met his gaze.

Picking up the knife once more he began to work away at the

antique mortar holding the bricks in place. It crumbled easily.

There was her voice once more. She was definitely in there. She was calling him on. He dug his fingers into the space he'd made between two bricks. They came free after some exertion.

The words were unclear but surely it must be a call for help. The sort he could never give her while she was alive ... the first time. Now, if he could only reach her, he could make it up to her.

Had she truly suffered the torment of resurrection? No matter! He knew she was waiting for him ... just a little further on. His hands shook as he dug them around a stone, pulling it backwards with frenzied movements before tossing it aside. It rolled across the grimy carpet, leaving a trail of blackness behind it.

Now that the bricks had been torn away, a wall of black earth lay before him. As his fingers began to grope and dig their way forward, his shredded nails struck something unusual. It was the wrong size and shape for a stone.

He ran his finger along a flat surface, knocking loose a layer of filth that covered the thing.

Someone had embedded a picture in the wall. Maybe they had been in such a hurry to renovate that they had merely buried the previous room beneath bricks, panelling, plaster, and paint. He dug his fingers around the edges of the frame and wrested it free.

Pulling a handkerchief from his pocket, he spat on the picture surface and began scrubbing at it. As the dirt was moved away from the image, he could see it was etched onto a metal surface.

The dull silver revealed a craze of lines that depicted two giant horns—impossible to say whether they were made of brass or stone. They stood in front of part of an enormous building, the detail of which had been sketched in quickly, lacking detail. The giant curved shapes faced each other, ready to reverberate together, loud and long, in an agony of sound. The detail was too small to make out clearly but there may have been two tether points on the base between the two horns. Presumably for some animal, though for what purpose he couldn't imagine.

Carefully he laid the wooden frame face down on the table and returned to his task.

He was several feet inside the wall now. He knew that was impossible, even in his befuddled state. By any normal measure of things, he should be hanging yards above the ground in the rainy evening air, the wall of his apartment left with a gaping hole in it.

His ruminations were cut short as his hand hit an odd-shaped object among the dirt. Pulling it free to examine it, he cleaned the thing off quickly with his thumb.

It was a doll, no more than three inches in length and made of some sort of wood. But it was unlike any child's toy he'd ever seen. It was terribly ugly with tiny eyes and a startlingly large mouth; he wondered what he might see if that mouth were ever to open. For a second, he feared that the mouth was opening. He clamped his hand over the thing, shrugging it off as an illusion in the dim light.

Pushing the thing behind him, he dug his fingers back into the soft, black earth ahead of him.

He felt his grandfather's hands on his own, ghost fingers meshing with his and doubling his strength. He pressed the big digits into the thick blackness, dislodging a large chunk of it. He hadn't thought of the old man in years but, recalling him now, he remembered how he died underground, toiling beneath the earth until it fell on him, grinding his bones into a ruddy powder. Buried forever.

On his knees now, he panted with the exertion, fearing he might collapse with exhaustion before he reached her.

There was just enough light leaking into the short tunnel from the apartment for him to see. He had no idea how far he'd have to excavate before he reached his goal. Not much further, surely? His mind wandered to the large torch that lay in the kitchen cupboard. That would do for illumination ... if he needed it.

Taking another deep breath, he laboured on. He let out a cry as he banged his knuckles on a metal object. Cradling his hand, he peered at the shape emerging from the dirt. It was some sort of rectangle. After the pain subsided slightly, he dug the thing out.

The box was well made, carefully riveted together along

the edges. Flipping open the unlocked lid, he saw it was full of large coloured glass marbles. He fumbled to pick one up and held it close to his right eye.

It was a blue beyond any colour he'd known until now: there were glints of near silver, a distant cousin of gold and something indescribable at its heart. When it shrank, as if releasing a pent-up breath, he dropped it with a start. He slammed the lid shut and pushed the box away down the impossible tunnel he'd created.

If these objects were meant as clues, they had failed in their intention. If they were intended to draw him on, they were completely unnecessary.

"Don't waste your time," he muttered to whoever had put the objects in his path.

When her voice came again he felt a sense of certainty. It was her—it had to be. And wherever she was, he was going to her. He felt an overwhelming lightness that he hadn't felt for many months. It was an ecstasy that lent him strength and he dug away at the dirt even faster. It was kinder than anything he'd found in a bottle and reminded him of the safety and joy he'd found in her arms. He was going to her!

He began panting and chanting to himself softly. "I'm here … I'm here … wait …"

Remembering the person behind the grey-blue eyes, he smiled to himself. The first night they met they lay on the roof, watching the moon cross the sky, putting the sleeping world below to rights.

While out walking once she'd picked up an upturned snail's shell filled with rain. After tipping the water out, she'd become sad that the creature inside had already departed. A little later, as they headed home and her mood had improved, they'd improvised a comic conversation with the missing mollusc.

He allowed himself a soft chuckle in memory of her, immediately regretting it as a small fall of dirt filled his mouth with grit. He spat several times to eject the filth in the hot, close space.

His sweat was black now, soiling his clothes heavily. "God, I could do with a drop right now," he thought, shaking off the swimming, swaying feeling in his head.

Digging his way forward another few inches, his hands hit something hard. Quickly clearing away the dirt, they scurried across the obstruction like two spiders approaching their prey. It was another wall. This time, the stones felt large, old, and uneven.

Cursing, he realised he'd have to go back to the kitchen and find something to help prise them loose. He put up his hands and leaned his weight against the wall, exhausted.

Then he gasped and lurched forward as the old stones gave way under his fingers. He'd broken through. There was just darkness. It couldn't be outside—there were no street sounds and no lights.

He hadn't heard the stones hit anything when they fell, so he assumed they must have rolled down just a few inches onto a soft surface. Twisting around, he pushed his arm through the gap and felt for the floor. He was almost shoulder-deep before he gave up in defeat.

The space beyond the missing stones drank his gaze. He squinted into the void to no avail. There wasn't a single drop of light. A slight coldness seeped through from wherever it was that he'd arrived at.

Her voice called to him once more. He couldn't falter now. She needed him. Whatever lay in the darkness, he had to go to her. He began to ease himself through the narrow space.

First one step. His foot didn't feel as if it had touched anything, yet it was being supported. He laughed softly to himself in disbelief.

Then the second. He made sure to maintain his grip on the lip of the hole he'd just climbed through. But he doubted it would support him if he began to fall.

Suddenly he felt as if he was floating face down in water, unable to catch a single breath. He flailed his arms, struggling hard to raise his face before the feeling passed, like the coolness of a breeze suddenly dying away.

He felt foolish. Almost childishly insecure. Forcing himself to do something rational—if that was the right word—he called out. "Hello?" The emptiness around him swallowed the word whole. "Is anybody there?"

His blood froze when her voice answered, calling his name. Tears tumbled down his cheeks as he called her name again. His own name rang out again. The voice was very loud now, as if she was standing right next to him.

When it called to him again, he felt like falling to his knees.

Her voice had a metallic edge to it. It wasn't the soft, enticing tone that he'd known for nine years. It was a trick, a cruel piece of mimicry that tore right at his core. He sobbed, desperately fighting back the desire to wail long and loud. He had no idea what such a sound might mean here. He was too afraid to risk the consequences, so he bottled himself inside, hot tears washing away the dirt from his face in tiny rivers.

When it called to him again, there was a blackness in the voice that made him shiver. It was a blackness that enjoyed his grief.

For a moment he imagined he could smell the stench of the disease that had eaten her away, day by day. Then it was gone, suddenly.

Blackness and silence. Blankness and cold. Unbearable stillness.

Nothing to be done.

He had no idea who his host was, but he was here by invitation. They were bound to turn up sooner or later. Gazing into the darkness, he waited patiently.

He had an uncomfortable sense that he had been created to be someone's toy. That he was meant to be led here. Wherever he was.

The truth was, he had been waiting all his life.

Slowly, all around him, the blackness began to come to life

...

Taking the Cure

Steve flung the car keys on the table and sighed heavily. She was few steps behind him, shoulders slumped.

As Ann passed him he grabbed her by the shoulders, being careful not to hurt her, and buried his face in her neck. "I'm sorry ..." He thought his voice sounded pathetic and infantile; just not up to the task of being adult and serious and supportive.

The consultant had given them the worst possible news. He was going to lose her, and he could do nothing to stop it. His brain and his guts knotted up in anger and frustration.

Ann pulled away and went into the bathroom, shutting him out. She sobbed alone behind the door for over an hour.

The next day Steve felt as though he was wading through grey sludge, though it had nothing to distinguish it from hundreds of other days in his life. Except today he knew that Anna was dying.

When he got home from work, Ann's friend Sayeeda was sitting in the kitchen with her. Steve's heart sank when he saw her and the look of pity she was directing at him.

He said a brief "hello," kissed Ann on the forehead and then went to change out of his work clothes. He loitered in the bedroom in the hope that Sayeeda's visit was nearly at an end. He was glad Ann had someone to spend time with but wished it was one of her other friends instead. He was worried Sayeeda wouldn't be good for Ann in her present state of mind.

The woman's near-mindless optimism and insistence of quick fixes and easy remedies annoyed Steve. He felt as if she never really understood the complexities of any problem set before her.

After nearly 20 minutes he felt he couldn't really leave it any longer and went back into the kitchen. To his huge relief Sayeeda had her coat in her hand.

As she left she tousled Ann's brown hair and kissed her on top of the head. "Hang in there. Think positive!" she chirped and was gone.

Ann turned her face to Steve. Her eyes were bottomless pits of despair, drilled deep into her skull.

That night Steve slept fitfully, a series of half-dreams rousing him each time oblivion seemed ready to claim him.

It was hard to tell whether he was awake of asleep when he felt water lapping at his sides. He struggled to get up but was held down by some unknown force.

He continued to strain to rise but couldn't. Making a huge effort, he turned his head towards Ann. She was still at his side but, as he watched, her body lifted from the bed as the water rose. As it covered him, he saw her bloated body float away, swelling with decay as each second passed. He wanted to shout out but was afraid to open his mouth in case the water rushed in.

He knew he was awake when he felt the pillow hot with sweat beneath his head. Ann was beside him, sleeping deeply as she moved through the depths of a drugged sleep. Making sure not to wake her, he went into the bathroom and sobbed into a towel.

Each day became more and more difficult.

It was like living with a death sentence of his own, knowing that mortality's malign children were growing uncontrollably in Ann, like a foul parody of the baby that had always failed to take root in her flesh.

The faces of his colleagues had taken on a grim, decrepit look; the office becoming a drably bleak prison for the eight hours he was trapped there.

His boss had refused to let him take any time off, even when he explained the situation. This was the busiest time of the year, he'd told Steve. Either Steve was a team player or he wasn't; if not, maybe he'd be happier elsewhere.

He was sorry, of course, to hear about Ann but he firmly believed his staff should leave their problems at home and not bring them to work, he'd added.

The man behind the desk mistook Steve's glare of hatred for a look that meant he agreed with his words of wisdom and would shoulder his burden with greater fortitude from now on.

When he got home Ann, her eyes haloed with red, was on the phone to her sister. He kissed her on the cheek and then left her to carry on her conversation.

After several minutes Ann came into the kitchen. Steve put down his glass of water. "Are you OK?" he said, pointlessly; he knew the answer. But she nodded anyway.

She sat down at the table opposite him. At first she seemed reluctant to speak before finally saying: "When Sayeeda was here she told me about someone who may be able to help. A man she's heard about." She pulled a leaflet out of her pocket.

Ann jumped in quickly when she heard Steve sigh. "I know what you think of her, but she says she's met people who've been ... healed by this man. And the thing is, he's coming here. Soon"

"He's not one of those American faith healers is he? All teeth and torment ..."

She flung the pamphlet at him impatiently. "No!"

He picked it up and opened it. There was no photograph of this mysterious miracle man. That's odd, he thought. In his opinion, these charlatans were usually weapons-grade egotists; only too eager to show you their plausible, smiling mugs that had been polished to within an inch of their life.

There was some vague gibberish about Chaos Therapy inside followed by the usual rubbish about uncovering ancient secrets. He studied it for a few moments before it gave him a headache, then turned back to the cover.

Below the heading "The Stars Are Right for You!" was the supposed healer's name. It was almost unpronounceable but given the number of Xs in it he supposed the man to be Basque.

Thoughts of the Spanish Civil War and the oppression of an

ancient Celtic people throughout recent history passed through his mind. It rubbed a guilty sore patch in his conscience. Maybe he shouldn't jump to conclusions, after all.

On the cover was a photograph of the Earth from orbit and some odd-looking constellations that Steve didn't recognise. But then, he was no astronomer.

Steve grunted. "Well, it looks like a load of mumbo-jumbo to me, love."

"It may be my last chance." Ann stood up and came over to him. "He may not be able to help but nobody else has been able to either. So what have I got to lose?"

Steve was about to say "money" but just managed to stop himself from being so tactless.

"If you loved me, you'd help me," said Ann, with a note of hurt in her voice.

Steve knew that was unfair, but he wasn't about to argue with her. He held her close, squeezed her hand and let the tears come slowly.

After lying awake for three hours, Steve rose and went over to the window. Darkness seemed to be his enemy lately, unwilling to let him enter the comfort of its soft, dream-filled depths.

As he stared out through the gap in the curtains, he saw that the city was lit by an unusual light. Looking up he saw that a gigantic black star was moving down out of the sky, leaving its previously hidden orbit to draw near the Earth. It eclipsed the half-moon as it drew nearer still.

Giving off rays of darkness, it flooded everything with its evil light, making things transparent so that the rot inside was visible. The only thing unaffected was him; he could still see his own hands and body clearly while all that was around him faded away into an untouchable part of the spectrum.

He was gripped by a fear at what he might see if he turned to look into the room, yet he knew he had to do it. He closed his eyes and turned around, breathing deeply. Steve waited for a vital few seconds as he gathered his courage, then opened his eyes and looked towards the bed.

Ann lay there, her illness shining through her flesh,

illuminating her skin with the dark and beautiful colours of a lingering death. Though it filled him with pain, Steve walked to the bed and looked down at her as the radiance of suffering and disease flooded out of her.

He sank to his knees beside the bed, balling up his hands and pressing them into his eyes, so he wouldn't have to look any longer. A life without her was unbearable—it would be like being buried alive—yet he knew that was what he faced.

Feeling too tired to drive, Steve took the train across town. In the second carriage he bumped into two old friends, John Quinn and Eric Wallasey. They talked about old times, laughed about nothing in particular, and whiled away the time pleasantly until the train came to Steve's stop.

It was only when he was on his way down the station steps that he realised he hadn't asked them where they were going.

And only once he was outside the station did he remember that John had been killed two years ago in a car crash in Turkey. He had no idea where Eric was in the world or what he was doing now but he was suddenly certain that he hadn't been on the train.

Steve felt sick. He sat down for a moment on a low wall. It was obviously his lack of sleep that was making him hallucinate. Or maybe he'd dropped off in his seat without realising it. But it had seemed so vivid.

He went back inside the station and bought a coffee to try and steady himself. Caffeine usually did the trick, whatever was wrong with him.

When he felt more himself, he set off to find the address he'd been given. The buildings in this part of town were old, grey slabs of forgettable architecture. When he found the place he was looking for, it was tucked away underneath one of these gigantic monoliths. It was a dismal, forgotten cafe.

Despite his enforced coffee break, Steve was early. It was just beginning to rain as he went inside. He was the only customer and the air itself seemed to have a coating of grease. The furnishings had a slightly dusty greyness to them. A small, bald man peered at him from behind an old-fashioned glass counter. Steve ordered a coffee and sat at a table in the centre of the establishment.

The chair was an odd design and not very comfortable. The walls were hung with odd-looking musical instruments and artefacts that he imagined were from Eastern Europe; or Eastern somewhere, at least.

Steve only had to wait a few minutes before a thin man in dark clothes came in and headed for the table. The man extended a gloved hand. "Mr. Johnson," he asked in a foreign accent. Maybe he was from Eastern somewhere, too, thought Steve.

"Yes," replied Steve, indicating the empty chair opposite.

The man sat down but didn't remove his gloves. He had an abnormally long, pale face with lank dark hair that hung over to one side. The man caught the proprietor's eye, and, within a few seconds, a second cup of coffee had appeared on the table.

Steve fished out the leaflet Ann had given him. It was crumpled so he smoothed it out and placed it on the table facing the stranger. "Are you him?" asked Steve, jabbing his finger at the name printed on the cover.

The man shook his head. "No. My principal does not make appearances outside of his healing sessions. He feels it dissipates his abilities. But I did speak to you on the phone, Mr. Johnson."

The man told Steve his name. But even though it was short name, when he tried to tell Ann what it was later he couldn't remember it but for the fact it began with a B.

Steve grumbled at the man about the vagueness of the leaflet. The man simply nodded and let him talk himself out.

When he got no answers, Steve tried the direct approach. "So what exactly is this "treatment" and how much does it cost?"

The man tried to smile. Steve didn't find it very comforting. "We ask no payment except your time and your belief. I can't really explain the details of it as I don't understand it myself. I have no medical certificates myself, you understand.

"But look on it as a focus of intent—a way of harnessing the necessary energies."

Steve shifted in his seat. "Yes, I ready all that in the leaflet.

But what "necessary energies"? Necessary for what exactly?"

"Necessary to cure your loved one, of course," said the man, patiently, as if dealing with a slow child.

At that moment, someone else came into the cafe and began to harangue the owner in a language that Steve didn't recognise.

Steve sighed heavily at the unwelcome distraction. He'd had enough and placed both hands firmly on the table, leaning forward. "Look if you and this so-called "healer" of yours are Snake Oil salesmen then I'll …"

The man opposite stared at Steve with his dark eyes. "Snake Oil is actually a very successful treatment for arthritis, Mr. Johnson. The phrase you use refers to fakery. I can assure you that what we offer is very real."

There was both a depth and a hollowness to the man's voice that took Steve by surprise. He was about to protest when raised voices and the sound of breaking crockery behind him claimed his attention. When he turned back, the man was already walking out of the door.

He'd left without giving any answers, without touching his coffee and without paying for it.

For a moment the whole situation angered Steve. He began to rise to his feet, to follow the man and remonstrate with him. Then he noticed the DVD case lying on the table in front of him. At least it was something tangible to show for his efforts.

Steve sat back down, sighed heavily and made a momentary effort to place the language being used to such good effect in the argument going on behind him.

That evening, he and Ann watched the DVD. As he'd expected, it was frustratingly vague about details of the therapy and its cost.

But he had to admit that the "patients" that it showed were in a pretty poor condition to begin with. Whereas, when interviewed after undergoing the therapy, they did look a lot better more alive. Though they seemed somehow different, too. They sat differently and there was something in their faces; it was nothing he could put his finger on.

He was aware how easily the camera and the make-up artist could lie but the people on the screen seemed not only plausible but compelling.

At the end there was an address, a date, and a time. Steve quickly scribbled down the details, as Ann hugged his arm.

Later, while she dozed on the sofa, Steve looked up the unfamiliar address. It was in an area of town he wasn't familiar with and had never visited. He'd heard it mentioned in connection with the army barracks. And he had a vague memory and some warehouses that were involved in a bizarre kidnapping case involving children and animals a year or two back. He was sure they were in the same district.

As he stared at the address, he felt an uncomfortable twinge deep in his gut.

Steve felt nervous about driving to the place, but it was too far to walk, and a taxi would have been an idiotically expensive luxury.

As they came close to the address, he drove down the street slowly. Small knots of people, some down-and-out by the look of them, drifted in the same direction.

A hand-made sign with the healer's name and the slogans from the leaflet stood in a gap between the buildings. Steve felt his heart in his mouth as he listened to the tyres crunch across the piece of waste ground that acted as a car park. The man that he'd met in the cafe stood at the end of the open space, directing people towards a set of dilapidated steps at the side of one building.

Steve got out of the car nervously. He didn't want to leave the car here. There were several others parked nearby, but he still felt as if he was being forced to swallow something that he knew would make him ill.

Ann clung to his arm as they made their way up the steps into the old building, then up a set of wooden stairs and through some double doors.

The room was laid out with rows of rickety-looking chairs and there was a low stage at the front. Steve imagined that someone must have been burning incense as the air was filled with a sickly-sweet aroma. Probably to hide the smell of the damp, he thought sourly.

They walked cautiously towards the front and sat in the third row. The room was filling up, but nobody seemed to be talking, not even to the companions they'd arrived with. Steve turned to Ann and asked, "Are you alright?" She smiled and nodded but he could tell she didn't mean it. Once more, he felt helpless.

Steve turned to look as a man raised his voice at the back of the room. He was obviously drunk and was being placated by the long-faced man. They were yabbering away in the strange language he'd heard in the cafe. He'd been unable to find out what it was. After a short while the man seemed content and took his seat with the others.

He turned to Ann to say something, and an echo of the night surrounded him. It was as if she was lit by the light from the black star once more. Vivid blooms of decay and morbidity showed through her skin as it had in their bedroom just a few nights ago. He'd dismissed it as a vision or a dream then, but now it was happening in a room crowded with people. He shut his eyes tightly and looked away for a few seconds.

When Steve turned back, everything had returned to normal. He would be glad when this evening was over, and they could head home.

After a few more minutes, the long-faced man walked to the front of the room and stepped up on to the stage. "Good evening everyone. Thank you for coming. I am sure that none of you will be disappointed and that you will all find what you seek here tonight." Steve was skeptical of this claim.

Then he introduced the "healer" and Steve discovered that his name was as hard on the ear as it was on the eye. He couldn't have repeated it if his life had depended on it.

From a door at the side of the stage a tall man in dark clothes entered. No one clapped or moved a muscle.

Like the long-faced man, his skin was pale, and his head was crowned with slick black hair. The man's eyes were the most striking thing about him. They were an unusually pale green and gave the impression they were lit internally. Steve looked around at the ceiling to see if a cunningly placed small spotlight was creating the effect. There was nothing.

Behind the man was a large black screen. Though, if you turned your head away slightly, it appeared to be a hole. He squinted and peered at it for a few seconds. It appeared to drink in the light around it, though the dimness of the lighting made it difficult to judge. He gave up wondering after a few seconds of eye strain and waited for the "show" to begin. Whoever had set all this up certainly knew their stuff, he thought.

The "healer" walked to the front of the stage and looked as if he was ready to speak. In an alarming trick of perspective, he seemed to grow taller as he took each step. Finally, we might find out what this is all about, thought Steve. The man simply cast his gaze around the room, scanning everyone's faces with his peculiar eyes. When it came to Steve's turn, he dropped his gaze, refusing to play the game.

Then the man stepped back from the edge of the stage and began to say something. Steve concentrated for a few seconds before he realised it wasn't speech at all. Rather than imparting any information the "'healer" seemed to be chanting in a buzzing, droning voice. Steve groaned; this was precisely the sort of pseudo-religious crap he'd expected.

And there was something happening behind the man. It was coming from the screen. Or was it? Maybe it was inside the screen. He felt confused.

A mantle of what looked like flies settled on the healer's shoulders and, within seconds, chitinous petals of disease bloomed on his skin. Behind him, there was a change, an opening up, an enormous blossoming in the blackness.

The man's droning voice continued. It was cutting through his head and Steve wanted to stop him, once and for all. He knew now that there was danger here.

He turned to those sitting nearest him and tried to speak but he could see straight through them, their vileness now visible in repellent clarity. An appalling coldness seeped into him.

He shouted out but his words became nonsense. Then silence.

Then blackness.

The Rolling of Old Thunder

(after R. L. Stevenson's *The Body Snatcher*)

That late summer Edinburgh had been plagued with thunderstorms, yet very little rain. It seemed to the inhabitants of the city as if the clouds were reluctant to release their balm, to ease the pressure and freshen the air. Instead, the storms insisted on oppressing them, doing nothing to relieve the heat.

The mornings were cool, on the other hand. Cold enough for the mist to cling to the streets until mid-morning, lending them a near-spectral glow.

The sun was many hours from burning away the mist one morning when a tightly bundled figure hurried across Surgeon's Square. Pausing briefly, the man checked one of his pockets before disappearing down a flight of stone steps leading to an almost hidden door.

Once inside, Macfarlane spent a few moments trying to brush the stink of the cramped, mist-wreathed streets from his clothes. He shook the thin layer of water droplets from his coat and hung it up. "Filthy weather again," he complained. "You're here early, Fettes."

The other man looked up from a small desk, where he was writing in a large ledger. "We had a delivery last night. I thought I'd best get things 'tided away.'"

"Very diligent of you. It does you credit," said Macfarlane. He walked over to the examination slab and pulled back the grubby sheet. The skin of the corpse was an unsettling blue. The doctor put his hand over his nose to block out the smell. "Uuugh! Hardly fresh, is it?"

"He was hanged yesterday, according to the orderly who delivered the poor unfortunate fellow," said Fettes. His companion snorted in obvious disbelief.

Fettes looked down with distaste at the black tongue and swollen face so typical of a victim of hanging. He'd seen so many hanged criminals come through this place over the years that he'd almost forgotten what the face of someone who'd died peacefully looked like.

"The head goes to Richardson again, I suppose?" he asked.

Macfarlane nodded. "I hesitate to speculate why he has such a liking for the human cranium. I have no idea what he expects to find in there."

"The soul maybe." Fettes saw himself as a rational man, who looked down on those holding religious beliefs as being worthy of nothing but pity. "Well, after all, his father was a preacher, wasn't he?"

Richardson sat in Mr. Killian's class later that day, gazing glumly down as the surgeon explained the intricacies of the blood vessels running through the arm.

Though the topic did not excite him much, Richardson knew that the mechanics of medicine had to be mastered if he was to become anything more than a merely competent doctor. Competence was anathema to him; he demanded far more of himself.

The stink of the cadaver laid before the students as they clustered around the dissection table was nearly overpowering. One, a young Englishman called Purcell, had already succumbed to the lethal combination of summer heat and the stench. Richardson wasn't about to follow him.

He watched as the surgeon parted a delicate blue vein from its shiny, fragile moorings, all the while explaining the function of the circulatory system in the anatomy of the arm.

Poking about in rotting flesh seemed an odd path to take to become a doctor, he thought. Indeed, it was an uncomfortable and vaguely obscene route into medicine, it seemed to him. Yet what other method was open to them? They had to have material to work on. There was no other way to learn.

There were even dark rumours of two detestable Irishmen, low types who weren't beyond the practice of rudely "resurrecting" those recently laid to rest. It caused him acute discomfort to think that the heights of science might be built on a foundation of filthy business conducted in graveyards and cellars. Yet like his fellow students, Richardson put whatever qualms he had to one side in the name of medicine and advancement, both scientific and personal.

When he was being honest with himself, Richardson admitted that, like his father before him, he hoped for resurrection. Not the feeble promises of his Christian counterparts, nor yet the unholy desecrations meted out by the so-called Resurrection Men, but something that spoke of true glory and a return to man's original form.

And now, finally, he was certain he'd found the means to achieve his goal.

"All right gentlemen, you may resume your seats." Killian's words broke the spell and the students all drifted listlessly back to their seats in the hot stench of freshly gained knowledge.

As they all filed out of the lecture room, Richardson glanced around at his fellow students. They seemed so small—both their bodies and their ambitions. They might as well be animated wax simulacra for all the good they'll ever do, he thought.

In his mind, he turned the book of miracles over and over in his hands, just as he'd done in his room last evening, relishing the uncommon texture of its strange binding. Its contents were a map to a hidden domain of strange and wonderful learning.

Why spend his time labouring with the other worker bees when he could be brilliant, celebrated? He might know in mere moments what it would take them years to discover—and then go on to learn far, far more than they would ever know.

He had the two keys that could open these unimagined new avenues of knowledge—the book and his serum, which alone allowed him to decipher it.

Outside the sky was heavy and threatening yet still, reminding Richardson of a hastily painted backdrop to a lacklustre play.

Although he was a highlander and not a native of Auld Reekie, Richardson had grown to feel at home in the place. He'd even been known to seek out some of the more disreputable taverns, where he'd find a secluded corner if possible, there to nurse a glass of ale and watch the behaviour of the inhabitants. He'd sit and watch their pleasures and their torments pass by like a spectator at the circus or, perhaps more accurately he often thought, a visitor to the zoo. The pastimes, half bestial and half angelic, of the tavern's habitues fascinated him.

He often pondered on what kept mankind in this semi-animal state. Surely it couldn't be natural? He returned to his studies with renewed vigour following a visit to the dirty, rowdy taverns. Then he was more determined than ever to release the secrets that lay locked within each person's head.

In his anatomy classes, he handled the cadavers with a degree of dismay at how life could be reduced to these cold, dead remnants. He'd asked Mr. Killian for the opportunity to study the brain as his area of specialism. The head of each corpse was duly delivered to his table, though he was always glad to extract the cold, white orbs and pass them to another student to study. His area of interest lay behind the eyes.

The more he'd studied the pinecone-shaped structure buried deep within the brain, the more he'd become convinced that the overlooked pineal gland, as small as it was, held the key to opening new horizons for mankind.

Like the Frenchman Descartes before him, he was fascinated by the strange little structure. But he'd gone far further than the illustrious philosopher ever had in probing its secrets.

With only the simplest of scientific instruments available to him in his humble lodgings, Richardson had made the best of his situation. Fortunately, all the hard work could be done at the anatomy class.

It took the secretions of the pineal glands of two average-sized adults to prepare the formula he needed. There was, of course, no other method open to him than to experiment upon himself. He knew it was a great risk, but in his mind the potential rewards more than outweighed any danger.

One remarkable piece of equipment was available to him.

Less than a decade ago, Dr. Alexander Wood had created the device not so far from the poor lodgings in which Richardson now sat. The hypodermic syringe that he'd "borrowed" from the dissection room allowed him to administer the formula himself. Without it he would almost certainly have needed assistance, and that would not do. This was a road he knew he had to travel alone.

He'd quickly learned that once his heartbeat began to elevate, he was able to read clearly the pages of the volume left to him by his late father.

The language was certainly antique and, he thought, overly reverential. Clearly some of the beings referred to as "gods" could be no such thing.

Once the solution had taken hold of him, his mind became illuminated from within. He supposed that this was because the preparation was enhancing his pineal gland's natural secretions. He ran his eyes over the pages of the book.

Some of the strange glyphs now became jumbles of letters that were either indecipherable or simply unpronounceable. They made little sense to him as words but somehow he was able to divine their meaning.

Yet, despite his enhanced abilities, some symbols still retained their mystery. And there was an insistence upon a type of geometry that was entirely unfamiliar to him from his schooling. He did his best but a true understanding of it still eluded him.

He knew some were words of death, but others were invocations and imprecations of great power. He could sense that the book was the key to an undreamt-of realm of hidden abilities and powerful allies, concealed just beyond the veil of the reality he saw about him. He knew his own world was partly illusion … any fool could see that … but how to tear away its mask and reveal its true face was a secret that he dearly wished to learn.

If he'd had that knowledge some years earlier, he might have been able to save his father from the wasting disease that had taken him. Instead, he and his mother and sisters had been forced to watch helplessly while the filthy thing had hollowed his father out while he still lived, dying a little more each day.

Richardson had become sickened by the two years his family spent praying to a God who didn't hear them or didn't care.

The doctors were stuck for a diagnosis, and the spectacle of his severely ailing father had strengthened Richardson's resolve to study medicine. For he was determined to do better than those men of medicine who had failed his father so badly.

Even the odd deformity of the middle finger of his right hand had not deterred him. When Mr. Killian, the surgeon and principal anatomy teacher, had told him he'd never be able to wield a scalpel properly, he'd learned to do so with his left hand instead.

He'd determined that nothing, and no one, was going to stand in his way.

The strange summer of lingering mists and unseasonal thunder almost passed Richardson by unnoticed as his fascination with the arcane book grew.

An odd, unhealthy smell clung to the volume, and its cover had a decidedly clammy feel to it. Richardson speculated that the binding might actually be some sort of skin, though from what sort of animal it came from was uncertain.

How it had come to be in his father's library was unknown, and it struck him from time to time that it was an odd thing for a churchman to own.

At first, it had seemed like any other book to Richardson. Then, some months after his father's death, a former colleague of the old man had called to pay his respects to Richardson's mother. His father's books lay scattered around, in the process of being sorted through. One particular book had caught the visitor's eye. The man, a Norwegian pastor named Saknussemm, commented on the volume and drew Richardson to one side, advising the boy to destroy it without delay.

Richardson had protested, naturally feeling proprietorial towards his late father's possessions. But the pastor had persisted, hinting that the book was a 17th century transliteration of a scroll from ancient Damascus. He went on to say that all copies of the book had been ordered to be destroyed by Pope Urban VIII. Richardson thought this an odd comment coming from a Protestant clergyman and decided to ignore the man's advice.

The following year when Richardson, convinced of the book's value, had tried to sell the volume to an Edinburgh book dealer, he was shown the door with a glare that could not have been any icier if he'd threatened to kill the man's entire family in front of him.

His curiosity piqued still further, Richardson had found references to the mysterious indecipherable text in libraries in Edinburgh and Oxford. These references, scant as they were, convinced him that he possessed something that could be a great asset to him, if not also a tool of great power.

It was not until he took up the study of medicine that the key to unlocking the book's mysteries had accidentally presented itself.

On the first occasion that Richardson had administered the solution to himself, he had expected a certain amount of sensory disorientation. But he was dismayed at how little about his surroundings had actually changed. Perhaps he'd got the quantities wrong while preparing the solution, he thought. But then his eyes happened to fall upon a pile of books that lay on his rickety shelf.

Most of his small collection of books had maintained their mundane appearance while he was under the influence of the solution. But one, tucked at the bottom of a tottering pile of texts, seemed to glow and writhe oddly within his vision. Richardson reached down and carefully drew out the strange old book that he'd inherited from his father.

He was astonished to see that the ruined cover had been restored to a soft fine-grained brown leather. He'd been right on that count, at least, but what animal it had come from was still not apparent. Near the top, picked out in gold leaf, sat the words "Al Azif." Whoever had translated the work had obviously kept the original title; maybe because it was beyond their skills to render it accurately into another language. Yet, though he spoke not a single phrase of Arabic, Richardson sensed that the title meant "The Voice of The Tempest," or something very like it.

Richardson reached out and, as he had done several times before, opened the volume at random. Astonished, he realised that the words were drawing him in as bold new ideas took shape in his mind.

It was as if a secret eye had been opened within his brain—one that saw through the surface of mundane reality to the truth behind it. His experiments had proved him right! He ran his hands over the book with a barely suppressed sense of ecstasy, like electricity transferring itself from his fingertips directly to the centre of his mind.

He had no idea what this book had to do with his father's pallid religion, or how or why his father came to possess it, but he knew instinctively that, just like a scalpel, if it could be wielded skillfully it could do much good.

Richardson's dreams that night were half-formed things, vague yet insistent, as if struggling to see a reflection in a mirror covered in cobwebs.

The sense that something was coming from a vast distance away clung to his sleep. There was an ocean to cross, vast mountains to overcome, but whatever it was wouldn't give up. It was on a peculiar quest to find him and him alone. And when it arrived, it would come with a tremendous gift, he felt.

Yet, as relatively benevolent as the dream had been, there was something appalling about it that clung to Richardson all the next day.

Once when under the influence of the solution, Richardson had been disturbed by his landlady, Mrs. Mackenzie. The woman was a widow and, while not unattractive, had clearly grown old before her time. She seemed fond of Richardson and treated him very like a son.

She had come into his room and begun talking about some mundane subject when suddenly she stopped. Something about Richardson's manner had alerted her to the fact that he was somehow different. "Not himself," she had put it. This had made Richardson laugh—for he'd never felt more like himself.

He remembered going right up to the woman and staring

at her, causing her to cautiously draw back a step or two as he continued to peer at her closely. Her skin seemed to be alive with tiny crawling creatures, normally invisible. The concentrated pineal secretions had transformed her from a mere person into a fascinating collection of fauna. Rather than a single person, she appeared to him like a walking menagerie, and he wondered if his own skin was similarly infested.

The woman had soon left, declaring Richardson to be ill and claiming that she would call a doctor to him. She must soon after have realised the absurdity of her words as no doctor had shown up. If he had, thought Richardson later, I could have told him a thing or two.

The next morning Richardson had woken late. Distractedly grabbing a number of books, he had rushed out to his class, not stopping for breakfast or to wash.

In the corridor he had collided with Macfarlane, who cursed him for a clumsy clod before stooping to help him retrieve his books. By chance Macfarlane's hand alighted on the strange old volume. Richardson's heart climbed up to block his throat when he realised that he must have picked it up in error.

Macfarlane turned it over in his hands. On his face was a look of disgusted fascination. "What's this?" he demanded.

Richardson reached out to retrieve the volume only for Macfarlane to hold it out of his reach. "It's a religious volume," Richardson offered.

Macfarlane looked down his nose at the book, which now fell open in his broad palm. "Indeed. And what language is this?" he quizzed, scanning the unfamiliar glyphs that filled the pages.

"It's Greek," replied the student.

Macfarlane smiled cruelly. "I know Greek, my boy. This is not Greek."

Macfarlane was only a few years' Richardson's senior, and the younger man detested being called "boy." "It's a very old form of Greek," protested Richardson. "You must understand, Macfarl … *Mister* Macfarlane, my father was a churchman and a scholar. He owned many obscure volumes of old lore and religious thought."

"If you say so, Richardson." Macfarlane equally disliked any attempt to put him in his place. "And you claim to understand this scrawl, do you?"

Richardson looked sheepish. It took him several seconds to answer, "Yes ... after a fashion."

"You are an extraordinary fellow," said Macfarlane, handing back the book. "It looks and smells as though you've literally dug this thing up." Then he dusted off his hands and walked away.

In his darker moments Richardson dearly wished that one day he'd see Macfarlane's head sitting on the dissecting table before him. He even speculated on how hard he'd have to press the scalpel blade into the soft spongy mass before all that had been Macfarlane, all the arrogance and cruelty and worldliness, began to seep out, ready to be collected and analysed. Not very hard, he wagered.

The cold corpse eye of the west moon looked down on Richardson as he left his lodgings that late summer night. His landlady had taken to her bed long ago, and the cold, narrow streets were empty at this late hour.

With the pineal solution flowing through his veins, the grey city about him was transformed. Colours formed and flowed in peculiar pools, streaming down the walls to gather and swirl along the gutters.

The paving beneath his feet throbbed with a previously unnoticed vitality, as if the city was a living thing. If he stared down for long enough he sensed a great dark river flowing beneath everything, connecting each thing to every other thing. But he also sensed that it was filled with corruption and that to know it too well would lead to despair and emptiness. He must not get dragged under. So instead, he raised his eyes to the blazing sky above, filled with its glittering supernal lanterns. He was almost sure he could see the dark star-winds, blowing life like a spore from shore to cold celestial shore.

He felt as though the thin veil of reality had been saturated with an acid that was now dissolving it, revealing the more beautiful truth behind it. Yet he also knew that the night's task that lay ahead would be grisly and require strong nerves.

Though he was no longer a religious man, something deep within Richardson baulked at what was required of him. Dissecting a cadaver in the cold light of medical knowledge was one thing; to do it under the moon's icy glare was quite another.

The book had quite clearly stated several times that the ritual needed to be performed in a burial ground and that certain materials would be required. As he headed towards the city's largest cemetery, Richardson pushed his doubts aside, musing that tonight he would find the secrets that he'd been longing to know for so long. Tonight or not at all.

As he approached a crossroads, something caught his eye in an alleyway off to his left. He was taken aback to see a naked figure moving towards him out of the gloom. At first he put the remarkable sight down to a restless sleepwalker, venturing abroad from the safety of his bed. Yet as the figure stepped into a pool of moonlight, he saw that he'd been mistaken.

The man took several more steps towards him before Richardson allowed the truth to fully dawn on him. The figure was that of his dead father.

Richardson began to walk away, uncertain whether his mind was not now unhinged. The strange figure began to walk beside him. Yet the man he saw before him was no animated corpse, come back to claim an unspecified revenge like some spectre from a Penny Dreadful. For his father had undergone a transformation.

He had clearly been dissected. Yet although he had been reduced to sections or collops of meat, still he hung together and walked like a man, keeping pace with Richardson.

From the top of his father's head grew a strange protrusion like a young sapling. Richardson recognised at once that this was the true form of the pineal gland. Though he was slightly disconcerted to note its grey fungous nature.

He pondered what role the gland might play after death. Was it the true seat of the soul, he wondered?

Richardson noted his own calmness with a small pang of pleasure. He put this down to the very pineal preparation that now coursed through his veins. If he had seen the awful sight of his dead father walking abroad at any other time, he was convinced he would have dropped down dead from shock.

What had been his father put its hand on his arm and turned him around. Richardson sensed that the "man" had something important to say to him.

He could clearly see the partly bisected tongue working in the gap left by several extracted teeth. But no sound came forth. "I-I'm sorry, Father. I cannot hear you," apologised Richardson to the phantasm.

In his left hand, Richardson carried a small sack containing a short-handled spade, the book, and a small lantern that he would need to read it by. His father pointed to the sack, mouthing wordlessly, as if he sensed the presence of the book. Richardson peered at him for a moment, but there were no words for him to hear and no expression was discernable on what was left of the man's face.

He shook his head and, turning, resumed his path. The paternal phantom fell into step again beside him. It seems he will be accompanying me on my night's deeds, mused Richardson.

Against his will, Richardson shuddered as the moonlit shadow of a church steeple fell on him, imparting a feeling of cold and immense distance. On the horizon, heavy clouds massed, moving towards him against the night wind.

Soon the moon was blotted out by swift-moving dark clouds, and, within minutes, the first peal of thunder filled the air. Richardson knew deep within him that this was a particular kind of thunder, one that had rolled around the Earth since life had begun.

Once more his father detained him by placing the remains of his hand on Richardson's sleeve. The phantom seemed more agitated this time, gesturing in an odd manner in an attempt to win his son over. The uncanny semaphore meant nothing to Richardson, and eventually he was forced to snatch his sleeve away. His father seemed more resigned to his failure this time.

As the thunder rolled overhead, it suddenly struck Richardson that perhaps his intuition of the title of the ancient book had been wrong after all. Maybe "The Voice IN The Tempest" was closer to the original meaning. For he was almost certain there was something in the crashing sound that called to him, urging him onwards.

The cemetery now lay directly ahead, and Richardson reached into his sack to retrieve the lantern in readiness.

At this, the figure of his father fell back, trailing a step or two behind him. When Richardson noticed and looked round, it was clear he was unwilling to follow and began walking away. Richardson called after him once but, eliciting no response, turned his mind instead to the task ahead.

He walked the last few yards slowly, resting for a moment as he reached the huge gateposts.

As Richardson pushed open the gate to the cemetery he saw he would not need his lantern after all. He was met by the sight of several corpses standing above their graves, burning like spectral candles set ablaze to aid his task.

Illuminated by the benevolent light of his curious guardian angels, Richardson selected a relatively recent grave and began to dig. The work went easily as if he had been granted added strength. The harsh sound of the spade scarping against the gravestone, striking off a shower of sparks, sounded like a symphony of dark desire to him. He felt on the verge of an extraordinary new life, with the path ahead filled with towering achievements.

Once the coffin was above ground, he dragged its contents free and opened the book. Its instructions were clear if unpleasant. He spent some minutes rearranging parts of the coffin's grisly contents, then began intoning the challenging and prolonged ritual.

Barely twenty minutes had passed when the noctilucent glow of the corpse candles flickered, faded, and then was gone. They had disappeared completely, as if blown away on the thin night breeze.

With the moon masked by clouds, Richardson was left in almost total darkness. He fumbled in his sack, managing at last to light the small lantern. By its glow, he saw that the marvellous tome had become a mouldering codex of unreadable antiquity once more. The syllabary of secrets had leaked away, draining out of his blood along with the false miracle of his serum; it had run its course and been purged from his system too quickly this time. But he hadn't finished the ritual …

Looking down at the destruction he'd wrought on the disinterred corpse, he was seized by a feeling of sickness. The decaying, dismembered limbs were twisted at unnatural angles, while a constellation of bone splinters stuck upright from the ground, spelling out the name of a black, unholy thing.

Despite the warmth of the summer night, Richardson began to shiver. The chill brought with it a sense of fear—what was he doing in this filthiest of all places alone at night? He must get out before he was discovered.

The cold creeping into him also brought an awful realisation. As he scrabbled for his coat and bag, he knew that the book, the blazing cadavers—perhaps even his vision of his father—had all been illusions born of his fevered mind.

Could it be that the pineal gland did not open a window onto a world of greater mysteries, but merely held up a mirror reflecting illusions? It sickened him to think he had merely been gazing at his own distorted features all along.

The book was no beginning. Instead, it spelled the end of everything he'd hoped for. All he'd done was to uncover a path leading to nowhere but a fool's paradise. In disgust he held up the book, its pages crumbling at the rough treatment, ready to fling it into the open grave, but something prevented him from moving.

Even if the words he'd spoken earlier had been incoherent, even incorrect, something had heard him … or, at least, felt his yearning. Thick dark clouds had gathered over the burying ground, slow thunder rumbling deep in their throat. Richardson raised his eyes as far as possible. He waited one heartbeat. Two.

Then something impossible—all angles and no body—dropped from the cloud like a stone falling from a high cliff. He struggled to make his eyes see it, for there was almost nothing there. Almost. But it was in his head.

The thing pivoted around the odd angles at the summit of an obelisk-topped tomb. If it had eyes then Richardson felt them on him. He'd been trapped by dreams, his own delusions, and now he was going to die. He wanted to yell out in protest but was still frozen like a stone.

The dark messenger reached out to him, too swift to see. When it gripped him, the worst thing wasn't the pain—though it burned like a branding iron—it was the secrets it told him, in a voice like a thousand buzzing insects crowding into his head.

Then, just for one moment, it allowed him to scream.

Fettes and Macfarlane met as they came into Surgeon's Square at mid-afternoon the next day. Fettes tipped the brim of his hat to the older man. "A wild night! Did you hear the thunder, eh?"

"I'd have had to be already in my grave not to," replied Macfarlane.

"And an odd storm at that. My sister has a view of Warriston Cemetery from her home. She will swear to you that not only was the storm centred upon the cemetery but that the lightning was going up into the sky from among the graves."

"Eh? Impossible! A trick of the light perhaps ...," offered Macfarlane.

Fettes shook his head. "Perhaps so, Macfarlane, perhaps so. Her neighbour said that something was seen flying, or falling, from the sky."

"Mmmm. A large bird struck by the lightning perhaps."

Fettes fished the large key from his pocket as they descended the steps, then slipped it quickly into the lock, eager to be inside.

As soon as he was through the door, he almost slipped on the topmost of the stone steps. "Damn it!" Then, as he examined the steps more closely, "There's some sort of filth all over the steps. Mind your footing, Macfarlane."

Macfarlane followed him down carefully, steadying himself on the iron railing. "Ah, you've had a delivery, I see. Excellent. Mr. Killian will be pleased."

Fettes stared in disbelief at the slab. A body lay under the sheet. "There was no delivery today. It's far too early for those foul rogues to deliver anything, you know that."

A look of slight alarm crossed Macfarlane's face. "Then, what ...?"

"T-there's no head on this one!" stammered Fettes, realising that the shape beneath the sheet ended just above the shoulders.

Now Macfarlane became angry. "If Richardson has taken it

already, I'll strip the hide from the whelp! What impertinence!"

Fettes drew back the sheet covering the body. Both drew in their breath sharply at the sight that met them. The head had not been removed surgically, but instead had been gnawed and twisted free by some sort of beast, the exact nature of which they dared not speculate upon.

Their nerves were further unsettled when the corpse's right hand fell from below the covering sheet, revealing the disfigured middle finger of the student Richardson. And clutched between the fingers, soaked in gore and filth, was a single crumpled page from an antique volume.

Red Walls

The air is too thick to breathe. Or there is too much of it and coming at him too fast. He has woken far too suddenly. Yet he doesn't remember even falling asleep.

To his horror, he is in mid-air. Flying along at an enormous speed, his mind races to match his velocity. He must have been in an air crash, he reasons. No, he hates flying. He has never flown—not until this moment.

Cries reach his ears. He strains to look around him. All is milky white, like some child's idea of heaven. But there are people in the clouds; not sitting on them but being hurled along at high speed, like him. Some cry out and try to twist in the air, limbs flailing. It is hopeless. Others seem half-conscious.

He is in the centre of a storm made of people. Suddenly a huge dark shape jumps out of the murkiness. He is going to hit it! There is no way to avoid it. He is staring at his own death.

Then a young woman intercepts his trajectory, moving in front of him, screaming. He hears her ribs crack within her as his body slams into hers, winding him. They hit the hard surface, her head making an awful cracking sound as it cushions his own.

She falls away below him, and he tumbles head over heels, falling for what seems like far too long. He lands heavily on his back with a loud grunt and blackness closes over him for a moment as he cracks his head against another bone-hard object.

When the light returns, he raises his head, gasping for air. She saved him. But for what? This life bought at the cost of another's. Alive. But dying still.

He lies on his back, stunned. His lungs strain against the

ribs that cage them too tightly. Above him is a poisoned sky of red and grey. A hungry sky. The stench of decay, blood, and opened bodies is choking.

Struggling against piled torsos, he forces himself to his feet. Gazing about him he sees a field of human wreckage. No one still lives. He staggers backwards, heavily dancing across the obscenely stitched quilt of corpses.

His mind reels at the numbers. There must be thousands stretched out on every side of him. And more arrive each minute.

Around him more bodies fall, adding to the undulating heap of corpses. He catches a movement over to his left. Someone has just landed hard with an audible grunt. Making his way awkwardly towards the man, he sees that he is still moving but is lying face down. "Hey. Hey! Are you alright?" he calls, thinking the sound of his voice might give the man some hope, just as he is clinging to his own small scrap.

Reaching the figure, he leans forward to turn the man towards him. "You're alive. You're going to be OK," he pants, hauling at the man's jacket, rolling him over. He pulls at the lapels, finally able to gaze down into the face. "Hey …" The man's ruined face lets forth one final bestial croak, then he is dead.

As he grasps the man's clothing a song from "The Wizard of Oz" strays across his mind; the man is not merely dead, he's really quite sincerely dead. His mind revolts at its own dark absurdity. He drops the fresh corpse he is clutching and lets out a cold, bitter laugh; one that is close to hysteria.

His skin formicates and a trembling begins inside. He begins to scratch his arms. But even after several minutes his skin refuses to stop crawling. His senses are screaming inside his skull. Taking deep breaths, steady and long, he forces himself to become calm. Or calmer, at least. It has to be some form of shock, he thinks.

Standing at the centre of the carnage, he holds his breath for a moment. He wonders if all these people have been thrown away because they are deficient in some way. He cannot imagine what that deficiency might be. As he is obviously also on the reject pile, he realises it would be one of dozens of things. No point in speculating.

Hoping to spy a way out the madness, he steels himself to climb a small pile of bodies that have fallen on top of each other. For a moment he hesitates—he'd want to be treated with more respect if that was him lying there. But then he was already walking over a pavement of people. He has no choice.

Once atop the miniature mountain of lumpen human meat, he sees no escape from the despair. From his vantage point he can see that the bodies are of all shapes, ages, nationalities, some naked, some still clothed. All these dead dreams; lost hearts that harboured empty hopes, now leaked away.

Clambering down once more, he struggles to stay upright. He averts his gaze when it meets the still-bright eyes of a small face.

Above him, more people are hurtling through the sky to their demise. As they fall, he tries to struggle away from the rain of death, fearing that if one falls on him he will become trapped or, worse still, buried alive. Even here, he still fears that. Something heavy lands near him, sending some of the bodies sliding his way or rolling past him. He staggers sideways, then is knocked off his feet, his leg touching something sticky as it slides into a cavity between several corpses. Pushing against them, he struggles to free himself, succeeding only in dislodging more corpses. Somehow their motion allows him to get his leg free, his knee coming to rest on the back of a small girl.

Wobbling upright he stumbles forward, nearly falling across the naked body of a middle-aged oriental woman, her plump buttocks pointing upwards as if presenting herself to a lover. Her scent is strong. He feels deeply ashamed at becoming aroused by the sight of her in this facsimile of hell.

Struggling to empty his mind, he looks up. They tower above him like two leaves of a gigantic open book, set at an obtuse angle to each other. Covered in detritus and bits of the wreckage of humanity, the walls are black in places, but overall they are red. Painted red by death.

He guesses that they must be measured in miles rather than feet. He lowers his gaze and peers into the distance, first in one direction and then the other. They must have an end, surely? If they do, it is hidden from him in the mist that gathers over the piled-up corpses. He is unsure whether they stand here alone or whether they are the outer wall of some gargantuan structure.

Every few minutes a dozen more bodies crash into the walls at a frightening speed. Few have time to cry out—like him they must be awakening in a state of shock, with no time to make sense of the terrible fate that is rushing towards them. There is very little sound, in fact. The sound of bodies slapping against the wall is a pathetically flat noise. The ending of someone's life deserves a more significant sound than that, he thinks.

His survival, he now sees, was due to the fact that he and his unfortunate, accidental companion had hit the wall quite low down. A fall from a greater height would certainly have killed him. Those hitting the walls higher up are falling farther out across this plain of the dead. Some even disappear into the mists before falling.

He pulls off his tie and opens his shirt. The sticky heat of fading life rises from the mountain of cadavers, the recently deceased shedding the last warmth they have to give. The stench makes him gag several times, but he manages not to vomit.

There was so much broken in his life, so much that was wrong with him, but he doesn't deserve this. Nobody does.

Too often he has settled for a walk-on part in his own life. It has been a strictly non-speaking part. His voice is never heard. He racks his brain to think of something left undone for which he might be judged so harshly. Something or someone knows there are a million tiny things that, added together, would be enough to crush his hopes.

He feels as if the few good things in his life have been incinerated in front of him, then the ashes have been spat into and rubbed in his face.

Dread alone has so far prevented him from imagining what might be next. Because there must *be* a next. This not an end for him, unlike those around him. They must all be here for a *reason*, surely.

Then he realises what is missing. There are no flies. Not a single fly in this stinking butcher's shop. That doesn't make sense—except if it is a feast so jealously guarded that not even flies, or their greedy white offspring, are invited. Where *is* this place?!

Is this hell? Has history finally ended, he wonders; has Judgement Day come and found everyone wanting?

Or maybe this is someone's—or something's—idea of heaven. If he is right, then the mind that conceived it must be rotted away with disease.

Maybe it is a monument. Or an altar to a foul religion, with an obscene dark god that requires constant sacrifice. Except for him.

But perhaps this is his curse—he was *supposed* to survive, he was *supposed* to see this. Those who died were the lucky ones. Oblivion. Maybe that is heaven.

A hundred hooks inside his mind, pulling him in all directions at once. The walls beckon. Just one last effort, one final moment of courage, and he can join the fortunate dead who lie all around him. He hopes he can summon enough speed, heading out over this nightmarish surface, to smash his brains out against the hard surface. He can stand no more of this.

Rushing forward as best he can, he is just feet from the dark hard salvation of the wall when he sinks to his knees in failure. He curses himself, aware that his own cowardice has cheated him of the mercy that oblivion would have brought. He is disgusted that he has been unable to overcome the simple-minded brute within him who wants to go on living, no matter what the consequences might be.

Shutting his eyelids tightly and praying to whatever foul god might be listening, he pleads for the towering walls to come crashing down on him and all the filth beneath them. At least that would obliterate the memory of this obscene situation. If only there was that much mercy here.

He slumps down against three large men piled atop each other and sobs heavily.

Sometime later, he forces himself to stand and face the wall. The fact that this giant obstacle is an execution device appalls him, yet he longs to know more about it.

Finally, he gathers enough tatters of courage together and

reaches out to touch the wall. His fingers hesitate, defying his will once more. Despite the rivulets of hot blood streaming over most of it, a coolness rises from the surface where the black shows through.

Gritting his teeth, he forces his fingers forward. The surface does not yield beneath his touch, but the cool clamminess is a shock. Snatching his fingertips away from the surface, he knows it is not stone. But it is not anything else his touch is familiar with, either.

He staggers back from it, fearing that it might not have been built at all but has grown there, a fungoid architecture of death nourished plentifully by blood and human flesh.

He staggers and stumbles away from the terrible, towering edifice.

Once every hour there is a giant lurch, as of some great machinery, and the sea of corpses descends, making way for more. He totters, trying to surf the wave of decay.

Every time this happens, a noise like razor angels burns from ear to ear, straight through the soft grey centre of his head, jolting the mush within. He covers his ears, but the sound is tenacious and refuses to let him go. Whether it is the complaint of old machinery in agony, or the triumphant bellow of some unimaginable creature is impossible to say. The sound transforms its 20-second duration into a black eternity.

Once the sound fades, he stands panting. Exhausted, thirsty. There is no food here and no water. This place was not made for visitors. He is deeply ashamed that, twice now, he has raised his head, opened his mouth and drunk in the rain of fresh blood that never stops falling.

Wandering back and forth, he looks for a familiar face among the corpses. An impossible task.

And he catches himself asking why he wants that anyway—it will simply add to his anguish. But at least it would be something familiar, something he recognises and can hang on to. Something to help him cling to the last thin sliver of sanity. Anything is better than nothing.

After what seems like an eternity of staring down into the thousand faces, face of human mortality, he abandons his insane quest.

He looks down at himself. After just a few hours stranded in this place he looks like a ruddied scarecrow. His clothes are torn and stained with filth and blood. For the first time in his life—if he is still truly alive—personal vanity becomes overly important to him. He tries to re-arrange his tattered clothes. He spits into his hand and tries to remove some of the dirt that has gathered there. After a minute or so he gives up his task, realising his vanity is all in vain.

Somewhere above the red mist, in the sky over the blood-soaked clouds, he sees a vast dark shape moving. Instinct takes over and he tries to flee back to the wall, tumbling over the tangle of tortured limbs, staggering gratefully to safety. Safety? He almost laughs out loud at the absurdity of the concept.

He has no idea what the shape might be. But even if it is a predator of some sort, there is carrion aplenty here to assuage its hunger. Supposing it did swoop on him and devour him—that would be a merciful release from this larder in hell. He yells. Incoherent noises, for what good is language here? He waves his arms in a desperate, idiotic attempt to attract this imagined saviour. But none comes.

His head slumps onto his chest. Eventually his mind will snap, he feels sure. But how much more terrible can it be to remain sane in a place like this? Whichever path he travels down, his eventual destination is death.

He starts as he catches some movement in the corner of his eye. A face. A human face. Smeared in filth and blood, two tear-reddened eyes stare at him from the distance. He is sure it is a woman. The head disappears from view. He thinks at first she might be hiding in misplaced panic at seeing another living being, but then convinces himself she has simply stumbled.

Heading in her direction he clambers over a raised pile of dead, pushing aside the face of an elderly man—smashed glasses, smashed teeth, gaping round mouth—and sees her kneeling there.

"Hello. Hello." His yells make the woman look up. There is fear in her face. Maybe she'd thought he was a hallucination. "It's OK. Don't be afraid," he says, sliding and stumbling towards her.

She still seems unsure. Maybe she thinks he's responsible for causing this carnage. "I'm a friend," is all he can think to say. "It's good to see someone else," he adds. Her face relaxes slightly at his words.

As he draws near to her, his foot gives way beneath him, and he grabs at her for support. She recoils, yelling. As she stands lopsidedly, panting with pain, he notices that her left arm has more than one elbow. "Sorry ... sorry sorry ... I didn't ..." he tenders his apology in a low murmur.

Looking around for something that might help, he quickly realises that there is nothing he can use to set her shattered arm. There is no help here.

As the pain in her arm slowly subsides, she takes a step towards him. At least another living face, one that doesn't stare back with hollow dead eyes, is welcome. She puts her arm on his and looks up into his face. "W—where ...?" she gasps, dryly. He shakes his head.

"IdunnohowIgothere ... I dunnohow ..." She lets the string of syllables slip from her lips like drool, her eyes darting back and forth from his face to the corpses lying all around. "Will anyone come for us?" she whispers, almost afraid of the answer.

The question drenches him in despair. He can't think of any way to tell her of his greatest fear; that mankind has been reduced to the plaything of some chaotic, chthonic god. That soon there might not be anyone left to care.

He looks at the vast dark walls, clamping his eyes shut as the latest arrivals appear in the air above them. "They'll come ... but they won't live."

She gasps, partly in anguish and partly from a twinge in her arm, then buries her face in his chest.

They cling closely to each other; a broken, bloodied Adam and Eve in their charnel pit Eden. Soon they will grow hungry together ...

Crashing into red walls. This storm of people, never ending. Under the feral sky.

Out of Stock

"What is essential is invisible to the eye."
-Antoine de Saint-Exupéry

Rowe often wondered if he was the only driver on the road who actually knew how to *drive*. Everybody else just seemed to aim their car and hope for the best. He felt besieged by idiots on all sides.

He slowed as he approached the junction. As the lights began to change from green, a large red car sped past him, vibrating to the persistent thud of loud music. Rowe caught a glimpse of the driver. He was in his late teens or early twenties with one hand on the wheel while the other fiddled with something. Probably himself.

The car didn't slow as it approached the lights but sped through the red signal, almost colliding with a blue van crossing the junction, before speeding away into the distance.

The driver of the blue van didn't even lean on his horn in anger. He probably thought the idiot was "cool" for speeding and putting other people at risk. Being an arsehole was a career choice now, it seemed. And a popular one at that.

Rowe shook his head. The stupid little bastard was like so many these days; they all obviously thought the rules of the road were for other, lesser mortals.

Although annoyed at having to make the trip in the first place, he was almost relieved to see the giant supermarket sign, signalling that he had at last reached the relative safety of the car park.

The huge uninspired double-M of the "MegaMecca" logo

stared down at him from the top of the hangar-like building as he turned into the car park and joined a short queue.

Rowe sighed to himself and tapped the steering wheel impatiently. He was only here because his wife was missing a vital ingredient for her recipe—ingredients were always "vital," he noticed—and she insisted on brand loyalty. The fact that his wife worked at the supermarket and, with just a *little* foresight, could have picked up the item before she'd left work earlier that day, was an avenue just not worth exploring with her.

He didn't intend to spend all day here, but the queue didn't seem to be moving at all. He was beginning to think of which Lucio Fulci movie he'd line up for this evening's entertainment when he suddenly noticed a loud beeping noise.

A large shape moved in the corner of Rowe's left eye. He turned his head quickly to see that a massive supermarket delivery lorry was backing towards him at speed. It was bearing down on him at such velocity that he was convinced it intended to devour him and his car whole.

His heart began to hammer in panic as he reached for the door handle. Then there was a loud hiss and the truck's red brake lights glowed brightly at him like the eyes of a predatory beast. They were head height, just inches from the car.

Rowe felt sweat bead on his brow as the lorry roared away towards the exit, and he noticed the name on the side of the van. Below the well-known haulage firm's logo was the slogan "Keeping the shelves stocked for MegaMecca." "Not much point if you've killed off their customers first," he thought bitterly.

After he'd managed to park, Rowe went through the sliding doors and grabbed a basket before heading towards the first set of aisles.

The air conditioning hummed agreeably behind the inevitable Muzak as he passed a notice saying "Eroteak—the sexiest wood in the world." On a raised platform a shop assistant who looked like Schwarzenegger's butch older sister was demonstrating a new line of furniture resembling standard pine lawn furniture. Customers were lining up to try it out.

He hurried past, puzzled as to whether the moans and sighs of satisfaction actually came from the people themselves or were a taped sound effect. Personally, he'd never found wood in the least bit "sexy."

His wife had been working at the new supermarket for over a fortnight, but this was the first time Rowe had been here. He'd assumed that all supermarkets were created equal, but he was staggered by the size of the place. The aisles of goods seemed to stretch away to infinity.

He glanced up, hoping to follow the overhead signs. But there were none. He shrugged to himself. He'd just have to use his eyes.

It was early evening, yet the place was surprisingly empty. He'd been walking for nearly a minute before he came across any other shoppers. But then again, he thought, this place is big enough to hide an army in.

Crossing the aisle in front of him was a small group of strangely-dressed women. Two of them had their heads covered and the rest were turned away from him. The woman at the front was pushing a trolley with a broken front wheel that kept veering off to one side. Every time she struggled to right the thing, the women sang softly to themselves. He couldn't understand the words but thought they might be Polish or Romanian.

The trolley was filled with brown paper bags. The thing that struck Rowe was that the bags looked old and crumpled and there was something leaking from each of them. He was about to raise his voice and draw the women's attention to the problem when he came up short with a start. A small dark-haired child was clambering about among the bags. As it lolled to one side, looking ill and very pale, Rowe caught its eye. The infant held him for a second with its large, dark gaze, and he could see that there were large clumps of hair missing from its head. Its skin looked dead.

The odd procession disappeared behind the end of the shelves, and Rowe stood frozen for a few seconds. When he'd recovered, he peered around the corner but, to his relief, the women and their weird cargo had disappeared.

Rowe continued along the same aisle, scanning the shelves for anything interesting. He stopped once to pick up a packet of sweet biscuits. The colourful picture of a winking cartoon fox on the packet brought back memories of his childhood. He had thought they'd stopped making them. In fact, the packet looked really old. He looked at the Sell By date; it had passed two decades ago. He replaced it and wondered exactly what sort of shop sold 20-year-old biscuits.

Ahead of him a woman appeared around a corner, her trolley piled high with DVD cases. As she began to head towards Rowe, a man with an equally heavily-laden trolley raced past him and crashed head on into the woman. Their trolleys tangled with a clashing sound. She squeaked and bleated in distress as the man pushed her back a few steps. He yelled "Out the way" and continued to force the woman backwards.

Rowe wondered whether he should intervene, but then the woman began to push back, and the duelling pair began headed straight towards him.

"Outthewayoutthewayoutthewayouttheway ..." The man continued his litany of impatience and anger as the woman now held her ground, blocking his way.

"This is ridiculous," thought Rowe and decided to reverse course. As he turned, he noticed that several other shoppers were approaching him from the opposite direction. They seemed intent on joining the fray, following some obscure tribal instinct. He was penned in.

Afraid that he'd be crushed by insane shoppers, Rowe abandoned his still empty basket and began to claw tins and packets from the shelves. Once there was enough room, he clambered up the shelves and sat looking down on the bizarre battle.

From his vantage point he could see that the covers of the DVDs in the woman's trolley looked like backwards dreams of awful events. The man's trolley was piled high with loosely wrapped chunks of meat; they didn't smell very fresh.

The trolley tug-of-war continued between the two for a few seconds more before three other jousters joined in the combat. One young woman with bleached blonde hair let forth a string of expletives and attempted to climb inside the first woman's trolley, clawing at her face as she did so.

An older woman with a hooked nose had begun to beat the man's head with a bottle of sauce. He yelped in pain but still clung onto the trolley, pushing and yelling. When the man began to bleed, Rowe decided he'd better go and find the manager and put a stop to this consumerist combat as soon as possible.

He got up on all fours and began to crawl along the top of the shelves. The lights flickered out for several seconds and there were gasps of surprise from every corner of the shop. When they came back on, Rowe made his way to the end of the section and gingerly descended the shelves, kicking goods off them to gain a foothold.

Jumping the last few feet, he landed on the floor to find himself engulfed by a cloud of fine brown powder. He coughed and fished out a paper tissue to hold over his mouth. Looking down, he realised he'd landed hard on two packets that he'd knocked off the shelves in his descent.

When the cloud had settled, Rowe bent to pick up one of the broken packets. Powder dribbled out as he turned it over to look at the swirling abstract design on the front and sides. "Choc Hotolate." The large colourful letters seemed perfectly harmless—and the name was probably the product of some bright young thing who had laboured long and hard over it— yet Rowe found the Spoonerism secretly sinister.

He quickly dropped the packet and wiped his hands as best he could, attempting to stamp the powder residue from his shoes as if it was dog muck. Come to think of it, the powder didn't *really* smell like chocolate at all.

As Rowe began to walk away, he noticed that the floor in this part of the shop was sloping at an odd angle. It wasn't anything very pronounced, but just enough to be bothersome and make walking slightly uncomfortable. Subsidence, maybe? And every now and again one of the floor tiles slipped under his feet, as if it was loose. He resolved never to shop here again, no matter how insistent his wife was.

He stamped off in search of a staff member, the sounds of the trolley tussle still evident above the insistently jolly music (it was a song he'd hoped never to hear again). Within a few seconds he came across a yellow "Cleaning In Progress" barrier that stopped him going any further. Next to it, a mop was standing upright in a cleaning bucket.

Rowe made a disgusted face as he peered into the bucket, which was filled with water the colour of liver. Something dripped onto the floor, and he looked up. Two tiles were missing from the suspended ceiling, and he could see that there was a dark shape hunched within the crawl space.

A young man dressed in a blue overall shuffled up behind him. "There's something up there," said Rowe, pointing. The young man grunted in affirmation as another droplet of red liquid splashed onto the floor. The cleaner picked up the mop and slapped it noisily onto the floor.

Unsure whether he was talking to the right person, Rowe told him about the fight going on in the next aisle. The sounds of battle seemed to have subsided, and he imagined one or more of the protagonists lying dead among deformed tins and slabs of dirty old meat.

The cleaner listened to Rowe then nodded his head, an untidy mop of dirty-looking sandy hair waving about as he did so. "OK."

Unsure of what to do next, Rowe simply shuffled off. For a few moments he concentrated on negotiating the difficult floor, wondering whether he should try and find someone more senior than the cleaner. But then he decided that he'd best concentrate on finding what he came for and getting out of this maddening maze.

Approaching yet another junction with a cross aisle, he could hear voices around the corner. Though they were indistinct at first, he caught one sentence as he was about to round the bend.

"We wear upon our heads the golden crown of divine thought. Yet how often do we appreciate this gift or even use it properly?"

Expecting to see two learned Jewish intellectuals, perhaps discussing the Kabballah, Rowe was surprised to bump into two supermarket shelf-stackers. The speaker had his back to Rowe. His companion pushed the man urgently and nodded his head towards the intruder as soon as he appeared.

The speaker turned round to look at Rowe while his mute companion suddenly remembered that he needed to re-arrange an already perfectly tidy shelf display.

Rowe told him his problem and the man smiled. "Oh yes, sir. You need the section marked 'Ritual.'"

"Ritual?"

The smiling continued. "Yes, sir. Two aisles over and carry straight on past 'Reclamation & Recycling.'"

Rowe thanked him and moved off, feeling slightly alarmed by the man. He had smiled, he had been pleasant and helpful. Yet his skin didn't seem to fit his face properly.

He noticed that the shelves here were rather old. The paint was bubbling and in some places spots of rust showed through. They'd obviously been used in another shop before. Perhaps that's what the man had meant by "Reclamation & Recycling."

There was something that looked like dried fish sitting on the shelves. Bombay Duck, he thought with a smile. But as he peered closer, he saw that it was a small, dark dessicated hand, possibly a monkey's paw. Rowe, imagining he'd strayed into the "Organic" section, hurried on quickly.

He slowed when he became aware of a sound like something large being moved around. Feeling sure he knew where the sound was coming from, he went to the next aisle over. It sounded like a giant pair of wings flapping in desperation, hungry for escape but penned within a confined space. Eager to see, Rowe rushed to the next cross aisle and hurried around the corner.

He was sure that this was where the sound had come from, but all he saw was an empty aisle with neatly stacked shelves on each side. Vaguely disappointed, Rowe returned to his previous route.

Ahead he could see what looked like a more open area, with a glass-fronted counter. If it was the delicatessen counter, they might have what he was looking for.

But as he got closer, he could see that it was closed, with hardly anything behind the glass. His mind flashed back to images of empty shelves that he'd seen on the news about the old Soviet Union.

It was then that he saw the figure of a young woman hunched over at one side of the counter. She was dressed in ragged clothes and was reaching behind the smeared glass to pick something up. She began to gnaw at it hungrily. Rowe was about to say something responsible like "You're supposed to pay for it before you eat it" when she turned, hearing him approach.

He was appalled at what he saw clutched in her hands and at what was smeared across her mouth. Her eyes were filled with anger and pain and something else Rowe couldn't identify.

He turned in mild panic and disappeared quickly into the maze of shelves. When he'd calmed down slightly, he began to question whether he should demand that his wife find herself another job. Any shop that would allow homeless people to plunder their produce was obviously not a safe place to work. And what on *earth* were they selling at that counter?

He'd only gone a short distance when he found his way barred. Someone had left a barricade of stock trolleys and cardboard boxes piled right across the aisle. Rowe thought of turning back for a second but was nervous of another encounter with the hungry young woman.

There was a gap in the very centre of the tangle, just big enough to squeeze through. Rowe struggled to get his bulk through the narrow opening, only to find that he was up against a wall of some sort. There was barely enough room to pass by into a narrow corridor left along one side of the structure. As he edged by, Rowe could see that the shelves were totally empty here. He hoped he wasn't entering a "Staff Only" area. But there'd been no sign, and he could protest if challenged.

The corridor continued along the front of the shelves for several yards before turning once again, allowing him to see an exit. Rowe caught his leg as he struggled out into the aisle, ending up on his back.

From where he lay he could see that what he'd thought was a wall was actually a huge plinth. Standing, he stuck his head back into the narrow space and looked up. Above him was a sculpture of a group of figures made entirely out of malformed and flattened tin cans. Stripped of their labels, the aluminium cans gleamed in the light that leaked into the claustrophobic gallery.

He could see that the figures, all young men, were leaning forward, as if yearning for progress against impossible odds. Someone had scratched some words onto the front of the hand-made plinth. Rowe had to stand back to read it properly. It said "The Struggling Sons."

Rowe shook his head in puzzlement and admiration before continuing on his way. How odd that the management should allow someone—presumably a member of their staff—to build a huge Social Realist sculpture in the middle of their canned goods section! Though it does make a nice change, added another part of his brain.

The small oasis of culture had lifted Rowe's mood slightly. But then the lights flickered off again. This time some of them stayed dark.

And now something else had changed, too. When he'd entered, they'd been playing the usual mix of characterless contemporary mush and "timeless" classics that were well past their Sell By date. But now the music had changed.

No doubt what he was hearing was the latest in ambient electronica, but it sounded like an orchestra being forced to play something slow and funereal while submerged in some viscous liquid.

The occasional pops and crackles of the failing PA system only added to the sinister phonics of the unearthly dirge. Though not unappealing, in a familiarly dismal way, it began to make him feel as if he was trapped underground. And that nobody knew or cared that he was here.

His mood had darkened again, but at least he was nearing the section he needed. There, ahead of him, stood the chest freezers he'd been seeking.

He lifted the lid of the first one and searched among the frost-rimmed packets. He moved on to the second one; still no luck.

The third freezer didn't have a lid. It looked as if it had come out of the Ark, and the motor made an unhealthy rattling noise. As he leaned over it, Rowe noticed that it was hardly cold at all. And it was all but empty.

He saw one solitary packet left at the bottom of the

casket-like freezer. It had the blue and yellow markings of the supermarket's budget range, but it would do. Rowe reached down and grabbed it, only to feel it deform under his fingers.

He picked up the soggy packet and a stream of thin, urinous liquid ran from it. His heart sank as he crumpled the packet in frustration, the word "Soul" becoming quickly unreadable in his clenching fist.

Then he noticed the red label on the freezer front. It said, "Out of Stock." Rowe groaned in despair.

A familiar voice behind him said "Sorry. Out of stock."

He turned to find his wife's hazel eyes staring into his. She was wearing her MegaMecca staff uniform. He couldn't work out what she was doing here.

Rowe's head ached. "Wha ...?"

Over her shoulder he saw a man in a stained white overall emerge from behind some plastic sheeting that was covered in long red streaks. He came to stand at her side.

Rowe looked at the man, but his expression remained blank, bored even.

His wife seemed amused at Rowe's confusion. "Don't worry, love. It's for the best," she said, as if to comfort him.

But even as she smiled, a bleakness came over her face, as if chilled by an ice-heavy blast straight from the guts of hell. "We've got to keep the shelves stocked somehow, haven't we?"

He muttered the phrase to himself as he felt his wife's hand laid gently on his arm. As she began to guide him towards the plastic sheeting, Rowe couldn't understand why he didn't resist. Did some deep, instinctive part of him somehow acknowledge that this was "for the best"?

He looked back just once. For a second he thought of running, of reaching the daylight ... if it was still there. Then, as the lights went out in rows and the music slowed soupily to a stop, an immense darkness fell upon the vast shop. And the screaming began.

Finest Garments Repaired

All the shops in the small arcade were in darkness now, except for the tailor's shop at the very end. The velvet soft light that spilled across the doorway showed that it was open until seven every evening, except at weekends.

Nick checked his watch. It was 6:50 now. There were unlikely to be any more customers today. He looked down the arcade for the hundredth time. It was still empty with only a few pedestrians passing on the pavement outside.

Stepping out from the deep doorway of the greetings card shop where he'd been waiting, he shifted the weight of the bag he carried over one shoulder.

The name "A B Kaltenbach" was written across the window in old fashioned gold letters, now flaking badly. Beneath, also in red-rimmed gold, it read "All Your Tailoring Needs Met" and "Finest Garments Repaired."

Nick smirked to himself, certain that he knew the truth that lay behind the supposedly innocuous phrases. As he turned the handle, a bell above the door rang to announce his arrival. And as the smell of slightly musty cloth filled his nostrils, he thought he'd stepped into a shop from a theme park or a museum exhibit. He scanned the shop quickly, noticing packets and tins that he remembered from his grandmother's sewing box.

All the fittings were made of dark wood. Everything seemed to have been plucked from its own time and deposited in the curious little shop.

The chimes of the little bell hadn't had a chance to fade away when a small, thin man appeared behind the counter. He dressed in a style reminiscent of the 1950s, thought Nick.

"We are closing soon, I'm afraid, but if I can help you quickly, sir?" The man's English was good, but his accent was unmistakably foreign.

"Yes. This won't take long," said Nick, assuredly. Despite his tone, he was unsure. Though this man looked like all the photographs he'd seen, he looked *too* much like them. Over twenty years had passed, after all, yet this man still looked to be in his 30s.

He'd also thought the photos had a fault with their contrast, but now he could see that the man's eyes were really as dark as they appeared in print.

"My name is Nick Laxman. I'm an investigative journalist." He hoped that this opening might provoke a reaction, but the man's face remained as still as a mask.

After several seconds the man said merely: "Yes?"

Plucking up his courage, Nick fished a small file out of his shoulder bag. "You don't remember an unnamed camp south of Prijedor in Bosnia?" He placed several photographs on the counter, fanning them out for the man to see. One showed a large white building with a yard at the front, surrounded by barbed wire fences. Several others showed lines of emaciated men with haunted faces, peering at the photographer through the same fences.

The man scanned the photographs for a short while. "What is this? Why are you showing me these? Please, we're about to close ..."

Nick leaned his hand on the counter, indicating the photographs with his other. "I think you remember this place because you helped to run it, Dr. Dodik. That is your real name, isn't it?"

The man tried to play dumb. Nick was not convinced.

"No, no. I have never been in the army. I have always been a tailor. I learnt at the elbow of my father in his shop at the shining market in Carcosa. Have you ever been to Carcosa, Mr. Laxman?"

Nick shook his head. It sounded like somewhere on the Mediterranean. He hated hot sticky places. And he wasn't about to let himself be distracted by tales of tourist destinations.

"They called some men who ran the death camps 'butchers.'"
Nick looked around at the bales of cloth, the line of shining
needles on the counter, the display cases full of bright-labelled
bobbins. "But not you."

"I-I don't know what you mean. Please leave now. I have to
close up. My wife is expecting me."

"There is a certain gentleman in Brussels who has a—
frankly—obscene private collection. I saw your handiwork
there. It drapes so beautifully, doesn't it ... fine young Slavic
skin?"

Even in the gloom of the shop, the man's face darkened
visibly, his patience clearly at an end. "Get out! Get out of my
shop! You've no right to come here making accusations. How
can you say these things to me?"

Nick wasn't about to be shaken loose. "My "friend" in
Brussels said that you would be more than co-operative if I
showed you this."

Once more he dipped into his capacious bag and brought
forth a carefully wrapped parcel, which he quickly opened on
the glass counter. A shabby yellow garment spilled out, grubby
and tattered at the edges. It looked as if it had once been an
expensive piece of clothing.

The man gasped softly but seemed unwilling to reach out
and touch the strange garment.

"Where did you get ... this?" he asked in an almost
reverential voice.

"I told you, I know a man in Brussels. He was reluctant to
part with it at first, but I convinced him that the police might
be very interested in his unusual collection. IF they found out
about it ..."

Nick watched the man's face carefully as he gazed down
at the tattered cloth. He let the man study it for a while before
speaking again. "If I offered you this garment in payment,
would you be willing to speak to me? I'm sure you'd agree that
it was a fair exchange—this piece of old, rare cloth for, say, 20
minutes of your time. Wouldn't you say, Dr. Dodik?"

"Stop calling me that—*they* gave me that title. I never told
them I was a doctor. I'm not ... I've always been a tailor. And I've

always gone where material is available."

Nick hesitated for a second or two as his mind danced off down a side avenue. "Then what are you doing here?"

The man spun around a copy of the local newspaper that was lying on the counter top. He indicated the headline. "Fourth Young Girl Missing."

Nick nodded as he took it in. "So you admit you are Elvir Dodik?"

He nodded. "That's one name I've used, certainly. Though not when I first made that garment you hold in your hands. It was my very finest work. It had to be, you see. Sadly, it has suffered greatly during the travails of the King."

Though puzzled by the reference to royalty, Nick pressed on with his questions. A small voice at the back of his head told him there hadn't been a king on the throne since 1952. But was that reason enough to question the man's sanity, he wondered.

Nick felt he should press home his advantage, now that he'd got Dodik's mask to slip. Time for some reassurances, he thought. "I wouldn't name you. There'd be no mention of where you live now. I just want the background on the camps—names, dates, the *real* criminals. You know the sort of thing. You don't even have to mention about your part in ... it all."

It was all lies, though Nick had faked as much sincerity as he could muster. He fully intended to expose Dodik's macabre line in human recycling but hoped to put the man at ease enough so that he'd condemn himself "on the record." Hell, he would crucify him! It would make a great story.

Dodik gazed at his shoes. "If ... if you weren't there, you simply wouldn't understand."

Nick saw his chance. "Then *make* me understand!"

"And where might all this appear?" asked Dodik. There was a distinct edge of suspicion in the man's voice.

"A few newspaper articles ... the quality press. Or maybe a book. A book might be best, thinking about it." Nick knew he sounded dangerously smug, in danger of losing his advantage. So he decided to appeal to Dodik's sense of honour ... if he had one.

"Don't you think you owe it to the families of those who

died to tell the truth? People were murdered in those camps! Don't you owe them something? The truth …?"

"Truth?! You pretend moral outrage. You pretend pity for those who died. But all you want is a story for your shitty little newspaper, so you can line your pocket and that of your masters with gold. That's the truth!"

"Actually, I'm a freelance," replied Nick, coolly.

"I don't care what you call yourself. You're still just a corpse worm." Nick caught sight of himself in a glass-fronted case. His face looked pallid, puffy.

"In any case, you fail to understand, *Mister* Laxman. Your supposed "victims" were all volunteers. Once I'd explained to them my intentions, they were only too glad to participate, following their deaths."

Nick snorted. "I don't believe you for a second!"

Dodik made a sour face and waved away his disbelief. "What you believe is irrelevant. You are a journalist … the truth is a stranger to you. Anything you'd write would inevitably be lies, even if you didn't realise it."

Nick felt he was losing the battle. He needed this story desperately; it was the only thing that might put him back on top, after the mess he'd made with tapping that teenage pop star's phone.

Maybe claiming the moral high ground might help. "But you have to talk to me. You owe it to the world … to history … to tell what really happened in those camps!"

For a moment or two, it seemed as if Dodik was actually thinking it over. Maybe I've succeeded in getting through to him, thought Nick.

But his mood plunged once more when Dodik spoke again. "Why should I? What's in it for me?"

"Well, you get to keep that." Nick pointed at the pile of ratty yellow silk to underline his point.

The man seemed amused by Nick's words, the corners of his mouth lifting slightly. "I could simply keep that anyway. Afterwards …"

"But don't you want the world to hear your side of the story? Not simply what was in the news at the time …?" Nick licked his lips, aware of how empty his words sounded. He doubted that, unlike most criminals, the man had any feelings of superiority. It seemed impossible to appeal to his vanity.

"NO!" The man's voice was lost in the no man's land between a hiss and a snarl. "You idiot!"

He swept the photographs from the counter, scattering them at Nick's feet. "You come in here with your pathetic claims, thinking you can blackmail me. You trashy little gutter press swine! I ought to ..."

Dodik calmed down slightly after his outburst. He paced back-and-forth behind the counter before stopping at one end, obviously mulling something over. Nick expected a counteroffer at any second.

"Animal skin is all very well, but human skin is so much finer." Dodik stroked the back of a small leather chair set back behind the counter. "Its grain is very fine in comparison. I much prefer working with it." Dodik's smile made Nick feel that, somewhere, he'd just been added to an exotic menu. What *did* Dodik do with the bodies once he'd flayed them?

Suddenly the man was on the counter, packets of needles crunching beneath his feet. Shocked, Nick took two steps backward, not daring to take his eyes off Dodik for a moment. The man was frighteningly agile for someone who was supposed to be in his early 60s.

Dodik crouched low, his eyes boring into Nick's like a serpent about to strike. Nick heard the glass of the counter top crack as Dodik shifted his weight, ready to pounce.

A voice in the back of Nick's head warned him to get out. "Run. This old bastard is capable of anything!"

Nick didn't want to turn his back on the deranged tailor, but he had no choice. Turning swiftly, he plunged towards the door. He hadn't realised quite how dimly lit the shop was until he reached for the door handle. It seemed to have vanished completely in the gloom.

He squinted, fingers fumbling swiftly for the brass handle. It just wasn't there.

Then Dodik was on him. His hands seemed unnaturally large, his arms wrapped around Nick's head and upper body, dragging him down to the floor with a loud grunt. The older man was all over him, pinning him to the floor. For someone who was slightly built, Dodik weighed a ton.

Dodik's mouth was next to his ear. "You want to know the truth about the camp? This is the truth. THIS ... is the truth!" He brought his arm down swiftly, plunging several sharp points into Nick's flesh. Nick yelped as Dodik pushed them further into the tender space beneath the back of his skull.

Big needles. He could feel them digging into soft nerve centres, pushing and probing as first numbness, then black rivers of pain shot down his arms to ball up in his fingertips. He whined in agony, totally unable to move.

"Normally I'd wait until post mortem to do this but I'm impatient to begin my work. And, in my opinion, you deserve to suffer." Nick felt the man's oppressive weight on his back; it was getting difficult to breathe. Then he was turned over; lying face up, he could only stare straight up as the shadows in the corners of the room reached their cold fingers down towards him.

Dodik's glittering eyes roved over Nick's face, as they might over a painting in a museum.

"You have such pale skin. *Beautifully* pale!" Dodik held Nick down with his knees, turning his head from side to side as if examining a specimen in a lab, stroking his face from time to time. Out of the corner of his eye, Nick caught a glimpse of light reflecting off steel. Then he heard the 'snick' of large scissors opening and closing.

"Time that I unmasked you, sir." The scissors snipped and snapped ever closer to the soft skin under Nick's jawline.

"I will be rewarded well for returning the Royal raiment to its rightful owner. Along with another small gift."

Dodik didn't rush things—after all, he was a dedicated craftsman—so Nick had plenty of time to scream himself hoarse.

A single candle was lit on the side table that the man had pulled into the middle of the shop. The light from it glinted in the warm amber liquid at the bottom of his glass as he sat in the comfortable leather chair. A certain volume lay open in his lap.

The yellow robe, which the skilful tailor had faithfully repaired as best he could in the circumstances, was draped carefully over one arm of the chair.

He picked up the mask that lay on the table, examining the careful stitching that tidied away the slightly ragged edges. The handiwork around the eye holes and the edges of the mouth was similarly painstaking. Not bad, he thought, considering how little time he'd had.

He ran his hand over the fine pale material, allowing himself a small measure of pride. And it was so rarely that such fine material actually walked into his shop and offered itself freely … more or less.

The man who had once been Elvir Dodik laid the mask down, sat back and waited for the King to visit his tailor. He knew he wouldn't have to wait very long.

In the Deeps of Dream

Through owlrain and mothlight she walked, collar pulled up against the cruellest cuts of wind. Smudged by clouds, a part-eaten pumpkin slice hung overhead, the man in the half-moon winking maliciously at her. "If you won't help me, don't hinder me," she murmured to him.

The rich stink of mould and rot rose from the leaf-littered ground. The sere trees scraped the sky with their wind-filled branches, scattering leaves over her as she went.

The moonlight illuminated the path ahead dimly. Just a single lamp still shone in the park but that was on the far side, nowhere near where she needed to go.

Although her eyes couldn't penetrate the darkness very far, she sensed there was something even darker out there, moving through the night; something huge, treading slowly. In answer, something small inside her whined pitifully, afraid that even her suddenly quickened pace would not be enough to protect her.

Twice she stopped and looked behind her. There was nothing except the occasional car passing on the nearby road. She'd felt certain she'd heard footsteps following her, always keeping pace with her but never passing. Your own shadow, said her small voice, hopefully. Not in this light, whispered her sensible self.

Three stunted figures appeared, dragging their feet. Then two more came into view, not far behind them, all illuminated by candles in moth-haunted glass jars. From their size and shrill voices, she realised they were children from the nearby houses, dragging their way along the moon-dappled path, all dressed in desultory costumes, on their way to a party of sorts.

She stepped aside to let them through as a taller figure, also costumed and masked, brushed past her, muttering "Hurry! Hurry!" to encourage her small charges.

As she watched them go, she gathered her courage to take the short cut through the woods. A gap in the fence beckoned her.

Her meeting was 25 minutes' walk from her house. She was reluctant to be dragged into this, but her sister had managed to persuade her after several phone calls. Uncertain of what she could do to help, the one thing she was sure of was that she didn't want this rendezvous taking place too close to home. However, she was now beginning to regret her choice of time and place.

Pushing aside an unruly branch, she soon managed to find the well-trodden path among the trees. It was drier under here where some of the branches still clung jealously to their leaves. In the park they had been like sodden breakfast cereal, squelching beneath her footsteps, but here they still crunched satisfyingly underfoot. From time to time, having saved up the rain, the black branches dripped on her. She started when the first drop hit the top of her hat like a soft explosion.

She stopped for a moment to get her bearings. Not too far now, she decided.

A bloated fungus clinging to the base of a tree exploded with a wet sound, spraying its spores into the damp air. She hurried away, brushing at her coat sleeve and collar, just in case. "The damn thing had to wait until I was passing by, didn't it?"

She made sure of her footing before descending a short slope, then relied on her ears to tell her where the shallow brook was. She leapt the gurgling waters and found her way out from under the trees, greeted by a spray of light rain.

In front of her lay the huge car park, almost empty. All the big shops were in darkness, asleep beneath huge signs in shades of sludgy yellow and grey. Most of the overhead lights were dead, too. The owners were obviously too miserly to either repair or replace them. Maybe they were right to save their money—the place was always deserted after dark, anyway.

Or almost deserted. The empty parking spaces were bathed in heavy pools of darkness. A gritty wind picked up as she started across the vast space.

At the far side of the small sea of tarmac lay her destination. To either side of it, lights were flicking off in shops as their owners closed up for the night. Even the big chain stores closed early in this part of the world, so there was nothing to draw customers to the retail park. No point staying open … unless you're the last coffee shop in the world.

"The Coffee Pot" was always open late. It stayed alive, she'd heard, on trade from late night lorry drivers doing overnight hauls. It was popular with insomniacs, too. And she'd also heard that insomnia was very popular these days. Personally, she'd prefer to be tucked up in bed, snoring happily to herself (she'd been told she snored by her unkind ex) … if she could manage it.

As she got closer to the single box of light in the encroaching darkness, she imagined it as a small submarine cell sunk at the bottom of a crushing ocean of black. At least this deep it would be safe from the depth charges of bad dreams, she thought.

She looked about herself uneasily, the wind forcing her to turn her face aside to avoid getting grit in her eyes. She picked up her pace. Even if her task turned out to be onerous, at least it would be warmer inside.

Standing outside for a moment, she looked up at the unimaginative name above the door before stepping forward and pushing open the glass door.

The amber and light brown decor was at least 30 years out of date. She found that slightly comforting, as if she'd stepped back into a time before … Her thoughts were snapped off sharply by the sound of the door slamming shut in the wind behind her. She felt sure she'd closed it tightly behind her. Catching the gaze of the woman behind the counter, she mouthed an apologetic "Sorry."

To one side lay a row of four booths. The tables in the rest of the place were empty. At first she thought he hadn't kept their appointment, but then she heard a snuffling sound from one of the booths and noticed an elbow jutting out from behind the partition.

Walking slowly over to the booth, she took in every detail of the man that she could. "OK, Holmes, what can we deduce?" she asked herself. As it turned out, not much from her present angle, so she took the plunge and decided to join him.

The seats were the colour of rotting leaves, or dirty brown seaweed. Her hat made a damp plop as it landed at her side. She peeled a few wet strands of hair from her forehead and re-positioned them as she sat down.

The man stared at her intently. He seemed so nervous that she was afraid he might fly apart at any moment—a bone bomb scattering deadly fragments in all directions. For a second she felt like ducking under the table in a futile attempt to escape the worst of the blast.

"Y-you're …," he began.

She raised her hand to cut him off. "No names. Please. It's just … easier," she told him, firmly. "Nothing personal."

He lowered his gaze and stared into the darkness gathered at the bottom of his large cup. She noticed that he wore nice clothes. Or rather they had once been nice clothes. His shirt cuffs were dirty and beginning to fray, while his coat had gathered various splashes and stains which he hadn't bothered to get rid of. Leaning back in her chair she could see his shoes were scuffed and dirty, unpolished for weeks.

He sat there slurping coffee nervously, almost chain drinking, the cup an extension of his hand. She looked at his red-rimmed eyes, the slight tremble in his hands as he raised the cup to his lips again and again.

"Trouble sleeping?" she asked him, as if she needed to.

For once he put the cup down, clinking it heavily, loudly, into its saucer. The owner glared at him from behind the counter, fearing for her crockery. "I daren't sleep," he said. "I daren't! That's when …"

She nodded, glancing down at the poisonously black liquid sloshing around in the bottom of his cup. "Yes, I know."

And things were always worse at this time of year, she'd noticed. It was when the sky changed, the constellations wheeling around to a different place. The new pattern they formed disturbed the mind, turning dreams against their dreamers. Some survived, but far too many dreamers lost their struggle beneath autumn skies, turning to dust and becoming mere grit in the eyes of the gods.

Perhaps bright Vega, gazing down from the West, had some sort of malign influence on the dreamers. Though she'd once considered the idea of stars somehow influencing people's lives was nonsense, now …

The cafe's owner appeared at the table, doubling as the waitress. "You ready to order?" It was a croaky creak of a voice with something metallic in it. And it was too old for her face. The woman scuttled away as soon as coffee—"*Just* coffee?!"— was ordered.

Once the waitress had gone, his imploring eyes settled on her. "Y-your sister said you could help me."

"I might have been able to … once." Amanda was four years her junior and was into ouija, tarot, Crowley—all that fake stuff. That wouldn't help anyone. She wished the clever little bitch would stop pointing hopeless cases in her direction. Amanda knew *nothing*!

She daren't tell him how many of those she'd tried to help were now dead. Several were hopeless derelicts, wandering the streets and sleeping rough. Occasionally she'd see one of them—the empty-faced children of her failure—and it would gnaw at her, sending her scurrying for her sleeping pills for several nights afterwards.

She had no way of knowing if the nameless man sitting across from her would be alive in a year's time. A month's time. Maybe he would be dead within a week.

The coffee arrived and she clutched it gratefully, willing the caffeine to make her feel less tired. These encounters seemed to take more and more out of her each time. And she was sure she'd been *noticed*. Followed. She was now far too conspicuous to ignore.

The silent TV at the end of the counter seemed to show a man demonstrating how to fit an unprotesting small dog into a jam jar, while enormous grey-green ropes were hauled across the background. Every time there was a gust of wind outside, the image juddered before exploding into a snowstorm of static for a few moments. She didn't have her glasses in any case, so she looked away, unwilling to see any more. Some bizarre sort of game show? Television seemed to get stranger every time she watched it.

"Listen, I can't guarantee anything. Nobody can," she warned him. He shifted in his seat, eyes roving over the detritus on the tabletop as if he'd lost the answer to his question there and such diligent searching would unearth it. This guy was obviously in no shape to hear the truth, she thought.

"But we'll see what we can do, eh?" She made a great effort to make sure her tone sounded more positive this time. He nodded, gratefully.

From time to time, the owner looked across at them as if she imagined they might be on some sort of sleazy first date, meeting in a lonely spot to cover up the shame of their unhealthy desires. The woman was clearly suspicious of this peculiar couple who were uninterested in any of the food on offer but simply guzzled cup after cup of coffee. Even her "delicious" homemade cakes were being spurned.

"You've had the dreams, too. You've heard the words. I'm not wrong, am I?" The pathetic, whipped-dog look in his eyes told her she couldn't disagree with him even if she wanted to. Which she didn't.

She sat patiently. Best to let him get it off his chest, she thought. There was a lot of apocryphal "dreamer" literature out there; the internet was crawling with it. Most of it was fiction masquerading as the truth—no harm there, in her opinion—but some of the self-help stuff was dangerous. It was obvious from what he said that he'd read some of it and swallowed it whole.

Some of it revolved around self-harm, and she was sure she'd caught a glimpse of some scarring poking out from his shirt cuffs. Maybe it wasn't related but maybe it was. Maybe if she let him talk, he'd let something slip.

"Sometimes there's something glistening in the darkness. But not in a good way. More like something you wouldn't want to touch ... or want to touch you. I always dream of huge places. Enormous. Places I've never seen in real life ... not even in photos.

"And the things I dream of … well, I feel that they're *old* … so very old. It just terrifies me …" he said. Well at least he's got that right, she thought.

"They're just dreams. They can't hurt you," she lied, as if reassuring a frightened five-year-old. "Everyone has nightmares from time to time, after all. It's just a normal part of life …"

For a moment she considered talking about the interpretation of dreams, of Jung, of a dozen other reassuring things. But she felt too weary of it all. After the events of the last decade, her energy reserves were almost gone.

Waiting until he'd come to a natural pause, she excused herself and headed off to the bathroom. "Buying yourself a little time?" she chided herself.

She looked at her tired eyes in the mirror. She'd seen enough horror films to know that this was the part where she glances in the mirror and sees something horrible standing behind her. She did as convention dictated but the only horror waiting there was the reflection of an earnest Victorian print of a shipwreck, hung there years ago and forgotten about. There seemed to be an awful commotion behind the small ship in the picture. She sympathised with the tiny sailors, fighting for their etched lives, forever frozen in their moment of greatest pictorial tragedy.

She turned her attention instead to the tingling tremor in her hands. They refused to be still, the chipped red nails like small tongues tasting the air for clues. One step closer, she thought.

She splashed some cold water on her face. After drying herself, she leaned her back against the wall and took three deep, slow breaths. The panacea that she handed out to others had long ago begun to fail her, like an over-used medicine gradually losing its potency.

He was still there when she returned, sipping and shaking. God knows what the cafe's owner thought of him. Probably assumed drugs were involved and would be delighted when he finally left.

"You probably think I'm mad or something, don't you?" He threw it at her as soon as she sat down, then obviously felt he should justify his aggressive words. "But I'm not. No. I just want to be like everyone else … to be able to sleep without being

…. persecuted. That's all. Just that. My family …" He stopped suddenly, his voice catching.

She nodded. "It's OK. I do understand." Now was the right time, she decided.

She fished in her handbag and pulled out a white card with a black brush-drawn symbol on it. She'd prepared it earlier that evening. If you tipped the card at a certain angle, the lines seemed to come together to make up a star. Covering it with her hand, she navigated it around a small heap of spilled sugar and slid it across the table towards him. "When I take my hand away, pick up the card."

He looked at her for a moment, dumbfounded, before nodding. In the back of his sleep-starved brain some small spark of sanity realised this might be the means of his deliverance. He was obviously ready to try anything. "Uuuh … OK. OK!"

She withdrew her hand, and he fumbled his fingers around its edge for a few moments before managing to pick it up. It trembled in his hand like a falling leaf. He gazed at it intently. Only slightly larger than a playing card. He was obviously skeptical that salvation could be delivered by something so small and simple. "Will this help?"

"Yes." Lying came too easily to her now, she decided. But what good would it do to tell him that she couldn't even help herself any longer? If he was still strong enough, it would work. At least this way he had *some* hope.

She'd heard of dreamers who'd sold everything, including their families, to set up bizarre cults based around their half-glimpsed dream images, the poisoned icons of a merciless Morpheus. One Russian billionaire—a minor celebrity in the Moscow press, thanks to his mutterings about dreams and recovered alien technology—was rumoured to have disappeared during a mission to the bottom of the Pacific in his newly-built mini submarine, searching for God knows what.

"Make copies of it and place it on every wall in the room where you sleep," she instructed. "But it has to be right. Follow the design exactly."

She glanced at his shaking hands. "Maybe you'd best get it photocopied," she suggested. "It won't affect the potency."

"But what is it?"

She gazed into his bloodshot eyes, unsure of whether to trust him or not. She'd found it when still quite young, after months of research in the strangest of books, hidden in the strangest of places. "It's best that you don't know, OK? Just trust me."

She started as a large black shape, illuminated in the brightness spilling out from the interior, almost flew into the window. The thing fluttered there for a few seconds, confused antennae twitching. It was the largest and darkest moth she'd ever seen. Then the creature, obviously growing tired of the cruel trick played on it by the unyielding glass, wheeled in mid-air, its wings working furiously to take it back out into the blackness.

She couldn't stop staring at the window, expecting an armada of moths, attracted by the brightness behind the glass, to strike the window at any second. She strained her eyes to peer out into the darkness. Beyond the reflections of the cafe interior, she was sure she saw a fluttering in the darkness, movement that was about to shape itself into something more visible, more tangible. It was like peering into a dark dream.

During her first dreams she'd seen nothing but felt everything. It was like watching without eyes as an enormous black flower began to bloom in the depths of the darkest night she'd ever known. Eyes straining until they were sore, she still couldn't really *see* it. But she knew it was happening. Once, she was certain, there had even been a suggestion of a face.

She'd always awoken sweating, the air crushed out of her lungs by the clinging demersal depths of her dreamworld. She'd told herself that dread imagined within a dream couldn't possibly be real. Because they *were* just dreams, after all. Weren't they? It was the pain in her mother's eyes that first made her doubt that.

She'd even resorted to trying experimental drugs proffered by various doctors, all peddling their own pet theory. But killing your dreams is like killing yourself, she'd found—the time has to be right. And she simply didn't have the courage back then.

The slap of the rain on the window grew louder, streaks and rivulets running down the glass, the occasional russet or yellow leaf blown against it to cling for a second before continuing its twisting journey. Night, older and deeper than any ocean, waited outside. She felt its eyes upon her.

Her companion's nervousness seemed to be infectious. She felt itchy. No matter where she went, she just wanted to get out of this drained fish tank. But her legs refused to listen when she tried to stand. Fatigue was getting the better of her. Her watch told her it was far too late.

Sitting there, she pressed herself back into the vinyl seat, as if the pressure of a wave had pushed her against her will. It felt as if the night had suddenly flooded silently into the small cafe, touching everything with its inky intrusion and draining all life and colour. Maybe it was angered at the impertinent brightness of this place in a world of darkness. And determined to put an end to it. She became aware that her breathing had become more laboured.

She forced herself to nod when the man suddenly stopped his jittery monologue to ask if she was all right.

Every time she helped someone like this, she felt as if she was writing another line in the final chapter of an invisible autobiography. One that nobody would ever read. You *can* fight this intangible oppression if you are strong enough, she would have written if it had been a real book … but there is a price to pay.

She'd asked too much. For some time, she'd known she would have to pay the highest of all prices. Payment was overdue.

He was now telling her something about his children that she simply didn't want to hear; about the sacrifices he'd been forced to make. Suddenly he stopped speaking. Or he stopped making any sound, at least. His lips still moved but there was only silence.

She was surprised by the fact that this came as no surprise to her. She knew it was a sign, a signal that now the time had finally come. She stood, as if in a mild trance, and walked out into the night, beyond the halo of light cast by the lights inside. Free of rain at last, the October wind sighed once, contentedly. And whatever was waiting in the darkness welcomed her in.

By a Scarlet Thread

With thanks to Patrick Meade

The station was cold and grimy and, at this hour, full of derelicts yet to be scared off by the morning commuter rush. John hadn't intended to be here this early, but he'd found there just wasn't a convenient bus.

And this was his one chance to fix things with Ann, so he daren't miss her. Better to be early rather than late.

But her train wasn't due for another 50 minutes, and he didn't fancy hanging around in the cold. None of the shops were open yet and, even when they were, there wasn't anything worth looking at or buying.

So when he saw the wrought iron gates of the old Park View Hotel were gaping wide, he decided to dash in and shelter from the wind behind the huge columns.

The portico of the grand old Victorian pile offered some respite from the chill, but when a particularly insistent gust came along, John moved further back towards the entrance.

He noticed that the main doors were open, though he was sure the place had closed down several years ago. He peered at a sign that had been fixed to the door. "TODAY ONLY! Exhibition—Textiles of The Unblinking Brethren," it read in a dusty orange hue against a white background.

Ann was always complaining about how uncultured he was. Maybe he could bring her to the exhibition once she'd arrived—that would impress her. It'd be good to get off on the right foot for a change.

John had no idea what that "unblinking brethren" stuff was

all about—probably just a pretentious name for a bunch of arty posers, he thought—and textiles weren't really his thing, but he may as well have a poke around anyway. And he was bound to be warmer in there while he satisfied his curiosity.

He flicked the last of his cigarette away into the gutter, where the wind snatched it up greedily, and went in.

Outside, the hotel had looked as grand as ever. But now he was inside, the place looked decidedly down-at-heel. He remembered something in the papers about the place being sold … probably to be pulled down and turned into "luxury apartments." Maybe it was being used one last time before the bulldozers moved in.

It looked—and smelled—as if something was rotting into the carpet directly in front of him. Unable to make it out in the gloom of the foyer, he walked around it and headed for the brightly lit doorway to the exhibition.

Just inside the open double doors a large room stretched off to the left. John had been inside the hotel just once before—for a friend's wedding—but this room was new to him.

One man close by was wearing an expensive-looking suit. He was speaking with some authority to a middle-aged couple. John guessed that he must be something to do with the exhibition organisers. There were also nearly a dozen men dressed in traditional monk's robes, most with their cowls down but one or two with their heads covered. Most seemed to be smiling.

Now he understood—the brethren name meant they were all monks. John knew that some monks in Europe brewed beer, but he supposed that textiles were considered more holy by this order. Beer has always had a bad reputation in this country, he mused.

He wondered what the unblinking part of their name was all about. He'd heard of religious orders taking vows of poverty and silence, but never anything to do with eyes before.

He was surprised to see so many people visiting the exhibition this early in the day. Some of them might be religious, he thought, and were followers of these brethren. He supposed that clean living meant you had less trouble getting up early. He ran his thumb guiltily along the edge of the cigarette packet in his pocket.

There was a textile hanging on a large frame near the doorway. He glanced at it quickly, presuming it would be of some religious scene.

Religion wasn't at all important in his life, so he wasn't that familiar with Bible stories, but this scene looked more like something from an action film. Figures tumbled and stumbled from one side of the frame to the other, presumably pursued by someone who was outside the frame. Some of the figures had already been ruined by their enemy, their corpses littering the escape route of their more fortunate companions.

Finished in threads of Hell red and night black, the thing disturbed him. Someone had sketched the design straight from one of his choking nightmares, he was sure.

It was a bit much to take early in the morning—and on a light breakfast of nerves and cigarettes at that—but he did his best to look impressed in case he was being watched.

The work was very intricate and must have taken hours and hours to complete. He could make out different thicknesses and textures of thread, making the surface highly uneven, with some sections standing proud of the surface while others threatened to sag inwards.

He could tell that it was all expertly woven. Ironic then that he should find his own life unravelling in his hands. It wasn't all his fault, despite what everyone told him. Anyway, he'd kicked the habit now …

Maybe these monks could help him tighten some of the loose threads of his life. The thought amused him.

John moved on to the next work, which was suspended from a simple frame attached to the wall. It looked like a cross between a shirt and a robe. Each sleeve depicted someone that John assumed must be a saint, one being broken while the other was flayed in public.

On the chest of the garment, woven in threads as fine as a child's hair, was a Biblical scene—though John had never heard any Bible story in which someone was crucified sideways.

The man in the expensive suit had finished with the couple

and now turned his head in John's direction. As soon as he noticed the man, John stood still. He felt like running. The man looked as if he was wearing eyeliner around his striking dark eyes. He walked towards John. His eyes almost shone as he approached.

John disliked being under such scrutiny and dropped his gaze, refusing to look the man in the face.

"Where have you been, Brother? We've been waiting for you to help us complete the grand work. All parts but your own are complete ..."

John seemed stunned. "I-I don't think ..."

The man merely lowered his head slightly, as if examining John's well-worn clothes. "Oh ...?"

One of the monks walked up behind the suited man. "We are ready, Frater Perdido," he said in low, reverential tones. John noticed that the man's left hand was covered in burn scars.

The well-dressed man turned his head towards the monk. "Yes. Please continue, Frater Ignio."

John watched as the monk walked towards a group of ragged women who stood in one corner, facing the wall. An under-nourished child dared to turn his head to look behind him.

"Why are they standing there?"

"They are waiting to enter," replied Frater Perdido patiently.

"But they're already in," thought John. Unless there was another part to the exhibition that he hadn't yet seen. He looked around but there was no other door.

He watched as Frater Ignio and two other brothers pulled a large, elaborately decorated screen into place, blocking his view. No doubt they required privacy while they gave this particular demonstration. Maybe I'll take a look at that later, he thought.

Along one wall was an enormous canvas draped across another work, hiding it from view. No doubt it was waiting for some dignitary to come and unveil it later in the day.

John scanned the room again while trying to be discreet. "You approve of what you see?" asked Frater Perdido.

Even though John nodded, he could feel himself being stared at. "It's ... interesting," he offered. The words seemed to placate the taller man, who gave a sigh of satisfaction.

Just as he thought he was going to be asked another awkward question, an odd sound from behind the elaborate screen claimed John's attention. It was a soft chorus of voices.

"We will all be claimed. We will all be found." The feeble voices repeated the phrase over and over, though they sounded as if they were fading into the distance until they had almost gone altogether. His ears were just getting used to the quiet when he heard the start of a scream. it was just the very start of one before it was shut off as if some enormous door had been pushed closed on it, choking it off.

It had definitely come from behind the screen. Breaking away from Frater Perdido, John began to walk quickly towards it, but he bumped into a wall of brown material. Looking up, he saw one of the brothers, standing well over six feet tall and blocking his way. His dark hood covered the upper half of his face, but his mouth opened, as if he was about to speak.

John found himself almost afraid of what the man might say. When a low, slow "No" emerged from his lips, John felt relief. But he also felt he should protest.

From somewhere a series of low chimes sounded. John couldn't see a clock anywhere, but he assumed this meant the exhibition was closing to the public. That was a ridiculously short day, he thought.

Sure enough, one of the brothers was ushering the handful of visitors towards the door. Under his arm was a "Work In Progress" sign, ready to hang on the closed doors.

Taking the hint, he was turning to go when Frater Perdido grabbed his arm. "I think you'll be very interested in this work," he said.

John had thought of fetching the police to investigate the scream but now he thought it best to hold the monk to account first. There was always time to alert them later if he didn't get a satisfactory reply.

"But that scream?!," said John.

Perdido simply tightened his grip. "It was nothing, believe me. Simply someone unaccustomed to sacrifice. People are so selfish these days, don't you think?"

Wary of having his words turned against him, John simply muttered "U-uh, well ..."

The suited man had deftly manoeuvred John to a spot before a small but highly detailed wall hanging. It was mainly in autumnal colours, with a dun sky over a scene of penitent monks heading in procession towards a huge bonfire in some woods.

It seemed innocuous enough, but John found it strangely disturbing. "Yes, it's very nice," he said, knowing Frater Perdido would insist on an opinion.

Frater Perdido laughed softly. "Yes, of course. But don't you recognise someone in the image?"

In order to satisfy his insistent host, John looked closer. The work was very detailed. If you stared hard enough, the tops of the flames showing among and above the trees almost seemed to flicker. The faces of the monks almost looked real. He searched for Perdido's face among them—assuming that was what he was expected to find—but came up blank.

"Recognise ...?" queried John, after a minute or two of rapt attention.

Frater Perdido's chuckle had an almost sinister edge to it. "Look closer, my friend. You will see yourself." His well-manicured hand reached past John to hover near the end of the line of monks.

Now it had been pointed out to him, John wondered how he could possibly have missed it. He felt like a fool. There was no doubt—that *was* his face under the cowl of the last figure in the dark procession. A feeling of dread crept over him.

"But how ...?"

"God moves in mysterious ways. At least, *our* god does."

John looked about him desperately. There must be an answer to this. "Why am I on there?" he pleaded.

Frater Perdido seemed puzzled by his question, even impatient. "That was part of the arrangement. That you be ordained, just as your father was before you."

"My fath—" As far as John knew, his father had never been a member of any religious order. And there'd been no mention of any "arrangement" before his death.

"No, no. There must be some mistake! I don't know anything about this ... you've got the wrong person. And my father wasn't at all religious. Definitely not."

Again, Father Perdido extended his arm as if to guide John, who allowed himself to be taken to another part of the exhibition. Before them hung another elaborately-woven scene, depicting appalling suffering and pain. In the centre was another procession of hooded brothers. Frater Perdido pointed to a figure in the centre of the row of walking figures.

John stepped forward and peered at the delicately worked threads at the point where the man had indicated. Certainly, the face looked like his father .... but this could easily be some elaborate trick.

John snorted in disbelief. "Look—just what is this all about? If what you say is true—and I very much doubt that—why would I be expected to join your mob now? I've never even heard of you before."

The tall man pulled himself up to his full height, clearly insulted at having his brotherhood referred to as a mob. "Because your mother and sister were spared, as per our agreement with your father. Everything has a price ..."

"Spared?" John didn't know what sort of a cruel joke this was, and he wondered what ordeal his mother and sister—both now dead, in the same car crash that had killed his father—were supposed to have been spared.

Before the monk could answer, John was startled by a loud sound from across the room.

Two of the brothers had begun to remove the screen in the corner. Suddenly one of the hooded brothers had grown weary of the burden and dropped the wooden screen, clattering, to the floor.

At last, their secret work was revealed. Seeking answers, John walked quickly across to the newly stitched scene.

There, marching across a desolate plain towards a place that hinted at an eternity of the same appalling suffering, was the line of ragged women he had seen earlier. Now they were in the large textile stretched on an elaborate wooden frame. Now he understood what the brother had meant.

He turned away when he saw the thin, hungry face of the small child staring his way.

The large, hooded figure who had blocked his path earlier had re-appeared. Once more, John bumped into a wall of flesh. "S-sorry," he stuttered, looking up at the man's face. His cowl was now lowered, and John was staring straight at him. With horror, he realised that what he'd thought was eye make-up on Frater Perdido was something far worse.

He walked to the centre of the room, from where he could see all the monks at once. His gaze darted from one face to the other. None of them had any eyelids. They couldn't blink if they wanted to.

The older brothers' wounds had long healed. But one of the younger men had scab-encrusted scars where his eyelids had once been.

John flinched at the sight, trying not to think about the image of their eyes suddenly popping out. The younger monk's eyes glistened just as brightly as those of his companion. Spiritual serenity had obviously granted him a great deal of inner peace and resistance to pain, thought John. He felt decidedly inferior at that moment.

Dazedly, John staggered to a part of the room where two straight backed chairs stood against the wall. He needed to sit down. The paint was peeling from the walls in this area, and it somehow looked older than the rest of the exhibition space.

The carpet had a gritty feel underfoot. He'd assumed at first that it was dirt—the building had been unused for several years, after all—but now he could see it was a layer of tiny insects. The vermin were everywhere underfoot. He lifted his one shoe in distaste.

Just then a brother appeared in front of him, smiling in a peculiar manner. "They are all our brothers," he muttered.

Then the man picked one of the larger insects out of his cassock and crushed it in his hand. He began to mould it, tugging hard at one end. As he worked he stuffed several more of the creatures in his mouth, mashing their crunchy carapaces between his yellowing teeth.

When he was satisfied that he had done his best, he held

something up between his fingers. It was a large but thin chitinous needle, its brown insectoid hues catching the light.

Though John had sought refuge in here from the cold, the room suddenly felt stiflingly hot. John tugged at his clothes to try and loosen them.

The brother continued to stare at him, smiling oddly. It was then that John saw that the man's eyes weren't following his movements. He felt a pang of pity, thinking the man was blind and maybe that's why he had joined the brethren and retreated from the world.

"My God!" John stepped back involuntarily as he realised the truth. He'd heard people use the phrase "glassy stare" but this time it had real meaning. As well as having his eyelids excised, the man had two glass eyes.

John looked around him. The monks all seemed to be turned in his direction and they all had that same stare. He had no idea what sort of sadistic sect they belonged to, but he knew he had to get out ... now.

The door was only a half dozen steps away, but John saw that he would never make it. The monks had formed a wide circle about him, one that was getting narrower. Then Frater Perdido was at his elbow again, having obviously sensed John's discomfort.

The monk put his hand on John's arm. He shook it free, but the man drew closer still, his lips almost at John's ear.

"We gave up our sight in order to see truly, brother. But you know this already ..." Frater Perdido raised his unseeing eyes to some imaginary heaven. "True vision. Perfect clarity."

John was genuinely frightened by Frater Perdido's constant implication that he knew about the brethren and approved of their disgusting practices. He did know that religious mania could be dangerous and didn't want it to taint his already complicated life.

"I haven't done anything! Just let me go, OK!?" He'd blurted out the words before he could help himself, knowing that it was the last thing they would do. They gathered around him, fascinated and threatening.

The brothers all took another step forward. Now they were crowded in upon him.

"A-are you going to take my eyes?" The words were cold in his mouth, sending chill pain up through his teeth into his skull.

The nearest brother turned his unseeing eyes to him and simply shook his head. John didn't think it possible, but the brethren moved closer still, hands reached out to grip him tightly.

He gave out a startled gasp as he was forced down into a heavy oak chair with embroidered upholstery. He caught a glimpse of the stylised image of a brutal stoning woven into the fabric. There was hardly anything left of the victim's face.

The chair was dragged, its back legs complaining against the floor, until it sat before the large, draped work on the wall.

"Do you believe in Heaven?" asked Frater Perdido.

John looked up at him, unsure of what his answer should be. He hesitated before shaking his head in honesty.

"Quite right," said the brother. "But I'm quite sure you believe in Hell."

He reached out and tugged the enormous canvas, which sagged and folded under its own weight, falling to reveal the gigantic tapestry underneath.

John pushed himself deeper into the huge chair, almost wishing that the brothers did intend taking his eyes. The image stretched over 16 feet across and a dozen feet above him. It was just another day in Hell—agony piled upon torment until a second death seemed like a sweet relief. Bodies were abused, bloodied, and bursting, in every corner of the work, while twisted creatures revelled in the pleasures of pain as they went about their work.

In one small corner of the appalling tableau there was a pile of bodies. Cadavers awaiting their renewed recruitment into the armies of agony. But something was missing, John saw. There was no blood—the red thread was missing, revealing unpleasant spaces in the design.

"It's magnificent, isn't it?" asked Frater Perdido. "And all it needs to be finished is your modest contribution."

John had no idea what the man meant but, whatever it was, he feared it like nothing else in his life.

The monks all turned their blind, glassy gazes down on him. Darkness glistened deep within their black orbs. As John watched, it leaked out to infect the air around them.

He gasped, tried to yell out. But he knew no help would come. He was alone. With them.

"P-please. I don't know what you want from me ...," offered John, feebly.

A thin old man with sagging cheeks, his grubby cowl sitting around his neck, pushed his face towards John's. "We do," he croaked hoarsely, grabbing John by the hand.

"Frater Senex will show you how you can help us," said Frater Perdido, mildly. The old man nodded; John noticed that there was a crack in one of his glass eyes. Filth had become ingrained along the tiny fissure over the years, giving him the appearance of a grubby old toy that had long been discarded and forgotten.

John tried to pull his hand away, but the old man was deceptively strong, his fingers curling around the wrist as if they were metal clamps. The man pulled John's arm towards him and peered at the open palm.

John followed his gaze, wondering what the man was looking at so intently. Surely he couldn't be intending to tell John his fortune.

Then John noticed what had drawn the man's interest. It looked like a tiny red scratch on his palm. Until the man's thin fingers plucked at it and pulled hard. John yelped in shock as a thin fibre of red pain tugged at the very core of him.

The old man worked away for some seconds, tugging insistently on the fibre reeling out from John's palm. Suddenly he stopped. "Thank God. It's over," thought John, until the brothers reached forward and grabbed his forearms.

They tore at his shirt sleeves, revealing more skin. Then they all stared in fascination as Frater Senex found more and more scarlet threads to pull from him.

Flakes of encrusted grime fell from under Frater Senex's long fingernails as he plucked, never stopping but pulling new threads and handing them to one or other of his brethren. The work seemed too delicate for the man's filthy old hands. And near impossible for someone with no eyes.

One young monk took a thread and began stitching it directly into the surface of the tapestry with a chitinous needle. Others wound the remaining threads around large wooden bobbins. "For later works," explained Frater Perdido, soothingly. "Our patrons will be very generous, I'm sure."

The monks all nodded, as if understanding how important their work was and how insignificant John was—fit only for sacrifice in this particular manner.

He saw now that all their faces were snarling underneath; their kindly flesh masks were just a cruel joke. As they worked they repeated a variation of the mantra he had heard earlier, chanted from behind the screen.

"We will all be claimed. We will all be lost. We will all be claimed. We will all ..."

John knew this was the end of his life. There was no escape. All that was left now was to hope for a quick death—but that hope seemed forlorn.

He screamed and thrashed as they pulled skein after skein of scarlet thread out of him. Crimson splashes rained down on the carpet all around him, the insects scurrying to enjoy the fresh feast.

Though his vision was tear bleared, John saw that the procession of monks he'd seen in the smaller work was there in the huge wall hanging, too. For a second he stared once more into his own face, as it looked out accusingly from the procession of the damned.

He felt Frater Perdido lay a hand upon his brow. "Thank you, brother, for your devotion. Bless you."

Inside there was less and less of him. He could feel himself being hollowed out, thread by thin thread. He was literally unravelling an inch at a time.

What would happen when he was just a sack of emptiness? Would they leave him draped across the waste bins in the filthy alley at the back of the old hotel?

As his head began to swim, the pain getting further and further away, he sobbed one last time. He would never see Ann's face again. She would never know what had become of him. Or how much he'd wanted to please her … and for her to love him. She'd think he'd just let her down again.

The moment before his eyes closed and darkness claimed him, he imagined he saw her being greeted at the door by one of the brothers.

The tapestry hangs on a bare stone wall in the study of an investment banker's upscale country dwelling.

The few who have seen it turn away quickly and never look back, afraid that the head of the final figure in the procession might once more turn and gaze into their hollow souls.

Side 1, Track 3

Every sound in the street seemed louder, every sight more vivid, every smell more pungent as Davey left the office building. The late afternoon sunshine almost seemed like an insult.

"Surplus to requirements." That's what Mr. McCarthy had said about him. He should take a look in the mirror sometime, thought Davey.

He wasn't the worst insurance salesman they had. There were worse. Ted Walters, for instance; that jerk hadn't sold a single thing in months. Davey guessed that you didn't have to if you were married to the boss's daughter and were a real creep into the bargain.

As he passed a newsstand, his eyes drank in the *Post* headline: "Nixon Resigns." Further down it said "The 37th President Is First to Quit Post."

He'd heard the story on the radio earlier, but the headline just made it seem more real. Damned crook! Hell, if you can't trust the President, who *can* you trust?

Somehow it seemed like the final insult. The country he'd grown up loving was becoming a ghost, fading away in broad daylight.

In his head, Davey wrote his own headline: "Great Day for America: Nixon and Davey Lawrence Both Out in Cold" before sniggering bitterly to himself. His mood plunged even further.

On his way home he passed a bar that he must have walked past hundreds of times. He remembered it as Murphy's but now it had a different name. Davey had no idea when it had changed.

The Promised Land. "Well, that sounds…promising," he thought. Maybe Moses and Nixon weren't able to enter the

Promised Land, but he was. And once he'd blown his last paycheck he'd just head back to Buffalo and throw himself on his parents' mercy for a while.

The last few bars of a Janis Joplin number were fading as he pushed open the door. He was more of an Elvis and Jerry Lee fan, but some of the newer stuff was good, too.

Behind the bar there was an impressive array of liquor. Davey felt spoilt for choice. The bartender came over and raised his eyebrows questioningly, so Davey ordered an Evan Williams on the rocks. It was smooth and would do the trick nicely.

Three stools along from him sat a girl with long dark hair. She was dressed in a blue top and jeans. Occasionally she glanced at him as he sat drinking. The glass that sat in front of her was empty and, every now and then, she looked at it sadly.

Several times she had tilted her head slightly towards him, peering at him through her hair as if studying a lab specimen.

It might have made some men feel uncomfortable, but Davey felt like a specimen right now, so there was no harm done. Hell, it wasn't the worst thing that had happened to him today...not by a long way.

The third time she did it, Davey turned to her. "Please, lemme buy you a drink."

"Thanks," she said, sliding across two stools to sit beside him. "My name's Willow." She smiled at him in a very sweet way. A way that made him think maybe she liked him.

"Hey, that's a lovely name," said Davey as she ordered a Jack and Coke.

Her smile faded. She shook her head. "I don't like it much. I'd have preferred Fern. Maybe I'll change it someday."

"Well, that'd be a real shame. I think it suits you," he said after another gulp of whisky.

"So what's your story?" she asked him. He picked out a card from his wallet and gave it to her.

She looked at it. It read "Mr. D. Lawrence, Senior Insurance Assessor."

"Wow. Pretty impressive," she said. He didn't tell her that everybody except the janitor at his company was a "Senior Insurance Assessor." She probably thought it meant he had a lot of cash. Well, for today at least, he had.

He noticed that she smiled a lot, though there was a darkness around her eyes that he felt unsure about. But another bourbon would fix that, he was sure.

The place was almost deserted apart from them; just one old guy on his own at the back, and the bartender who kept the drinks coming.

Davey began to tap his foot and nod in time as The Doors came on the jukebox. "Do you like rock music?" chirped Willow, brightly. "They've got a *great* jukebox here."

"Sure. Sure." Davey nodded. The music was worming its way further inside his head by now.

"I've got a great new album by an English band called Black Dog. Have you heard them?"

"Nope. Named after the Led Zep track, I expect." Davey took another slug of his drink. Willow smiled at him, seeming not to understand.

"You know, *Led Zeppelin IV*, the Four Symbols album, yeah?" Davey nodded, knowingly.

Her smile grew wider, but she still didn't seem to understand him. "Oh, well, maybe."

When she lifted her drink he noticed she had a small tattoo on the inside of her wrist. He didn't get a chance to have a long look, but it looked like foreign writing. Davey was itching to ask her about it, but he didn't want to blow it with Willow. Maybe he'd ask her later. Because he hoped there'd be a later.

They talked for a little while longer as the drink began to warm them. Then she drew closer to him and slipped her fingers over his. "My place is just around the corner."

Davey wasn't sure what he saw in her deep, dark eyes but, just this once, he was prepared to take a chance.

Willow's apartment was small but neat. Against one wall, pride of place went to her expensive-looking stereo deck. It seemed out of place in these cheaply furnished surroundings.

There were dozens of LPs lined up neatly in a cabinet and leaning against its sides. True to her word, Willow really did like her music.

Davey sat on a chair while Willow lolled on the floor, holding a glass of wine and talking, mostly about herself. The wine was cheap, but it tasted good.

They were listening to some Deep Purple. "Just to get us in the mood," Willow had said.

Then she got to her feet and went to change the record. "This is the one...side one, track three," said Willow as the needle clunked down onto the vinyl.

The music started up suddenly with an emphatic beat and a soaring guitar. Then the singer was telling Davey how much love he had to give and how good it would feel. There were two short but pleasing guitar solos between the verses.

As the music wound its way around their heads, Davey picked up the album cover. *Black God*. The elaborately designed lettering definitely said *Black God* and not *Black Dog*. No wonder Willow hadn't understood his Led Zeppelin reference. He giggled to himself, feeling stupid.

He looked closer at the illustration on the cover. "Inchantation" was written across the top in writhing letters; Davey smiled at the weak word play. He usually spent hours staring at the artwork on some album covers, but he thought he'd make an exception tonight. It was difficult to pick out details on the illustration...it was dark, and the lights were low...but something about it made him feel upset, even slightly nauseous.

He put it down and concentrated on the music instead. Just as he did, the song came to an end. It must only have been about two-and-half minutes long. Somehow he felt let down.

Then Willow was at the record deck again. "You've got to hear it backwards; it's incredible!"

Davey wasn't sure he'd heard right. "Backwards? Hey, my stereo only plays records forwards," he chuckled.

Willow flicked a switch at the side of the record deck. "A friend modified this for me. I was very grateful. It sounds really...well, out of this world!"

Heard backwards, the music encompassed all the wrecked and wretched rhythms of despair. And there were words weaving themselves into the desolate cacophony. "...We seal our mouths…our hands work for his return…stuttering in from the outside…"

Davey licked his lips. He looked for more wine at the bottom of his empty glass. He could do with a drink right now. Willow picked up the bottle and held it upside down. A single drop of wine emerged, reflecting the dim light of the apartment; she made an apologetic face.

"…arcs of black reveal…the rape of descending energies… the maw that swallows aaaaaallll…"

There was something about Thoth, too. Davey remembered the name belonged to an Egyptian god. Hadn't Crowley written about him? But then the singer added another couple of syllables, separated out by strange stuttering words. Somehow, Davey's mind instinctively gathered them together until they sounded like "A-Za-Thoth…a-ZA-thoth." Davey shook his head to clear it. He didn't know what it all meant. Probably just gibberish.

He slumped back in his chair, feeling heavy. He tried to ask Willow what sort of wine he'd been drinking but his tongue failed to co-operate.

He struggled to turn his head to look at the wall to his left. Something was happening to it. Suddenly it had become dark, as if he was peering into a corridor beneath an archway. Something was moving towards him down the corridor.

A procession of pale figures shuffled past, their naked bodies covered in large black snails. A dirty beige fungus grew where their eyes should have been, while their mouths were fixed in an "o" of praise to whichever dark god they served. A string of silver drool hung from each bottom lip as they seemed unable, or unwilling, to close their mouths even for a second.

Davey mustered enough energy to reach out but was unable to touch them. "Hey…Hey, you…" Either he couldn't reach them, or they were merely in his head, but Davey just couldn't touch them.

He stared after them as they moved on, leaving bloody footprints from their ruined feet on the carpet. They looked as if they'd walked a thousand miles, thought Davey. Then, one by one, he saw them drop away into a dank pit filled with fungoid rot, their voices only ending as their mouths filled with the filth.

The stench of rot was overpowering.

His mind struggled to grasp what he'd just experienced. There couldn't have been any pit, of course, but his addled mind had found a way to shape the unbelievable into something familiar.

When the last voice had faded, Davey looked back at Willow. "Where did they..." he began, then fell silent as Willow began to dance.

He tried to shake off the odd sensation that lingered after what he'd seen. His very soul felt filthy. "If I could wash it, I would," he thought.

But now the music was taking him over completely. The drums hammered impossibly inside his head, beating against the fragile walls of his skull.

Now the short guitar solos sounded like a thousand enraged demons, sawing the air apart with their curses. It went on and on and on. Panting and moaning, Davey knew that this inhuman chanting had already lasted longer than the song had first time around.

He gathered as much strength as he could and yelled "St-stop, STOOOPP!"

Before him, Willow kept on dancing, blackness weaving out from her fingertips. It began to spill out of her eyes, too, staining the floor at her feet then creeping slowly towards where Davey sat.

Behind her, the blackness seeped from her and spread up the wall like huge dark wings unfolding. Now Willow joined in with the insane chanting coming from the stereo. Except it wasn't, because now it was coming from everywhere. It was even inside his head.

Davey slumped onto the floor, the blackness finally reaching him. It swallowed him up and he seemed to fall backwards as the room ceased to exist around him. Instead, he lay on his back, gazing up with burning eyes. There were a billion stars gazing back at him.

In the wide vista above him the brilliant points of light began to darken. One by one, the stars all stopped shining. They dimmed quickly, light bulbs fading as the switch was flicked off. Davey squinted. It was a trick; they had to still be there.

As his eyes adjusted, he could see that their shapes were still there; they were just darker now. Black shapes against an even blacker night sky. Then they all began to move, plunging straight towards Davey as if they'd found the path home after being lost for so long.

Suddenly they stopped, filling his sky and blotting out everything, even thoughts. He screamed as the night sky poured into him.

Now he understood the music.

He felt immensely solid and heavy and desperate. It was as if every individual atom of his body had been staked to a sacrificial stone. And now he was being pulled apart, his body crushed and stretched, extending to impossible lengths as his mind evaporated into the unbearable blackness.

The meagre thing that was Davey Lawrence was stretched thinner and thinner across the width of the ever-darkening cosmos, becoming a part of the writhing emptiness between the black stars.

He had become one with the master.

Willow sat at the bar and waited each night, listening to the jukebox and watching. Sometimes, between one heartbeat and the next, she remembered the echo of Davey's last scream with a shiver of delight.

Whenever a stranger walked into the bar, she always smiled at him.

Treading the Lost Path

(Descending Aklo Songs)

There were days when each footfall felt like a glyph in some secret alphabet, hidden and compelling, confiding secrets in him and drawing him to places he would never normally go.

But much of the time he merely felt sodden with misery and dragged down by the weight of the everyday.

When he lay in bed each morning, before rising, he tried to divine which sort of day it would be. He found the task impossible as he was at the mercy of unfeeling circumstance.

He lashed out at the hideous sound, knocking several objects to the floor before collapsing backwards onto his grubby pillow.

When he eventually swung his unwilling body out of bed, he picked up the alarm clock along with a photograph that had been next to it. He placed the image of himself and his brother Michael carefully back on the bedside table.

It was the only "family" photograph he had from his childhood. Like most other things, it was partly a lie as he'd folded the photograph so the children either side of them were hidden. He didn't want to see the other children from the orphanage. He'd obscured them both literally and metaphorically.

After a shower followed by toast and weak coffee, he climbed the steps from his basement flat and pointed his feet reluctantly in the direction of work.

The swirl and fret of the city ran on around him. People called it vibrant, but he just found it unnerving.

The near-hysterical grins and grimaces of fellow pedestrians made him want to shrink into himself or to break into a run and leave this place far behind.

An insipid, pale blue carpet dotted with islands of faded coffee stains formed a map leading to the outer door. The view from his cramped cubicle across the main office aspired to be uninspiring, even on a good day. Today was not one of those.

His workmates came and went like ghosts, never stopping to speak to him unless it was to complain about some work he'd done or something he'd left undone. He looked out of the window at the building next to theirs. It looked almost identical, and he guessed that it was full of identically miserable and distracted people.

Just then Mrs. Ferndale entered the outer office. She walked between the grey desks that rose like monoliths from the pale blue. Dressed in dark business blue, she glanced sideways at him. It was a look bereft of kindness.

He knew she no longer found him a satisfactory employee. He lacked almost every quality she valued in one of her workers and she did little to disguise her unhappiness.

When he started here he made every effort to fit in, to be liked by his colleagues. None of them returned the compliment, and now he regarded them as his secret warders; his captivity ensured by sidelong glances and conspiratorial information exchanges by the coffee machine.

At the end of the day, he always left promptly and was always surprised when no one tried to stop him. He took the stairs down to the street, disliking the sensation of being crammed into a small metal box with others.

After waiting far too long for the lights to change, he took a chance and dashed across the road during a break in the traffic. He dodged down a side street, intending to take a short cut.

He often took this route but tonight the street seemed different somehow. It felt colder, less crowded. In fact, it was empty. The street lights were dimmer. And, strangely, he noticed the sound of traffic from the main road was beginning to fade.

He stood still, holding his breath, as the quiet crept across the street towards him. Only when it had surrounded him did he dare to breathe again.

After several seconds of perfect silence, some notes of lost music came floating on the night air, returning from the future. Or from the dim past.

He strained his ears, not wanting to miss a note. It was definitely singing of a sort, though the notes seemed too high, the voice too perfect, to be human. Or entirely human, at least.

The song—he was certain it was a song, even though it followed no musical rules he was familiar with—aroused in him a feeling of having lost something incredibly important. The lost thing was primal, deeply loved, supremely vital … but now it was gone, leaving a gnawing hole. The feeling of something mislaid or stolen from him was heartbreaking; he found himself kneeling, tears running hot down his cheeks under the foul, yellow light of the streetlamp.

Near the far corner of the street, he saw a girl standing staring at him. She wore a light garment that looked far too flimsy for this late month of the year. Short and pale, she raised one arm as the music coming from her mouth stopped. Then she turned suddenly and was gone.

He staggered to his feet, feeling as if he weighed a ton or more. He needed the song to continue. He could not let it end so suddenly. He croaked out his plea through dried lips. "Wait. Wait …"

One foot fell in front of the other as he found himself compelled to follow the frail-looking girl along the nearly empty streets.

The song began again. Intermittently it floated to him on the chill air, calling him on, urging him not to give up. Everything was so close, he felt. Just a little further. His feet had gained traction by now and he was making better progress. Still the girl evaded him, always rounding another corner just as he caught sight of her once more.

Scuttling around the corner of a building, almost losing his footing, he saw a white shape move swiftly through a darkened doorway. There was a loud clang as something metal swung into place, barring his way. The rotten wooden door inside had been taken off its hinges.

He worked his fingers through the gaps in the antique iron grille that denied him access. The song continued, weaving around him as he peered into the darkness. He gazed intently as strange shapes danced inside his eyes, struggling to grow accustomed to the deep gloom. Eventually he saw some pale shapes moving slowly down the steps. Three shapes that resolved themselves into what seemed to be people, watching him.

What had sounded like two voices now became one. He saw a female face, looking pale and worried as it receded into the darkness at the bottom of the steps, still singing. He gripped the iron grille and shook it hard in pain and frustration.

He stayed like that for several minutes after the darkness had swallowed the sounds, echoing off into what sounded like an impossibly vast underground space.

He hadn't called after the girl and her companions, he realised afterwards, as he dragged himself reluctantly back to his basement flat. But he hadn't wanted to spoil their song; that would have been a desecration. The worst thing of all, in fact.

On his lunch break the next day he went back to the same street. The doorway was where he remembered it, but now it was open and there were workmen going in and out, carrying sacks of cement.

One of the workmen saw him staring at them. "Orright, mate?" he asked, cheerily.

"Yes. Can you tell me please … where do those steps lead?"

"Lead? Well, nowhere, mate. Just down to the basement. We're doing it up for the new owner." The workman seemed puzzled by his question.

He leaned closer to the man, lowering his voice. "Can … Can I see it?"

Amused by the almost conspiratorial nature of their conversation, the workman smirked. No doubt he was unable to imagine what could be so interesting in a basement. "Yeah, I suppose so. C'mon."

He followed the man down the steps, expecting to find a room that stretched away under half the block and worthy of a far grander name than a basement.

Instead, he found a medium-sized room, brightly lit by an unshaded bulb. It was crowded with the three workmen and their equipment. Otherwise, it was quite empty. There was no other way in or out. Shaken, he began to back up the steps.

"You orright there?" asked one of the workmen, chuckling at his odd behaviour.

Out in the daylight again, he felt unsteady on his feet. There was no other doorway in the basement. No way out and certainly no entrance to a huge underground cathedral worthy of the mesmeric song he'd heard. Where could the strangers have gone?

He felt suddenly and uncomfortably as if he'd been witness to something that perhaps wasn't meant for him. A sense of mild panic kept a hold on him until he was at his desk once more.

For days he played the song he'd heard over and over in his head. It wasn't even so much the song, whose words were unknown to him, as the way it sounded.

His memory clung on to the sound of the music swelling to fill an enormous space—an impossible space, as he'd seen for himself.

And the feeling it had given him! It was a promise beyond anything that mere words could deliver. It too seemed impossible, as if everything he knew was wrong ... too cheap, too dull ... and that it could all be made anew. Who knew what sort of life might be waiting for him?

The week passed slowly, and the nights were filled with fractured sleep, riven with dreams filled with those extraordinary sounds.

Finally, he realised that he must force himself back down to earth. He had a job to go to, a life of sorts to live. Hard though it was, he pushed the hangover of the bizarre incident to the back of his mind.

He'd had to beg for the time off work, but it would be worth it. He got to see his daughter so rarely these days.

The rain began to fall as he headed towards the shopping centre where he was due to meet her and his ex-girlfriend. Once inside, he ran his hand through his hair to rid himself of some of the droplets. He felt sure four-year-olds would object to being showered with water, even by their fathers.

Sofia was the best thing in his dull life. He didn't want to miss a rare chance to see her and certainly didn't want to upset her in any way. It took him a few minutes to find the small burger restaurant where Jen had agreed to meet him.

They were at a table covered in the detritus of a meal. A glass of orange juice and cup of coffee sat half empty.

"Hi there," he said, rather shyly. Jen rose and gave him a half-hearted hug. "Hey, how are you? Say hello to daddy then," she told the small girl sitting next to her.

He bent down as his daughter clambered from her seat.

Sofia gave him a hug, then stepped back and stared at him as if it was the first time she'd ever seen him. Her eyes were a little less bright with joy every time he saw her. Bit by bit she was forgetting how to miss him.

He sat and stared at the little girl as she ignored him, happily peeling the wrapper from a piece of chocolate.

The plastic seats and the glistening surfaces seemed painfully fake to him. There was an ache just above his stomach. He sat up very straight, hoping it would subside.

"Are you OK? You don't look very well." For once, there was genuine concern in Jen's voice.

He rubbed his eyes. "Yeah, I'm OK. I just haven't been sleeping too well lately. Got something on my mind."

"I suppose it's a girl again, isn't it?" The look on Jen's face narrowly avoided becoming a sneer.

"No … yes … I mean, it's …"

She nodded. "I thought so. You just don't change …" There was a slight sourness in her words, fed by bad memories barely tempered by the passing of time.

"I do. I have." He'd stopped drinking heavily, that much was true, but he wondered whether he was fooling himself about having really changed.

Jen slurped her coffee, displaying the lack of manners she

seemed so proud of. Her frequent mantra had always been "no one's going to tell me what to do."

He searched for something endearing or engaging to say but his mind was always blank when he was with Jen. Eventually he decided something practical might impress her.

"I send something every month. So you can get Sofe something nice. You are getting it, aren't you?" It was a thin umbilical connecting him to his past life—he couldn't bear to think that it had been broken.

"Yeah. Thanks," Jen said quickly, swatting his words away like a bothersome fly.

Trying again, he fished in his pocket. "Hey, Sofe, I've got something for you." He pushed the brightly wrapped packet across to the girl, who picked it up a little too eagerly. The paper was quickly torn off to reveal a small box containing a doll.

"It's the latest one," he said, hoping to elicit a joyful response from Sofia, who seemed slightly bored. When prompted by her mother the girl said a quiet "thank you" before quickly losing interest.

"Don't you like it?" he asked the girl. Jen jumped in to answer.

"She's not really into them anymore. It's all your computer game now, isn't it, sweetheart? MooniMoo!"

The girl's head wagged obediently up and down, followed by her waving her arms and chanting "MooniMoo!" over and over again. Eventually she got bored and turned her attention to the remains of the chocolate in front of her.

He hated to see Sofia eat burgers and chocolate. Jen, who was now carrying some extra weight herself, had told him in the past to mind his own business.

"So, ummm … p'raps we could go out for a meal, the three of us. Saturday evening, maybe? My treat." At least that way he could choose where they ate, he thought.

Jen looked at him as if he was a child who simply wasn't listening.

"I've told you that we're just in town for a few days visiting mum, OK? We're leaving tomorrow." Jen lowered her voice and surreptitiously glanced around her. "She's not been very well."

He nodded his head as if in understanding but, in truth, he couldn't even imagine what it was like having a mother, let alone one that was ill.

The conversation wound desultorily around the wreck of the meal before them. Only at the end of 20 minutes did he realise he hadn't ordered anything for himself.

Jen started fishing around in her handbag. She checked her phone and looked up at him with an expression of impatience on her face.

"Look, we've got to go. I promised Mum we wouldn't be too long. Like I said …"

He nodded. "Yeah, I know. Well, I hope she feels better soon." He didn't send his regards, as her mother probably remembered him best as a tearful drunk hammering on the door at two in the morning, demanding to see a pregnant Jen.

They walked out of the burger place together, into the stream of scurrying shoppers. "Well, it's been nice to see you," said Jen, probably because she felt she had to.

He nodded before squatting down and stretching his arms out to Sofia. "Goodbye then, Sofe."

The tiny girl pouted, turning her face away from him and burying it in her mother's coat. Jen grimaced apologetically at him.

When she waved at him as they walked away, there was an air of finality to the gesture.

That evening, Jen wasn't returning his calls. He sat at home and realised that perhaps he might never see Sofia again. Despite what the court had said about access, Jen had always made it difficult. She had moved just far enough away for regular visits to be out of the question.

He'd fooled himself for a while but now he was aware that, for years, he hadn't been able to see the forest for fallen trees.

He stared at the wall and wished he could see his daughter one last time.

It had been another day of grinding tedium. Yet his journey home revealed an astonishing transformation that seemed to have crept over the city while he had been secreted away in his over-lit office.

Until now, buildings and other physical structures seemed to have been wearing masks of crude mundanity that hid their true, astonishing nature. He could barely stifle his laughter as he realised his ideas about the place where he lived were so far from the truth.

The marvellous and bright seemed to peep out from behind grey facades at every turn, instilling in him a feeling close to ecstasy. Promises of marvellous things and feelings were presented to him as he walked his usual route home. Shop fronts displayed objects of unbelievable purity and truth. Yet he didn't attempt to purchase them, knowing they were merely objects and, in any case, had slipped far beyond anyone's ability to own them.

Even the people he passed had a serenity and beauty about them that he had never seen before. He should merge with the early evening light, he felt, and remain there forever.

It took him almost three times as long to reach home. Every step down the stone steps to his dingy two-room retreat was filled with an odd, shivering delight.

When he opened the door and stepped inside, every colour within the sparsely furnished living room radiated a feeling of reassurance and pleasure.

Feeling sleepy, he went straight to the bedroom and lay down on a bed that felt wonderfully comfortable and suffused with dreams of perfection. Within minutes he was asleep.

When he awoke in the small hours, he dared not breathe for a few seconds. Waiting for the sensations to flood in upon him once more, he felt only stillness and emptiness surround him. Then, when he could bear it no longer, he let the tears come.

For the next day or so, he wandered through his life hating all about him. He felt as if he was being insulted at every turn and that everything he saw was a cheat, a lie. It was as if he was being fobbed off with a cheap, plastic imitation of what his life should truly be. And that someone, somewhere thought this was good enough for him, and even as they were having this thought, they were wracked with laughter at his plight.

Somehow he was aware that the pale girl and her companions were connected with this feeling, and the journey home filled with an almost unbearable ecstasy a few days previously. He had no idea why anyone would do this to him. He needed to know why he was being toyed with in this manner.

The cafe wasn't convenient anymore. It had been when he'd lived in his previous place but now it was a bus ride and a walk away. But he had nothing better to do and it always served good coffee. If he felt relaxed anywhere, it was here.

Mulligan's was in the basement. He'd known Mulligan years ago, but he was long retired and now the place was run by a young Polish couple. Filip and Anka were pleasant enough, but they lacked the Irishman's easy wit.

He sat gazing into the cup as a whirlpool of milk and froth spun to its doom. No escape.

Suddenly he felt as if he was being stared at. He looked up and was startled to see the pale girl sitting opposite him. He started backwards, tipping his chair onto its back legs. He hadn't heard her come in or move the chair to sit down.

He looked around quickly. There were no other customers in the place and Filip had disappeared for the time being. A slight feeling of panic accompanied the knowledge that he was alone with this strange creature.

Forcing himself to relax, he put all four chair legs on the floor and grasped his coffee cup, for some sort of imagined safety. "How did …? Never mind."

She looked as if her clothes had been pulled on awkwardly, that she was enduring rather than wearing them. It was almost as if she didn't understand them or know why she should bother to wear them.

Her eyes were the palest grey he'd ever seen. When he saw her first, he thought of her as blonde but now she was nearer he could see she was almost white. He supposed she must suffer from a form of albinism.

He dismissed the thought after just a few seconds. The girl's eyes were extraordinary, with a dark grey limbal ring which grew lighter as it crossed the iris and approached the dark pit of the pupil. It was a pure colour the like of which he'd never seen in any other person's eyes. He couldn't stop staring at her and realised he must appear rude or threatening, so he forced himself to look away.

He stared down at her hand instead. It sat perfectly still, contrasting sharply with the busy tablecloth design. The nails were the colour of milk without even the slightest hint of pink.

He reached out and touched her with just three fingers, feeling that wouldn't be too much of an intrusion. He drew in a breath involuntarily as his fingers touched her skin. Her moonlight hand was as cold as ceramic.

Outside the sunlight had been stifled as the clouds closed in. Then she said something.

"Ikla ib'nar llan'st ..." As she began speaking, he looked about nervously. He was sure there must be eyes on them. But then he remembered with relief that they were the only customers.

"Slow down ... slow down," he muttered, waving his hands at her.

She took a gulp of air and began again. "We ... know ... you ..." Like her clothes, the language didn't quite fit properly.

"We? Who are "we"?"

She shook her head, somehow aware that communicating with him would be near impossible. Instead, she reached out and touched his hand. Again, the coldness of her touch was shocking.

It made him feel queasy, but the sensation soon subsided, to be replaced by one of yearning ... no, now it had become belonging. The feeling was so pure and so strong that it brought him close to tears.

Withdrawing her fingers, she whispered one word to him and then was gone. He mouthed the word in turn as he watched her leave, quickly and gracefully. "Home."

He felt as if he had found the thing ... or at least someone who knew about that thing ... that had been denied him all these years.

The days all tasted and smelled the same to him. The only difference seemed to be whether he walked to and from work or got the bus. Today he felt drained after what felt like a long day at the office, so he got the bus.

He sat near the back, next to the window. He was surprised that the bus wasn't busier at this time of day. At least I've got a choice of seats, he thought.

At first he thought the passenger behind him was talking quietly on their phone, or maybe even to themselves, until the voice became more persistent. It was difficult to say whether the voice was male or female, but it had a tone that demanded attention.

"We know all about your name …. all the letters, all the syllables, all the secrets." The voice was barely audible. So somebody knew his name—it was public knowledge, after all. But something in the voice, the way it had said what it did, turned his blood cold.

He twisted around quickly in his seat. There was nobody behind him. The rear seats of the bus were empty except for a middle-aged woman reading a magazine. She was sitting too far away to have spoken to him. As he continued to stare, she peered warily over the top of the magazine at him.

Turning around, he looked down at his feet. Was it that girl again? But there was nowhere for her to hide on the bus, as small as she was.

Then the voice started speaking again. He forced himself to keep looking down and gripped the edge of the seat in front of him, desperate to hold on to something real.

"Your name … your name," said the voice. And then, in an unfamiliar tongue, it spoke a word several syllables long.

He heard it with a shock of recognition. It *was* his name. Not the one that he'd been given in the orphanage and that he now called himself, or the one that sat on official pieces of paper or blinked softly away in data files, but one that was much, much older. It felt like cold water pouring through his soul. It filled him with a sense of freedom … and a knot of fear.

He sat in his seat as if he'd been turned to stone. The voice was silent now and he prayed that whoever the speaker was had gone and would leave him in peace.

The bus drove on through the city's crowded streets as he sat there, totally alone. He barely pulled himself together in time to get off at his stop.

He stood at the bus stop. The girl must have had been on the bus … somehow, he thought. Impossible though it seemed, she *must* have been. He felt as if he was being hunted.

This city had been so familiar to him until very recently. While he hadn't grown up here, it had been his home for over twenty years, and he'd settled into its streets and habits.

Everything felt like second nature to him, though familiarity had not bred contempt. But the favour had not been returned, he now realised.

Now everywhere was like a minefield within a labyrinth. Nowhere was familiar, nowhere safe to walk more than a few steps at a time, and then only cautiously.

Everything was hollow now and the mere possibility of her presence was beginning to haunt him.

There had been a small library in the orphanage. Its shelves were mainly filled with donated books, years out of date, but at least it was a haven where he could escape the others.

He'd been in there one day, sat at the big table, reading a large book about British myths and legends. There were some tongue-twisting names on those pages, but he just skipped those bits and read about what they did instead of what they were called. There was a drawing of one of the creatures stealing into a house. Its face was long and pale, and the eyes burned with malice. He'd never seen anything so evil.

He was reading about changelings and the way the "fair folk" made off with human babies when the door creaked open.

His brother Michael's grubby face appeared. "There you are …" he half yelled, triumphantly. "I knew you'd be hiding here."

"I'm not hiding," he protested. Michael was already at his elbow. He knew the book was in peril and tried to hold onto it tightly, but his brother was too quick and too strong for him.

"What's this then?" he demanded, peering at the open pages. "Reading about fairies? You big sissy!" He clambered onto the chair at the end of the table.

Outraged at his brother's rudeness, he tried to retrieve the book. "Give it to me! I haven't finished reading it ...."

Michael held the book above his head. He wasn't going to give up something that someone else wanted, even though he had no use for it.

When the chair was shaken, he lost his balance and fell to the floor, yelling in anger. The book sailed through the air and ended up by the window.

Then Miss Wilkins had come in and they'd both been in trouble ... again.

When he had a chance, he'd slipped back to the library to look for the book. It wasn't on the floor where Michael had dropped it. He supposed that someone had come into the library and put the book back on the shelf, where it belonged.

But it wasn't where he'd first found it on the shelf. He searched the other shelves but couldn't find it there either. The problem was, he couldn't remember what the book was called, just that it had a blue cover.

Subsequent searches proved equally as fruitless and eventually he simply gave up.

Years later he'd read a book of stories by a Welsh writer who mentioned the same creatures. But it was the drawing of the face in the first story book that stayed with him, even though he didn't know the name of the artist who'd drawn it.

The kettle had just boiled, and he decided to watch some TV to pass the time. A documentary about Ancient Egypt would be good. He'd begun walking towards the TV when he stopped in his tracks.

He was astonished to see three pale figures standing near the door. They were covered by scraps of strange clothing. She was among them. He dropped the cup he was carrying. "How did ...?"

He didn't finish the sentence as they all opened their mouths and began to sing with a heart-stopping clarity. His mouth hung open as he became immersed in its beauty.

The song. Was it something he half-recognised? But it was

so strange, almost unearthly, that he couldn't possibly have heard it before. He decided he must be suffering from a sort of auditory déjà vu.

Now and then the music would stop unexpectedly only to start again a few moments later with a series of strange trills.

He noticed that the strange harmonies had an odd effect on him, creating a slight dizziness and the beginning of a sense of panic.

He could hear her voice now, singing alone as the others fell silent.

Something beneath his feet changed. The old carpet now seemed to feel more solid and, slowly, he became aware he was standing outside, in the night air. Peering through the dimness, illuminated only by a sliver of silver in the sky above, he saw that he stood at the bottom of a natural hollow.

It was a small, flat area. On every side the ground ran uphill away from him. Several yards in front of him, embedded in the mossy ground, were two light-coloured stones about three feet high.

As he watched, his eyes gradually becoming accustomed to the dim illumination offered by the moon, he saw something move between the stones. Then, as if being knitted together from the surrounding gloom, he noticed a number of small animals appear from between the stones.

Standing on all fours and about the size of a cat or dog, the creatures began to walk towards him. It was difficult to make out their features in the poor light, but he was sure they were growing or changing shape as they advanced. Now they seemed to be roughly the size of small deer, with jagged antlers jutting from either side of their heads.

They were closer still now and seemed to be melting, shifting or re-arranging themselves with each step. He drew in a deep breath and took a step back. It was as though he was being granted a glimpse of a time before any humans walked the land, before the laws of nature had been settled or fixed as they were now. Or maybe those laws were simply being subverted.

He became aware of a feeling of freedom, a certainty that he could become whatever he wanted to be for however long. And then he could become something new, something different, if he wanted. It gave him a feeling of power and a sense of perfection that seemed to form the very ground in this mysterious place.

He could still hear the girl's voice, tripping lightly from note to extended note, as the shifting creatures moved closer. They were enormous now, far taller than him and partly walking on their hind legs while dropping on all fours from time to time.

He had no idea what they were, but they were huge. Just a few steps away now, their dark outlines continued to change and move without any pause. Their bulk gave them an air of menace as they advanced on him. Despite his best intentions, he yelled out and sank to one knee, covering his head with his arms.

The beasts passed by him, padding softly through the moss on either side as they ignored him. He let a few seconds pass before daring to glance under one arm to check their progress. Just as they had been seemingly knitted together from the air, they now began to fade into the moonlit night. Within a mere few seconds, they were no longer visible.

He looked around, puzzled. He saw the girl standing behind the two stones. She smiled at him, and his vision dimmed a little. Putting his hand to his head, he swayed slightly.

The familiar feel of his carpet was beneath his feet. He looked up to see the girl and her two companions.

"What was that? Where was I?" He knew that even if he got an answer he wouldn't be able to understand it, even if she spoke English. But he had to try.

Even before the words had finished leaving his lips, the three figures had been swallowed by the small portion of night that was crammed into his living room.

A sense of uncertainty swept over him. It became a kind of fear unlike anything he'd known before. Perhaps the girl had thought she was being kind in showing him those things, but it was a very peculiar sort of kindness, he thought.

Aware that walls were no longer an impediment to his strange visitors, that they might come to him at any time, he retreated into the bedroom, barricading the door.

He only emerged when morning came, and he needed to go to work. A perfunctory shave and a clean—or nearly clean—shirt and he was out of the door. Breakfast was a luxury he couldn't afford.

For once he wanted to be surrounded by people and decided to take the bus instead of walking. He waited in the bus queue nervously, almost dancing on the spot.

His fellow commuters gave him plenty of room.

That Sunday morning, he sought refuge at Mulligan's again. There was no bus on Sundays, so it was a long walk, but he had nowhere better to be.

Absorbed in the abstract world of his coffee, he wondered what these white people wanted of him. Why did they keep appearing to him? He had nothing to give them—he wasn't rich, or talented in any way.

Without warning, there was a moonlight white hand on the table in front of him. He'd been half expecting her to be here again. Maybe that was why he'd come.

Again, they were alone. He supposed the couple at the corner table must have left quietly without disturbing him.

He gazed at her as she sat there, saying nothing in her strange language or her halting English. Her clothes looked slightly less dishevelled than the last time she'd sat there, but she still looked uncomfortable.

She reached inside the pocket of the ill-fitting jacket she wore and grasped something. She didn't remove whatever it was from her pocket but instead turned her head and stared at the wall.

It was a plain tiled wall, yet she gazed at it as she would have at an ancient tablet revealing secrets beyond normal human reach.

The girl's hands were in constant movement, the small fingers drawing a complicated pattern in the air in front of her face. Her head turned from side to side, her lips twitching into a brief smile, as if she was speaking to invisible companions.

In astonishment, he stared as something like smoke emerged

from the cracks between the tiles. He almost rose, ready to shout in panic that the place was on fire, before he noticed that there were images in the smoke. Within seconds it had enveloped him. He expected to choke, but instead he felt the scented warmth of summer surround him.

A vision of blanched fields lay before him, filled with tall pale figures moving towards him from all directions. Strange fur-like ferns waved here and there among the grasses, as if scenting the air, perhaps for fear or some other inadequacy.

He had no way of knowing if he was seeing through her eyes or if these were his own visions.

A strange, rustling music came and went as the breeze ebbed and flowed. He could feel it on his skin.

Her words continued unabated. Though he couldn't understand her strange language, he somehow got a sense of what the girl was saying to him. She seemed to be telling of a land below the grey sea of the streets. It was something he had always suspected. Except suspected wasn't the right word … the thing he meant was closer to a dream or a wish. Something that could never be fulfilled.

Yet sometimes he felt as if the entire city was underground and that the sky was merely the bottom of a vast, barren field filled with broken stalks. But the land he saw wasn't barren—it was filled with vibrant, strange life.

The figures moved swiftly through the grass, heading towards him. He tried to count their number twice but failed. Eventually he was surrounded by them on all sides. They stood more than an arm's length from him. Then they all raised their left arms and opened their hands.

The things they held out to him were too awful for him to gaze at directly. Several of them stretched their hands further toward him, enticing him with the foul objects.

For a second he was tempted. It seemed right to him, this evil, as if he was born to it.

The appalling cargo they bore somehow promised something beyond the material; a personal renaissance, a restoration of something that had been missing for so long. Beyond that there might even be a righting of all the wrongs done to him, a re-balancing of the very universe itself in his favour, even if it did cost the blood of others less worthy than him.

If only he accepted what was being offered so freely …

Struggling, he turned his head away, heedless of any price he might have to pay for rejecting their offerings.

This was obviously some form of hypnotism, he told himself. He clamped his eyes shut, bit down hard and tried to make it all go away.

When he opened his eyes all he saw was the cafe and the girl. He exhaled heavily.

She gazed at him in expectation. He had no idea what he looked like, but he felt terrible—drained and shaking, as if he had been battling a persistent illness for weeks.

Although no words had been spoken, she looked at him as if she'd misunderstood something he'd said. An expression akin to panic suddenly filled her eyes. She rose and darted towards the door in one swift, smooth movement.

"Hey …!" He rose to follow her, feeling like something huge and ungainly. Outside, the street was empty except for an elderly man struggling along with heavy bags. There were no doorways into which she could have dashed quickly.

Puzzled as to where she could have gone to so quickly, turning his head to gaze in both directions, his eyes sought her in vain. He felt like an abandoned child, dumbfounded at his fate.

She held his daughter's hand and led her onwards into the maze of streets. Each grew longer and narrower, occasionally taking an unexpected turn. He felt that he was being pulled back with every forward step she took, prevented from going to her.

With every step the colour drained from her hair and her skin. With every step she laughed in delight, her voice becoming higher and thinner. And, with every step, she became more like them.

His daughter's face, always small and wan, had become deathly pale and doll-like. Hardly human at all.

A scream in a dream is no scream at all—merely a pathetic,

voiceless thing to be laughed away upon waking. So he saved his breath and forced his feet to trudge to the bathroom.

He stood in the shower, seeing her face growing smaller and paler and further away as the cold water ran over his head, making it ache.

He could not let them have her. If he was being presented with a choice then it was no choice at all.

Somehow he had to save her from the treasury of agony that he had unwittingly saved up for her.

The nights were getting more and more difficult. Previously they had always been his refuge from the strain he felt during the days.

But now they were just as fraught. Shallow sleep and constant worry meant he was more-or-less sleepwalking through his already difficult days.

He thought of sleeping pills, but he'd had bad experiences with them in the past. He slept well every third or fourth night—from sheer exhaustion, he supposed—and would have to rely on that until *they* stopped visiting him.

On returning home that evening, he found something waiting for him at the top of the steps that led down to his front door.

It was a small domed rock, surrounded by an intricate pattern of sticks, encircling it like a halo.

Perhaps it was meant to represent a castle surrounded by a moat. Or a city on an island. Maybe a prison. Or all three. Somewhere safe, he thought, or maybe just desolated and abandoned.

At first it seemed almost beautiful to him. Then, within the space of a few seconds, its true meaning dawned on him. It was a message—something ancient and menacing which threatened to overwhelm him. Its meaning tore at him.

Struggling to control his breathing, he stepped forward and raised his foot above the thing. A mixture of fear and anger filled him as he stamped on it, snapping the delicate wood before kicking the heavy rock into the gutter.

Magic had never been a part of his life. He simply didn't

believe in the occult, but he felt deep inside that he had to destroy that trap for his soul.

Ignoring the pain in his foot, he stumbled down the steps and fumbled his key into the lock, gaining sanctuary within and slamming the door hard. He stood with his back to the door, feeling the sweat dry on him as his breathing calmed gradually and his foot began to throb with pain.

As he sat at his desk, the computer screen told him things that he no longer understood. The words and images seemed as if the meaning had melted and run down onto the floor, leaving only their ghosts behind.

The white girl was never far from his mind. In fact, he had to force her out of his mind to simply perform everyday tasks … and even then he did them badly.

He speculated that she and her companions were ghosts. That might explain how they could come and go so quickly. Maybe they were echoes of a distant past, their skeletons lying deep in some cavern waiting to be discovered. Even that didn't make them any less unnerving. If anything, it made things worse. He didn't relish the prospect of being haunted. He had no idea what he had done to deserve such a thing.

Besides which, he had touched the girl. She had definitely felt real. Far too real, perhaps. In some ways, he wished he could simply dismiss her and go back to his former life of tedium.

He was asking for the impossible.

As he descended the steps to his flat, he noticed something propped against his front door. He put down his bag of groceries and fished around for his key, all the while peering down at the unwanted thing.

The object was wrapped in an old newspaper. Or maybe it was a kind of comic book, written in a language he didn't understand and illustrated with mystifying drawings.

He walked through the door backwards, struggling to juggle the wrapped object and the heavy bag containing his supplies.

Placing everything on the table in the centre of the room, he shrugged off his coat and picked up the strange parcel. It hadn't been posted, that much was clear. He couldn't think who would simply leave something in the open like that.

He unwrapped it quickly, sparing a few seconds to examine the unusual wrapping before casting it aside. Inside the parcel was a crumpled cardboard box that looked as if had been very roughly made.

He opened the lid and gazed down at the bundle of sticks inside. Then he saw that it wasn't just a random collection of bits of wood but something woven. He gently pulled it from its resting place and gazed at the intricate thing. It was a tiny hand. His delight at the workmanship in the piece of five-fingered craft faded almost instantly.

The thing was unbearable. He turned it over and looked at the other side. His eyes told him it was only made of sticks—a small and elaborate piece of folk art—but some unknown sense told him it was a child's hand. He dropped it and backed away against the wall, suddenly feeling very sick.

His gut told him that this was the worst sort of warning.

There was a mixture of darkness and delight in Mrs. Ferndale's eyes when he stepped into her office the next morning.

Sit down, she said. Would he like a coffee? She had some news for him. Bad news.

It was unfortunate, of course, she said, but hard decisions had to be made. And his work hadn't been satisfactory of late. The company was having to let him go.

He left the office and drifted back to his work cubicle, followed by a forest of furtive glances. No one spoke. The office was silent as he began to clear his desk.

He couldn't pretend he felt any grief at his fate. He hated his workplace and was as indifferent to his colleagues as they were to him. In fact, it had become a soft, grey hell with every day revealing new ways to demoralise and belittle him.

Now that he was freed of work, his mind seemed to float above the world, free of its mooring. Things seemed clearer to him.

He had the inescapable feeling that he was wandering along a lost way. It was a path that had been lost by his forefathers—whoever they might be—but discovered anew by him.

But he only trod it now thanks to the pale, strange girl whose name he didn't know and might never know, unless he found a way to learn her unusual language with its odd inflections and sudden reverses.

Where this path led he couldn't be sure, but he was sure that the lost way wound itself through a land that lay somewhere in the scrubby, inhospitable and misunderstood wasteland between terror and ecstasy. He was uncertain if he could choose between them—if his choice to turn this way or that might allow him to find either one.

The pale girl and her companions were almost certainly never far from the path of mist and dreams he trod. At times he felt they walked alongside him, matching him step for step, always unseen.

On some days he felt sure he could hear the pad of a thousand unshod feet following him.

His brother Michael was sitting at the corner table in the bar, wearing his usual brown leather jacket. He raised his hand in greeting.

His brother lived on the other side of the city. It was an effort for him to get here and he was aware he'd kept him waiting. "Have you been waiting long?"

Michael raised his glass. "About half a pint."

He went to the bar and bought his brother another beer, while he stuck to mineral water.

They exchanged pleasantries for a few minutes before Michael asked: "So why did you want to meet up? You said something about the orphanage?"

"Well, it's something to do with our name ..."

"Our name? What about it? Smith is a perfectly good, ordinary, everyday name. One of the most ordinary, in fact." His brother furrowed his tanned brow.

"But it's not our real name, is it? It's just the one they gave us in the orphanage. I think I know our ... my *real* name."

His brother took another sip from his glass. "Oh, right. Been doing some digging, have you? Well, I don't want to know, quite frankly … our mother abandoned us and that's that. If she didn't want to know us then I don't want to know her, the bitch!"

"I can't let it go like that … I've met someone who has shown me the truth."

His brother looked at him with a mixture of concern and disbelief. "Look, why dig all this up now? I don't understand your sudden concern." He let the silence grow larger for a few seconds before adding: "Are you sure you're alright?"

"Yes!"

"Well, you don't look alright. In fact, you look terrible. You're pale and you look like you could do with a good meal. Are you sure you don't need to see the doctor again?"

"No. No. No. It's nothing like that. Really." Michael's concern was diverting him from what he really wanted to talk about. He gritted his teeth in frustration.

His brother's face broke into a sudden grin. "Why don't you come and stay with me for a few days, eh? We can have a few beers, have a laugh!"

"That's the answer to all my problems, is it?"

His brother sighed, heavily. "No, but it's a start," he said before lifting his glass high and emptying it. He began to rise. "Do you want another?"

A slow shake of the head sent Michael on his way to the bar. After ordering he turned back to his brother, intent on asking if he wanted anything to eat. The chair was empty.

The world was running away with him. He feared that, wherever it took him, he might not be able to return.

Perhaps that wouldn't be as bad as he first thought.

His mind was coming apart as if tearing itself into pieces from inside. He hyperventilated, thinking of the alternating threats and promises—all unspoken—that he'd endured over the past few weeks.

Looking around, his possessions now seemed like grisly souvenirs from a war he'd fought with himself.

He stumbled to the bathroom and gazed at his reflection, hoping for the solace of the familiar. In the mirror, behind his face of crumpled paper, he saw a soul of sand, trickling away, grain by grain. He wondered how much of it was left.

Staggering back to his dishevelled bed, he sat down heavily, making the mattress complain. He fished about on the bedside table for the bottle of sleeping pills he'd bought recently. It was empty.

He picked up the photograph of his brother and himself and studied it intently for a few seconds. We barely look like brothers, he thought.

He stumbled across a bruised landscape covered in bushes whose branches ended in pale, pleading hands clutching at him. They snagged his clothes, piercing them. He tried to push on, but they tore his clothes, digging into the flesh below. He winced in pain as blood began to stain the fabric. Soon he couldn't move a single step forward. He was trapped and the tiny hands began to grow into his torn flesh.

He gulped down a huge lungful of air as he awoke. He lay panting in the darkness, relieved that it was only a dream. Then he had the uncomfortable feeling that someone was there in the room with him.

He squinted into the darkness but could see nothing. "H-hello?" There was no response. He began reaching for the bedside lamp.

Before he could find it, a pale hand reached towards him out of the darkness. He gasped in panic, but then her face appeared from the dimness.

Even though her fingers were open, they held promise. Perhaps even a sort of salvation.

He tried to untangle himself from the twisted sheets. She put her hand out and pushed him back down. He noticed that she was naked and that even her pubic hair lacked any colour.

"Wha—what do …?" he began. Then her lips were on his.

His skin tingled as she ran her hands over him. Arousal mingled with fear as he realised what she wanted.

They began moving together, responding to each other's touch. She began to murmur strange words in a rhythm he thought he remembered from somewhere. Pausing to kiss him now and then, she continued her stream of words.

He remembered touching her in the cafe and her skin was shockingly cold. Now she was warm and felt more alive than any other woman he'd been with.

His body began to ache. Moaning slightly in pain, he realised this was something he'd known about all his misshapen life but just couldn't remember. The next words she uttered seemed to dive down into him, taking away the pain and forcing his limbs to move in new ways.

Their bodies twisted together, sliding over each other in an unnatural way. His flesh and bones were not meant to bend like this. He found it both repugnant and arousing at the same time.

She sang—almost whispered—one of her people's odd songs as they licked and clawed at each other and his blood hammered through his head, rearranging his thoughts.

The air was filled with words unspelled since before man first sat on the throne of his ruined world. His name ... his true name ... was in the song. The music, winding and descending, was calling to him.

Whispering the rare, ancient words into the darkness, she sang the words without music, flinging open the doors of the mundane to let in forces unknown and unseen for more centuries than there were days left in his life.

Grown together at the groin, they fitted together perfectly, beginning now to flow into each other. Everything was changing.

One moment they were in his tiny bedroom, the next they rolled together in ecstasy on the soft feathery grass and cool air of a place that he felt was so very near. At last, he recognised the words as being the ancient, natural language of his people.

Now he could sing the song, knew every word and phrase, raise his voice at the precise moment of ecstasy so that the world was bathed in a secret splendour. And his name was a part of it all. That's why they had sought him out, he now saw. His name had been missing.

But no longer. He was joining with everything. The gates reopening.

Reduced now to a few scraps of flesh and wisps of thought,

he bent to kiss the lips of a face that was no longer a face.

Transcript of a message left on Michael Smith's phone on October 29th:

"Hi. It's me. I thought I'd best … let you know. I owe you that much. I tried to tell you the other day, but you didn't want to listen. There are some people … well, a girl … I think I have the chance to change things … for good …"

"Things are created just to be broken apart. Is that really it? All that our lives are? They've shown me another way … a way to remake the world …"

"There are secrets … places … I wish I could tell you about."

"They are waiting for me. Her gaze is resting on me … it's pale … so beautiful. I must descend with them …"

There was a pause, dead air. "Goodbye, Michael … I'm going home."

A Meeting Beneath the Moon

The stars overhead defiled the darkness, drawing unsettling silver patterns against the black backdrop, and the moon was larger and paler than any waking sky had ever held.

The garden stretched a long way from the house and the man with the pale complexion wasn't sure whether he'd ever seen the full extent of it. He anticipated that some obscure, previously unseen corner of it might one day yield a sight that would fill him with wonder or joy. Or perhaps some other, less wholesome, emotion.

Once he'd been certain that the sea touched the garden at one point, far distant. But when he'd tried to find it again he'd become lost, unable to re-visit the place where the tang of brine and ozone in the air made him feel as if he was setting out on a long voyage of discovery.

He turned and looked back at the impossibly tall dark house from which he'd emerged. The darkened windows of the forbidding structure seemed to hold his attention for longer than they should have done.

He tore his attention away and finished tying his sturdy gardening apron at the back. Frowning slightly, he reflected on how demanding a garden this large, and this unusual, could be.

The layout of the vast garden appeared to change regularly, yet he always retained a map of sorts in his mind, so that whatever happened he could find his way back to the house from within the heart of the leafy labyrinth. Though that didn't stop it from surprising him at almost every turn.

Nearby a small tree, stirred to life by a lazy breeze, uttered a sentence of alien sibilance.

On nights like this, when the starlight was so cold, he could sense the presence of a darker dreamer, reaching towards him through the icy blackness.

At first it was tiny and faraway, like the sound of a single candle guttering in the vast darkness of a cathedral. Then it drew closer and closer. Finally, it was as persistent as an unwelcome visitor hammering on the door of night.

It was then that he headed for a small grove of trees not very far from the house. They had tall, slender trunks crowned with upward-facing branches and he had no idea why he had first sought them out. They each bore a symbol on their trunks.

At first, he thought they had been carved into the light-coloured bark of each tree individually. But on closer examination, the strange five-pointed symbol seemed to have occurred naturally, growing there in some inexplicable fashion as each tree developed.

Whenever he stood within or near the tiny grove, the unwelcome sensation receded until he could no longer feel it. This was a place of peace that he cherished.

The gardener looked around at the plants waiting to be tended and mused that he had planted none of them. They had all seeded themselves. He had no doubt that each of them had come here from a very far off place, seeking a very particular nourishment.

The moon tonight was so large, so bright that he felt that it could be reached quite easily, if you had the right sort of craft. Its brightness brought an ancient coldness with it.

He was constantly surprised that those chill fingers of night had little effect, either positive or negative, upon the plants, even though they affected him quite keenly.

Indeed, the growths seemed to thrive in any sort of weather. He attributed this to their alien origins and, in no small part, to his care, which was always diligent and appropriate no matter what their uncommon demands.

Dutifully, he lifted out the implements he would need from a small box he'd secreted under a large bush. He put on a pair of heavy fabric gloves for safety's sake.

He scooped a handful of loose pellets from a small bag

marked Starfeast Fertiliser Company and spread it liberally around the thick base of the nearest plant. The fat leaves spilled over the path, making it difficult to pass by without touching them.

Nearby, odd triangular insects, trailing frail tendrils behind them, flitted from flower to flower, gathering nocturnal nectar. A group of them, seemingly mesmerised, hanging in mid-air before the large purple bell of a gargantuan flower. They waited patiently as a long tongue emerged slowly to devour them one by one.

He stood and gazed at them, wanting to turn away but being held there perhaps by the same fascination that enraptured them. He found the idea of them hanging in midair, waiting for death, quite repugnant.

Then he paused. Was the human condition really any better?

Like all men, he knew he must someday exchange the coolness of the night for the eternal cold of the grave. Until then, he mused, I shall make the very best of this remarkable place.

He reached up to pull a flower closer, intending to inhale its unfamiliar perfume but quickly let it go when an angry clicking began. A multi-legged creature crawled from within the bell of the flower, dropped to the floor and scuttled away.

When he finally inhaled the flower's scent, it was disappointingly insipid.

Continuing along the path, he came across a gaping pit barring his way. The deep hole was just long enough and wide enough for a man to lie down in the pool of darkness at its bottom. A snug fit, he thought, but not tonight.

The garden had provided him with several graves in recent days. But he still had things to do. If the place really was able to anticipate his thoughts, he found this particular intervention a great impertinence.

The enormous bell of a highly scented flower nodded at him, as if in silent agreement. He scooped some food around its base as a slight reward.

He stooped now and then as he made progress to those plants that looked most in need of nourishment. Soon he found that he was some distance from the house and the air had taken on a distinct chill.

The wall was high and sturdy in that part of the garden, yet still the ice had encroached. In the snow at the vanguard of the chill whiteness, he'd noticed several giant plants, barely buried beneath the thin layer of frost. Atop their enormous bodies were large star-shaped flowers.

One day, he knew, he would have to find out exactly what sort of thing grew there. But he had more pressing matters this night.

Bending to feed a large, proud flower with an eye-like centre, he was sure he felt the ground tremble slightly beneath his feet.

He imagined the earth from the garden running through a hole in its hidden centre, like sand in an hourglass. Perhaps the garden was as temporary as everything else and, once he was no longer able to tend it in his unique way, it would fall into desolation and decay.

There was already a definite stink of rot in the air. Yet all the plants here appeared healthy. Healthier than in the average garden. Although "average" was a word that was definitely out of place here.

Following the overgrown path around a red flower-laden bush, he was slightly startled to see a figure standing with its back to him. Hearing his approach, the man turned around.

He wore slightly old-fashioned clothes but had a kindly expression and a head crowned with silver hair that hung below his ears.

The gardener felt that he should be wary of any stranger in this place, and yet there was something curiously familiar about this person.

Although they had never met before, an odd expression of recognition appeared on the faces of both men. Stepping forward to welcome his visitor, the gardener extended his hand. "It's Arthur, isn't it?"

The older man returned the handshake with some vigour. "Yes, yes. Hello!" he replied, as if greeting an old friend. "It's very good to see you. I was just admiring your splendid garden. It is *your* garden, I take it?"

The gardener paused for a moment as if unsure. "Yes. It must be. I am the one who always tends to it."

Arthur nodded. "Always? There is no one to help you?"

"No. I feel a compulsion to come here each night. The plants need tending. Some require a very particular sort of care."

Again, a nod. "Do you never feel a little trapped by that regimen?"

The moon high above dimmed its light, making the darkness deeper and thicker. Does it somehow disapprove of our conversation? wondered Arthur.

Despite the blackness of the night, the two men could see each other clearly in the curious luminescence given off by the larger plants. It is as if they are drinking in the moonlight and then releasing it once they are sated, thought Arthur.

The gardener stood, shaking his head with a half-awake expression on his face. "No. Not trapped exactly."

From the high black house somewhere behind them, came a sound like an enormous object crashing against its walls, shaking it tremendously as if something was being born. Or was dying.

Arthur and the pale man stood looking in its direction. Their expressions were a mixture of awe and fear. They waited several more moments, but the sound did not repeat itself.

"Is that a regular occurrence?" asked Arthur, once he'd found his voice once more.

His friend merely shook his head slowly and returned his attention to the plant at his feet.

Arthur wandered off a little way to examine more of the bizarre flora.

One plant that drew his attention seemed to be made up entirely of stalks. He nearly walked straight past but then noticed an unusual pink flower almost hidden in the centre.

Stepping closer, he saw that the flower looked uncannily like a woman's face. It looked peaceful, as if it had recently fallen asleep.

From the mouth extended a tongue-like stamen. On its surface was yet another face—this one looking as though it lay in a troubled sleep—and, if he peered even closer ...

Arthur pulled himself upright with a jolt. He would not look at the thing.

Composing himself, he ambled over to where his companion was tending a low liquorice-scented bush with fleshy leaves.

"Yes, you have quite a remarkable collection of plants here. Did you choose them all yourself?" Given what he'd already seen, Arthur hoped the answer would be in the negative. He was more than a little relieved when his companion shook his head.

"No. Most, if not all of them, have seeded themselves. But I welcome their appearance, I must say."

"I believe that each of these extraordinary growths may represent a fresh idea or a remarkable tale. Quite literally, the seeds of a story."

Arthur blew into a pipe he'd produced from his pocket, making a loud snorting noise. He considered whether to light it or not.

"A gift from the gods, you might say." He waved the pipe around, pointing at individual plants in turn to illustrate his point. Observing the look of consternation on his friend's face, Arthur stopped fumbling for his tobacco and slipped the pipe quietly back into his pocket.

"I admit that tending this garden does help me to formulate my ideas. Whether I can carry them beyond this place is another matter."

The leaves of one plant hung down like the spread pages of an oversized, inverted book. The gardener paid particular attention to this one, Arthur noticed, feeding it generously, fussing over it and picking off dead leaves.

Arthur suddenly felt compelled to look over his shoulder. A strange, tree-like shrub behind him now seemed particularly fascinating. A few steps and he was standing right in front of it. It gave off a musky scent.

On the enormous bole of the plant were a series of raised mounds with a notch running down their centre. From each ran a thin trickle of clear liquid.

To Arthur they appeared like a superfluity of vulvas. Or weeping eyes, ready to open and stare at him.

A slight sense of unease crept over him as he speculated as to what could be born from such a fecundated growth. Or what the thing would see were it to look at him—a friend, or food?

Suddenly he became aware of the gardener at his elbow. "Please come away, Arthur. I have reason to believe that this particular plant has an actively hostile nature."

Arthur looked around, unsurprised. "Really?" He was glad of an excuse to step away from the plant.

The bag of food was now empty, so the gardener folded it and put it in the pocket of his apron before brushing off his hands.

"Let me show you where this place lies." He indicated a narrow path that led off to one side, away from the main promenade through the garden. Arthur followed as the tall man led the way through a gap between the plants.

Luxuriant growths shot up on either side and the light became dimmer as they squeezed between the narrow green walls. Leaves caressed them and once a twig tugged at the silver hair that hung down past the older man's ears. He was beginning to feel a mild claustrophobia when the path suddenly opened out and he found himself on a stone platform.

The two men stood on a small outcrop that seemed to stand proud from the garden itself, where green walls curved back in either direction. They were within an oddly decorated stone and wood gazebo. The stone looked so ancient that Arthur feared to touch it, in case it crumbled beneath his fingers. He stuffed his hands into his pockets to deter any temptation to do so.

He looked out from his vantage point, astonished at the fact that there was nothing to see. There was no landscape stretching away from the garden and its heavily overgrown walls. The strange stars seemed to fade out just as they met a horizon that was not there.

Arthur looked at his friend, who simply said "The void."

Daring to lean forward slightly to peer over the low wall, Arthur gazed down into the blackness, hoping to catch a glimpse of something. "An abyss above us and abyss below," he muttered.

But surely there was something, he thought. Was that the

sound of waves? Were they in fact on an island of some sort, lost in the wastes of some vast aetheric ocean? He turned his head to one side, listening intently to the sound, which seemed to come from miles and miles away.

Arthur turned to his friend and opened his mouth to speak. He didn't know whether it was possible to be interrupted before you'd even said anything but that's how it felt to Arthur. "Voices," said his companion.

"But—?" began Arthur, then stopped and leaned over to listen even more intently to the sound coming from far below. "I-it ... it ..." he began. There were words within the faraway, echoing chaos of sound.

"I thought at first that I was hearing the sound of waves," said his friend. "I'd imagined once before that the sea lapped against the garden, but I was mistaken. It is not the sea, just an ocean of voices."

Arthur's face twisted into an expression lost somewhere in the wasteland between hope and fear. The strange, whispering siren sounds refused to let him stop listening. He wondered if this was a place of inspiration or merely desperation.

As if in answer, his friend spoke once more. "It is a place where all the voices are dead. They simply repeat empty things. Sometimes they grow louder but they are still divorced from life. Or from what we know of our life, at least."

The pale man now stood beside Arthur. He closed his eyes and listened. Unsure of the sturdiness of the ancient stonework, Arthur stood back from the edge. He was afraid it would not support the weight of two people and he was certainly the heavier man.

He watched his friend intently, expecting some further revelation from him about the curious nature of the phenomena. Instead, his friend's face took on an aspect of grief, as if he recognised the tones of a familiar voice in the distant tumult. It seemed to grow more profound with each passing second.

"Come. Let us go back," said Arthur, hastily. "I have seen—and heard—enough." He laid his hand on the pale man's arm as if to guide him away, afraid that he might succumb to some wayward instinct within him.

Back where they had begun, the two men sat on a large, decorated rock for a moment.

The gardener looked down at a plant whose dried leaves were drooping so much that they nearly touched the ground.

"Some of the more fragile plants need watering. It hasn't rained here for some time." He held a leaf gently between his fingers but even this was too much for the plant, which crumbled at his touch.

"I will fetch the watering can from the house later. There is a well in the garden, but it has become unaccountably poisoned. Anything watered from it undergoes an unwarranted and quite bizarre transformation."

Arthur couldn't help but wonder what exactly that must look like in this hothouse of wonders and horrors.

Once they were on their feet again, the tall man led the way.

To one side of the path was an object on four sturdy iron legs. It stood on its own paved section and was around two feet long.

As the men passed by, a sound came from inside the box-like object. "What is that?" asked Arthur.

The other man shook his head. "I have no idea."

They stepped closer to examine it and saw that it was made of glass, almost completely covered with a green film. Taking his handkerchief out, Arthur tried to clean off the mouldy layer. As he did so, there was movement inside.

"There's something alive in there," noted the gardener, as he leant closer to look inside. The reverse of the glass was similarly grubby, obscuring everything but the impression of movement within. A faint blue glow penetrated the murk. A low grumble or growl accompanied it.

He and Arthur looked at each other with mild concern. "Might it be dangerous?" asked Arthur. The other man acknowledged his lack of knowledge with a slow shake of his head.

A small brass plaque was attached to the front of the odd display case, but it was impossible to read it in the gloom. Arthur struck a match so his companion could examine the sign. "We are no wiser, I'm afraid. The writing has been worn away," he said, indicating the pitted and weathered surface. The only decipherable letter was a capital "S" at the top right-hand corner.

A dozen pinpricks of blue light appeared through the twilight inside the box, then disappeared in the blink of an eye. It was difficult to work out if they were looking at a single creature or a whole colony. Whichever it was, the commotion from inside was growing the longer the two stood looking at it.

"I don't think we'd better open it," whispered Arthur, suddenly surprised at himself for lowering his voice.

The other man checked around the back of the box. There was a curiously fashioned brass clasp at the rear, but it seemed not to have been designed to be opened, or at least, not by human fingers. "I agree. There's no way to open it without breaking it, in any case."

As they walked away, the noise and movement inside the glass case grew even more frantic. They talked of other things, deliberately ignoring it until it was out of earshot. Both men secretly congratulated themselves for escaping something that would have been exceptionally unpleasant, if not deadly.

The two relaxed sufficiently to carry on their conversation as if the sinister glass case had been merely something from another dream entirely.

Arthur was regaling his companion with the finer details of an extraordinary novel that he had read recently and was not paying full attention to where his feet were going. "... and on the very last page, at that."

He was so absorbed in his tale that he nearly pitched forward into a deep pit that had opened up in the ground ahead of them. Only a restraining hand saved him.

"Good Lord," he muttered, recognising a grave when he saw one. There was a headstone already in place at the far end of the mortuary trench.

As the men watched, letters began to form as tiny chips of stone fell from the upright stone slab.

"Come on. We won't want to see this ..." The gardener began to part the foliage nearest to him, finding a way around the obstruction. His companion followed, placing his feet carefully so as not to be snagged by protruding branches. If we keep going we must come across the path again, he reasoned, as the undergrowth crowded about them. They trod slowly and carefully in the gloom.

Neither man had anything to cut through the foliage, and the going soon became difficult. After a few minutes of struggle, they came to what looked like part of an old, cast-iron fence. At first glance it looked as if it had been allowed to rust but, on closer examination, they saw it was entirely organic. It had grown straight out of the soil at their feet, barring the way.

"Where are we?" asked Arthur.

"I don't know," said the younger man. "I've never been here before."

On the other side of the obstruction could be seen a clearing where three or four enormous stone blocks stood. Three had become obscured almost completely by vegetation, but the fourth, which stood slightly apart, was free of any growth. It looked, in fact, as if had been freshly deposited there.

Finding their way along the obstructing plant, the men discovered that it decreased in height, then trailed off along the ground before finally disappearing into it. Having cleared the obstruction, they decided to examine the huge stone blocks. These were obviously ruins that required exploration.

As they neared the closest block they could see that, unlike its companions, its surface was smooth and clean. The dark grey block was nearly ten feet in height and looked as if it had been part of something much larger. On one side of it, picked out in the moonlight, were several large glyphs, both whole and partial. Some of the shapes were carved right up to the edge of the stone and looked incomplete, as if it was meant to join with a companion carving on another block.

As they took their next step, the indecipherable letters appeared to invert themselves for a second before returning to their former position.

"Extraordinary! Did you see that?" When no answer came, the younger man turned to his companion. He saw that the older man was standing with his head in his hands. "Arthur? Are you not well?"

The older man staggered forward a few steps before being steadied by his companion. "My head … it's so …"

Within a second or two, the gardener began to feel an odd pressure building behind his eyes. It was as though a huge, yet silent tocsin was being rung inside his head. The pressure came and went in waves, reverberating against the inside of his skull.

The two men stumbled into each other, almost ending up on the ground. Grabbing at their clothing to support one another, they retraced their steps as quickly as they could. At a certain distance away, the throbbing waves began to ease. It was clearly a warning to stay away from the ruins.

Disorientated, Arthur staggered off to one side, bumping into the trunk of a very large plant before tumbling sideways.

He suddenly found himself in a tiny space surrounded by the enormous fibrous trunks of several plants clustered together. What little space lay between the trunks was filled by the thick stalks of yet another plant.

Confused, Arthur looked around. How on earth had he got here? There was no entrance to the cramped space. He pressed against the trunks and the stalks but neither gave way even an inch. He could only imagine that the plants had suddenly and impossibly sprung up around him.

He then noticed that each of the thick trunks had set into it a narrow, hollow space suggestive of a coffin. They were just large enough for a man to fit inside.

Standing was difficult. He had hardly any space to put his feet and, struggling for balance, he toppled backwards into one of the tight spaces.

Arthur lay still for a second or two, tilted backwards at a slight angle and wedged in place. He got his breath back and tried to stand. His arms were pinned at his side, and he was wedged in place.

Managing to free one hand, he placed it on the side of the plant and exerted all his strength. He moved an inch or two before becoming stuck fast once again.

He felt a slight shiver run through the plant as thick, sticky liquid began to trickle down the sides of the hollow he was lying in. The smell was quite unpleasant.

Realising that the plant knew it had fresh prey to digest, Arthur was on the point of panicking when he saw a hand appear between the thick stalks directly in front of him. "Take my hand," a voice commanded.

Angling himself as best he could, he heaved his one arm free and grasped the outstretched hand with gratitude. With a tremendous effort, he pulled himself up and through the plants blocking his way.

Out in the open once more, Arthur did his best to clean the viscous substance from his clothes with some large leaves from a nearby bush. "Are you alright?" asked his saviour.

"Yes. I think so. Thanks to you," he answered, before glancing back in the direction of the gigantic stones.

His companion followed his gaze. "That's one mystery that can remain a mystery for today, at least. Though I'm reluctant to give up on it altogether. After all, it may reveal that the entire garden is planted over ancient ruins."

Arthur glanced warily over his shoulder as they picked their way around the site. "Menhir of some fashion, maybe ..."

Within a few minutes the pair found their way back to the path. Picking tiny hair-like seeds from his clothing, the gardener indicated which direction they should take.

As they continued, the soft luminosity around them faded. The eldritch growths, fallen from the stars or risen from the seas, were suddenly aglow with a deep orange light. The effect on the two men's faces was alarming. In the infernal illumination, Arthur fumbled for his matches again. As he struck one, he noticed there were only a few left.

The halo of light returned their faces more-or-less to normal.

"That's never happened before." The two men looked about them warily, fearing that the odd livid light might foreshadow something more sinister. After a few minutes the light began to change once more, the previous white glow returning as the redness faded into the night around them.

Then, above them, the stars blinked out slowly, as if being obscured by gigantic petals as they closed over the garden. Soon only the doleful, ashen eye of the moon remained, gazing down at them from directly overhead.

Suddenly, the taller man gasped and doubled over. He seemed helpless for a few seconds then, panting hard, he regained control of himself.

Arthur rushed forward to help him. "Are you alright? Can I help?"

"No. No. I'll be alright, thank you. I have some pain from time to time." He stared into the distance, seemingly at nothing at all.

"How long have you been suffering from these pains?"

His shoulders moved in what might have been a small shrug or a reaction to a final small spasm of pain. "Several weeks now, if my memory is correct."

"Do you think it may have something to do with some noxious emanations put forth by these remarkable plants?" asked Arthur.

The thin man looked at his silver-haired companion. "Well … some kind of radiation, you mean? I hadn't considered that."

Arthur nodded, though he wasn't sure that was exactly what he'd meant.

"Have you sought your doctor's advice? After all, it might not merely be a passing problem but a more serious malady. It is not good to ignore these things."

The tall man had an uncomfortable expression on his face. "I distrust the medical community. They pretend to more knowledge than they actually possess, it seems to me."

He took in the view of the vegetal and floral kaleidoscope surrounding him. His next remarks indicated to Arthur that he had indeed considered his own mortality.

"Whatever might happen, if I have taken some of these dreams and made them real—at least for myself—then I think it may have been a price worth paying."

"They are more than dreams, I think," muttered Arthur. "I am sure they are …"

The gardener nodded. "Perhaps. Or perhaps I am merely storing them up against a time when there will be no more dreams."

Again, an enormous crashing sound emanated from the dark house that towered over the far end of the garden.

"Your guests seem to be growing ever more restless," commented Arthur.

"I don't have any guests. At least, none that I know of."

Arthur seemed embarrassed at his friend's response. He stepped back and sat on a convenient bench, making some general remark about tiredness in order to cover his obvious error.

His companion ignored the remark. "I am tired now. If you don't mind, I believe I will go inside. Thank you for your visit, Arthur. It was so good to see you."

When no reply came, he turned to look. There was no sign of the other man. In his place on the bench was a jumble of sticks and roots, twisted together to approximate the shape of a seated man. Several lightly browned leaves, curled and misshapen, made up the face, with two dark berries beginning to wither below a brow of smooth bark. Some downy white seed heads had settled atop the plants.

After contemplating the sight for a few moments, the solitary man turned and walked away. Heavy night-borne aromas filled the air as he rounded the bend in the path, passing beneath an enormous drooping overgrowth of *Orchidaceae stellam natae*, to face whatever waited for him in the dark house.

In the near darkness, the house opened up like an enormous flower to welcome him in.

For the Love of Insects

The small station was deserted. It had a run-down look as if it had always been deserted: abandoned before a single train had either arrived or departed. Each discoloured tile told a tale of neglect. Filth clung to every corner. No timetables or posters had ever been hung on its walls, it seemed.

Had he got off at the right place? There were no signs anywhere. The train sounded its horn once, a mournful farewell, as it rounded the corner and disappeared behind a hill. Alex clutched his shoulder bag to him; it contained the few essentials he'd brought along.

He noticed a dust cloud moving towards him from between a line of houses. Suddenly a large black car appeared, slowing slightly as it negotiated a crossing over the railway tracks. Grinding gravel under its big tyres, it crunched to a halt just a few yards away.

The car was a huge black Soviet-era limousine that glistened even in the milky sunlight. The artist obviously took great care of it; he'd probably had it restored at some expense. Inside, it looked roomy but not particularly comfortable.

The man seated behind the wheel glared at him for a moment before opening the door and climbing out. He was tall and wore a baggy black shirt and grey trousers. The gravel crunched dryly under his huge work boots as he strode forward.

He extended his hand, closing it again tightly. The handshake was surprisingly soft. "Modril," he croaked before coughing loudly and repeating his name in a more audible tone. Although taken aback by the extraordinary volume of the man's cough, the new arrival managed to squeeze out "Hello. I'm Alex McCarthy."

Modril let go of Alex's hand and nodded. "Yes." It was said in a tone of satisfaction, as if he was pleased he'd found the right person.

The big man walked around the front of the car and opened the passenger door. Alex noticed that he walked with a distinct limp, as if the leg was malformed or injured in some way. "Get in," barked Modril, his voice now obviously fully recovered.

Modril settled himself into the driver's seat and bullied the car into life. A small, sad-faced cat watched the car speed by. As the driver put his foot down, Alex was shocked to see that the end wall of the station was pock-marked with bullet holes.

He'd been warned by a gallery owner in Bucharest that Modril disliked empty flattery or idle chatter, so Alex decided ahead of time to hold his tongue for the duration of the journey to the painter's home. Now that he was face to face with his intended interviewee, Alex knew he wouldn't find it difficult to keep his promise to himself; the man was huge, and his eyes held a stern expression beneath large, dark eyebrows.

Alex felt relieved that at least Modril's English was likely to be good. The few words he'd already spoken were in a slight but distinct accent, but he could clearly be understood. Alex's own language skills were poor, and he'd struggled to understand the few dialects he'd heard on the exhausting train journey from Brussels.

He didn't know where the artist had learned English, but he was grateful that his tutors had done such a good job. Of course, he'd known Modril could speak English already—otherwise, how could an interview even take place—but it was one of the few certain things that was known about the enigmatic painter.

No one was even sure if Modril was a first or last name. Just Modril. Always.

In the few monographs and catalogue notes on him, there were very sparse biographical details. "Originally from Eastern Europe" was the most detailed that Alex could find. But the man's face seemed somehow more exotic than that. There was something about his eyes.

The car ascended a narrow road with unfamiliar road signs dotted here and there. At one point, Modril nearly ran three workmen off the road, sending them scurrying into the trees for safety. But he seemed not to notice.

They'd been driving for less than 10 minutes when the landscape levelled off. Another few minutes and Alex could see another hill ahead, with a large house built near the top. Modril grunted softly and nodded as if to indicate that this was their destination.

The hill was covered in trees. Probably the remains of ancient woodland, thought Alex. The mist still clinging between the trees, even this late in the morning, looked like deftly spun spider gossamer.

He looked at the big man sitting next to him. According to some, he was the heir of the great Surrealists like Max Ernst and Dali. And there had also been comparisons with Giger.

But he was greater than any of them, in Alex's opinion. Modril's exquisite and terrifying images of humans and enormous insects, locked together in curious embraces or puzzling dances, were quite unlike any other work ever created. The look of rapture on the faces of the people he painted was inexplicable, haunting.

The trees made the approach to the house dark and Alex kept craning his neck for a glimpse of the building around the next bend. And the next. When the house finally loomed up before them it came as a great relief to him.

Modril parked the huge car in the courtyard before the house with less than diligent care. The machine rocked for several seconds on its tortured suspension before the big man leaped out with a grunt.

The house was large. In fact, Alex wasn't sure "house" was the right word, as it seemed to be more a complex of buildings joined together by low corridors. Maybe it had been used as something else once, mused Alex.

Modril almost bounced up the few steps to the front door and threw it open with a flourish. Alex followed him obediently.

Just inside the door, he stopped in his tracks. On the wall was a John Curtis illustration of a crane fly, its perfectly delineated long limbs reaching up into the air. The slight yellowing of the paper told him that it was an original and must have cost Modril a small fortune to obtain.

"This way. This way." The artist's voice sounded impatient, so he followed him quickly into the inner darkness of the house.

Modril stood holding a large oak door open for him. "Down here, Mr. McCartney," he said.

"Uhhmm … McCarthy. My name is McCarthy," corrected Alex.

The big man nodded. "Yes, sorry … I must have been thinking of The Beatles."

No doubt, thought Alex as he caught sight of the numerous examples of coleoptera displayed on the wall. Beetles had always made his skin crawl. For the next few days, he'd be running the gauntlet.

The corridor was lined with deep glass-fronted picture frames, each containing delicately mounted butterflies, moths, various other insects or spiders. He stopped before one frame. It contained a single specimen of a large, remarkable-looking creature. It seemed as if the thing within the frame couldn't decide whether it was an insect or a spider. Certainly, it was an arthropod, but he'd never seen anything like it before. It was horrifying but fascinating.

His host had lingered, waiting for him to catch up, so Alex took the opportunity to ask what the creature was. Modril merely chuckled and gestured to him. "Come on, there'll be plenty of time for all this later. You need some rest and refreshment after your long journey."

The two men sat facing each other in a large lounge at the centre of the house. There were no windows, but a large, decorated skylight revealed that the room was stuffed with art and artefacts. Some were by Modril himself, but others were of more obscure origin, Alex noted.

A large coffee table stood between the two sofas on which they sat. The table looked as if it had been carved from one solid piece of wood. Alex guessed that it must be immensely heavy.

"Thank you for your hospitality, Mr. Modril," ventured Alex.

The artist frowned slightly. "I am not Mister. I am just Modril. Please just call me that." Alex nodded, feeling suitably chastised after his clumsy attempt to divine the artist's full name had fallen to pieces.

An emaciated-looking maid delivered a tray to the table. She wore a neat black uniform and looked to be in her late 50s. She looked briefly at Alex with dark, sad eyes before Modril said something to her in an unidentifiable language, after which she left quickly.

"Please," said Modril, indicating the coffee pot and cups on the table. As Alex reached forward to pour himself some coffee he almost snatched his hand back in panic. There were various books and objects scattered about the table, but Alex hadn't noticed the evil-looking piece of sculpture at first. He took his eyes off it only to ensure he wasn't spilling the coffee while pouring it.

Although of poor craftsmanship, the statuette was obviously of the odd creature he'd seen on display in the corridor. Whoever had created it had made it a hideous mixture of antennae and multi-jointed legs. They'd very obviously got the details wrong, giving it an impossible number of limbs and appendages. It was a nightmare. One roughly cast in some dull grey metal that had barely been polished.

When Modril caught him looking at it and said, "You may pick it up if you want," Alex did his best to conceal a shudder at the thought. He didn't want to touch the repellent thing.

Yet, the more he looked at it, the more he had to admit it had an odd allure. He disliked it, most certainly, but something in him wouldn't let him look away. When he found himself reaching for the foul looking object, something inside his mind snapped in desperation, and he let his hand fall to his side.

"It's from Indonesia, in case you were wondering," said Modril. "It's quite rare. I don't think they are made any longer."

Alex took the opportunity to press the matter further. "The insect itself is also from Indonesia, then?" Modril simply dropped his gaze and nodded, pouring himself some coffee.

"I've never seen anything like it. What's it called?"

Once again the painter simply ignored the question. He

clattered his cup down onto the saucer, placing them on the table before springing from his chair with astonishing grace and speed. "We will talk tomorrow. Tonight, we will eat, and we will keep the art until the morning. I should show you to your room now. If you've finished ...?"

Alex nodded, not wishing to antagonise his host, even though he still had half a cup of coffee left.

As he ushered Alex out of the room, the artist added: "My wife will join us later ... before dinner."

Despite all the interiors being painted in light colours, the rooms of the house were cool and dimly lit. There was an odd chemical aroma everywhere that Alex didn't recognise. It wasn't paint or anything to do with painting, he was sure. He eventually dismissed it as being due to some cleaning product that he was unfamiliar with.

Alex opened the small window that looked out upon a line of dark trees. He unpacked the few things he'd brought and lay back on the bed in a feeble attempt to recharge his batteries. What he needed was sleep but he was too keyed up to drop off.

Who knows, maybe this will be the only interview Modril will ever give—it will certainly be the first—and I'll be the one to get it, thought Alex. He'd be "the man who talked to Modril.". By definition he'd become the world expert on the artist. At the very least he'd get his PhD and a book out of it.

He remembered Professor Aitchison's remarks on the day he'd received the summons from Modril. "Be careful. Some called him Madman Modril, you know." Alex had assured him he would be. "You can forget the rest of your work towards your PhD if this comes off. This interview will be enough to secure you your doctorate ... and make your reputation on top of that!" his tutor had added.

As he'd closed the door, he'd added one final caveat: "And you'll have to do something about this idiotic fear of insects that you have, Alex. That'll hold you back."

Easier said than done, thought Alex. He resented the Professor dismissing his fear so lightly. His fear of the multi-limbed creatures had been with him since his early childhood when a picnic had been ruined by a veritable swarm of ants. The miniature monsters had been everywhere; they'd coated the food with their awful black bodies, and they were in his mother's hair when she'd bent to pick him up. As she'd held him close to her, they'd begun to crawl over him, too. Some had even got up his nose. He was only five and it'd taken his mother nearly half-an-hour to stop his crying and shaking.

Alex had paid a hypno-therapist for three sessions before leaving London. He hoped to God that would be enough to hold off his phobia long enough to get this interview over with.

Alex got up, went into the small bathroom and splashed some cold water on his face. He felt exhausted. In a way he was glad Modril didn't want to give the interview until tomorrow.

He had dozens of questions that, even if the artist was evasive, should shed more light on the mystery of Modril.

There were only nine of his works in public collections. But they'd been enough to excite several laudatory articles and monographs on his work. Those, and some learned catalogue entries, had been sufficient to provide him with an enviable reputation.

But there wasn't a single interview with him. Much of what had been written about him was simply guesswork.

About four years ago, there had been rumours that Theo de Caestecker was writing a book with the artist's co-operation. But the book never appeared, and then de Caestecker died suddenly, so that was the end of that.

Then the note had arrived. It had said simply "Come for an interview" and given a time, a date and a place. Brief and to the point but equally unsettling, Alex had thought.

He could only assume that it was the reputation of his tutor, Professor Aitchison, that had secured this rare opportunity. The Professor had contacted the artist through a friend of a friend of a friend who owned a gallery that had shown Modril's work. After six months had passed with no reply, they'd assumed that the message had sunk without a trace.

But now he was standing in the artist's home with his heart in his mouth. He sat on the bed and surveyed the small but comfortable room.

On one wall hung an enormous painting, dominating the room. It was nearly eight feet wide and depicted a bizarre landscape filled with entwined figures. In the foreground lay a pair of figures locked together. The insectoid creature was as large as a man and lay atop a woman, its proboscis extended around her neck. The woman's expression was difficult to read but he found the impression of erotic asphyxiation impossible to escape.

Behind the two figures the picture plane tipped up sharply towards the viewer. It showed a flat area with a building of some sort a little distance back. The building was painted in such a way that it might have been ancient or very modern. The terraces of the structure were all but obscured by similar insect and human figures; whether they were embracing or struggling was impossible to determine from this frozen snapshot. In the background of the painting there was the suggestion of trees.

To one side a dense patch of foliage, sensuously painted with long brush strokes, gave Alex the impression that the scene depicted a humid place.

In the bottom left-hand corner, just below the artist's familiar signature, were some words. He presumed they were the title but there was some slight damage to the canvas and the paint had been scratched away. All he could read was "… tual."

It made him feel uneasy. The more he stared at it, the more uncertain he became as to whether he was spectating on an orgy or a slaughter. Every other one of the artist's paintings that he'd seen had an indefinable air of eroticism clinging to them, but not this one. Perhaps he'd been unable to sell it, and that was why it was here.

He didn't know if the painting normally hung here or if Modril had deliberately placed it here for him to see. But Alex knew it was unlike any other of his paintings hanging in museums or public galleries.

Quickly he took a photograph of it. He felt like a criminal but didn't want to lose such a rare opportunity. He didn't yet know if he'd dare mention it in his thesis, at the risk of angering the artist, but at least he would be able to gaze on it in private.

Alex had managed to doze off on the soft bed. He didn't know how long he'd been asleep when he was woken by a knocking sound. Dazed at first, he thought it might be part of a dream. But when it came again, he realised it was the door.

When he opened it, he found the maid standing there. She looked concerned and then opened her mouth to speak haltingly. "He zay to coomb now and tork. Now." She laid a hand on Alex's arm to underline the point. "Now."

Alex was surprised, delighted. Maybe Modril had changed his mind, and this would be the "big interview." He grabbed a notebook and pen and followed the maid. "Where are we going?" he asked.

The maid did not answer but simply kept on walking, glancing just once over her shoulder at him. She'd obviously learned what she'd been told to say parrot-fashion and had no grasp of English.

Alex followed her into a part of the house not visible from the front. Part way down a long corridor, the maid stopped and turned to him. She looked flustered and began to hiss to him in her own language. Staring back down the corridor the way they'd come, she jabbed and pointed. She repeated what she'd said then fished a piece of paper from her pocket.

Unfolding it, she showed it to Alex. On it was a crude ink drawing of what looked like two people dancing. Or perhaps engaged in something more intimate. It looked like it had been scrawled by a child. If it was the maid's own work, then Modril clearly hadn't employed her for her artistic ability. She insisted on repeating her words for a third time, still in a low whisper.

He had no way of understanding her, so he just said "Umm … yes. Yes" and nodded emphatically. She stared at him as if he'd just made a very bad and cruel joke at her expense. Then she walked past him and went back down the corridor.

Alex watched her go, then turned to look towards where Modril must be waiting. He presumed that he was expected, so he continued on his way.

The corridor was relatively dimly lit but there was a skylight at the far end. Alex headed for the two doors lit by the pool of illumination.

Near the end of the corridor was a large-ish photograph, elaborately framed and hung just at eye level. It showed an obviously younger Modril, very smartly dressed and standing next to a seven-foot-tall version of the hideous statuette he'd seen in the living room. The craftsmanship of this version was far superior to the object he'd seen earlier. The sunlight glinted off its smooth surface, each segmented section of its underbelly sculpted precisely enough to make Alex shudder. Although partly obscured by a spray of leaves, there was a disturbing suggestion that some of the limbs were disappearing behind Modril's back. Impossible, of course, he thought.

Alex was speculating as to whether the giant thing was an idol, worshipped by the Indonesian natives, when one of the doors a few yards away opened and Modril's figure filled the frame.

"Alicks. Here you are. Didn't that stupid maid show you the way?" The big man took Alex by the arm and almost threw him into the room before slamming the door emphatically.

Alex found himself in a large studio with the last of the daylight streaming in through two elaborate skylights.

The artist insisted on showing him his brushes, manufactured nearby from the finest horse hair. "Very soft, very good," he kept repeating.

Again, Alex noticed Modril's difficulty in walking, just as he had at the station. Alex tried not to stare or draw attention to his interest. But it appeared as if the man's knee worked the wrong way round—bending backwards instead of forwards— and that he was struggling to conceal it.

Unsure of whether this was to be an interview or not, Alex asked polite questions about the brushes and the house. If he could put Modril at his ease, then maybe Alex would get what he wanted.

After several minutes, Alex asked the question that was burning a hole through the very centre of his mind. "Why do you paint insects, Modril? And such large ones?" The query was almost child-like but it had the desired effect. The artist turned to him with a new light in his eyes.

"Without the insects there'd be nothing. They are the most successful and numerous creatures on the planet. And they render us so many useful services ... they are the base that we all stand upon. You ... I .... everybody ...

"They were here so long before us—I have no doubt they will endure once we are gone. After all, they were building cities while our ancestors still slept each night in the trees.

"They have far greater nobility then a mere race of contemptuous simian upstarts ... Compared to them we are pathetic creatures, don't you think?"

Alex disliked Modril's attempt to get him to agree. It was obviously some sort of test but, at the risk of appearing ungracious, he remained silent.

"Mankind." Modril pronounced the word with a chuckle. "So many battles fought, so few victories won, hhhmm?"

Alex felt uncomfortable with having to listen to Modril's ramblings. In his opinion a little madness was desirable in an artist, possibly even essential, but this was taking things too far. And there was no way he could agree with his host's musings about the many-legged monstrosities, though he knew better than to say so.

Alex's belly was beginning to complain, as well, which didn't put him in the most receptive mood for such extreme views. He was looking forward to dinner, which he hoped would be quite soon. He hadn't eaten properly since breakfast. If only Modril's wife would hurry up and make an appearance.

"Errr ... will your wife be joining us soon, do you think?" asked Alex, attempting to move the topic on to more pressing and mundane matters.

Modril looked at him as if showing pity for some terribly slow pupil, finding his lessons too hard. This was clearly not the interview Alex had hoped for.

By now Modril was standing in front of a huge canvas, largely obscured by a cloth. It was obviously a work in progress.

"They are gods. They deserve to be worshipped." Seemingly intent on not being deflected from his favoured topic of conversation, he pulled at one edge and the cloth fell away from the huge canvas.

Alex's mouth dropped open involuntarily. The painted scene was vast and horrifying.

The figure of the insectoid creature was familiar; it was a variation on the horrifying form seen in his other paintings. But the human figure was unlike any other he'd seen in any of Modril's other works. It looked like something splitting apart or flying back together after being torn to pieces, all frozen in a moment. The absurd phrase "Francis Bacon with a hangover" came into Alex's mind.

The figure appeared to be in a kind of delirium, its mouth gaping open in a sigh of surrender.

The artist ran his hand slowly across the surface of the canvas, smudging the paint into one corner after nearly erasing half of the human figure. "I like to think there are worlds beyond our own where the order of things is very different."

Alex didn't know how to respond. Best try to sound professional, he thought. "Perhaps we can talk about that in the interview tomorrow, too."

"My paint stands in for my words," spat Modril. "I don't need to give interviews."

"Then why am I ...?" Something deep inside Alex turned black and withered in the light of new knowledge. "No-no ...," he breathed.

Modril smiled and pointed to a spot behind Alex's left shoulder. "Ah, here is my wife now ..." Then the man made a bizarre series of clicks and scraping sounds with his mouth. Alex's scalp crawled with fear as an answer to Modril's greeting came from somewhere behind him.

Frozen with fear, he was unable to turn his head more than a fraction. Yet, out of the corner of his eye, he saw a dark shape lowering itself from the ceiling a mere yard or two behind him.

Slowly the shape moved around so it was almost directly in front of him. Alex gasped in terror as he recognised a gigantic living example of the bizarre insect displayed in the hall. It dawned on him that the photograph he'd seen minutes before had showed Modril not with a carved idol but with the nightmarish thing that stood before him.

The creature was enormous, stretching upon its rear legs to tower over him. It hissed softly but didn't make any threatening moves. Alex heard Modril cooing to the huge monstrosity in his own language and wondered if they were instructions.

The thing moved closer to him. The strange chemical tang that Alex had noticed on arrival was nearly overpowering now. He gagged and coughed at its intensity.

His head began to swim, and he saw images of a vast green plain. Where and when it was, he didn't know, but he'd seen it before in the large painting in his room.

Then the huge creature came into focus once more. Lost in the great hollow of dreams, as if adrift amidst the humming, insect-heavy summer air, he watched as a bead of light journeyed across the compound lenses of each eye. He was fixed to the spot, unable to think, let alone move.

The sunset sent rosy light through the skylight as the sun prepared to depart. The creature clicked with what might have been pleasure. The light caught the sensuous sheen of her carapace, highlighting its lustrous blue-green hue. Her mandibles moved with a softly clattering nervousness.

He could see now how beautiful she was, how elegant and sleek. At last, he understood Modril's intoxication with her and her kind. All Alex wanted was to belong to her, to be with her.

In the gloom behind her the wall was now crawling, alive with invertebrate witnesses to their outlandish union.

He almost lost consciousness, overwhelmed, as her impossibly long limbs enfolded him. The blend of terror and ecstasy was close to unbearable, forcing him to gulp down each breath painfully.

Now he was almost immobilised. Suddenly there came an agonising pain in the middle of his back as the huge creature stung him. He bucked hard against the thing's segmented body as the pain bit into him, his arms too tightly pinned to escape. Alex couldn't feel exactly where the wound was, but a hot numbness began to spread through him. He tried to cry out, but his voice failed to reach beyond a whisper as the creature clicked excitedly.

"Don't worry. She will be most gentle," whispered Modril.

"Isn't she exquisite?" he added in a tone filled with almost idiotic reverence.

As Alex's eyelids swelled, closing one eye altogether, he caught a final glimpse of Modril sketching furiously. The last sound he heard was of charcoal scratching roughly across canvas, faster with each stroke. He couldn't help wondering if he'd be on public display or part of a private collection.

Mere seconds before the numbness spread down his body, he felt his abdomen being pierced by something large, his previously empty belly filling to near bursting point.

Alongside the bitter tang of the venom on his quickly swelling tongue, Alex felt a deeper bitterness when he realised that he wasn't to be her lover after all but merely a larder for her young.

Late Night, Caradoc Street

The funeral was the following Monday. And the town was just as small, grey, and dirty as Dave had remembered. No, not quite as dirty; not these days.

Pulling up outside the house, he turned off the ignition and told himself: "This will be the last time."

Clicking the car door shut, he looked up at the sky. Grey and threatening rain, as usual, he thought.

The house was built of the same dingy stone as every other dwelling in the narrow street. Only the colour of the doors and window sills differed. The dark windows stared at him, uncaring.

He ran his finger along the window sill. It came up dirty, but not coal-black like it would have when he was a boy.

It was like one of a thousand identical terraced cottages, thrown up to house those who laboured in the ground beneath his feet. The dignity of labour and the glamour of filth had never appealed to him, so he'd left as fast as the bus to Cardiff would carry him.

He pulled his bags out of the boot and closed it again with a satisfying clunk before locking it. You can never be too careful around here, he thought. He'd just begun thinking of the list of tasks ahead of him when he was interrupted.

"An Alfa Rome-ee-oh, eh? I bet you drive that round like a right Juliet, too, don' you?"

He turned, sure he recognised the mocking tone in the voice. "Oweeeeen, man! How are you?"

The two shook hands. The last time they'd met was five years ago. "Good to see you again, Davey," chuckled Owen.

"It's just Dave now. Got to sound professional and all that, haven't I?" There was the smallest hint of self-mockery in his words.

"Oh, right ... all grown up and that. I get it," said Owen, nodding in mock sagacity.

"The old place doesn't seem to have changed," said Dave, after a few moments' silence. It was the only thing he could think of to say.

"No, we're still top of every league where you never win anything ... bad health, unemployment ..."

Dave lowered his gaze to the floor. "Hmmm."

Owen brightened then. "Still ... you're doing alright, eh? What a beauty!" he said, indicating the sports car.

"Well ... um, yeah." Dave suppressed a shiver of outrage as Owen ran an appreciative hand along the curve of the bonnet.

"Sorry to hear about your mam," said Owen, suddenly serious.

"Mmmm, yeah ... thanks." Suddenly the sky above their heads seemed to turn a dark slate grey, to match Dave's mood. Rain began to fall. He shuffled uncomfortably. "We need to catch up on things. Listen, let's have a pint tomorrow night in the New Inn, eh?"

"Can't," said Owen, glumly. "It's been a discount carpet warehouse for over a year now."

"Whaaat? No!" Dismayed, Dave didn't intend to give up. "OK then, the Cambrian."

Owen shook his head sullenly, pulling up his collar against the raindrops. "That's closed, too."

"Bloody hell," hissed Dave, suddenly realising how much in decline his old hometown was. "What about The Crown?"

Owen nodded. "The beer's shit but at least it's still open," he chuckled. "Better dash anyway. See you there at 7 tomorrow?"

Dave nodded as Owen dashed away into the rain. He stood outside the front door of the house where he'd grown up. The door looked a bit more care-worn but nothing else seemed to have changed.

He was almost afraid to open it, afraid of what he might find inside. Nothing ... but everything. Finally, the strengthening rain made up his mind for him.

Digging in his pocket, he found the old keyring. It had been used so seldom in recent years. The familiar soft clunk of the lock brought him close to a sob as he turned the key and pushed open the front door.

He put down his small overnight bag just inside the door and walked through to the living room.

The small house seemed even more cramped and dark after his own high-ceilinged apartment. The stale smell of his mother's overly floral perfume clung everywhere.

He eyed the half-empty sherry bottles ruefully. The handwriting on a pile of Special Delivery envelopes was his own. Picking them up, he saw they were all unopened. She'd never even used the money he'd sent her every fortnight.

He pushed open the door to the front room, which his mother always kept spick-and-span for visitors. This was where his mother had "held court" after his father had died.

In the small room, dark behind curtains kept closed out of respect, they'd all trooped in to see his mother. There was plenty of pity for her but never a word spared for his father. He'd been puzzled and hurt by that.

"Didn't none of 'em like Dad, then?" he'd asked his mother later.

She'd pulled him to her, burying his face in her skirt. "It's not that, love ... it's just .... well, it's hard to explain ... maybe one day ..." That had been the last she'd ever said on the subject.

Dave gave a start as he heard the front door open. It was the sound he always associated with his father returning home from work. But that had been nearly two decades ago.

"I knew you were here," his aunt called out. "I saw the car outside." Dave almost breathed an audible sigh of relief at her voice. The very next second, he stiffened himself ready for the onslaught to come.

His aunt, short and gaunt, walked into the room as if she owned the place. She gave him a stiff, uncomfortable hug. "Hello auntie, how are you?"

"As well as can be expected," she said, shortly, glancing around the room. "Have you started going through your mum's stuff yet?"

Dave shook his head slowly. "I've only arrived this minute."

His aunt nodded. "Well, you'd best make a start soon. Have you seen how much stuff is in this house?"

Dave nodded, though it had been years since he'd visited. His aunt must know that.

"How long are you here for?" she asked, tartly.

"Just until after the funeral ... I've got to get back ... work, and ..." And, if truth be told, I simply can't face what might be in this house, he thought.

"What, is that all? Well, there's *lots* to do ..."

He nodded vigorously. "Yes, of course. Don't worry. I'll ... sort things out ... I'm sure mam has kept things in order ..." He knew those last words were a lie. His aunt saw her opportunity and didn't hesitate.

"A pity you never came to see her, isn't it? She was bad in bed for three months and you never came near. Too busy, I expect ..." There was a cold gleam in her eye.

He looked away. "I—I knew she had you and Uncle Will," he muttered. "That she was OK."

"Yes, well ... she's dead now. So she's not "OK," is she?"

He wanted to spit back that she'd been a stupid, drunken old woman who barely had a good word for him when he did visit. But he held his tongue, feeling ashamed and lonely as a knife twisted in his guts.

Something prevented him from telling his aunt about the only time he'd phoned his mother from New York. She'd seemed fine when she answered his call, but it became clear after a few sentences that she thought he was his dead father. It had been just before 11 in the morning where she was. Dave had to put the phone down when she'd asked when "he" was coming home.

He had to say something to his aunt in his defence. "I made sure I always sent money."

"Money." His aunt made it sound as if the word had been dipped in something corrosive and didn't belong in her mouth at all. "Money is the least of it ..."

The air in the room seemed colder somehow. Dave stood in silence, looking down at his mother's favourite chair, unable to speak.

He was relieved when his aunt finally broke the silence. "Well, I've got things to do. You call round tomorrow and I'll give you the papers we talked about on the phone." Dave nodded. She let herself out.

After his father had died, his mother seemed to lose interest in everything, including him. The bottles she brought back from the supermarket replaced any kind of life she'd had previously.

On the last occasion he'd visited, Dave had walked over to where the pit used to stand. For several minutes he'd stood in the car park of the sports centre that had replaced the colliery, wondering what on earth was going through the minds of the people going in and out of the main door.

Behind the building, a gigantic wheel from the colliery's winding gear had been set up on a concrete plinth as a memorial to those who'd died underground. He remembered thinking how insultingly ugly it was. His father's name was among the two dozen or so listed—when he'd read it a cold emptiness had come over him that had taken days to shake off. Only when he was back home in London had it finally left him. Only then did he feel that there were no eyes upon him, watching for every expression or facial tic that might betray his true feelings.

Just one week later he'd accepted the job in New York. Sometimes even that didn't seem far enough away.

Dave spent several hours going through his mother's papers. Many of them were inconsequential or long out of date.

But one or two items he put to one side. An insurance policy. Gas and electricity bills that would have to be paid.

Of most interest to Dave was his mother's diary. A large, blue-covered book. He wasn't exactly sure what to find in it. When he opened it, the contents were mundane enough—the old woman had kept it as a memory aid rather than a true journal. But the "Notes" section had some very strange contents.

The back pages of the diary had been filled with strange symbols or half-words in his mother's handwriting, grown spidery with age. He peered at it for several minutes before putting it down to her declining mental powers. It was probably just gibberish.

Feeling the need for a cup of tea, Dave had ventured into the dismal main street of the town in search of a pint of milk. Many of the shops he'd remembered were gone now, replaced by discount this or cheap that. And, as Owen had said, many of the pubs had simply shut.

As Dave made his way back to the house, he heard his name being called. Looking round, he recognised an old friend of his father's.

He remembered Mr. Hughes fondly from his childhood. Now the man was grey and stooping, wearing a ratty-looking tweed jacket that had seen much better days.

"Well, hello stranger. Good to see you. Sorry that it had to be like this—you know, with your mam passing away."

Dave nodded. "Yes … well, ummm … I'm only back until just after the funeral really. Work, you know."

"What are you doing now, Davey? A banker, is it?" he asked.

"Well, a trader … it's similar."

"New York, too?" There was a twinkle in the old man's eye at the mention of this mythical name.

Dave nodded. "Among other places, yes."

The older man leaned forward and punched him in the arm softly. "I knew you'd do well for yourself, lad. And that you'd get out of this *bloody* place …"

He stopped himself suddenly, forcing a half smile as if his last comment had been a joke. He was fooling no one, least of all himself.

"Well, not much of a future round here for a boy like you …" He looked nervous now, as if he felt he had to defend what he'd said a moment ago. But Dave wasn't quite sure if his words were a defence or a condemnation.

The old man carried on with a string of platitudes for a few moments, then made an excuse and shuffled off quickly. He lowered his gaze as he went, as if conscious of having committed some misdemeanour that he would have to account for.

Dave felt unsettled after his meeting with Mr. Hughes.

The town was grey enough on a good day, but now the streets felt narrow and confining. They might have been a maze built deliberately to confound and entrap him.

Too tired to make up a bed, he slept fully clothed that night on his old mattress. A rolled-up coat shoved under his head served as a pillow while he struggled to fight off the thousand ghosts that crowded in on him.

A grey-washed sky dragged over his head as Dave set out for the undertaker's the next morning.

It was a 10-minute drive outside town. Uphill, of course. Not a problem for the car but it seemed to Dave as if he was heading into a place even bleaker than the one he'd just left.

Past the empty shops and boarded-up pubs, the road climbed up the side of the valley. Greenery struggled to take over from the bleakness of the streets. The undertaker's was along a short road to what used to be a farm.

The farmhouse had been given a serious refurbishment. He remembered it as a scruffy, half-collapsing place run by a curmudgeonly old man. Now it looked clean and respectable, with dark wood everywhere to imply dependability and, perhaps with deliberate irony, continuity.

He was met at reception by the senior undertaker, Mr. Jenkins, and led through to the viewing room.

There was a dusty emptiness in the man's expression. He imagined that the undertaker had been hollowed out by mouthing endless expressions of sympathy to people he hardly knew.

"I'll leave you alone with your loved one for a moment," said Mr. Jenkins in a baritone whisper as he indicated the open casket a few feet away.

Dave took four hesitant steps forward and forced himself to look down at the corpse of the woman he'd known better than any other.

His mother's cheeks were sunken, and he was shocked at how white her hair had grown. Her face was now a mask that parodied her life. Her skin had a glossy sheen that he had never seen before. He refused to let any tears come.

Stepping outside, he stared down at the grey paved path. He felt like thin, wet paper, as if he might tear down the middle at any moment, to be trampled into the pavement and then kicked into the gutter.

His gaze was still fixed on the floor when he heard a soft voice call his name. He looked up to see his cousin, Elin, walking towards him.

"Hello, Dave. My mother said you'd probably be here. I'm so sorry about your mam," said Elin.

They'd been close as children but then life had got in the way. He and Elin hadn't seen each other in years but kept in touch by e-mail and the occasional phone call.

Dave nodded. "I saw your mam earlier. She wasn't that ... sympathetic."

Elin stepped forward and touched his arm. "She can be hard work sometimes, I know. I'm sorry. It's just that she really misses your mam and, well ... looking for someone to blame, I guess ..."

"Well, that isn't me," said Dave, quickly. He sounded unconvinced.

"No. No, of course not." Elin sounded equally sceptical of his too-swift denial. "I know it's hard but try not to take any notice of her .... you had your own life to lead ..."

Elin looked around. Words weren't going to come easily today, she decided. Whatever she did say would only be what everyone else said, so she decided to keep quiet.

"So are you off to visit your parents now?" asked Dave, glumly.

"No, I'm off to visit my friend in Cwm," said Elin, indicating a battered VW in the corner of the car park. She nodded at his black Alfa Romeo. "Nice car, by the way. Very flash," she said, making a comic grimace, glad to be off the subject of family grief.

Dave nodded and chuckled. "I'll let you ride in it if you're lucky."

"I'll try to be a good girl then." She grinned and climbed into her car. Dave waited for her to leave the car park, waving as she headed off in the opposite direction to him, before he drove off.

He was at the bottom of the road back into town when a large car came out of nowhere. All he saw as it flashed past was a snarl of teeth beneath a pair of glasses as the driver grimaced at him; all he heard was a grinding sound as it scraped the paint off the driver's door.

Dave gripped the steering wheel hard and gritted his teeth. The car sped away. A big, silver-grey Ford was all he was certain of. The number plate had been too muddy to read … probably on purpose.

He got out and examined the damage, cursing. It could be fixed but it would be expensive. In bitterness he hoped that the other car had been damaged, too. The driver's face had looked almost animal, but it seemed familiar somehow.

Dave got back behind the wheel and waited for a bus to pass before pulling out. "No point telling the police. They won't be interested," he thought.

It had been years since he'd even thought of Bryant's Cave. Riffling through some papers of his mother's, he came across an envelope of his childhood drawings. Dave leafed through the crumpled, discoloured papers covered in childish crayon marks.

One showed a small figure at the mouth of a cave. The dark opening looked like a mouth, ready to devour the inexpertly sketched version of his younger self. He remembered that it was a drawing of a particularly vivid dream.

He must only have been around eight or nine. It was a night when his cousin Elin was staying at their house—because his aunt had gone into hospital for a "minor op."

He remembered that, in the dream, he was standing in the cave. Several of the other kids were there, all standing behind him. Suddenly the back wall of the cave came towards him, as if it was falling, or as if something was coming out of the rock at him.

He'd woken up crying out and sobbing. Looking up, he was surprised to see Elin standing over him. Then his mother came in and asked what was going on.

"We were just playing games in our sleep," said his cousin.

"Weren't we?" He was about to say something when she shot him a dark glance that made him simply nod.

His mother had looked at Elin strangely and then taken her back to her own room. When she returned, she told Dave not to be scared and that nothing could hurt him.

Despite her words, he didn't sleep for the rest of the night. He knew her words weren't true. Lots of things had hurt him already.

At the end of Victoria Road, the tarmac simply crumbled away, turning into an overgrown track for some way before disappearing. The road past the last house hadn't been used for years and nature was having her revenge, reclaiming what was rightfully hers.

Avoiding the copious amounts of dog mess, Dave picked his way through the brambles and overgrown bushes, following the barely visible path.

He presumed the cave—which was really no such thing— had been named after the quarry's owner. That was usually the way things worked around here; outsiders came in and claimed ancient places by putting new names all over them.

The so-called cave was little more than a shallow hole left in the side of the mountain after stone to build the houses had been quarried. But it had been the place where all the kids had gone when he was small, despite the dire warnings of their parents and the punishments that often followed upon discovery.

The floor was covered with a very dark earth, soft underfoot, that gave off the stink of ancient rot, so familiar from when he was young. It was a moist smell unlike anything he'd smelled since.

The back wall was now covered in streaks of bird lime from pigeons nesting on the high ledges. The wall was covered in graffiti made up of the usual obscenities and inexpertly scrawled swastikas but mixed in among them was something new. There were odd symbols, carefully drawn in red, interspersed with the childish rubbish. They reminded him of the symbols used in the keys to maps, but one in particular caught his attention.

Crunching over the discarded lager cans, he noticed it in

three separate parts of the cave. It resembled a child's simple drawing of a house, turned on its side with a bar struck through it. It was nearly identical to one he'd seen in the back of his mother's diary.

He stared at it for some moments before he was distracted by an insistent sound, which grew slowly clearer.

It sounded like a chorus of anxious voices stumbling and stuttering over some demonic doxology; repetition running round and round till it ran out of road.

After nearly a minute the sound stopped. Dave looked around for its possible source. The knot of soporific pigeons on the higher ledges seemed unlikely culprits. Then he remembered that the cave used to "sing" in the winter when the winds blew through the fissures at its one side.

He made his way to the cracks in the rocks. They seemed larger than when he was a boy and he doubted they could have caused the sound now.

The sound had had an odd effect on him, as if he'd just heard a few bars of a familiar but long-forgotten tune ... one that used to be one of his favourites, maybe.

Dave didn't know what he'd hoped to find at this local "beauty spot." Whatever it was, it was absent and didn't seem to matter now anyway. He began to retrace his steps back to Victoria Road.

There was a movement somewhere off to his left. He was sure he saw someone in the nearby bushes. Probably one of the local kids—maybe even the son or daughter of one of his old school friends. Or enemies, more likely. Maybe the sounds in the cave had been a prank after all.

It reminded him of another reason he'd left this place; there was never any privacy. Wherever he went or whatever he did, he always felt watched.

Sometimes at three in the morning—when sleep seemed like just the memory of something he used to do when he was younger— he'd imagine walking through the pitch-black tunnels to the place that had never been found, where his father lay crushed and buried, abandoned to the darkness and his death.

Suddenly there would be light, just enough to make out some shapes. Despite the tons of rock and coal on top of him, his father still had a face and was able to talk to him, though he could never make out what he was saying. It looked as if he was struggling to form the syllable "Day ... Day ..." as if trying to say his son's name one last time. But Dave also felt it must be a warning of some sort. The darkness would then come down once again and he wouldn't be able to make out the face any longer.

Outside his apartment, all around him, snakes of light slid across the night-time glass as the dreams he thought he wasn't dreaming dragged him deeper still.

He'd put it off as long as he could, but now he sat in his aunt and uncle's living room staring at the awful pattern on their carpet.

His aunt put a tray of tea things down on the coffee table in front of them before sitting down. Tea was poured and biscuits handed around.

"You'll need these, I suppose. The undertaker's already seen everything he needed to." His aunt slid a thin sheaf of official-looking papers across the table to him. Dave saw that the top one was his mother's Death Certificate. He didn't need to look at it—he knew that she'd died years ago from loneliness and pain. But nobody had dared say it.

He put his hand on the papers, acknowledging their existence. "Thanks, Auntie Sian. For everything ..."

His aunt pursed her lip and played with her tea cup. "Yes, well ... your mam was like a second mother to me ... when we were growing up."

Dave knew the stories and, for a second, he was afraid he was going to have to hear them all over again. But to his relief the silence that had settled remained unbroken.

Uncle Will sat looking at him over his cup of tea, his horse's nostrils sitting uneasily on his long face. The smart casual look didn't suit him at all. If there'd been a look called "'pinched, conservative, and painful" he'd have been a style guru, constantly splashed across the front of every men's fashion magazine. But there wasn't ... at least Dave hoped to God there wasn't.

"Long drive, was it?" asked his uncle, who obviously felt he should say something.

"Hmmm," he muttered, nodding. He wasn't sure which leg of the trip from New York his uncle was referring to, so a non-committal answer was best, he felt.

He drained his tea and stood up. Picking up the papers from the table he muttered "Thanks for the tea. I'll give you a ring later ..."

"Yes, if you need a hand with anything, just let us know, David."

Dave nodded. "I think I'll manage, thanks. You've sorted everything out so far—I'll be able to give mam a proper send-off. I'm sure that's what my father would have wanted ... if he was here ..."

There was a drop of poison in her voice every time his aunt mentioned his father's name. This time was no exception. "Your *father*—"

"Sian!" Uncle Will's bark cut her off in mid flow. Dave looked up, astonished. It was the first time he'd ever seen the old man stand up to his wife.

His uncle smiled weakly at him. Dave returned the smile while his aunt glared coldly at both of them in turn.

"Someone scratched your Batmobile? That's not on, is it?!!"

Dave shook his head. "It can be repaired but ... it's just it seemed as if it was done on purpose ... so maliciously!"

Owen coughed pointedly. "Not being a touch paranoid are we? It was probably cock-up not conspiracy, knowing this lot 'round 'ere."

"You didn't see the look on the driver's face, though ..." Everyone in the dimly lit lounge of The Crown seemed to be listening, while making it very plain that they weren't.

"Perhaps they 'don't like my sort 'round 'ere,'" he said in a mock rural accent.

"No, they don't like anyone 'round 'ere—not even themselves!" Owen chuckled. "It's probably bad old-fashioned jealousy, aye. But then you were always an outsider. We all knew that."

Dave bridled. "What do you mean, an outsider?! I was born here ..."

Taking another gulp from his glass, Owen gazed at Dave over the rim of his glass. "Well, you know," he said finally. "That you *felt* like an outsider."

Dave couldn't argue. He had. He still did, wherever he went. But that was why New York was the perfect place for him— everyone seemed like a stranger, all of them outsiders, even those that were born there.

Owen was obviously about to ask Dave a question when an old school "friend" appeared at his elbow. Lewis Thomas had a broad, freckled face and untidy ginger hair. Owen seemed to get on well enough with him, but Dave glowered at him, remembering the schoolyard misery that had been meted out to him by this intruder.

Owen seemed interested in the conversation that followed. Dave stared into his pint, trying not to listen as Lewis went on endlessly about the irrelevant minutiae of some local rugby match.

After his final words to Owen, he turned his beefy, freckled face towards Dave. His hard, black eyes had lost none of their menace. "Good God, I thought you were dead," he almost yelled.

Dave forced some sort of smile. "Just wishful thinking."

As he walked past Dave towards the door he said "Aye, it was and all!"

"That bastard hasn't changed, I see," hissed David. He kept his voice low in case any of his friends overheard.

"No, not much," said Owen, shaking his head slowly. "He married Jeanette, you know that?"

Dave shook his head, slowly. Jeanette Williams had been a pleasant girl in their class at school. He didn't know her that well, but he was sure she deserved better from life than that. "This bloody place ... I tell you."

Owen chuckled, darkly. "Glad you got out, eh? I bet you count your blessings every day you wake up somewhere else."

"If I'd stayed here I'd have ended up working for the bloody Counc—" David stopped himself suddenly. "I'm sorry."

Owen's face was a mask of mock fury. "None taken," he

growled, comically. "Nah … I know what you mean, though. If it wasn't for Mari, I'd have left, too. But she won't leave her mam on her own. Anyway … another pint?"

Dave was about to put the key in the lock when he noticed something odd by the light of the streetlamp. There was something daubed on the wooden panel of the front door.

Peering closely, he saw that it was the same image of a house turned on its side that he'd seen before. Above it was another symbol but this one was unfamiliar. It resembled a spiral maze, skewed to one side.

He peered at it. Maybe it was the work of some local drunk, with a grudge against his father from years ago. Or perhaps someone who'd harboured childhood resentments and thought he was "being clever" by being clever. He was baffled by the repetition of the strange symbol.

The images were drawn thickly and crudely in an unusual-looking substance. Leaning forward, he breathed in an oily, tarry odour. It smelled like something that had been beneath the earth for a very long time.

He decided to scrub it off in the morning. Pushing the front door shut behind him, he reached for the light switch. It didn't work. Dave flicked it up and down a few times. There was an old-fashioned fuse box somewhere, but he'd need a torch first.

As he took a few cautious steps towards the kitchen, he heard something move nearby. He held his breath for a moment, standing stock still.

He pressed himself against the wall, next to the window. Faint light wept through from the street. Just enough for him to see something move further back in the shadows.

"Who is it?" he hissed. His enquiry was met by a creaking, cracking sound and a foot appeared out of the darkness. It was made of wood.

"Hello, cousin." It sounded like Elin's voice but changed somehow, as if heard down the end of a long, bad telephone line.

As she stepped forward, Dave pushed himself back against the wall. He wished he could push himself into the wall and escape as he caught sight of the thing his cousin had become.

She looked as if she'd been hewn out of wood by a weekend sculptor; any beauty she'd possessed had disappeared under their chisel.

His legs refused to work as he tried to run for the door. He half-collapsed onto a chair. His cousin reached forward and grabbed his arm. "Careful, David. We don't want you to hurt yourself. We've been waiting for you."

As she pulled him up, he saw that the carpet was streaked with the same tarry stuff that he'd found on the front door. The smell was much stronger here. "What the f—?"

The thing that had been his cousin moved forward awkwardly on stiff limbs. "You mean you do not recognise it … the signs of the Ahn Ny'hoo ritual …? Our lord, Nyogtha, has blessed us with his gifts." She stretched out her arms to either side as she spoke; his aunt and uncle stepped forward as they were summoned. He nearly yelled out at the sight of their overwhelming transformation.

"We are one with the world around us … not like you," said his cousin, almost mockingly. "Did you never feel it? What about those times at the cromlech in the woods? Did you not hear the black goat calling?" she hissed.

"But that's not a real one, it was …" Despite his fear, part of his mind wanted to rebel. He needed to tell her how wrong this all was and how he didn't belong to their world.

She pinned his arms to his side. His cousin was surprisingly strong for such a small woman … if she was still truly a woman. "Those day trips to Three Cliffs Bay—do you remember how Dagon's horn called to you from the sea? How your mother had to pull you away from the water's edge time and again?"

He shook his head vigorously, but it did nothing to mollify her. "Or all those times the wind stole your umbrella, or blew rain in your face day after day, week after week for all those years. Did you not feel Ithaqua reminding you of your promise? You really do not remember?" He continued to shake his head.

"I told you so. That'll be his father's blood," his aunt's voice clattered, flints shaking from her in agitation to litter the wooden floor. "He is perfect for the ritual of replacement …"

Elin nodded in agreement. "Once there were plenty of worshippers, down there in the dark. But the people have turned from him. Just when we need him most … when we've grown weak."

"We need to reach him now," she whispered. "And you'll be our fuel. You're part of the ritual."

His aunt moved closer to peer at him with eyes that could surely no longer see. "Oh, pray that great Nyogtha will return my sister to me in place of *him*!"

His uncle chanted something in the darkness. The words sounded harsh and almost alien, but he recognised his father's name among them.

"What are you saying about my father?" He was disgusted that he sounded like a small, weak child complaining about some puny injustice.

"Your father lived a fool's life and got a fool's reward," said his aunt, her voice like shale tumbling down.

"He should have stayed away from our family," added his cousin.

Dave's head began to ache as his uncle continued to sing and bellow. Within a few seconds the room had grown measurably lighter. When the words ended, his cousin let him drop from her grip.

On his knees now, his headache throbbed like repeated chords of darkness in some insane symphony.

Uncle Will, anthracite-black and crumbling with every movement, came towards him. "Listen, boy. He's coming! This house is built from stones quarried from Bryant's Cave. It's his altar!"

From each of the monstrous figures a stream of darkness flowed out and up, congealing along the edge of the room before streaming across the ceiling.

Something in this shapeless form shifted. Then the very darkness itself moved swiftly, sweeping down towards him like an enormous wave, intent on knocking him off his feet and swallowing him.

Somewhere, deep within the darkness and down a million miles, he heard his father's voice, as he always did in his dreams.

Now he could hear what the dead man was saying—it wasn't his name, after all, but a warning, heard far too late. "Day-n-jer … day-n-jer …"

Dave screamed—or at least did something that he thought must be like screaming—but he knew it wasn't enough to express the absolute pain that burned through him. His voice was a maddening melisma of agonies.

A deep, thick blackness brushed against him. It was darker than anything he'd seen or known before and, at that moment, Dave realised he *did* have a soul after all and that it was convulsed in terror.

He felt himself being overwhelmed, consumed whole by whatever it was. This was the promise that, unknown to him, had been held like a knife against his infant throat. *This* was what his family had worshipped since God alone knew when.

Voices from a race of whispering giants filled his ears, forcing their way into his mind. Lightning snakes, tongues forking out to entwine each other before separating again, danced through the broken orbs of his eyes.

He heard familiar, familial voices yelling in near-ecstasy and fear as the rest of his senses were blotted out. Then the blackness thundered in its silence and the world disappeared.

He felt as if his chest had been immersed in icy water. Chill fingers forced their way into every tiny tributary of his lungs as he struggled to breathe through the cold agony.

His limbs became too heavy to lift and, though he couldn't tell which way was up any longer, he was sure he felt himself crash heavily to the floor, assaulted by broken salvoes of putrescent blackness.

If he had hit the floor, it suddenly offered no resistance. What was left of Dave felt himself descend unendingly.

Under everything. Deep below, where tunnels dug by man finally met those dug by ancient elementals in a cathedral filled with darkness.

In this lost labyrinth of permanent, unrelenting night, time turned black, stopped, folded in on itself.

Dead voices calling to each other in the echoing emptiness.

His own voice joining with the chthonic chorus.

He had no feeling anywhere, yet he trembled and screamed. Saturated with blackness. Never to see the light again.

The Sixth Guardian

For Eddy C. Bertin

From two or three miles down the railway track, the town looked grey and old. It almost looks dead, he thought, as he drew closer.

The classical architecture of the station reminded him of an ancient mausoleum instead of a mundane transit point. It felt hot and claustrophobic inside the vast structure.

His twisted childhood—stolen by the coldness and cruelty of his uncle—had brought him back here, despite all the promises he had made himself.

He wanted to gaze on that hated face just one more time, mainly because he wanted to assure himself that the old bastard truly was dead. But, as his only living relative, there might also be something in it for him, even if it was simply a delayed legacy from his poor, dead father.

He left the bulk of the station behind him and passed the tall, narrow houses that lined the wide road.

The sunlight drew hard shadows under the bridge over the grey, sluggish canal.

His uncle's house was further from the station than he remembered. The intervening span of years had obviously warped his memories. Or maybe it was just the stifling summer heat that made the journey seem longer.

For the last 30 years, the old man had led the life of an anchorite. Most presumed his allegiance to be to the martyr of the cross, but Jan knew the truth was very different. He'd never understood his uncle's occult predilections, despite being

forced to participate in them, but he knew he wanted nothing
to do with them.

The tall grey house at 27 Schemeringstraat stood in contrast
to those around it. Those on either side were freshly painted
and looked well cared for, while his uncle's house appeared
unkempt, like an unwashed old man. "How appropriate,"
thought Jan.

He pulled up the old brass knocker and let it fall. The metal
felt pleasantly cool but oddly greasy. It made the dull sound of
a sledgehammer hitting a coffin lid.

He was about to knock again when the door opened, and a
small elderly man peered up at him.

He took a second or two to focus on the visitor. "Yes?"

"I'm Jan."

"You have come for the funeral?" The dusty-skinned man
gazed straight at his mouth, awaiting a reply. Evidently he was
deaf, thought Jan.

"Why else would I return to this place? To fall down dead
myself and allow the worms to gorge themselves on my bitter
memories?" Jan made sure he enunciated every word carefully.

The old man kept staring at his mouth, not moving an inch.
"Out of the way please," said Jan, losing patience.

It was barely any cooler indoors that it had been in the
street. Once inside the bare hallway, he left his holdall near the
door. Draping his overcoat across it, he entered the open door
on his right.

Nearly two dozen pairs of eyes turned to him as he entered
the large room. Except for the door, nearly every inch of wall
space besides a large ugly sideboard was taken up with a chair.
Each was occupied by a withered, black-clad figure.

Jan took in the room quickly before stepping across to
the antique catafalque in the centre of the space. The coffin
containing his uncle's body lay on top.

He had been a tall man, but the huge black coffin lent him a
dignity he had lacked in life. His enormous vulturine nose stood
proud above his withered cheeks. The corpse reminded Jan of
a plundered statue of a pharaoh that had been taken from its
enormous pedestal and laid on its back ready to be dragged away.

He was tempted to lunge forward suddenly and sink a pin into the waxy flesh, to test whether the life had truly left his body. He had always suspected dishonesty from Bernardus.

Jan wiped the grim smile from his face as he noticed a man at his elbow. Turning, he was met by a short, smartly-dressed man who he guessed was in the legal profession. He extended his hand. "Mr. ...?"

The man spoke in a low voice that was intended to be confidential, though his voice could be heard easily by all the occupants of the still, hot room. "I am Julian Walton, your uncle's solicitor. There are certain matters to be taken care of over the next few days, Meneer de Vries."

The man's heavy voice exactly matched the pronounced bags under his eyes.

Jan nodded. "Yes, yes ... of course. Your note caught up with me in Edinburgh. I do understand ..." He gestured towards the coffin. "What did he die of?" he inquired, only half interested.

"His heart gave out," the solicitor informed him.

"Impossible—he didn't have one!" snorted Jan. Hatchet-like faces turned towards him with disdain. He stared them all down.

Jan looked around the room at the disappointed, decrepit faces. Every visage looked as if it was made of melting wax, with two marbles glistening above their pendulous noses, as if pressed unwillingly into the grimy material.

He noted sourly that all those in attendance, who he assumed to be all his uncle's acquaintances (for he certainly had no friends), were all ready for the grave themselves. He was the youngest one there and even he was fast approaching middle age. Anything filled with the vitality of youth had wisely steered clear of the old man.

He remembered from his childhood that a kitten he had brought into the house once lasted a mere four days before it died. He'd been heartbroken. By way of consolation, his uncle had given him a book about the occult with black covers and grubby page edges. It was presumably meant either to explain why the kitten perished or to toughen Jan up to the point where he no longer cared about "lower" beings. It failed to do either.

The sun was now no longer shining through the window. Outside, the grey sky flowed overhead. It did little to alleviate the heat.

Jan loosened his collar. Trust the old bastard to die in the middle of a stifling summer, he thought.

On the huge, dark wood sideboard stood a heavy picture frame. The photograph showed him with his father. A dark figure stood at his father's shoulder, as if waiting to pounce on them both.

Uncle Bernardus always had the air of a bird of prey. He'd been tall—taller than his brother—but always shabby in appearance. This added to the impression that he was a half-starved vulture.

Jan looked away from the image. He was surprised Bernardus had kept the photograph. It reminded Jan of the most terrifying moment of his childhood.

It was the evening that his uncle had come into his room and announced, with an awful attempt at a smile covering the lower half of his face, that Jan's father had died. "I am your father now," he had added.

Jan shrank inside and begged with God to kill him. But, as usual, the deity ignored him.

Walton and his even more elderly assistant produced a bottle and glasses from a large wooden piece of furniture. Everyone was furnished with a glass, which was then filled to the halfway point with a tawny liquid.

After what seemed like an hour, Walton turned and spoke. "To the memory of our benefactor, Bernardus de Vries." The old man raised the glass of pale brownish liquid and made another toast. "To all those born with blood."

"… and bone," muttered the ancient fool next to Jan, touching his withered lips to the glass without drinking a drop. Jan noticed him lower the glass and tip its contents onto the carpet.

Jan was puzzled by the toast and by the reference to Bernardus as a benefactor but, after a cautious sniff, he downed the liquid in one gulp. It tasted rich and grapey, but he wasn't able to place it. For a second, he hoped he hadn't unwittingly bought into some sort of occult suicide pact with his vile, dead uncle and his hangers-on.

After a few uncomfortable minutes, Jan decided he would survive. "I need some air," he announced to Walton before taking his leave.

In the hallway, he gazed down ruefully at the hideous tiled floor. It depicted an all-seeing eye, gazing up at all who passed. It sat in the midst of a stylised serpentine design that nodded towards some early 20th-century art movements.

Jan had always hated it and noted with pleasure that even more of the tiles were crisscrossed with dirt-encrusted cracks than he remembered. As he swung the heavy front door open, he wished it had been ground into pieces by the passing years.

At a small bar nearby, Jan ordered a jenever and a beer. After a few mouthfuls of the near tasteless beer, he took the opportunity to phone Saskia. He'd insisted his wife stay away from this poisonous place.

When she asked how long it would be before he could return, he answered "Not too long. A few days at most."

After he'd hung up, he enjoyed the cooler air rising from the canal as the day crept to a close.

He had some more questions for his uncle's English solicitor, but he wanted to ask them without a room full of vultures eavesdropping.

The following morning Jan found himself in Walton's office, hoping to clear up the small matter of whether or not he was going to inherit anything from his uncle. He supposed that he was.

Walton looked even dustier today than he had at the house yesterday. Jan supposed that the light was better here.

"Your uncle left very specific instructions as to his funeral and eventual interment in a private cemetery just outside the city." Walton placed a thin brown folder of papers in front of Jan, who flipped it open at once. He hoped some revelation of hidden wealth that was coming his way would leap out at him. The papers remained stubbornly confusing at first glance.

Walton's treacly voice began to warp itself around Jan once more. "The will is to be read immediately before the funeral service which, if you care to glance at the chart enclosed, will be in two weeks' time."

"Two weeks?!"

Startled by Jan's outburst, Walton's raised his gaze. "Yes. As I said, the chart left by your uncle indicates the most propitious date for his burial will be the 23rd of this month."

Jan stared at the calendar-like chart that Walton had indicated. It contained an odd graph to one side and unfamiliar markings crawling across the dates on the calendar.

"Yes, I see." Jan sighed. There was no way he was staying in that old mausoleum of a house for another fortnight. He would phone Saskia later; they would just have to make other plans.

"Can you tell me, Mr. Walton, if I can expect to benefit from my uncle's will in any way?"

The old solicitor shook his head. "It would be highly unethical of me to discuss the contents of the will with anyone prior to its reading, Meneer de Vries. I'm sure you understand."

Jan didn't understand … or didn't care, at least.

"However, I believe that Vrouw Kantner is safeguarding a small legacy for you. One that is completely outside the terms of the will and therefore unaffected by it."

Jan nodded slowly. "I see." Vrouw Kantner had been his uncle's housekeeper … and much more besides, he imagined. He hadn't seen her at the gathering around the coffin earlier. He'd imagined that she'd moved on years ago or died.

As if he could read Jan's mind, Walton added: "She still lives in the house."

Jan scooped up the folder from the desk and shook the old man's hand.

Confused, the solicitor began "Oh … but there are other matters that we must … as your uncle's only living relative … ummm …"

Jan nodded. "Perhaps tomorrow. After all, I'll be around for the next fortnight.," he said, knowing full well that he wouldn't be.

This bleak town was where he grew up—if one could truly use that phrase about his childhood. It was more accurate to say that he reached a kind of premature maturity, at which time he realised that escape was the only real option.

The grey sky lowered overhead as he walked back briskly to the house. That house had been the place from which escape had once seemed impossible.

His young life had been an endless round of harsh discipline, deprivation, and fake devotion to his uncle's obscure occult obsessions.

He remembered the insane, endless incantations. And how he had been forced to kneel in "prayer" hour after hour by Bernardus. Sometimes he even imagined that his fingers still ached from the odd hand gestures he had been forced to adopt, his fingers twisted at unnatural angles.

Jan had understood none of it and had viewed it simply as his uncle's peculiar brand of cruelty. He also remembered being struck hard if he stumbled over the gibberish he was forced to repeat.

And every night that maddening music; a violin that sounded like a dentist's drill. When he asked about it in the morning, he simply got a cold stare in response. He'd supposed it had come from Bernardus' own room, but he had no proof. His uncle had once even claimed it was his own "over-imaginative young mind."

As Jan approached the door of the house that he imagined he now owned, he noticed a bent old man hurrying to intercept him. Jan slowed for a moment in astonishment at the sight. The man looked like an odd black bird that had grown in size and now insisted on pretending it was human.

Then it spoke. "Meneer de Vries, if you please. Will you now be taking over your uncle's role?"

Jan didn't remember seeing the man at the house earlier. Taken aback, all he could mumble was, "What?"

"Are you an adept at the sacred geometrics, too? We need someone to lead us, you see. We all need a benefactor."

Jan shook his head. "No. I'm sorry. I don't know what you

mean." It occurred to him that Bernardus had gathered a group of followers since the last time he was here, despite Walton's claim that he had been a recluse. A coven of some sort, no doubt, thought Jan.

"But … but … We need someone, Meneer de Vries." the man had placed his unpleasant, nicotine-stained fingers on Jan's sleeve. Despite his previous resemblance to a bird, the man now looked more toad-like.

All Jan wanted to do was get away from him. "Look. I don't really know what …"

The man's grip grew stronger. "… when our lives could be snuffed out at any time by the accidental footfall of a behemoth from a hidden realm, existing beyond the reach of our poor senses … we need help." The man had laid particular emphasis on the final word.

"Old man—make some sense, will you?" Jan had lost patience and began to pull his arm away.

The old man staggered back a step or two. The rebuff seemed to run through him like a small electric shock. He stood muttering to himself. "Not the one—not the one—"

Jan stared at him for a second before putting the key in the lock. He left the man standing in the street with a look of stunned finality on his face. When the heavy door clunked shut behind him, Jan let out a delayed breath he hadn't realised he'd been holding.

Once inside the house, he went from room to room looking for his uncle's former housekeeper. She was nowhere to be found on the ground floor, and every bedroom except his was nearly bare of furnishings. There wasn't even any indication as to where his hated uncle used to sleep.

Giving up in frustration, Jan went to the room that Walton had furnished for his stay. He still hadn't recovered from the rigours of his previous day's travel. He lay down on the large bed and napped on and off until early evening.

At just before seven there was a knock on the door of Jan's bedroom. Rising from the bed, he opened it to be confronted by Vrouw Kantner. Despite his fruitless search earlier, here she was. Jan was slightly shocked to see that she was now wheelchair-bound.

The Vrouw had always been a woman of few words but her silence as she sat in front of him was unnerving.

Suddenly, she took one clawed hand from the rim of the right wheel and picked up a parcel that lay in her lap. She looked at it for a moment before thrusting it towards him.

"Your father wanted you to have this." Her voice was almost a whisper. "Now that you are old enough—and your uncle is no longer with us—I can fulfil the promise I made."

Jan took the parcel from her. It was wrapped in a thick brown paper that had become discoloured over time.

"Well ... uh, thank you." The woman had never helped Bernardus to abuse him but then she'd never tried to stop him either. Jan still felt uncomfortable in her presence.

"So, how have you been, Vrouw Kantner?" he asked, awkwardly.

The woman raised both arthritic hands from their grip on the wheelchair and spread them in front of her. "As you see, Master Jan."

He pursed his lips in sympathy. Before he could utter any uncomfortable platitudes, Vrouw Kantner had spun her wheelchair around and headed back into the darkness that swallowed the end of the corridor.

He closed the door and laid the parcel on a small side table then carefully unwrapped the crisped, old paper. It was obviously a book, but Jan was slightly fearful of what its pages might contain. The volumes he'd been allowed to read in this house had been a far cry from those that most children were accustomed to.

He looked at it for a few seconds before daring to lift the front cover of the book. He recognised at once the small, crabbed letters of his father's handwriting. Each page was dated at the top. He'd had no idea his father had kept a diary. Though he supposed it was something Willem was unlikely to share with a seven-year-old boy.

The diary pages cracked and tore as he turned them, drinking in the entries, struggling to understand.

The words seem to burn into his mind. At last, he was able to decipher the code. The words he'd heard issuing from Bernardus' twisted mouth during his bleak childhood were all here. All the phrases he'd been forced to repeat, while kneeling on the hard floor before his brutal uncle, now made some sort of sense.

The word "Cyaegha" was part of almost every sentence spoken during those rituals. Jan now discovered the awful truth behind the word—that it was a creature of dreadful power, worshipped as a god by some and capable of bringing eternal darkness to humanity.

Some of the images Bernardus surrounded himself with were of the foul entity under the hill, he now realised.

At first Jan's rationalist outlook fought against the truth contained in the words. But an older, perhaps wiser, part of him could not deny the dreadful certainty revealed by the shapes made of discoloured ink.

He wept for his father's fear and courage. He could only imagine what a struggle it had been to battle Bernardus secretly while also keeping his small son safe and untainted.

His father could only speculate on exactly what Bernardus intended with his ceremonies. Maybe he had wanted to harness the power of the slumbering deity somehow … or, worse, to release it from its captivity.

But one thing was certain from his father's words—he had done everything in his power to thwart his brother and prevent him from attaining his goals.

One section of the diary made it clear that his father had been given custodianship of a sixth Vaeyen—one known to very few and protected diligently down the years by men like Willem. He referred to it as "The Keeper of Light and Fire" and there was a vague suggestion that it was somewhere within the house.

Jan read that these powerful guardians, demonic servants embodied in carved statues, both protected and imprisoned the dreaded star-born thing beneath the hill. It was always supposed that there were only five Vaeyen. But now he knew the truth and it was imperative that he seek out the sixth.

The diary ended the day before his father's death. The final entry mentioned Willem's fears that his brother was growing stronger.

Jan lay on the bed for an hour as the light faded outside. It was difficult to believe all that his father's diary said. If it had been written by anyone except his father, he would have dismissed it as a lurid fantasy.

Had his father, in truth, been the caretaker of a lost Vaeyen? It appalled him to imagine that this dark, cloistered place, filled with misery, could be the front line in a battle that must be won—and quickly—if the world was to survive.

His suspicions that Willem may have been killed by his own brother were underlined by his father's avowed role in trying to halt the sorcerer's deviant plans.

He picked up the book and reopened it many times, refreshing his memory and trying to glean even more from his father's words. The phrases "under Bernardus' very feet" and "beneath the eye of Cyclops" stuck in his mind.

Had his father hidden the precious Vaeyen from his brother? If so, those who worshipped the god may be glad to have it back. It was bound to be very valuable to them.

It soon dawned on Jan that the clues could only lead to one place in this hellish dwelling. Jan headed downstairs to Bernardus' study. He was convinced that his father had secreted the object in a location where it would have the maximum effect on his vile brother.

The dark wooden door faced him defiantly, but Jan resolved to invade his uncle's former sanctum boldly. Gripping the handle, he turned it and pushed hard.

The door almost flew open, revealing a room crowded with furniture and books. On the wall hung prints and fabrics bearing arcane symbols and images, which Jan glanced at with renewed repugnance.

Jan took two steps inside, fighting back memories of his past, and let his gaze drop to the floor. He pulled the heavy carpet aside with some difficulty. There, etched into the floorboards using God only knows what magical means, was the curious circular symbol that his uncle had spent so much of his time sitting inside. At its very centre, was a huge eye, returning his gaze.

On several occasions, Jan had been forced to help his uncle in his rituals. They had lasted hours, with the stench of foul incense and the man's rancid sweat filling the air.

There was still a faint whiff of the incense trapped in the furnishings.

Jan ran his fingers along the floorboards. They were solid but old, and he needed some tool in order to force them up. A sturdy metal poker that had been left by the fireplace would do, he decided.

The wood splintered with an alarming crack. Jan was sure the rest of the house must have heard it. Then he remembered that the cook didn't live in the house. Besides her, there was only Vrouw Kantner, hidden away in her bolthole somewhere.

He swung the poker high and hard. Again, the floorboards cracked and split, complaining loudly as they flew apart. Sweat dripped from his forehead, making wet islands on the dusty boards.

He dug his fingers under the last board and tugged with all his might. Inch by inch, it came free, and he pushed it to one side.

When Jan gazed down into the space between the floor joists, he sucked in a great heaving breath.

There, lying on his side, was his father's corpse. He recognised the remnants of dark hair and the badge sewn on to his favourite jacket. There wasn't even the decency of a shroud or other funeral wrapping.

His father's head bore a terrible wound that had undoubtedly killed him. Bernardus' story of a heart attack had obviously been lies.

The desiccated fingers clutched at a two-foot-long carving of a bird-like creature. It had to be the sixth Guardian mentioned in his father's diary. All these years it had lain beneath his uncle's feet—no wonder the old fool's magics had never worked.

Jan chuckled in delight. His father had defeated his uncle even after his death. He presumed that the evil occultist had no idea his brother's corpse and the mechanism that had frustrated his life's work lay beneath his very feet.

Even after all these years under the floorboards, the sculpted figure was an almost fierce white. It seemed to repel dust and decay.

Jan reached down to touch it, wondering who had snatched his father away from the fire of cremation to bury him here? He had his own supporters, no doubt—those who were opposed to his uncle's foul dealings. Maybe Vrouw Kantner was a secret ally after all. Maybe she had arranged to have him buried here, to guard the Vaeyen even after death.

As his fingers closed around the neck of the sculpture, it sagged. His nails dug into the dried material, and he watched, appalled, as it crumbled away before his eyes.

As the dust of the false Vaeyen began to rise, the mirage of his father's corpse faded like mist in sunlight. He had been tricked.

Jan cursed his own stupidity. How could he have allowed himself to be trapped like this?

Bernardus' sorcery was reaching out to control him even now. Even in death, he had won. Jan imagined the evil old man's corpse grinning in its long, black coffin.

A deep cold began to invade the room, stealing the sticky warmth of the summer and squeezing the air from his heaving lungs. Beads of sweat began to freeze uncomfortably on his skin.

Ice crept impossibly across the inside of the window pane.

His frozen fingers refused to move any longer as he fumbled with the door. He slumped down onto the floor as he felt the cold grip him tighter. A darkness invaded the room, dissolving its details like an acid as it came.

In his confusion, he thought he saw Saskia's soft brown eyes looking down at him. He blinked and her gentle gaze was replaced by the terrifying stare of an enormous orb, looking into him, replacing his memories with confusion and pain.

Cold fingers stabbed towards him out of the darkness. No, not fingers … something much worse.

The god under the hill. That dreaded thing. It had failed to seduce him when he was younger but now here it was. Even from his coffin, Bernardus had summoned it.

As the cold stabbed further into him, he gasped, expelling his last breath. Cold filled him. Darkness and cold.

So deep. So cold … under the hill.

Doorgrave to the Bittersea

As he tried to open the doorgrave, muscles tensed and yearning in anticipation of release, he felt the ground slide away under him.

Again, the landscape sought to escape, or to expel him. He was not welcome here, it was saying. You are unnatural and should not be here. "Why do you seek to do this ... to know what you must not know?"—it was a silent question, asked by the act of denying him what he wanted more than anything else in his life; his so-called life, the shell he inhabited that now passed for a life.

The portal he sought to open was the only one that he wished to pass through. No other would do. Any substitute would be a cheat, an evasion of the truth. Because there was only one way back. And this way back was the only future he desired.

He clambered to his feet again, brushing the filth from his knees. The sky overhead had a tinge of purple at the edges, like coloured paper torn up and pasted at the horizon as the day prepared to turn its back on him.

"I'm coming," he yelled defiantly as he dug his feet into the ground, struggling slowly forward.

As a child, the sand had always infuriated and delighted him as it slid away under his soft shoes, his small feet. A million, million tiny creatures crushed to pieces and thrown upon the shore for his childish delight.

Everything was so bright, so alive—too bright and too alive, it now seemed—as he laughed and slipped towards the sea.

The water had hissed and roared, reflecting splinters of

summer at him as it hurled down its ancient challenge. Even at that age, he knew better than to accept.

Even then, before it all became a lie and the brightness faded into memory.

Was it safe to think about it now? Even though it was locked away in the past, he was wary of approaching it.

But the past was the land where he was born. He had moved away as soon as he could but, in his sanest moments, he wished he could return.

Propped up as a sunshade, the rotten casket lid provided some shelter behind which to work.

He took a deep breath, feeling trapped at the twisted crossroads where the carnal and the charnel met.

Then he jumped down into the open coffin, his feet landing in the crumbling mess that had been her guts.

For possibly the hundredth time, he stared down into his beloved's empty orbits. "This time, it'll be right," he whispered to her. Her rictus smile, rimmed by parched and peeling skin, seemed a deliberate mockery of his efforts.

He began reciting the formula, treading among the words as carefully as if he was being asked to dance in a minefield. Suddenly, he felt himself plunge into the darkness that his beloved harboured within her empty skull, falling through her and into a place that tried to deny his existence. The door had opened …

Yet how could a charnel pit be a doorway of any kind? He didn't believe it at first. But after certain dark sacrifices had been made he dared not deny the truth any longer. And he dared not admit to himself how much such sacrifices had cost him.

He'd had no choice but to believe.

During the long years of his incarceration, every dark hint he'd read, each vague supposition he'd heard about, all pointed to the same supposed solution.

That day—during that long-lost summer—they'd walked to the

shore slowly, passing through the flower-jewelled meadow that ran down to the sea.

They'd sworn about the miserliness of her father. Just because he had money, he thought he could turn everyone into his whores.

"I'm not like that," she told him. "And neither are you. We know better ..." Then she'd grabbed his hand and brought his fingers up to her lips.

He'd felt his heart being imprisoned then by her sirensong smile and deep, hazel eyes.

He'd utilised a bootlegged science in extremis; each step calibrated along the cusp of insanity. He's wandered down lost passageways, long abandoned to conjecture and misguided speculation.

Sorting the wheat from the dubious chaff took time, of course. Too much time. And time, he knew, was at the heart of it all.

His calculations induced frequent migraines of agonising intensity. The depredations of the ritual of the void gnawed at him constantly.

But time ... time was getting away from him ...

The place was in darkness except for three figures; standing, glowing, in the space between times.

He reached out to her, and the darkness tugged her out of reach, dousing her glow, swallowing her in its near solid absence. The door was beginning to close ...

He turned then to the other, unrecognised figure, only to find that it, too, had disappeared, perhaps erasing themselves purposefully.

The investigators had kept asking about a weapon. Time and again. He didn't know what they meant.

There were no other footprints. Where was the weapon? For months he'd heard the same thing, day after day. After a month they stopped asking.

Then the long years had stretched before him. A room filled with sadness and loss. A prison both outside and in.

He checked his pocket one last time, removing the object and carefully unfolding the cloth covering it. The scrying lens had been obtained from three sisters; practitioners of a science of the mind long condemned, its adherents persecuted. Subtle symbols etched, around the edge, snaked between his fingers.

Having performed their lunar rites, the device was now perfect, they said.

They told him of what it might reveal. They'd seen it in their skysight glimpses, they claimed. When he'd dismissed their concerns, they had simply chuckled while rearranging their serpentine locks and exchanging knowing glances. They'd looked at him as if he was nothing more than a misguided child, acquiring a dangerous toy that they knew would destroy him.

He'd left quickly, carrying their precious creation as if it was a newborn.

He'd resented being treated like an idiot by the beautiful old hags, but he'd needed their help too much to risk upsetting them. He'd borne his humiliation before them, as all men must when in their pristine domain.

The scent of her hair, the silk of her skin, drops of sunlight and water dappling it, all trapped in the past, thirty summers ago.

This was his memory of her. He supposed most men would think of sex; the first time or the best time. What he remembered most was lying naked next to her, stroking her back as she drifted off to sleep. The flat of her shoulder blade as she lay on her left side, the dip and hollow of flesh as his hand slid across her smooth skin, down to the hard mound of her hip and over the rounded curve of her right buttock.

He traced the freckles that appeared like constellations of desire on her milky skin.

It was like touching a fragile piece of living sculpture. And he felt as if he alone was allowed to touch this unique beauty.

"It has to be believed to be seen," the white-clad sisters had told him.

When he'd expressed his concerns, his weaknesses, his fears

of facing what might be, they looked at him scornfully.

"Turn the pain into a game. It's so simple," they had advised him. He shrugged off the memory. Despite his investment in their wisdom, he still distrusted their perverted science.

That lost day he'd been for a swim. Not too far out and not for too long. But it had still been far too long.

The blood-soaked sand was already drying around her by the time he came out of the water. There were no footsteps around her, yet her throat and stomach lay open, as if sliced into by something vicious and sharp.

He'd cradled her body in his arms until the sun had taken its heat away and left him to shiver.

He felt the sand beneath his palms as he knelt panting, fighting back the nausea. His body felt like a nest of snakes, all venomous.

Fatigued from swimming against the tides of time, he brushed the grave dust from his clothes, then struggled to stand. The heat of the beach was a shock after the chill of the graveyard.

He'd succeeded. This was where he needed to be. As soon as he was able he checked his pockets, sighing in relief when his fingers found the object they were seeking. This time it would be different … it had to be.

The sunlight was as sharp as glass, reflecting harshly off the cutting granules that made up the wide expanse of the beach.

The light dazzled him, causing him to close his eyes for a second. It gave him a moment to forget himself, basking in the heat.

He remembered not remembering, as if his mind was a toy for someone else to use. When this game was over, he'd be discarded, locked away from the light. But that was the price, he knew that.

He had to focus. This was where he could change everything. Distractions had to be kept at bay. He squinted hard to block out some of the summer dazzle.

A figure down the beach took on a shape he recognised. He began heading towards it, feet sliding in the uncooperative sand, making him work hard for any progress.

She lay alone on the sand, kissed by the wind and the sun.

"It has to be believed to be seen." Remembering the sisters' words, he reached in his pocket for the scrying lens and, closing his eyes, lifted it up before his face.

When he snapped his eyelids open and gazed through the lens, the beach seemed distorted, and the sky was an unnameable colour.

He scanned the scene before him, struggling to ignore the beginnings of another crippling headache. There was nothing out of the ordinary, nothing he'd not seen a dozen times before. Had the sisters been lying to him, after all?

The sky seemed to dip and swoop as he swept the lens across the landscape, just as the ground appeared to heave upwards to join the stray clouds. A bird or two warped their way through the air. Despair began to clutch at him.

Then, movement. There, cutting through the water like a knife of light …!

It was a creature of some sort, previously invisible to him. The sisters' device was doing what they'd promised. His heart began to beat faster and breathing became difficult.

Holding the lens before him, he began to move down the beach as quickly as he dared.

The thing stood just where he had stood. But where was his younger self? Why didn't he emerged from the water to save her, the fool?!

Suddenly, she seemed to see the creature. At first she didn't seem at all alarmed. Then her yelp of surprise cut the air in half.

He almost dropped the lens. He couldn't bear to see her life seeping out into the burning sand again.

He was getting closer now. Just as the shining, formless thing raised itself above her, he yelled. "Hey! Hey! Over here!" It turned towards him. Something in its movement revealed that it was not pleased by his intrusion.

The thing now appeared to have limbs, detaching from its body in frustration or anger as it ran towards him.

Then it hit him. He had no weapon. There was no way he could know what he'd find here but he should have brought some protection. It was a stupid mistake. He came here intending to save her life, now it looked like he might lose his own as well.

He didn't dare take his eyes off the creature as it advanced towards him, but he needed to get away. Gripping the lens in his sweat-slippery fingers he began to move away swiftly. He stumbled backwards before regaining his balance.

But the creature had the advantage of forward movement. Its momentum brought it uncomfortably close, far too quickly for his liking.

Something long reaching out—fingers—antlers? All made of diseased light, filtered down from a dying sun perhaps a million lives away.

Its broken bone longarm reach seemed to pass through him, falling and failing as he ran backwards into the water. Lapping, hard waves broke on his calves and shins.

For a moment, it seemed to hesitate. That couldn't be for fear of the water as it had come from there, he reasoned. Whatever the cause, he was grateful for the momentary respite.

The creature moved towards him again, forcing him to move back even further into the razor surf. Relentless pain cut into him. Shatter stick bones, cracking open on rocks. He gritted his teeth, ignoring the pain, which now seemed only half real to him anyway.

Now it was barely a foot from him. His breathing came with difficulty, as if he was sucking air in through a thick veil of fear.

He lunged forward and struck out at it with one hand. He pulled it back instantly, covered in blood. The light was … razor sharp! That explained her wounds, he thought. And why the investigators had found no weapon.

Black and white flashes exploded across the sky of his mind. Thunder like the cracking of God's knuckles filled his ears. Each breath came like a rare blessing.

And he recognised himself in the fierceness of the creature. Something like a face formed words behind the mask of intense light. To look at it hurt his eyes, but if he wanted to learn what this thing was, where it came from, he needed to see.

His eyes watered with strain as he peered at the rough

facsimile of a mouth. He concentrated hard to try and lip-read the words.

Adjusting the scrying glass, he struggled to hold it in front of his face. He must know the truth.

Suddenly, it was like looking into a mirror. A moment's shock froze him as he stared into a bright, twisted version of his own face.

Tears brimmed over and ran down his face, stinging his already burning cheeks. It was he who was killing the one thing he'd ever truly loved. His worst fears were being realised.

He didn't think it was possible to hide something like this from oneself … and for so long. And how could he feel such rage and anger toward her?

The thing moved what passed for its head back and forth, as if enraged by his very presence there. The face distorted, as if shouting repeatedly.

There was no sound, but the word was clear. "Murderer!" The creature repeated it over and over, as if it was the only word it knew.

"Yes," he whispered to himself.

He dropped the scrying glass for a second. When he raised it once more, he stared again at the awful reflection of his own face, surrounded by writhing light. Then, suddenly, he flipped the glass around so that the side he'd been using now faced the creature.

The image was lost to him, but the creature began to thrash back and forth, as if unable to bear what it saw through the lens. Perhaps it was able to discern exactly what it had cost for him to be here, to be able to see exactly what he didn't want to see. Himself.

For the first time, the creature emitted a sound. It was a form of agony that no human ear could bear.

Suddenly it turned, seeking escape, the light leaching from it at every step.

Its limbs turned grey, flaking away as it moved. Parts of its body blackened and fell away. Soon it could run no further as its legs crumbled under it. In a diminuendo of hacking coughs, it fell face down in the sand.

He stepped over to it, cautiously. Looking down at it, he felt as if someone had walked over his grave.

Then the remains began to sink into the soft sand. It disappeared quickly, as if the world, in shame, wanted to dispose of an unfortunate error. But the error had been his, all along.

He walked over to where she lay, dazed. Reaching down, he touched her shoulder as the incantations and calculations ran through his head.

They were both gripped by a sense of dislocation as a wave of darkness crashed down upon them.

He moaned and rolled in the blackness, reaching out for her but not finding her. For a moment, he feared that all his efforts had been wasted. He couldn't bear to think of her trapped in the past without him.

Then there was cold, hard earth beneath him, and his breath felt like ice inside him.

He rolled onto his side, ready to vomit. Then he saw her. They were two bedraggled puppets, dragged forward through a crumbling wall of time, lying side by side again.

She lay panting softly. He closed his eyes in grateful disbelief. He had atoned for his sin. She was safe now.

He didn't believe in luck. Yet it had been there with him all along and now, for the first time, he could have what he wanted.

He struggled to his knees and, eventually, to his feet. Walking over to where she had been buried, he saw that the soil around the edge of the hole had begun to crumble inwards. The grave was empty. He smiled to himself.

There weren't even the remains of a coffin—just dark soil and some busy earthworms. He turned back towards his beloved.

She had come to herself now and was sitting up, looking around her. "Where am I? Who are you?" she asked, eyes wide with fear.

He should have known that she could never love the wasted, withered thing he'd become. She didn't even recognise him. Still, it hit him hard.

She shivered in her flimsy beach wear as the cold of the late evening crept into her.

He took off his coat and held it out to her. She flinched away. "Who are you? I don't know you!"

He swallowed hard. "But my love … it's me. Don't you recognise me?"

She looked at the old man before her and began backing away from him, shaking her head. "Stay away from me. Stay away!"

She turned and began picking her bare-footed way gingerly along the gravel path to the cemetery gates. Just once, she turned and glanced back at him with a look of disbelief on her face.

He waited until she had passed through the gates and then walked the same way.

Behind him, he left all his hopes, tumbling backwards into an empty grave that would remain empty, forever.

About the Author

Mark Howard Jones was born on the twenty-sixth anniversary of H.P Lovecraft's death and grew up in a town in south Wales where it once rained fish. He has had dozens of short stories published around the world, some of which are collected in *Songs From Spider Street* (Screaming Dreams), *Brightest Black* (Screaming Dreams), *Dreamglass Days* (ISMs Press) and *Flowers Of War* (Black Shuck). A regular contributor to *Weird Fiction Review* in the U.S. and to PS Publishing's Black Wings series, he is also the editor of both volumes of *Cthulhu Cymraeg: Lovecraftian Tales From Wales*. His Cthulhu Mythos novella "Still Life With Death," was published in the 2020 anthology *The Book Of Yig: Revelations of the Serpent* (Macabre Ink).

Curious about other Crossroad Press books?
Stop by our site:
www.crossroadpress.com
We offer quality writing
in digital, audio, and print formats.